Nobody's
Empire

Nobody's Empire

A Novel

Stuart Murdoch

 HarperVia

An Imprint of HarperCollins*Publishers*

Dear Mum

You are in every page

I always thought you would read this book and chuckle
and wince
and occasionally tut at the memories

Instead, this book is in memory of you

Thank you for everything

Love Stuart

We are out of practice
We're out of sight
On the edge of nobody's empire

Belle and Sebastian

Nobody's
Empire

1

Getting Chucked

When Vivian broke up with me I cried a bit. A few crap tears. It felt obligatory, it was the end of my first major adult relationship. I squeezed the tears out, in a kind of "woe is me" way. She didn't cry. She's quite unsentimental. She was the unattainable beauty I attained. But I couldn't hold on to her.

I had started crumbling from the effort as soon as I was with her. It wasn't her fault. I said to her, "What will I do now? You're the only person I like. You're the only person that knows me now."

"You're just going to have to be friends with Carrie, someone like that."

Fuck off. Don't chuck me then try to palm me off on someone else.

Carrie was this girl I met once. She's in the same basket that I'm in, so I can see that Vivian has a point. But Vivian was making her point as she ran for the door, for a life of delicious sexual, artistic and everything-else freedom. I was just getting the hang of having a beautiful girlfriend, that's the thing. After two and a third years of clenching my stomach, not sleeping right, not eating right, falling down a massive hole and becoming a completely different person, I think I was getting it. But here I am, numb and burnt out. And a tiny bit relieved.

I should tell you how I met Carrie. I was getting sick all last year. And the year before actually. Finally I went to the doctor and he told me I had this thing called ME, or chronic fatigue or post-viral fatigue syndrome. Take your pick, I had it. He couldn't really help me much. All I knew was that I was "done in," I felt ill most of the time—like someone had pulled the plug on me—and my strength had gone.

They sent me to a specialist, but that guy didn't know anything. He kept saying "You can tell us more about this thing than we know," which was nice of him. He was being ok about it considering he was the specialist. But it didn't do me any good. Vivian said that Samara's mum knew about this girl who had ME, and she'd been in bed for five years, and she didn't move and she didn't eat and she hardly spoke, and did I want to talk to her?

To be honest, right at that minute I didn't really want to go there. I was just trying to keep things going as normal as I could. Fast-forward nine months, things got a lot worse for me. I ended up in hospital. I was in there quite a long time. I wrote postcards to people—that was the limit of my strength and my concentration. I wrote to Carrie, and she wrote me a postcard back. Turns out she was in hospital too at the same time, her in Glasgow, me back in the town my folks lived in.

I finally went to visit her, five months after we both got out of hospital. She lived in Glasgow with her parents, in a big house in the West End of the city. Her mum let me in, showed me into this big living room with a high ceiling and big windows. It felt like the trees outside were a continuation of the room, like the house and the trees had grown up together to form a perfect unity of grace and privilege. Anyway, there she was, tucked away in the corner of a sofa, frail, propped up on pillows, wearing an old rugby shirt, book on knees.

"Hi."

"Hi."

"Sit down," she said.

I sat at the other end of the sofa.

"How are you?" I asked.

"Fantastic," she said.

She smiled. She pushed her hair away from her face, her frailty dropped away for a moment, and there was a dark, resolute beauty.

"I got your postcards," she said.

"Oh yeah," I replied.

"My family think you're a bit unbalanced."

"What do *you* think?" I asked.

"I don't know."

I thought about it for a second.

"I mean, I *was* in a psychiatric ward. But I don't know if I should have been there. I think they just put me there because they didn't know what else to do with me."

"They did the same to me," she said.

"How long were you in?"

"Six weeks. What about you?"

"Three months."

"God, what did you do for three months?"

"I put on weight. They fed me, like a turkey before Christmas."

"You're not fat."

"I was really thin when I went in. So did they help you?" I asked her.

"A bit, I suppose. Before I went in, I was just in bed, with the curtains closed."

"Me too. Except curtains open."

"You didn't have a problem with the light?" she asked.

"No, for me it was more noises."

"Noise is big for me too. And headaches. Do you get the head-aches?" she asked.

"Not so much. Not now I've put some weight back on."

She looked down at her hands.

"So what's your worst thing?" she asked.

"Just feeling ill all the time. And being weak."

"Same," she said.

I thought for a moment and said, "The ward sister asked me what I was going to do when I got out and I said I was going to go water-skiing, and she said, 'Great. That's amazing!' She totally didn't get

3

that I was being sarcastic. I think in the whole hospital there was half a person who believed that I was physically ill."

"Same with me."

"So how did you get by?" I asked.

"I just did what they told me to until I couldn't do it. What about you?"

"After a while I realized that I could handle their regime. It was mostly sitting, listening, eating, trying not to look unhappy. I went to the classes, I sat in on the groups. Even though I was thinking, *This doesn't apply to me*, it was ok."

We paused. She looked out the window, and I looked out the window. So much green.

"What are you going to do now?" she asked.

"Dunno. Try to get better. What about you?"

"The same."

2

Somewhat Stricken

I was talking about the hospital the other day. You know, the stuff I was saying to Carrie? That I felt like I was the only one there that was actually ok. That I felt like I was just a visitor, a casual observer. In one sense it was true, and in another way I never felt like I belonged somewhere so much in my life. Not for a long time, at least. I mean, where did I belong before that? Nowhere. I was on my own.

They took me in. I don't want to tell you the whole story just now. Let's just say that I was in a really bad way before I went in. I'd got to the stage where I wasn't even eating, I was just lying in bed. My prospects weren't good. Later I was told that the doctor gave me about a week to live if I carried on with my regime. My whole life had been collapsing for years, and this was the natural culmination.

My dad scooped me out of bed one morning and put me in an ambulance, and they drove me to the nearby psychiatric hospital. My intellectual response to what was happening to me may have been shock and humiliation, but the hospital probably saved my life. I'd bottomed out; it was a turning point, a flushing out. It was getting rid of the poison of one way of seeing life and starting again, really simply. I wasn't who I was before and it didn't matter. I wasn't a prospect, I wasn't cool, I wasn't clever, I wasn't a boyfriend, I wasn't a DJ, I wasn't an undergraduate, I wasn't an athlete, I wasn't angry, I wasn't *as* confused. What was I?

I was a son. There was my mum and dad. I was a person. There were other people around me—patients and nurses and auxiliary workers. I was part of this thing called a hospital. I was just a person again, and it was not for me to think about what I couldn't do anymore. I just had to focus on existing. Life was stripped right back to the basics. I started to eat again, and that's all they really asked of me. That was my only real treatment. They weighed me every morning, and as long as the arrow went a little higher every day, they couldn't be happier. Most of them were nice, but there was a misunderstanding deep at the heart of it all. I had this thing called ME that had caused me to be so ill in the first place and had certainly been the trigger to all this calamity—and it was never mentioned.

They weren't interested in it. And right now I had to admit that it didn't matter. Because if I could get by at the hospital, if I could get through the day without being in bed all the time, if I was relieved of the threat of possibly dying next Friday, then I could go for that. I could do their bidding. I knew deep down though that the dream of a "full recovery" was just a dream. Towards the end of my stay, they thought I was "cured." They had done their bit. As far as they could see, I *looked* better now. My actual psychiatrist, who I only saw a couple of times the whole time I was there, was an asshole. He was the only bona fide asshole in the whole place. Unfortunately, he was also the top guy. The nurses and student nurses were all differing shades of kindness, but the psychiatrist set the treatment. I made it through this time despite him. I floated by. There was no understanding there, no attempt to meet me in the middle. At least he didn't drug me up.

One night in the hospital we were all sat round watching *Top of the Pops*—it was a Thursday. They announced this band, and I couldn't believe it. It was a group called the Soup Dragons. They were from Glasgow or close to Glasgow. The singer guy used to come into the shop I worked in and sell me his old records, and we used to chat. He was really nice. They were also one of the first bands I ever roadied for at the university when I got a job on the stage crew there.

Anyway, I was sat in the common room at the hospital, and I said, "I know those guys!"

Neil, one of the younger patients, tapped Maxine on the shoulder and said, "Steph says he knows those guys." And he laughed, and Maxine laughed, and James laughed, and even Janice, the nicest of the student nurses, smiled a bemused smile.

"I do. They played a concert and I sat on the stage while they were on."

My voice trailed off. It didn't seem to matter to anyone very much; it was like nobody believed me, and I hardly believed it myself. As the band on the TV threw themselves around the set and the beautiful young audience swooned over them and tried to grab a piece of them, there was too much of a gulf between them and me, sat in a psychiatric ward in a provincial town.

Someone farted loudly. People laughed.

Maxine said, "Aw, who shat? James?"

"I cannae help it, it's my medicine," James said.

"Ok, shut up," said Lorraine, gesturing at the screen. "New Kids on the Block."

When I lived in Glasgow before I got sick, I used to see bands every night. That was my job—it was what I liked. I was the number one seer of bands in the greater Glasgow district. I couldn't avoid seeing them. I was either playing records at shows where bands were playing, or I was on the crew helping the bands to perform, or I actually paid some bands to come and play, put up the posters, let them sleep on my floor, the whole thing. It all seems so far away and exhausting, though I know that it was thrilling too. So when I did finally get out of the hospital and I was back at my folks', I started tuning in to music again. I watched this grungy little show on BBC Two called *Snub*, and there was a grungy little band from Glasgow playing called Teenage Fanclub. The announcer said, "Out of the ashes of the somewhat stricken Glasgow independent scene lies many people's fave new noise outfit."

She was describing the band, but I heard the phrase "somewhat stricken Glasgow independent scene" and decided she was talking about me. I had been in that scene, and I was "somewhat stricken." I watched the group and they definitely seemed to be the right sort of thing. They were a bit more raggedy and loud than the groups that had been around Glasgow before I got sick, but that wasn't a bad thing. I felt so out of it. If I hadn't got sick, I would have sniffed them out in a second. But there they were, mincing about on national TV.

Many people's fave new noise outfit!

So only a few months after getting out of the hospital, I took a risk, went on the train up to Glasgow to go see them. Lift, train, taxi, show, taxi, train, lift, home. I could do this. They were playing at a club called King Tut's Wah Wah Hut. It was rammed full. The last time I was in this place it was called something else and it was me that was booking the bands. Hardly anyone had shown up. This time I felt like a tourist. I was just here to watch. It did feel like a bit of a miracle to be there though. I didn't recognize anyone in the crowd, but I kind of liked that. I felt like one of the kids in *Tom Sawyer* when everyone thinks they've died, but then they turn up at their own funeral. This wasn't a funeral. Quite the opposite—this was a party.

The guys started playing, and the music and lights and vibe in the place were so rich and warm. I looked for a little perch at the back; I couldn't stand for long. The back was still near the front in a place so small as this. I could see everything. I didn't really know the songs, hadn't heard their records, but that never mattered to me. I'd seen so many shows, I actually preferred the thrill of hearing a song unfold for the first time in its tremulous live form.

The drummer seemed kinda agitated, in an excited sort of a way. Between songs he would step from behind his drum kit and come down to the front of the stage as if he had something to say. This was unusual. It was unusual for any of the bands that I was used to seeing

8

to have anything much to say between songs. This guy had a lot on his mind.

"See, just for tonight, could you watch your language? I don't want to hear any swearing. My sister's in the audience, she's pregnant, and I don't want that wean learning any bad words." And then he went back behind his drum kit and looked at the singer.

The singer looked back with a quizzical gaze. "Are you done?"

He raised his sticks to show his willingness to begin the next number.

"Ok, then we shall continue. This is a new song called 'Star Sign.'"

And they crashed into a number that was so clearly great. It was funny and tuneful and surfy and Byrdsy and heartfelt and heavy all at the same time. And I just loved it—the music flowed into me and through me. And in my new guise as the indie scene ghost, I could enjoy it in a different way. I didn't *have* to have an opinion on it, I didn't *have* to play their records at the club, I didn't *have* to try and pal in with them. I just liked them, and it.

3

God at the Piano

Something happened the other day. I did make a note of it in my jotter at the time, but I think I should expand on it. It has to do with God. I believe in God now, but I don't really know when it began. There wasn't an exact moment, but it seems somehow that while life was being stripped away from me, when I was getting ill and giving everything up, something else was being revealed. It was like a river going down and exposing the wreck of a ship. I'm not being particularly lucid, but I think the bare fact is that God stepped in and saved my neck. He put me in the hospital. It feels as if I could have just as easily died. Ever since I went into the hospital I've felt as if I'm being looked after, and I don't just mean by parents and nurses. It's like there's something else there.

Maybe that's what has to happen, maybe life has to go all quiet around you for you to realize there's something else going on. I feel now that there is another facet to life that is new and interesting and profound and definitely mysterious. I used to have these odd moments in the last five years or so. I called them "flags"—just small warm moments when I felt like things were going to be alright. Genuine moments of well-being; little nudges towards the light. Now I'm thinking that was probably God all along. It had to be. If it was, and without wanting to be too cheeky, I'm thinking, *Did you really have to rough me up so bad? Was I such a bad guy? I thought I was getting on ok. I would have believed in you if you had just said "Hello" or something.*

But this is the deal. This is the real thing. I was at the very nadir of my life and You somehow crept in. And now I'm having conversations with You because I don't really know how to pray. But maybe the conversations are ok for now. So that's the background, that's what I've been quietly thinking. I don't want to crow about it because I don't want the feeling to go. I feel less each day that it will go, however. My mind is now open to thoughts of *otherness*.

The thing that happened the other day, I'll tell you about it. I was sitting at the piano at my folks' house, sometime in the morning. I had just sat down, hadn't played anything. All of a sudden I got this feeling that this life is just an introduction to something else. A prelude. I could feel "life" stretching ahead, but it went way beyond me sitting at the piano, it went beyond me even as a person. For a moment I had been allowed a glimpse of something bigger. I'm quite certain about it. It just happened, it was a gift. It was up to me to decide how to react to it.

Do I change my life or has "it" already changed me? Either way, there's no going back. I may as well say I was never ill, I was never in hospital, I was never close to death. I may as well deny what has happened to me as a person this last year. That's how real this feeling of "otherness" is to me. I have come out the other side, and God is here. Since the hospital, I have been feebly praying sometimes. I suppose I went back to the Lord's Prayer from church. That happens to be the one I know. But it works for me. The glimpse I had while I was sat on the piano stool, on a quiet Tuesday just before lunch, seems to correspond to the bit in the prayer:

Thy kingdom come

There's something coming afterwards. That's what I felt, and it's what I feel. I just hope I can stick with it, not disappoint. There are no guarantees. How can I be good enough? But the great thing is the next line. It's special. There's a lot of comfort in it.

Thy will be done

Thy will. God's will. You can't control life. It's pointless to try. I used to try. Now I'm listening, and waiting.

4

Me and Richard, Richard and I

So we decided to get a flat in Glasgow together. Me and Richard. Richard and I. Richard is a friend of mine. He went to school with me. We were never big buddies at first, but then we got to be good pals near the end of school. We bonded over heavy rock music. He was a quiet guy at school; really, really quiet. He was quite tall, but even when he was in the middle of the playground he would always stand next to a bin or a post, hoping that people would just think he was part of the bin or the post.

When I think back on it now, I wonder what his plan was. Actually, I know what his plan was because it was the same as mine. Survival. And then get the hell out as fast as you could.

This was a big, tough, Scottish, redbrick, glass and plasterboard, built-in-the-sixties, comprehensive secondary school. The comprehensive bit meant that you would get a comprehensive kicking if you did anything that hinted at smugness, smartness, braininess, poshness. Richard's dad was a teacher at the school, so he was pretty much doomed from the start. Hence he assumed the cloak of invisibility.

For him it was extra hard though. He was almost the only non-white guy in our year, the only black guy. *And* he was English. There were a couple of other guys, some girls in the school, that came from different family backgrounds, different country backgrounds. But not many. It would have been different if he had been outgoing and cool. I'm guessing that the other boys would have taken to him. And he was a pretty good-looking guy. All it would have taken was for him to get a girlfriend, then the world of school would have seen him differently. Or if he'd knocked someone out with a punch. But it didn't happen. He was as open as I was to the everyday harassment of being a non-fighting male.

I'd go over to his house. I remember his younger sister, Johanna, was much more outgoing and funny—she was cut from a different cloth. She would kind of tease him, but kindly.

"Richard has lots of friends. Do you not think Richard has quite a lot of friends?"

"Johanna, what are you talking about?" Richard replied.

"I'm just asking Stephen if he knows that you're actually quite popular."

She didn't wait for me to answer though.

"What are you going to do? Are you going to go to Richard's room to talk about music? Do you want me to come up—I'll bring biscuits?" she asked hopefully.

"No, thank you, Johanna, we're fine. Do you not have homework?"

"I did all my homework before I even left school. I'm really clever."

She was balancing between two banisters at the bottom of the stairs.

"Stephen, do you want to hear me play 'Für Elise'? It's by Beethoven."

"Erm, I suppose so."

"I think we're just going to go upstairs," said Richard.

He gave his sister a bit of a look, as if to say "Stop embarrassing me."

"Ok, I'm going. See you later."

She detached herself from the stairway and let us go up.

I left school the year before Richard, but we both ended up "studying" in Glasgow. I hadn't seen much of him the last couple of years. I think he got his degree and then went off around the world, just drifting and thinking. At the same time, I ended up back in our little hometown, on my downward slide to near oblivion. He came to see me in the hospital. I was surprised to see him; I imagined he was off doing great things. He was practically the only person that came to visit apart from my mum and dad. When I got out of the hospital around Christmastime, we met up, and I just got the feeling that something wasn't right with him either. He was moving even slower than usual; he'd slowed right down. He'd been to see his doctor and the doc had suggested that he had some sort of post-viral thing going on too.

Ironically, his mum was a doctor, but sometimes that doesn't count for much, especially with something so slippery as ME/CFS. Unexplained chronic illness is like the doctor equivalent of a detective's cold case. It usually ends up in the bottom drawer of the filing cabinet. Whatever it was, we quickly got on with it and accepted that we were in the same boat. A leaky, directionless little vessel— but at least we had each other for company. I could paddle, he could steer. We'd take turns.

So for the next six months we'd do the small-town hang. We'd rest in the mornings, then go out somewhere in the afternoon. We'd watch sunsets, we'd lie on the grass if it wasn't too damp. We'd play each other at Scrabble and chess at the same time. While one person was considering their Scrabble move, the other person was playing their chess move, and vice versa. Thus our minds were always occupied.

I'd picked up the Scrabble bug in the hospital. When I'd got my strength back a bit, I'd always want to play Scrabble. I'd play anyone, anytime. It occupied the hours between lunch and dinner. There was a woman called Carol. She'd had a pretty bad time on account of her husband leaving her for someone else. She didn't have kids, it was just her in a semi-detached house on a new town estate. She kinda lost it and ended up on the ward. I liked to play her because she was a crossword type of person, so she wouldn't get huffy if I used a "big" word.

"What are you going to do when you get out of here, Stephen?" she asked.

"I don't know. I haven't thought about it."

"Don't you think you should have some sort of plan?"

"No. I had a plan before. Plans don't work."

I was wishing she would move. I had a possible seven-letter word on my rack. But then I thought I'd better ask her something back, out of politeness.

"What are you going to do?"

"Try to get my life back in order," she replied.

"What does that mean?"

"I still have a house and a job. I just need to get back to normal."

"What's the big rush? It's not as if normal was working out so great for you before."

I didn't look up from my pieces; I was just hoping she wouldn't block the double word. I could lay all my tiles down as long as she didn't block the double-word score. She'd gone quiet though. I looked up. There was a tear trickling from the outside left corner of her eye. She caught it with her screwed-up little bloodless fist.

"Shit, I didn't mean to upset you."

"No, it's ok, Stephen. You're not to know."

"Are you ok? You want me to go get Janice?"

"No, I'm ok." She found a tissue in her sleeve.

"I mean, it's ok, people are nice here. And the food's ok," I offered, as some sort of compensation.

"But we can't just sit around for the rest of our lives playing Scrabble, can we?" she said a little more forcefully.

I didn't reply. My plan was to sit around playing Scrabble. That was my horizon and my sunset back then.

But now, with Richard at my side, perhaps I was finally "getting my life back in some order," like Carol was talking about. No job, no partner, no mortgage; it still feels like a big deal though. Even though

I had lived in Glasgow for five years already, it feels completely different going back. If you can imagine a couple of young cats that have just moved to a new house and you put them out in the garden for the first time—that's me and Richard right now. We're moving gingerly, putting our paws out carefully and then pulling them back in. Smelling everything. Sitting for long periods in pools of sunlight.

I looked for a place back in the West End of the city, back in the old leafy neighborhood. This time, though, I was going to get extra leafiness, extra ambience, older stone, quieter, deeper streets. I knew the area so well, Richard left it to me to find a place for us. It was on the second floor of a converted Victorian townhouse. There was quite a grand entrance hall and then the building was split into apartments as you went up or down the stairs. Ours was divided up curiously. Somebody had put in fake walls when they were making the flats, and there was a long squiggly sort of walk between the kitchen at one end and Richard's room, through the living room, at the other end. That was a good thing. We could cut ourselves off from each other when we needed to. He could do his meditating, me my half-arsed praying. I took the best bedroom. I got more sunlight. I figured I had found the place. I made a vague promise that we'd switch after six months. Let's see what happens.

So that was us back in the city. We just wanted to live quietly, slowly and cheaply. Our ambition was to wake up healthier than the evening before. We were both on invalidity benefit, so the council paid for most of our rent. We had about £34 to get by on every week. We were going to take turns cooking, try to make stuff from scratch, no expensive luxuries, everything budgeted. We could make it like a game—how to get by, cheap, sick and nasty, in a northern city of your choice. Winter was going to be harder. There was no central heating in the flat, and we couldn't afford to run it anyway. Let's worry about that later.

In some quarters I'm already known as "the World's Coldest

Boy." It's maybe not such a curious thing, but one side effect of having slowed so much from one's lithe and athletic best was that one became icy cold. I did anyway. The cold seemed to affect me more than anyone else I had met with ME, before or since. I went from a two- or three-layer person to a seven- or eight-layer person. If I dropped below a certain temperature, it seemed to activate dormant viruses in my system that were just waiting for their chance. The first shiver I felt, they leapt out and took their grip, making me sneeze and snuffle with a quickness that many took for playacting.

At least we were heading for summer though. We were moving in at the best time. Everything was so lush and green. We were feeling every moment. All life was now ambience. We noticed everything. Because we had slowed and stopped, we had more in common with the peonies than the postman. Funny thing—have you ever stopped in a place that you would usually be moving through and just sat? It seems so different; in fact you would swear you were in a different place because the experience is so changed. I was always moving before, especially in *this* city. Now I was settling. As I sat at bus stops for long stretches, I saw the community slowly unfurl. As I sat in the laundry window waiting for pants and socks, I saw the hippest, the heightened and the homely pass in front of me. The experience was like looking at a painting, one you never noticed before because it wasn't gaudy and didn't shout out. It just *was*, full of love and insight. Richard and I continued to be the cats in our neighborhood, stretching out our paws a little more each time.

The flat nestled. It was one row back from the city. If it had been just one street forward, we would have heard the noise of the city floating up from Partick. But we were tucked in behind a heavy terrace of other Victorian townhouses. They had the view, but we were cooried in. The back lanes—where foxes dined, where magpies fought, where humans rarely bothered to go—that was my new real estate. I claimed it and owned it. From this point on I would walk in odd places, never fearing the polite but pointed inquiries from other stakeholders.

"You know that lane doesn't go anywhere?" they would say.

"Are you sure you're not lost?"

"Are you the gardener?"

I quite liked the last one. Didn't someone mistake Jesus for the gardener after the Resurrection? Shortly after we moved in, we did in fact go gardening at night. There was what they called a "pleasure garden" at the front of the house that was shared between the residents. It was fenced and locked. These curious entities were all over the West End. I'd never thought about them too much before because they were inaccessible. Also, no one ever seemed to be in them. We wanted in, obviously. But they wouldn't give the key to renters. We were fine to live in the building and pay rent, just not good enough to share an unused social space.

So we broke in.

We went down at dusk, around nine thirty. We walked around the perimeter and found a bit where the fence had been repaired. It was weakened and, really, the bolt was hardly holding the thing on. We gave it a shove and a shoogle and we were in. The grass was soft and mossy. We stepped into the center, near an ornamental thingy, and with theatrical timing a cloud moved, the moon was there, and our elf-like shadows leapt out over the lawn. It was a nice place to be in. I didn't feel like we had violated anything, we had just loosened a screw. We lay on our backs in the center of the lawn and tried to spot and name the elusive summer stars, but we were failing.

"I'm going to come and sleep here," Richard said.

I believed him. That was the sort of thing he did.

"And our new neighbors will love you for it," I replied.

I came up on my elbows and looked both ways. There were two lawns separated by shrubbery, but they were long.

"Perfect place for a Frisbee," I said.

"We don't have a Frisbee."

"We could get one?"

"It's not in the budget."

"Nuts to your budget."

We let the quiet come in again.

"We could cultivate food crops," I suggested.

"Where?"

"Over there." I sat up and pointed to an empty border. "I could put potatoes in."

"They wouldn't let you," Richard said.

"They wouldn't know."

"Do it then."

"I will."

I wouldn't though. I wouldn't follow through. Richard would. If he said it, he would. If I say it, it's because I like to say it. I say many things. I'm not sure Richard liked *hearing* many things. Thankfully, off through the bushes, within a twelve-minute radius of where we lay, as the fox went, there was someone who I was pretty sure would put up with my extra need for saying things. Carrie was somewhere over there, with her own complexities and her own pleasure garden. Over the next few weeks it seemed like I started going round to see Carrie pretty much every day. It was a destination, and she was always in. I worried that her folks might think I was being intrusive, and I was a little concerned that I didn't take Richard with me more often—but I went anyway. Sometimes she was passive, sometimes she was active, sometimes she laughed, some days she was too ill and she sent me away abruptly.

But I still went. I was like the boy that climbs the beanstalk. There's a path ahead with a castle at the end. Where the fuck else are you meant to go?

20

5

Girl Sweat and Pleather

This room isn't so bad. There's a pool of light that comes in during the morning that warms you. I wrap myself in a duvet and sit cross-legged on the carpet. I'm wedged into the corner between the MDF doors of the fitted wardrobe and the chipped magnolia of the wallpaper. I should really try a bit of meditation.

I look around the room. I have two plants for company—a cheese plant and a fern. They are both what I would call ME survivors; they managed to bridge my old and new lives through the crisis of the last two years. This was not easy for them. There has been a purge on both sides. I have purged, and the rest of life has purged me. These two plants have escorted me through a narrow wormhole and made it to the sunny uplands of Glasgow, 1991. I'm being optimistic. I'm trying to be optimistic. I may have lost a lot, but from the void I have returned. With each disability income voucher, I am proving my resilience, my capability to survive. I am going to live and thrive like my cheese plant and my fern (if the cold of this new flat doesn't get them).

Here I am—no job, no essays, nobody phoning me up for a gig, no one phoning me to play records, no girlfriend, one flatmate, one friend. It's amazing how easily it can all fall away. Materially, I had disappeared long before they dumped me in hospital. I had a good nine months of invisibility in Glasgow before that. No one noticed. It's funny how easy it is to disappear from your own life. I kept my mum at bay with sparse but regular enough phone calls. I moved into a house with total strangers and never came out of my room. Vivian wasn't even sure where I was in the end. She had gone to Spain with Sam and Hannah.

When she came back and found me, she turned me in to the authorities, namely my poor parents. But that was then, and this is the sunny uplands. And even though Vivian is gone (and Samara and Hannah, by strict, unbending, end-of-relationship rules, are gone with her), I will remain upbeat and unbent, and jammed into the corner of my new, dappled room. So now that I'm upbeat, why can't I just be like a normal guy and go out and get another girlfriend? Move on.

Prior to Vivian, I was so used to not having a girlfriend, so resigned to being single, I just shut my brain off to the whole idea. When she chatted me up (and she did; she had the whole thing planned out), it was like trying to open a tin of sardines when the little key thing had fallen off. It was tricky. It took negotiating, it took belligerence. It took determination. She was around me for a while before an acquaintance of mine pointed out that he thought she was interested in me. I was playing records at the time, controlling the dancefloor in a dark and busy club. It took a lot just for me to notice someone was talking to me.

My point is that when Vivian finally pried my tin open and exposed my fishy sides to the world, all silver and gleaming, I didn't just fall for her, the opener of the tin. I fell for everyone. I fell for beauty in numbers. I fell for beauty in squadrons. I fell for beauty in formation. In this case, the formation was four young women walking into a club wearing long, ornate floral-print dresses, costume jewelry, stacked boots. It was an ambush of the senses.

Let me explain.

There was a uniform in the club. There was a uniform plus a couple of outliers. I liked the uniform. *I* was in uniform. My uniform was, approximately:

Doc Martens;
trousers—black flannel, wide and straight of leg;
t-shirt—striped, crew-necked;

jacket—zipper, reversible, cream/black or houndstooth;
hair—number two shave at sides and back, overhanging flop
at front.

That was me.
The clientele, the boys anyway, wore variations on a few different
themes:

band t-shirts aplenty;
jeans with hems tucked up;
some flannel shirts, plaid, country style;
the occasional cravat;
white denim jackets;
the occasional punk;
the occasional psychobilly;
the occasional goth.

The girls were either dressed just like the boys—

denim; Docs; flannel shirts; band shirts; Harrington jackets

—or they wore:

cutie dresses,
kinda fifties,
polka dots,
checks or flowers,
often belted;
hair could be short,
bobbed or tied up
in a pigtail;
lots of make-up,

red lips,
dark eyes;
into the sixties,
mixing it up,
short skirts,
stripy tights,
leather boots,
mod dresses,
psychedelic;
and . . .
the occasional punk;
the occasional psychobilly;
the occasional goth.

Ok, I'm generalizing a bit, but the kind of music I was playing drew a certain crowd. Also, I think pretty much everyone went to this one shop called Flip. It was a bit of ritual for me anyway. It was a retro, vintage superstore. The people that owned it went to America and bought up bulk loads of all the clothes I previously described. I guess they dug them up in warehouses or something. There seemed to be an endless supply of plaid shirts and old denim. But aside from that there was all this quirky Americana that seemed to come straight from the set of *East of Eden*. Rows and rows of zipper jackets with real guys' name patches sewn on. Chad and Ralph and Jody and Billy. All those guys that had jobs in the fifties and sixties *parking cars and pumping gas*.

So that's where everyone went to dress, and I wasn't any different. It was cheap, and you could invent a character for yourself. I went in every Saturday, usually for something that I would wear that night, even if it was just an accessory, like a burgundy-roped shoulder bag or a pair of James Dean glasses. A trip to that store was such a wonderful hors d'oeuvre to the weekend. I could get a tantalizing glimpse of some of the crowd that would come to the club that night. It helped me think about the night and what tracks I would play. Funny thing is, I never really talked to them, even the regulars. Just the odd glance and nod. I mean, I *could* have talked to them. I didn't have anything to say though. I was channeling everything I wanted to say through the records I was playing.

There was a basement in Flip that was so deep in piles of odd clothes, you could get happily lost. It was a kitsch jamboree. They had the idea that they would get these old silk pajamas and dye them black and sell them. And we bought them. I bought US Navy gear, leather-sleeved baseball jackets, Holden Caulfield hunting hats. There were windbreakers and car coats, college jackets and checked sports jackets, all straight out of *Happy Days*.

They played great music too. Not quite as brilliant as the stuff I played at night, but then they didn't have to keep the dancefloor assiduously supplied with perfect grooves. It was excellent browsing music. Did the Clash or the Cramps or the B-52's ever sound as good as they did in there, blasting out of the changing rooms while all the young bucks pouted and fought for the best mirrors? Never. It was the ideal setting to hear certain songs. There was a leather jacket—a black, stripped-down, sixties, biker's thing, real simple. I shouldn't have bought it, it was too much money. But they played "Pretty Persuasion" by R.E.M. and I handed over the cash in a rush of intoxication I just couldn't fight.

My point is, and I do have a point, that Vivian and her friends didn't look like any of us. They started floating into the club around that time, a little like they had come by mistake. They seemed young and fresh. If one of the staff had gone over to their table and asked, genuinely, "Are you guys in the right place?" it wouldn't have been surprising. For all the concentrated coolness in the club, it could be a little suffocating. Everyone was very serious about how they looked, and everyone wore their musical proclivities on their literal sleeves. These four girls, however, would have taught any old zealot how to breathe again. They were beautiful, from what I could gather out of the corner of my eye as I glanced across the record decks. That beauty would swirl around me over time, all that hair let loose, all the hot breath of gasping girlfriends, the different smell of the four of them trying to outdo each other in fragrance, the paisley scarves, the big hoopy jewelry, ornate patterns, suede and skin, girl sweat and pleather.

That was then.

Here I am now, sitting between cheese plant and fern, looking for peace in the quiet morning void. I'm trying to meditate. I don't even know if I'm doing it right. I keep emptying my mind, but I keep getting pulled back to those times.

6

Nature Boy

I'm so tired today, I feel battered. If I don't come across as coherent, you know why. This is a typical day of my life in Glasgow so far, and it goes pretty slow . . .

This morning I stayed in. Richard's off at his brother's, so I can move real slow, drink my tea, look for a warm spot. I'm reading *Kidnapped* by Robert Louis Stevenson just now and I love it. After lunch I walked slowly round to Carrie's. I take the lane route, which is 385 yards longer but if you have the time and the leisure is often worth it just for the leafy vibe. It was one of those still August days when you can hear someone's voice clear as a bell coming from an open tenement window. I stopped and *heard* a woman filling in the *Herald* crossword at a kitchen table. That sort of day.

I travel in the land of no traffic. There are always copious amounts of grass pushing up between the cobbles of these in-between passages. Cats and old tin wheelie bins. Bits of an old Jaguar that someone was working on once. Opportunist birches squeezing between garages. Trees, trees, *trees*—my greatest friends!

Carrie already calls me "Nature Boy." Her sisters, as reported elsewhere, call me "the World's Coldest Boy." Funny to fall in amongst that lot. When I'm round there, I cleave to Carrie. I don't make a move without her, I try to stay quiet and still, I try not to offer an opinion unless I'm asked. It's a family, after all; they have the family thing going on. Furthermore, they're a brainy sort of high-functioning family. You could imagine them in a documentary about brainy sorts of high-functioning families. And they talk about things, things that aren't just "what's for dinner." A subject is introduced, it gets thrown about the room and spat out a little worse for wear on the other side. If you are going to be a talked-about subject in that house, prepare to be cajoled, mused over, held up to scrutiny and ultimately chuckled about.

When I arrive round at the big house, Carrie and her younger sister, Gillian, are sitting on the steps to the front door. A tartan rug covers the top step; the sun catches the whole scene. Half-empty cups are there. If I was a painter, I would paint that scene and I would make you fall in love with it and them.

"Ho," I say.

"Ho yourself," Carrie says.

"Well, I'll leave you to it," says Gillian, and she gets going. She always does that, slinks off like a svelte and uninterested cat. It's a bit annoying because it makes you want her to stay even more, but she never does.

"Do you want to go to a garden center?" Carrie asks. "Dad says you can drive the car as long as you promise not to crash. He says he doesn't care about us, he just doesn't want to be hassled by the fuzz."

"I can drive," I attest.

They had a big orange bus of a square Volkswagen, which the sisters called "the Bop." See what I mean? Quirky. Who calls their car a name like "the Bop"? Luckily, I had retained my capacity for driving. Carrie did drive once but learned to drive in a far-off farming community on an island where all you had to do to pass was not kill a sheep. So she was rusty. And incapacitated besides.

We drove out of the city. Glasgow is a really easy city to drive out of. Eight minutes from the door, you are in the countryside, looking at hills that turn into the Highlands quite quickly. We pointed the Bop that way and headed for the last homely house, which was Rivendell Garden Center. We parked up and walked slowly through, heading straight for the nirvana that was the garden center tearoom. It was nirvana for us anyway. There be scones.

Carrie and I called this whole process "sconery." As in:

"How was the sconery?"

"Pretty good. On the whole, pretty good sconery."

"Sconery" was meant to designate the whole scene. Centered around the possibility of getting a nice scone, it was a scene that we were part of but preferred to think that we weren't. The "just visiting" thing again. Like when we were in the psychiatric unit. We were there but not really. Just observing.

And observe we did. Us off to one side, a cozy corner with a view onto a grassy slope running up to . . . nothing, just sky. It was enough to give us a sense that we were "out." We draped ourselves over the chairs, made the table our island. It felt ironic that the elderly couples we gazed upon, the harassed family men, the fifty-something whip-thin crop-haired women that we observed, all seemed to move with a sense of purpose far beyond our ken and capabilities.

"How are you anyway?" I asked.

"Ok, you know . . ." That meant the usual; no change.

"What about you?" she asked.

"Aye." That just meant the same.

Still, that was better than "bloody awful," which would be her stuck in bed, curtains shut, head throbbing, muscles aching. I was definitely less "bloody awful" than her in general. Carrie seemed to have an unswerving physical limit, a threshold to her movements that she had accepted a long time ago. It didn't so much cast a black cloud as maybe a mottled gray one. I liked the challenge of trying to puff the cloud away.

"Last boyfriend," I said.

Carrie had settled into staring into a void, letting her milky Earl Grey go cold.

"Last boyfriend," she repeated, staring into the middle distance. "Marcus Dempsey. Ginger balls, narrow penis."

"And that's it? That's all he amounted to?" I asked.

She turned to engage in the conversation.

"No, he was good, he was sweet. He was my lanky, student halls guy. He was on the committee, I ran the tuck shop. We were a Davidson Hall power couple."

"Did you have shoulder pads?"

"Not shoulder pads, but I did have thighs like Jennifer Beals."

"Who's she?"

"The actor from *Flashdance*."

"And she had good thighs, I presume?"

"The best."

"And that was enough to make you one-half of a power couple?"

Carrie thought for a moment.

"Well, obviously I had other things going for me, but yes, kind of. I had a great body, really nice definition. I used to work out."

"Like Jennifer Beals?"

"Like Jennifer Beals."

She poured more hot water into her mini teapot and gave it a stir. She always got the most out of her teabag.

"What did this guy Marcus do to deserve you?"

She looked at me in a more pointed way.

"You know what? He was lucky to get me. It was just a student halls thing, a corridor deal. I thought it was going to be a jumping-off point, something to start with, but we were together for a year."

"And then?"

"Well . . . this." Meaning ME, dropping out . . . sconery.

"It started that far back?"

"December '87. Started feeling ill. Four months later, I had to leave uni. Easter '88."

"That was pretty quick."

"Yeah, it all just kind of . . . unraveled," Carrie said. "Then I was in bed for three years."

She went back to her middle-distance staring.

"Hey, at least we're in Rivendell now, that's something!"

"That's something, yeah."

"What happened to Marcus, did he ever visit?"

"He did at the start, but then it was too much. He is actually *married* now."

"*Married!* Fuck, do people actually do that?"

"They do. At least, people called Marcus Dempsey do."

We both stared off and tasted our lukewarm tea.

"Good for him," I said gently, without meaning or motive.

7

Alone Is Not Lonely

I was back at my mum's, and it was just after lunch. I got this feeling. I was thinking about Carrie. I felt like writing about her. I know it's funny, because I haven't known her for *that* long. But I had a definite urge. I was near the piano. So I sat at the piano, and I let the words come to me, and they seemed to attach themselves to a tune in my head. The tune was like the arc of a rainbow. I know that doesn't make any sense, but the little tune felt like an arc in my head, and the words were attached.

I placed my hands over the keys, looked around for the chord that seemed to match the notes in my head. I don't think I even sang it, I just played the chord and heard the tune. Then I felt for another chord further down. I knew that if I played that with the same tune, it would work. This time I actually sang out loud, a second line with the second chord, then back to the first chord again. Just like that, I was writing a song. I wrote some words in my jotter that fitted the tune. I wrote about Carrie, or at least used Carrie as my jumping-off point, and I called it "There's No Holding Her Back."

I had thought about trying to write songs quite a few times before I got ill, but I couldn't. It was a mystery to me. It was a closed door. It wasn't just closed, it was invisible. But just then the door appeared to me. And I have this feeling that now it's open, I'm not going back. There's no holding *me* back. It's a thing. I can do a thing. I can write about anything. Sing about anything. I'm not crowing about it. I'm whispering here. I'm just saying, it felt good. In the absence of anything else, maybe I can do *this*.

*****

Back in Glasgow at the flat, I'm sitting on my beanbag between my two plants, trying to suck up the extra oxygen they're producing. It's pissing down outside. Richard and I did our supermarket run this morning, so that was today's outing. Now we're stuck in. I'm thinking about the hospital again, and I'm thinking about creativity. I have hardly done anything really creative since . . . well, hardly ever. I've been thinking about other people's creativity constantly, though, in the last five years, especially while reading or soaking up music.

While I was in hospital, I did go to a creative writing class. It was the ward sister who suggested I go. I had nothing else going on. It was in an old three-story sandstone building on the edge of the hospital grounds, surrounded by pine trees. The bit of the hospital that we stayed in was newish, built in the eighties perhaps. There was a core of old buildings in the trees that hinted at less enlightened times in the history of psychiatric care. They had really small windows near the top, I assumed so that the patients couldn't jump out.

The building with the writing class was in the old part but was friendly enough now, if a little musty. The lady that took the class was called Mrs. McCallum, and she was kind, schoolteacher-like and dressed in a plaid suit. It was a small group: just me, then an old boy called Damian Caster (who dressed like the major from *Fawlty Towers*), Brian from our ward, Jacqueline, a skinny, howling girl from Craig Ward, and Mia, one of the student nurses.

Mia I fancied, in an obvious kind of way. The nurses never talked about their personal lives too much, but I had a feeling she had a boyfriend tucked away somewhere, whether in the town or back home. Even if she didn't, nothing *ever* was going to happen between us. And not just because it was "not on" between a nurse and a patient, but just *because*. I think maybe hospital was all we had in common.

The student nurses all lived in the accommodation blocks at the other end of the campus. I overheard talk about "legendary parties." It all sounded way out of my league. Regardless, I did my best to flirt with her in my stuttering, subtle way, and she condescended to converse with me on matters trivial and to play the odd game of Scrabble. I told her I was going to the writing group, and she was quite enthusiastic. I said she should come along, and I was pretty surprised when she took the wooded path with me to Mrs. McCallum's lair.

I can't remember much about what I wrote. I put no great store in it, but it was no thriller. Something to do with trees and rain and confusion. The reviews were mixed. Damian had written a descriptive piece about a lovely ship. It was pleasing in a neat sort of way, especially as he did seem to have more than a hint of salty air about him. Mrs. McCallum asked where he got his idea from and he said, "From the television." She asked if anyone else had done their piece while the TV was on and everyone put their hand up except me and Mia.

Mia read her piece next, and it was called "Alone Is Not Lonely." I mean, it didn't say much, but I still liked it.

I'll tell you what I liked:

- it was being in that room with her reading it out, steadily, intently;
- it was being in that room with the fading sun through the window as the NHS strip lights flickered into life;
- it was being in that room with the moaning of the pine trees in the wind as they rocked and rubbed against the building outside.

Mia's piece must have been ok because it put me in such a relaxed place. She described a cup of coffee and her kitchenette. She described an ironing board and her two hamsters. She talked about being far from "home" (which was obviously in the north of England somewhere, given her north-of-England-somewhere accent). I was thinking while she read that the only thing that stopped me being actively and rudely in love and lust with her was that she was wearing tights under her uniform. And I'm kind of glad that she was, because I might have said something after she finished her story, something whimsical yet inappropriate. And if I wanted to maintain the image of being the only person in the psychiatric ward that really wasn't meant to be in that place, then such things were not to be blurted out.

I don't know what she did that triggered me, but any combination of beauty and kindness at that point would have done it. It's no wonder that patients and nurses sometimes have "things." The patients are just puddles of emotion ready to attach themselves blob-like to any passing uniform. At least I was. It's a little worrying that I seem to be talking so much about the hospital when I'm meant to be getting on with this new life. But the one thing the hospital had that the last six months haven't had was a feeling of a society. A community. Something. It had it. When I left at Christmas to go back to my folks, the lack of a common room full of recovering alcoholics, anxious mothers, pill-popping goons, runaway tearaway teens and a smattering of the mentally incapacitated was a real drawback.

One of the first mornings in the hospital, maybe the third day, I think I had slept a little better, like a few hours, and I was up early. I crept into the day room. It was about six thirty, mid-September. It was light outside, so I went over to the big windows. The trees were growing right up against the windows and I loved that. I went over to feel their embrace.

I had my Walkman with me. I had stopped listening to music when I was at my worst. It just irritated me. But this morning felt like a miracle. This morning it felt like my life might be saved. I put on my favorite song by the group the Sundays. The song was called "Can't Be Sure." It is a miracle of a song, so it matched the mood of the morning. Her voice was ringing in my head, saving me and calling me. It was the first time in months I had the energy to entertain an emotion, so I cried.

Shortly after that, the first staff started coming in. Lights turning on, voices in the corridors, confident morning steps, swinging briefcases, swinging doors. Patients began drifting in to get breakfast. They called us up to the tables. I was giving it my best go with the porridge and the scrambled eggs. I still felt out of it though, completely alien, like this all wasn't really happening.

One of the nurses, a big, beardy guy, started singing a song I immediately recognized:

> "*Oh, they built the ship* Titanic,
> *to sail the ocean blue.*
> *They thought it was a ship*
> *that water would never go through.*
> *But the Lord's almighty hand*
> *said that ship would never land.*
> *It was sad when the great ship went down.*"

We had to sing that at school when I was eight. It had gone into my head and never left. All my life I thought if I ever had to stand on a chair and sing one song, I could sing this one. I wanted to say to the guy, "That's my bloody song! Why the hell are you singing it now?" But I didn't. I wasn't up to it. I wasn't up to bantering. I just let the memory swill around my head for a minute. I ate what I could, then retreated to the chair nearest the trees and put on the Sundays song again.

The Sundays were a bit of a surprise when they came along. In '89 I was at the height of my powers as a DJ. I was filling floors three nights a week in clubs around Glasgow. My core thing was post-punk/indie/new wave. That's what it said on my posters. Everything

'77 and after. When I was employed by the university, I would play goth for the goths, some psychobilly for the psychobillies, and ska for the ska kids. Then came hip-hop, acid house, baggy and the start of grunge. The Sundays were lovely though. They just snuck in at the end of the eighties. They were what I listened to when I got home.

I'd arrive back outside my bedsit in my crappy Peugeot at three in the morning. I had to lift my crates of records up the three flights to my flat. I'd shut the door, get my Shredded Wheat and tea, go to my desk by the window, find the page in my book, try to lose myself in a different place. For years, this bookish and quiet existence had been a brilliant complement to my going-out life. Lately I had been favoring books and quiet. That's when my legs had started failing me, when those crates started getting heavier.

Instead of anticipating the madness of Saturday night, I started to shy away from the people I was there to entertain. I was being drained. This was the ME coming, though I didn't know it then. I couldn't believe people managed to work and then drink and then dance and *then* go to parties afterwards to drink more and be sick and snog and shag and take drugs and talk until the sun came up. I had always drawn the line after the club shut. I liked to get up in the morning and see both parts of the day. I didn't drink, I didn't take drugs.

And, as discussed before, I didn't do girls. I'd kind of given up on that one. I hadn't had a girlfriend since I was thirteen. How the fuck did that happen? Easy. It's easy to not have a girlfriend or partner. Just live your life and you will be single. That was my west-of-Scotland, spotty twenty-year-old, late-developer perspective. I *had* tried. I'd hung around at a few clubs in my early days. I'd propped up walls at parties, wanting desperately just to go home because no one ever, *ever*, talked to me. All that relationship stuff was about competing. I figured out that if you had to compete for beauty, that was the kind of beauty I was not interested in.

Back at my flat, I'd put on my headphones, put a record on the turntable. The '89 comedown. The Sundays, Cocteau Twins, Felt, the soundtrack to *Betty Blue*, the soundtrack to *Paris, Texas*. When I wasn't reading, sometimes I'd write letters to people in bands, sometimes to the singer in the Sundays, just telling her about my day, thoughts, occurrences. As for what I was reading, I glanced over at the books I had just taken out of the university library. They were:

Men Without Women — Hemingway
All the Sad Young Men — Fitzgerald
Deaths for the Ladies — Mailer

I remember at the time, even with the almost zero capacity for irony and self-awareness that I had in pre-illness days, thinking to myself: What is this saying? What is this telling me? Vivian invaded this space. Vivian changed it all, chucked in a wrench. I don't regret it though. I think it had to happen for me to become a human being. I was on course to being a robot, a non-functioning person, a strange uncle.

Was it this hard for everyone to have a relationship? I knew my life had become rigid. I had fallen into patterns, I lived by a strict set of rules. I was just holding on to things by the fingernails. I think Vivian was partly to blame for all this — the ME, the hospital, the collapse — in the kindest way. She was a catalyst. Like in a chemical experiment, you introduce a certain substance and the whole thing kicks off, goes wild — smoke, steam, explosions — but the catalyst is unaffected, walks away unscathed, leaving a bench of broken and scorched test tubes.

On one hand I'll never get over her beauty and loveliness, her spunk and her laugh, her smell and her artiness, her sex and her dimples. My other hand, however, was still writing admiring letters to a girl who was just a disembodied voice, an idea, a comfort, a solace—reliable, dependable, never yelled back, never sulked or criticized or took up too much of the bed.

That was Harriet, the girl from the Sundays.

8

Will Your Anchor Hold?

I was singing in the kitchen. I often sang around the flat, probably much to the annoyance of Richard. I don't know if I always used to sing, but I was singing now, like a bird. Richard and I were getting in each other's way in the narrow kitchen as I was making tea and toast. He sat down with his porridge. Finally, he said, "You know, you should probably just go to church and get it over with."

"Get what over with?"

"The church thing that's going on with you."

I honestly didn't know what he was talking about.

He continued. "The last couple of days you've been singing old hymns almost constantly."

"*Really?*"

"How could you not know? 'Will Your Anchor Hold?' You were singing that two minutes ago."

"Was that song from church?"

"Definitely. And then we had a few days of 'Bread of Heaven.'"

"I don't know the words—what's that one?"

Richard proceeded to hum a few lines of the theme tune to *Songs of Praise* on BBC One.

"That's the theme to *Songs of Praise*."

"Still, it's a hymn."

"How do you know so much about hymns?"

"I went to church every Sunday for sixteen years."

"I went to church too. I suppose a lot of the tunes are knocking about in my head. I never remember the words though."

"I think you should go back."

"To church?" I laughed.

"Seriously. You probably should."

He went back to his porridge, but he'd got me thinking. I knew that I believed in God, and I said my rubbish prayers at night and in the morning, but surely that didn't mean that I should go to church? I think in the back of my mind I had a vague notion that at some point I might be coerced into joining some spiritual discussion group for the hip and young who had heard the call—some little clique that met on a Thursday night for coffee cake and board games, with a passing acknowledgment that there was now an extra dimension in our lives and did we think that we should do something about it? Answer: probably not. Maybe just enjoy it and feel a bit superior.

Church. Stuffy old church. What did it mean anyway? That place that I used to get dragged to as a boy. "Mumbling in cold buildings" I heard a comedian describe it as once. That seemed about right. Richard was ok. He was already a dedicated meditator. He seemed amazingly sorted for someone whose scope of life had been so viciously narrowed in the last few years. There he was—meditating, being calm, eating Marmite, writing a few letters, wearing socks in bed, playing classical guitar. There didn't seem to be many rumples in his outlook.

Carrie and I had crash-landed into our situations though. I think it's fair to say we had gone through our respective crises at a different level. And it might be fair to say it was still an hourly mystery to Carrie and me what was happening to us and why. We had questions, and while there were few answers to be found, it helped that we could sit in the same room hogging the same imagined question mark.

I wasn't going to church though. What good could it possibly do? And anyway, Jesus was in church and what the hell did he have to do with anything? Why not a mosque or a synagogue? Or with the

Buddhists. All that stuff was cool. If Richard could sit cross-legged for ages and be happy with his porridge, maybe I could? Did the Buddhists have God?

I'm not going to church.

The next morning I woke up kind of late and my first thought was: *Is there even a church around here and could I make it to the service?* I pulled my big trousers over my PJs, grabbed a big coat and ran out. I seemed to remember there was a big church tower up on the main street, ten minutes away. I jogged along, which really was walk a bit, jog a bit, walk a bit more.

I got to the place—big tower, big church. The massive doors were closed tight. There was the sound of a church organ inside, and singing. That was it. That was the sign. They had started early and without me. I was locked out. God wanted me to contemplate his nature, but he wanted me to do it on my own. With some relief, I retreated down the church steps to the main road, puffed out from the rush. I turned back towards the flat, but I noticed that there was another church on the opposite corner. This one was a bit more tucked away, didn't have a tower or a steeple. *How many churches do these people need?* I thought.

I moved warily towards it, reluctantly. It was in the way anyway. I had to walk past it to get home. On the corner nearest the road there were people still going in, up the steps to the big doors. I peeked up there but turned left up the smaller street, along the side of the church, away from the entrance. As I got to the other corner of the building, an old lady in a blue coat was coming towards me.

"Good morning." She smiled, waved a hand in my direction, then turned into a little alley. I looked in after her. There was another way of getting into the church.

I followed her in. There was a bespectacled gent with a low, low voice there to welcome me in. He gave me a sheet of folded paper and ushered me through a swinging wooden door. Here I was, in church.

From what I could remember of such things, it seemed to be the same flavor as the one I went to when I was a boy. But here I was on my own, and it wasn't even Christmas. The minister soon asked everyone to say "Hi" to everyone else, and the people that were close by came over and shook hands, wishing me well. A couple of the sprightlier ladies even leapt halfway across the church to say "Hi" to me. My anonymity was punctured.

The organ started. I knew *all* the songs. Richard was right about that. My ability to absorb songs from my youth, whether from TV adverts, cartoons or hymns, was seemingly well developed.

I liked *half* the hymns.

I liked the prayers—I was there already, no problem with that. In fact I liked the feeling of bowing my head at the same time as everyone else, like I had been practicing for this moment and here it was—the one bit when I didn't feel like a fraud. Some might say I was acting meek, like a sheep, but I wouldn't even mind that description so much. Meek is ok. Prayer is a giving in, after all. It's only in the yielding that the good stuff has a chance of creeping in. That had been my experience so far.

When I was on my own, I didn't have to think about how to pray. It was as natural as talking. It was asking, remarking, beseeching, thanking, wishing. Things that the average human did every day. I was usually happy to get around to it. No one forced me. I did often *forget* to pray though, and when I finally did it, often coerced by the stress, worry and discomfort of everyday living, I'd think, *Why didn't I do this before? This is the best part of the day, the only time when things feel peaceful.*

Back in the church, the prayer was over. The minister was tall; he looked like one of the youngest people there. There were a few kids down the front, and as he talked to them specifically, I looked around. The building was one big vaulted open space on the inside. No balcony, no side bits, just really big and dark. There were massive stained glass windows on all sides, but their slightly dour illustrations seemed to block the light rather than send it through with a heavenly sparkle.

There were maybe eighty people in the place, which looked like it could take eight hundred. Some families, but mostly older people sitting alone or huddled in groups for warmth. (The comedian was right about the cold bit.) I made it through the service. I kept waiting for a telltale moment, something said from the pulpit that would make me cringe. I was certain I would hear something that didn't sit right with me, something that went against what I stood for, something lame, out of date, something too mainstream, too establishment, too . . . restrictive. It never came. It all seemed pretty reasonable to me. Maybe I'm getting soft, but there was absolutely nothing I was offended by. Maybe I just got a lucky week? (And what did I stand for? In these days of ME, I just wanted to be warm.)

We sang the hymns, we prayed to God. Someone read from the Bible. Some of that seemed random at worst, but the last reading was clear enough. It was about a tax collector. (There always seems to be a tax collector. There must have been loads of them back in those days, just hanging around the fountain, rubbing their hands and bothering widows.) This was the one that climbed the tree to see Jesus because he was too short to see over the crowd.

Jesus said, "Ho, you, short arse! Yes, you. I'm coming to yours for tea."

"Mine? I'm the tax collector. You can't come to mine!"

"I'm Jesus, I can do whatever I want, and I'm coming round to yours later, so get out of the tree and start making a few bannocks."

And he did. He went to the guy's house for tea, and the crowd moaned about it, especially the disciples, and they said, "You can't go to his house. He's a real bastard! One of the worst!"

And Jesus said, "I can and I will. I'm not here just to talk to you lot, I'm here for the tricky bastards too."

You couldn't fault that. He was here for the tricky ones.

I was sitting there thinking, *Stupid disciples. If I was a disciple I wouldn't doubt him, I wouldn't answer back.* But I was no disciple.

I thought about it later.

I was the tax collector.

9

Traditional Matters

Masturbation is such a waste of time and energy. It's totally mince. I am of course speaking after *la petite mort*, "the little death," as the French call it. Ejaculation. You find me but a shadow of a boy. I don't know what your situation is, what the average person's situation is, but it really knackers me for days after. I know that's partly an ME thing. It piles depletion on depletion. Depletion squared. Not pretty.

I used to hardly ever do it anyway. Went for long periods without even thinking about it. Now that I'm more open to it (especially on account of having had a proper girlfriend and therefore something to think about when wanking), I end up falling back to it—on a Friday night when nothing is happening, no prospect of anything, a few dreams, some distant shadows, faraway encounters.

It's a bollocks.

And I've got God staring over my shoulder, watching and judging everything that I do now. I mouth an apology, pull the virtual curtain between us and give in to "traditional matters," as I think Kenneth Williams once called it. But seriously, sorry, God. I am sorry, and I hope that you forgive me. And I hope you don't mark me down too badly every time I do it. I do want to stay on the path, you know. "Your will" and all that.

I never asked Vivian if she did it. We never really got that far in. Funny thing—I have just about got to that stage with Carrie, even though we are definitely destined not to be a couple. She is a prisoner, just like me. We are in an exclusive club, the chronic illness club. So we trade information like bubblegum cards. When you're cellmates with a person, you tell them everything, right? You have to; you've got to spill the beans eventually. Those beans are all you have. It's your duty to entertain your fellow detainee with Proust-like fantasies and memories—if you can muster them.

Like the other day in her room. We were lounging as usual.

"I kissed his neck," she admitted.

"Why did you kiss his neck?"

"It was just there. I couldn't help myself."

Carrie was telling me about a night out with "the football lads." She could only really make it out for a short time. Like me, she was just a tourist, even on a visit to the pub. As she was saying goodbye to one of the boys, her head shot forward and kissed his neck like a snake taking a bite out of a pig.

"Oh God! What did he do?" I asked.

"Recoiled. Yelled '*Carrie!*' Everyone looked. Everyone judged. It just adds to their deepening conviction that I'm desperate and horny."

"Why don't you just have a wank and be done with it?"

She laughed. "Ha! It's not the same. Come on, you know it's not the same."

"But, really, he's not *that* good-looking," I added.

"The lips, the hair, the leather jacket. It's a devastating combination."

Thank God Carrie isn't into me. I've known her for one summer, but it feels like we are established best friends without even making a thing about it. We were just meant to be. She thought me and Richard were a couple for most of that time. She only admitted that to me when she realized we weren't, on account of the fact I was always pathetically going on about some girl or other, real or invented.

"So, when you wank, do you feel depleted?" I asked.

"When I walk to the toilet I feel depleted," she said.

"So that's a yes?"

"It's just a lot to build up to. It feels a bit like trying to get Frankenstein's monster going. You need the electricity to get started.

When you're on your own, it hardly feels worth it. Do you do it?"

"Occasionally. But I always feel rubbish afterwards. And I don't mean that I get a good night's sleep and wake refreshed. It just seems to borrow so much from the ME bank account."

"Ah yes, the ME bank account. The bank manager's a real cunt," she agreed.

"A total cunt. He doesn't give you anything. What a frigging bank! You keep saving and saving, but there's no interest, no free coffee. It's a no-frills safe with a big hole in the back of it. Someone's taking our money."

We always talked in metaphors about our infirmities. The doctors often talk about the bank of our energy, and how you couldn't keep drawing and drawing without penalty. You only got what you put in, and all that. The trouble was that sometimes with ME, the more you rested, the more you saved, the iller you got. And the more you did—that is, the more you spent—the iller you got too. It really was a stupid fucking metaphor. Someone needed to take some TNT and blow that fucking bank sky high.

"Are you giving it up then?" asked Carrie.

"Yeah. Until the next time."

"What got you going this time?"

"Film on Channel 4. Arty, nudie, French thing."

"*Vive la France*," she said.

"Exactly. We were watching it with electrical tape over the subtitles, cos Richard's trying to practice his French, but we got the idea anyway."

"And you just whipped it out in the living room?"

"No-oh! No. I excused myself and went to bed."

"With a facecloth and a tub of hair gel?"

"Shaving foam and a sock."

She sniggered and went back to flicking through the late-afternoon shite TV. Thank God we weren't a thing. It would take all the fun out of it.

48

10

Tidy Beard

Sometimes it's scary being ill. What is illness anyway? It's only when illness impinges on your life that you actually *feel* it. Up till that point you can kid yourself that you're not ill. But even if you lie on your floor not thinking about it, listening to music and daydreaming, it starts to leak out, like hot treacle bubbling under a tin lid. That's when it gets scary. What is the escape? I couldn't even make it to church yesterday, I was too ill in the morning. Richard's away at the weekends. Carrie does the family thing too. I could have gone with her, but I wasn't up to it. *Thank God I'm not as bad as this every day*—that's what you have to tell yourself, and of course I'm much luckier than some.

I know I could get on the train and go back to my parents'. Maybe it's weird that I prefer to tough it out in the city. It still feels like there is something here for me in Glasgow, even on a day that I can hardly get out of the house. Ironically, I feel like I'm starting to belong in this city in a way that I didn't before when I was super-active, always moving. Back then I used to tell myself that I "owned" the city, that the city was mine. I was Glasgow's champion. I used to run up its tallest hills at dawn and box shadows like a madman, then run along the frozen canal paths and into the city center as rush hour was happening. I would tear back through the streets to my flat with the papers and rolls, make myself a champion's breakfast, plan the work for the day, plan plan plan all my dubious exploits.

Now I see the city in a different way. I see myself, but I think about people. I want to be around people. I want to talk about big things, I want to figure out what is going on with me, and it would be nice if there was someone around who felt the same way. It wouldn't be so lonely.

I forced myself out as the light was starting to fade. I heard that there was an evening service that we "shared" with other churches from adjoining areas. It was a long shot that it was going to turn my day around, but what the hell. I took the lanes as usual. I waste so much time. I realized that when I'm out walking in the city, I'm constantly evaluating the life behind every window I look through. Even though I believe in God now, I'm still looking for a solution in every lit window, in this tree-heavy environment of entitled families. There are the old ladies with stories, there are the floppy-haired students with bikes; everyone else seems so set, so comfortable. I'm guessing they can't all be, but they look it. I have to find out what makes their lives ok. Are they happy or are they just braver than me? I'm not very brave, I can feel it. It's pish poor.

I arrive at the building where the service is, an old Victorian edifice behind the main street in the West End. The big windows are dark, the only light on is coming from a side door down a few dark steps. There are the shadows of two humpy old ladies behind the frozen glass. I pause for a second to think about if I will go in. I feel like a ship rather than a human. A ship that someone else is captaining. A sad old hauler of junk, moving slowly through the water. I can't stop. It would take me two hours to slow and change my trajectory.

I go in.

I'm shown into the "committee room" by one of the ladies. There's not much light in there either; there's a circle of about twenty chairs lit by candles in the center. If I didn't know the church scene by now, I would have thought it was a séance. There's no minister present. Even though this meeting represents five different churches, they couldn't get a minister to show up. The man next to me introduces himself as Stanley. I tell him which church I'm from. He passes me a piece of paper and asks me if I'd like to do one of the Bible readings. Ok.

It's nineteen old people and me. Again, it's a bit like the hospital—there's a part of my brain that's saying "I shouldn't be here, I'm the odd one out." But I should be wise to this by now. I'm not odd, I'm not different, I fit right in. In the last seconds before we start, a younger woman comes in, smiling a broad smile to folks. Latin-looking, long dark hair streaked with blue at the tips, tattoos on her ankles, serene hazel eyes. We bow our heads to pray.

The service is all about trees. The lady that is leading the worship asks us to close our eyes and imagine a wood. We can each find a tree in the wood and settle beside it. She is describing the scene, and then she asks us to meditate awhile on the wood. Well, this is fine. I'm already there. I'm sitting at the foot of a tree, a broad trunk, between two jutting root collars. It's an ash tree, my favorite. I suddenly feel at rest and completely at home. I want to stay there for a while. I feel like I'm in a bit of a trance. The wood is working for me. I am changed in that time. The day swung like a pendulum from dark to light and I knew that I had achieved what I needed to get me through the night to Monday morning. Just by imagining a tree.

It might be a small thing, a small trick with a small consequence, but where does it end? Why couldn't there be more? Is this feeling guaranteed? Does the magic work every time? I'm not sure, but I'm not turning back. God has his roots in me.

*****

The summer had been pretty good to us, but it was time to try something new. Out of Richard, Carrie and me, I would say I was the pioneer when it came to trying new therapies. I wanted to attack this thing, and I was certain that we could all get over it and back to "normal." Carrie had been at this longer, and she did seem more trapped in her day-to-day struggles with the illness. Richard was deeper. I think he had a plan; he just wasn't letting on so much. He was also the one who seemed most at peace with the whole situation.

During the summer we had tried to keep moving. We had the feeling that if we could exercise, push ourselves in healthy ways, we could train our bodies back to health. Richard and I had always been active before; maybe we could get it back. There was an old tennis court round the corner from where we lived. It was attached to the bowling club, but no one ever seemed to use it, so we took to sneaking on. We tried to build ourselves up that way, swinging at tennis balls and padding about on the ash court. Richard was marginally better than me, he had the edge. I tried pretty hard; he didn't seem to try at all but usually won. He had longer arms and he also had the skill. Carrie often got dropped off by her dad and she used to come and watch us. She seemed happy enough soaking up the sun, lying on her ubiquitous plastic-backed tartan blanket. And if ever any of the old folk from the bowling club came over, she was there to sweet-talk them.

We were all on the rug one afternoon, in between games, lying on our backs like three candy cigarettes.

"You do realize that we can do anything," I said.

"What do you mean?" Carrie said.

"We can do anything that we want. I feel unfettered. Nobody can tell me what I can or can't do. I don't care anymore. Being ill has made me not care. In a good way."

Richard raised his eyebrows for a second, under his sunglasses, then decided not to say anything.

"What are you going to do?" asked Carrie.

I thought about it for a bit. "I don't know yet. Just let me feel good for a minute."

"I let you feel good." She made a queenly gesture towards me with her hand, without getting up, to show she was letting me feel good.

I shut my eyes. I thought about our various therapies, tactics and cures. Richard had his meditation. He also did cold baths. He would soak in there for forty-five minutes. I did not have to try that to know that it wouldn't work for me. All of us were skeptical about special diets. I had done the whole diet thing before and it had precipitated disastrous consequences. I'd been reading the only book I could find about ME and it suggested cutting out certain foods. In the end I had omitted almost everything from their exhaustive list of "bad" foods in a bid to exclude anything that might have been doing me harm. That didn't really leave much, hence the disastrous consequences—I just lost loads of weight and felt much worse. I wasn't about to try that again. We were veggie anyway, me and Richard. We cooked almost everything from scratch, so I think we did eat pretty healthy.

There were more therapies. My own doctor had sent me up to the homeopathic hospital. I took these little powders every day for three months—no change. Carrie and I had been to see a healer, a young Irish chap, one of those charismatic sorts. It was a public gathering and we lined up with another hundred or so poor sods. We were momentarily touched, physically if not metaphysically. Then we went in search of a nice scone. No reported effect.

Carrie had gone to a psychic fair at the local library, where a woman offered to read her aura and predict her future. Her dad was with us when she went in, and he was shaking his head, obviously thinking this was a waste of time. She came out twenty minutes later, crying. Evidently she had heard something that she didn't want to hear, either about her future, or her present condition or something. I gave her a hug, which is something we only did when one of us was crying. Her dad caught up to us and saw what had happened.

"Oh, for fuck's sake," he said, not uncomically, as Carrie gulped and choked on my shoulder.

It was now coming to the end of the summer. While we walked back to the house, I thought it was about time for me to try something new. I had been to ME group meetings when I was back at my parents', and I still had a list of therapists that promised a variety of treatments. There were no ME "specialists" as such. Information was hard to come by, and information without expertise could be damaging. If you were working on your own (like I was with the diet thing) or acting on hearsay or unsubstantiated claims, you could end up worse off.

For instance, back in the grim days when I was getting worse all the time and I seemed to be falling down a pit, I'd heard or read somewhere that some doctor said you should simply go to bed for six months—you could get better with complete bed rest. I'd like to get hold of that fucker now. The whole trick, I realized later, was *not* to go to bed for six months. Because where are you going to be in six months? Still in bed. And the fucking ME would have seen its chance to take over and dominate you—physically, mentally and spiritually. Secondary symptoms would then sneak in and compound what was wrong in the first place. Muscles would waste, digestive systems would go moldy, torpor would set in.

I wasn't to know that then, and this little gem of information was one of the only things I had to go on at the time. It certainly didn't help my already addled decision-making abilities. I'm maybe being a bit hard on myself here. I felt bloody awful at the time. If you've never been ill before, like chronically ill, how the hell are you to know what to do? No one, not even the doctors, had a scooby-doo what I was supposed to do and how I was supposed to act. So you rest; you try and get over it by resting; you try to get to a place where you don't feel ill by exertion. And if that place turns out to be at a very low level, then you will exist at a very low level, like a warmed-up corpse.

Ok, so that seemed a long time ago, and the three of us were just looking forward now. From the list I had, I'd heard about a guy in Fife who'd had good results with some people. His therapy sounded like a bit of a mishmash, but he seemed to be the best option. It involved a pilgrimage to the other side of the country, but my mum said she'd pay as a birthday present. A few weeks later I was taking the train to Perth, then taking a bumpy wee bus for another hour to a small coastal town, all to put my hope in a new cure. It felt good to be out of the city though, a nice excuse for a day trip. The town was pretty ordinary and I felt conspicuous as I picked my way slowly up the side streets, looking for the doctor's house.

As I got higher above the main street, I ran into bunches of kids going the other way, out of school at lunchtime, heading to shops or home. I definitely didn't feel like a young person anymore. I felt a million miles away from those schoolkids. I didn't even feel close to being a student anymore. I didn't know what I was. I was just a nothing guy walking slowly up a hill.

The doc greeted me at the door. He was a smallish man with a tidy beard. You might almost say there was a twinkle in his eye. He ushered me through to his medical room. There were a couple of contraptions in the consulting room that if you weren't confident about why you were there might have made you a bit worried. They didn't quite make sense—a mixture of tubes, electrodes, wires, oscilloscopes and substances.

"The good news is I can make you feel better."

That's what he said after I told him my story. So far, so good. I know I had heard this before and nothing came of it, but hope is the thing. He explained that his therapy was a mixture of the Eastern arts, a pinch of homeopathy and a lot to do with allergies. Finally, once his speech was done (and it was quite a fine one, his eyes twinkling away), he plugged me into the machine. I grasped an electrode in each hand and he passed an electric current through me.

There was a gap in the circuit. In that gap he would place a series of substances that were housed in glass capsules with metal caps. When the circuit was complete, the current would register and he would take note of what substance had what effect. In essence, he was passing current through me and, say, arsenic, or bromide, or copper, or garlic, or dried mushrooms or condensed milk. I just went with it, obviously. As a previous student of science, I might have stopped him and asked how much the current would really be affected by the garlic, even if it was suspended in a salt solution. But I just let it float by. I think he was trying to build up a picture of what was going on, and this was his way.

When Dr. Tidy Beard finished his work, he gave me some tidy wee white pills. I made an appointment with him for two weeks' time. I paid him £70 for his trouble and I bade him a cheery farewell at his front porch. Before I was in the hospital, I wouldn't trust anyone to guide me as far as a bus stop. I didn't exactly end up doing so great. So my new thing was to trust people. He said he could help, and he was trying to help me. Even though I was paying him, it was still a nice thing—to be helped.

11

Industrial Life in Scotland

When we moved back up to Glasgow, I decided to form an ME group. I had been to one when I was home at my parents'. I suspected there might be a lot of people stuck in the same situation in the West End, so I thought we could get together and discuss our problems. With the summer waning and people drifting back towards Glasgow, I figured it might be the right time. I thought I would make the group for "young people." The one I had been to before was all middle-aged women except for one man and me. I just figured there were bound to be some young people with ME close to the university, and I thought it could be a good social thing.

I went at the task of designing the poster for the group in the same way that I designed posters for shows in the years before. I had a nice photo book about the French film director Jean-Luc Godard, so I pinched one picture from *Breathless* and one from *Pierrot le Fou* and went to work with the photocopier and colored paper. There was no reason why this little group couldn't be a little hip even though it might be a little fucked. I even went down to the university newspaper, and they ran a snippet about the club: *A social club based around a disease, for young people. Is that morbid? We don't think so.*

On the allotted evening, Richard and I splashed out on herbal teas and honey cake. The buzzer started going at seven thirty and by eight we had twelve people in our front room. I must admit I was a little bit unprepared for the group that was finally assembled. Everyone seemed quite normal on the surface, but that is of course the thing about this condition. Look at us there—twelve soft pilgrims of the way, expectant faces, hopeful, cheerful. Twelve very different people, working hard underneath to keep it together, as it turned out.

There was Adrian, English, rosy-cheeked, polite. Got ill, life stopped, moved back with his folks, stabilized, moved to Glasgow to live with his sister for a while. Nicola had come from way in the south of the city. She was particularly frail-looking, in fact her mum waited in the car outside for her the whole time. Karen and Liv, short for Olivia, were sisters, both with ME. Karen, the older one, was in a wheelchair. We had to leave it downstairs. On the phone I said we'd get her up the stairs somehow, and we did, me and Liv on one side, Richard on the other.

Yvonne—seemed a bit posh (east coast Scottish posh), frankly gorgeous-looking—breezed in, all mohair and teeth. Martin: suspiciously not young; looked a bit grizzled, but then maybe that's what we'll all look like in ten years with this thing. He was on the cusp and he must have known it—he was in his late thirties at least—but what were we going to do? We weren't going to kick him out. *And* he was having a cigarette at the door when he came in. An ME person smoking was like . . . well, it was something.

Asha was an ME veteran, with lots of twists and complications, as we would hear throughout the evening. A bit of an activist, she had been fighting the authorities for quite a while. It was interesting to hear that stuff, and it's a path that seemed admirable. We admired her. Just couldn't quite be bothered going down that road ourselves though. Or maybe we weren't at that stage. Who had the energy to fight? Then there was Josie, who seemed particularly hacked off with the whole thing and who hadn't been ill for too long. Finally, there was Dave. Tall, quiet, he sort of folded himself down into the sofa, and there he stayed.

The chat was typical introduction stuff: how and when did everyone get it, what were their main symptoms, how did everyone try and cope best. Medicines and methods and so forth. It went off ok, and we agreed to meet again in a couple of weeks. I was pleased I'd had an idea and it had worked. It felt like a while since that had happened.

Before we even had a chance to have another meeting though, Yvonne invited us to stay at her folks' house for a couple of nights. It was an hour and a half away in the countryside in central Scotland. I was surprised; it seemed quite soon for something like this to happen, but it seemed a genuine offer. Richard and I said yes straight away, Nicola too. Karen and Liv were going to come, but in the end it was too much for Karen. And Josie wanted to come too, which surprised us because of her aforementioned annoyance at it all.

Carrie thought it would be too much for her.

"I don't think I can make it," she said. She was sitting up in bed.

"Will you be fed up if we go?" I asked.

"No, I just can't make it. There's no question, so I'm not conflicted."

"Nicola is going."

"I know. I hope she will be ok. I didn't think she was doing *that* much better than me."

"I think maybe she's got a thing for Richard."

"Yeah, I think she has too. And if she has, then that would give her the final push out the door."

"Chance of a snog will always do it."

"And in that regard, do you fancy the Mitchell?" she asked.

"Who doesn't fancy the Mitchell?" I said straight away. "The Mitchell" was Yvonne Mitchell, our host for the weekend.

"Everyone fancies the Mitch," said Carrie. "She's just got that thing. And she's got tits like the Death Star, they just draw you in."

"What have her boobs got that your boobs don't?" I asked.

"It's a good question. I have good boobs. I like them, I'm very attached to them. But she just has the Rodin of boobs. They are laughably perfect. They are Oscar-winning shneb-lits."

"They're not *that* big."

"I know—they don't have to be. But I saw you and Richard looking, drooling all over your faces."

"There was no drool!"

Carrie is funny. I must admit she surprised me. I wasn't looking at her boobs. I had just taken an impression with me.

"Do *you* fancy the Mitch?" I asked.

"Well, mm, I've said what I said, but I don't want to go there." I caught a cold little whiff of a north breeze coming in there, so I didn't say anything.

"So how are you going to proceed?" she asked.

"With my usual caution."

"Never put your hand in—"

"—if you can't draw it out! The ME motto. One day, however, one of us will have to leave our hand in," I said.

"Yeah, ok. As long as you always tell me everything." She looked a bit pale and fed up suddenly. She turned over in the bed.

"I tell you everything before it's even happened," I said.

"I know," she said, facing the wall.

"I tell you everything even when I've got nothing to tell you," I added gently.

She turned halfway back around.

"I know you do. Ok, leave me to my boudoir, and have a lovely time. Say hi to her artful mounds for me."

And off I went.

The next day, Carrie called.

"How are you getting to Yvonne's?"

"Richard and I are going to get the train and a bus."

"My dad said we can take the car. Can you drive up?"

"Ok," I said, a bit surprised. "Will *you* be ok?"

"I feel a bit better this morning. I can lie down in the back seat and rest when I get there. Screw it, let's go!"

So Richard and I picked her up and we drove to the land of Clackmannanshire. It sounds made-up, but it's real—look it up. It was the smallest piece of my favorite jigsaw when I was a boy, the Victory Jigsaw Puzzle of Industrial Life in Scotland. The puzzle depicted a map of Scotland with all the old shires, their main industries, crops, commodities and transport systems. As I was now one of life's spectators, the old jigsaw held even more allure for me. I just loved the notion of a nation in motion. I felt the emotion.

So there we all were, the Fellowship of the Retiring. Yvonne's parents had gone off somewhere, but they'd left plenty of food and good cheer. It was the kind of house that you imagine semi-posh people of a certain ilk to live in. Out on its own, not quite a farmhouse but in a field somewhere. Lush grass rolling down to an actual stream. A copse within the big garden, with rope swings and an actual dad-built treehouse.

I wonder how Yvonne managed to get ME. She seemed so atypical. The rest of us were within the psychological Venn diagram, but on paper she should have been dancing around the edge of the universal set. She was smart and sexy and assured. A wee bit cold, or at least she seemed that way to me, but she might have been putting out that vibe to me to make sure that I knew I didn't have a chance with her.

Richard and I got a room up in the rafters, which suited me. The roof sloped, so I wedged the bed in underneath. It seemed cozy. We all milled about the big kitchen, the way you do, everyone waiting for the weekend to coagulate. Me and Carrie and Josie took a big blanket outside to the slope, Nicola went to rest for a bit, Richard went to the wood to meditate, and Liv helped Yvonne in the kitchen.

"How have you been, Josie?" said Carrie, lying down, dark glasses, knees in the air.

"I'm ok. I still don't really know what's going on. My useless fuck of a GP doesn't know anything."

I pulled myself up onto my elbows. "None of them do. Not even the specialists know anything."

Josie thought for a second. "Does that not make you mad?" she asked.

"It's a bit annoying, but what are you going to do?" said Carrie.

"I think that when it's your whole life that's gone down the toilet, you should be mad. How come nobody is doing anything at all to cure this thing?"

"They don't even have a test to tell what it is that's wrong with us, never mind a cure," I replied.

Josie looked at me, in a not completely kind way.

"Well, I'm fucking mad." She sort of lay down for a second, and so did I. Then she sat up.

"Why are all of you so weird about it?"

"Weird?" I said.

"You're like a cult or something. Like sheep."

"Erm, Josie, I'm not sure that's very fair," said Carrie.

"If you just lie down and accept everything that's happening to you, how can you expect to get better? It's like you've all given up."

"I haven't given up. Richard hasn't . . ." I responded.

"You two are like monks though. I'm just saying, I'm not letting it happen to me."

"Let what happen?" said Carrie, dark glasses off now.

"I'm just not going to be an ME basket case." Josie glowered at the stream.

"What, like me?" said Carrie.

"No, I didn't mean it like that. I just don't want to give in."

Carrie got up.

"We haven't given in, Josie. We're just trying our best to live with it."

She took her sweatshirt and headed inside.

Josie looked at me with a shrug. "She nearly got mad. That would have been a start."

"I've never seen her mad," I said. "Not proper mad. She wouldn't. She knows it would be like a day's worth of energy wasted."

"Jesus! How can you live like this?" She got up and walked towards the stream.

I suppose Josie was at a different stage to the rest of us. She'd only been sick six months. Maybe she wouldn't get so bad as Carrie and Nicola and the rest of us. I hoped she wouldn't. But I hoped she'd stop being such an arse around Carrie.

Pretty soon we all went inside. Yvonne and Liv had made veggie chili.

Nicola came down the stairs, looking a little shaky. Carrie helped her over to an armchair, which supported her on three sides, and we pulled it up near the table and everyone sat down. Asha had arrived too, with a flurry of apologies about being late, but no one cared, we were happy to see her. So now we were eight. Yvonne served up the chili, and there was rice and tortillas, chips and salsa. Yvonne had some wine, so did Asha and Josie; everyone else stuck to water.

Josie asked, "How do you explain ME to people around you?"

There was quite a long pause.

"I don't actually bother anymore," said Asha. "I'm in a place where I can get by with the people that know me best. I don't have to explain it."

"Aside from my mum and my sister, I don't talk to non-ME people about ME," said Richard. "It's just easier. People don't get it. By the time you've explained it you've used up a lot of energy, and then they don't know whether they should run away from you or feel sorry for you."

"I know that me and Karen mostly just tell each other stuff," said Liv. "Karen has the wheelchair, so it's almost easier for people to take her seriously, and I just float by. When we're outside, I think people just assume I'm healthy."

"Unless you're passed out on the ground," said Asha.

"Ha! Even if you are flat on the ground, it doesn't help," said Carrie.

"What do you mean?" asked Yvonne.

"One time I was in the supermarket near my house," Carrie said. "It was a big effort to get there, and then suddenly I felt I just had to sit down. There were no seats close by, so I sat in the aisle. While I was down there, I felt I needed to lie down and put my knees up."

"You actually lay down in the supermarket?" said Josie.

"It was the natural thing for me to do. But it caused a commotion. The people close by came to help, and I said it was ok, I was just resting, it would pass. And then the assistant manager came, and he was going to call an ambulance, and I thought, *Aye, call an ambulance. I need one, I feel terrible. But I feel like this all the time. And what are they going to do? They'll take my blood pressure, they'll listen to my chest, they'll tell me there's nothing wrong with me, they'll send me home, they'll note that I am under the supervision of a psychiatrist, they'll add them into the report. And they'll send me home. In a taxi that I can't really afford.*"

"So did they call one?" asked Liv.

"No. I just asked if I could lie there for a minute more, and he said no, they'd have to move me. So they put me on a bench near the tills, but they really just wanted me out of there."

"They don't like a gray area, and you were a gray area," I said.

"I was a fuzzy gray area. I gave them the dry boke," Carrie said with a smile.

Josie still looked a bit puzzled by it all. You could tell she was wrestling with all this information. Even the way she sat was tense. The rest of us had settled in like we had never been so comfortable. It was easy, in this company of people who understood.

"What about relationships? What about where you live? How do you manage?" asked Josie.

Another pause. Nicola poured more water for people.

"Is anyone in a relationship?" Josie asked.

"I'm just out of one," said Yvonne.

"Me too. Thank God," said Asha.

"I live with my boyfriend, Ben," said Liv.

"Does that work ok?" asked Asha.

"He's really nice. He's been brilliant actually. I'm not saying it's perfect, but he's been a good support. I can't imagine getting through this without him."

"Wow, that's great!" said Carrie, sounding genuinely surprised, as if such an arrangement seemed completely foreign.

Asha fiddled with her wineglass, then began. "I was so relieved when me and Duncan broke up. By the end of it I was just like 'Go away, just let me be ill, leave me alone.' He didn't change the whole time I was getting ill. It's honestly like he didn't notice or didn't want to deal with it at all. He always made it about him. I realized that's what our relationship had always been like. Him making it about him. When I got sick, nothing changed. He certainly didn't."

"That must have been really hard," said Yvonne.

Asha continued. "It was just annoying more than anything else, being stuck with this tosser during the big crisis of your life. The sicker I got, the clearer I saw things. I just wanted out. But he kept guilt-tripping me. He really kept the pressure up, acting like he was the one hard done by, like I was deserting him."

She paused to think for a second. "It would have been so much easier if I hadn't lived with him. Oh my God, I could have gone anywhere, especially when I had more strength. I let it drag on though."

"What did you do?" asked Liv.

"My doctor helped me get a council flat lined up. She was good. We arranged it all on the quiet. Then I just announced to Duncan I was leaving. I had somewhere to jump to."

"What was it like when you got in the new place?"

"Heaven, at first. It was quite a bit of work, it took a while to get settled. It was lovely to be on my own. It's almost like I finally had permission to rest, nothing was stopping me. So I slowed down, the ME got its teeth in for a while. Eventually I leveled out, and I was happier."

Asha took a gulp of her wine and sat back. "Does anyone mind if we move to the sofas?"

"No, good idea," said Yvonne.

We all moved over to the sofa section of the large living and dining room. We got around the fire even though we didn't need to light one. Richard and I dragged Nicola's seat over to where we all were, so she didn't even have to get up. She giggled; I think she liked it. She liked Richard anyway—anyone could see that. I liked Yvonne—she could probably see that. Why is it that if we like someone, we think we can hide it? We think we're being so clever and aloof, but we're not. It's so obvious. She could probably feel my look.

Asha and Josie and Richard did the clean-up. I think they wanted me to help too, but to Asha and Josie's annoyance I went over to the piano instead. I always just leave tidying up till I have the energy to do it. It used to bug Richard too. I played them part of a little instrumental piece that I had been working on called "Belmondo." I still couldn't play it right, but I thought it would be good to perform when there were people there. It was politely received. People started to drift off to bed after the clean-up. A few went on the blanket outside on the bank as the daylight started to fade, taking coats and layers with them against the night. We waited for the ragged constellations to reveal their dark-sky glory, something we'd never see in the city.

The next day we were all a bit weary. Yvonne, Liv and I drove to the nearby artesian well to get water for the day. We filled up two five-gallon containers. Everyone was going to be replenished by these life-giving waters. We hoped. The plan for the morning was: no plan.

I looked in at one of the sitting rooms in the house, all lined with books. I asked Yvonne what I should read, and she said, "Read *The Pigman*." She gave it to me. It looked like a book for a kid or a teenager.

"Is this not for children?"

"Maybe. But it's good."

I took her at her word. While people were finding their favorite spots around the garden, in the treehouse and by the stream, I got back into bed under the warm eaves of the house and absorbed *The Pigman* by Paul Zindel. I felt partly guilty and partly relieved to be reading a book that was obviously written for a younger person. I'd always thought about reading as the "meat" of my day, and so I always had to tackle something worthy, something to make me think, improve my vocabulary, improve myself. The "improving book." That was quite often the punishment imposed upon Bertie Wooster, the protagonist from the Jeeves books. Bertie would have a lover and she would press an improving book into his hand so that he might raise himself to the standards expected of a gentleman. Poor old Bertie just wanted to be happy. Jeeves usually got him out of it though: "You would not enjoy Nietzsche, sir. He is fundamentally unsound." Jeeves always knew best.

There was a psychological test in *The Pigman*. It was a little sidestep from the main story. I was reluctant to take the test. The last time I took a psych test was when I was still with Vivian. My results were appalling. They said that I was running from life, scared of everything, and that I would like to have sex as much as I would like to be plunged into a cold river at night.

The Pigman test was a bit curious. It didn't seem to relate to life in a real sense. It was something about a woman begging her husband not to go to work because she knows that while the husband is away she will go to her lover. She can't resist. The husband does go to work. The wife goes to the lover, but then the wife gets murdered by an assassin on the way home. There's a boatman too, because there's a river to cross, as there often is in strange fables. You had to decide which of the characters you thought was most responsible for the woman's death. I picked the boatman for some reason. This corresponded to magic being the most important thing in my life, as opposed to money, sex, love or fun. Bit silly, right? I was satisfied enough with the magic thing though. I took magic to mean God and all who stood with him—the supernatural and so on. I wanted to give in to the possibility of a little magic. I had to. We needed it, all the sad weekenders draped around the patio.

The day passed peacefully, though I think I continued to irritate a few with my reluctance to help with meals and clearing up. Asha went in the afternoon, the rest of us were going to go the next morning. Carrie had lasted well, though she did have one of her headaches coming on, and they could last a couple of days, so she went to bed early. The rest drifted off. Richard was out in the tree-house with blankets and celestial hope as he wondered at the stars.

I eventually, by waiting, saw Yvonne alone in the kitchen, checking we had enough for breakfast in the morning.

"I finished *The Pigman*," I said.

"Did you like it?" she asked.

"Yeah. I did. The end was a bit of a disaster, but I liked it."

"There's meant to be a warning in it."

"Yes, a lesson for all to learn."

Yvonne went back to her cupboards.

"Do you remember the test?" I asked her.

She thought for a sec. "The one with the assassin?"

"Yes."

"I think I do. What did you choose?"

"Magic."

"Ah, you are more mysterious than me."

"What did you get?"

68

"Money and sex."

My mouth was dry. I swallowed.

"Yvonne, is there a possibility that I might kiss you?"

Without blinking, without looking away, as if with perfect understanding of the gulf in dynamic between us, she said, "I don't think so."

Hurt, and without the nous to know when to quit, I half whined, "Why do you have to be so beautiful?"

She half smiled to my half whine. We both knew the question didn't merit an answer.

"Do you want some tea?" she said.

12

Harmony and Counterpoint

I signed up for university again. Third time lucky. At least this time I was going to do music. It was a part-time course and it cost me £325. I still had some money left over from selling rare and autographed items from my record collection earlier in the year, so that was ok. It seemed worthwhile, and if everything went ok, I could then transfer across into a full-time degree course next year.

It's fair to say that my relationship with tertiary education up to this point had been a strained one. A strange one, in fact. I had liked certain things about it, but not the things that got you closer to a degree. I don't know when things started going "wrong" for me. I could trace it back, I suppose. Alternatively, I could take the optimistic view that the moment when things started going wrong was really the moment things started going right. You have to be pretty optimistic to have that view.

I had a simplistic view when I was sixteen about the future. It didn't involve doing things I liked doing. I looked around me. There were people having fun and getting away with it. But it wasn't for me. That would have been too easy. It seemed to me that if you were to make a success of yourself, you had to go down the darkest route. That's just the way it seemed. Fun wasn't an option. I had given in to being grim, male and Scottish. I had pretty much stopped having fun ever since my first girlfriend had finished with me. Everything emotional inside had been stymied, a lesson had been learned, gayness had been vanquished, the sharp forces of reality had been revealed. I hunkered down to a life of after-school jobs and spotty anonymity.

Now I was back in a classroom. The very schoolteacherly music professor, Ms. Galbraith, was just getting warmed up.

"Listen! Do you hear that? Do you hear the change? The vibration, the tension, the release. What life there is in that one moment, what abandon, what a chord!"

I can't remember who the offending composer was just in that moment. This was the first of my Harmony and Counterpoint classes. I hadn't meant to enroll specifically in this class, it was just part of the bundle. It was intense; it was seven years since I'd dallied with any formal musical training. The people in the class around me sat up really straight and grinned. They all looked as sharp as the pencils that lay before them, neatly lined up with their manuscript, rubbers and rulers.

"What a combination of notes," she continued. "I feel like one single chord could change the world, if it was played in the right way and put in the right place." She paused, obviously waiting for the class to find humor in her remarks. She was rewarded with a smattering of appreciative amusement.

"Do chords mean *anything* to you?"

Her tone had shifted to one of mock exasperation. For some reason I had chosen to sit near the front, and there was no avoiding her question.

"I suppose so," I offered, trying to wriggle up from the slouch that I was in.

"You suppose so," she said back to me. "You *suppose* so," she repeated as she turned to face the board again, letting the phrase roll around the four walls of the room, searching for a golden ripple of laughter. She got it too. All the ponytailed rookies, all the steely-eyed orchestra types straight out of school with great hope and great energy having a chuckle at my expense. It hadn't taken long, but I got the feeling I wouldn't last in that class. I was out of my depth.

I started worrying that the music course was going to be more counterpoint than harmony. With my energy limited, I couldn't do parties. I couldn't do pubs, really, so I wasn't going to see these people socially. I didn't play an instrument, at least not anywhere near the standard that would have been required to make it into the orchestra. They did put me in the choir though, and that's when I got my second shoe in the nuts.

At the first rehearsal they threw out a load of music manuscript, notes all over the place. They cranked up the piano and everyone started singing straight away. I couldn't do it. I didn't even know where on the page to look. I couldn't sight-sing. Sight-reading had always been my worst discipline from piano days, and I'd never sight-sang. I was lost again. If this had been a college movie about determination and the eventual success of the academic underdog, I would have retired to my garret and worked on the old sight-singing. There would have been a music sequence that showed me getting up super early, drinking a mix of three raw eggs and singing at the piano in a tight t-shirt while time sped up around me.

None of this happened.

Back at the practice: I felt dizzy from the combination of standing up too long and pushing too much air out of my lungs. So I sat down and kind of disappeared in the crowd. And the music got muffled and bass-y. And I wondered if I was cut out for this at all. I hung about to have a word with the choirmaster.

"I'm not so good at singing."

"Everyone can sing."

"I'm not so good at the reading bit."

"It will come, surely. You can read music?"

"Yes, just out of practice."

"Ok, then just give it a go. Take some music away."

"There's no chance . . . ? I couldn't bash the occasional drum? Do you have a vacancy in percussion?"

"Ah. Ha ha!" he said, and he started clearing his things away.

"Hmm. Ha ha. Hmm," he said as he popped his baton into his satchel.

I took it that this was the conversation over. I'm still not certain as to the cause of his amusement, but it was probably in the same category as Ms. Galbraith from the other day.

I waited for everyone to filter out. We were in the university chapel. I liked the feeling of everyone leaving. Before becoming ill I'm sure I would have been the first out, rushing hare-like to some engagement. Now I was happy to be last. There were advantages to that. Everything got quiet. I could enjoy the ambience for a while. If I had just stumbled into the chapel right now and sat down, I would have felt like I didn't belong. I would have felt uneasy and wouldn't have settled. Because I had been in the class beforehand, I felt I had earned the right to stay for as long as I needed. Or at least until someone came to turn out the lights.

The chapel was what you might imagine a university chapel to be like. Narrow, tall, ornate, with stained glass all over the place. It was a Gothic chapel within a big Gothic double quadrangle. It seemed a waste to find myself in the conveniently quiet and sacred setting of a university chapel without offering some sort of prayer:

Dear God,

Hello. I hope you are ok. I'm sure you are ok because you have pretty much everything sorted out. It's a bit strange that you have everything all tied up in your part of the world when everything is all so uncertain over here. I don't mean to sound ungrateful.

I'm thankful that you chose to save my life. It does occur to me that because you chose to make such an intervention, to reveal yourself and all that, and put me into hospital, that you might think that this life is worth saving?

Either way, the ball is back in my court. It feels like you might say "Make something of this life."

I don't know how to do it.

I'm just going to have to keep asking you for help. I hope that is ok?

Help me, Obi-Wan. You're my only hope.

Sorry, I didn't mean to call you Obi-Wan. That's from Star Wars. *I know you know that.*

Bless and look after my mum and dad, and Carrie and Richard, and my brother and sister, and my sister's kid, and bless the homeless guy who sits outside Roots and Fruits. Over and out.

I said "over and out" pretty fast because I heard the creak of the swing door opening to my left. I was secreted behind a gargoyle in a carved wooden corner. I don't think they could see me. Into the chapel more people started coming, in groups and alone. Chatting and busy. Most carrying instruments. They started setting up stands in the space between the two banks of pews. Most of the instruments were stringed, but I did notice a few woodwind instruments. One wild-haired guy went up to the holy end of the church and with one movement whipped the cover off what looked like a miniature piano. He played a few notes while he was standing. It was a harpsichord and it made a pretty nice sound.

I scanned the players. I saw this one person who stood out straight away; she was pretty, but you could tell she also had the confidence, the purpose, the ease. I couldn't help noticing *everyone* now; they quickly became my heroes. Lithe, intelligent boys. Why hadn't I noticed *them* before? They moved around the girls and the girls moved around them, and they were all caught up in a sort of dance. She fancied the boy, and the boy fancied the other boy, but the other boy couldn't care less, and that made him more attractive, so he was the linchpin, and he brooded over scores, while a plainer girl giggled with her dumpy fellow cellist, and on and on. Social cartwheels, cascading collegiate life, hand-knitted scarves, manuscript and bow resin—observed in a second.

They began to play, and it was so pretty and accomplished. I stayed silent and still because I was liking it so much. And I liked her—the confident girl with the purple velvet trousers, mucky boots, turtleneck jumper and dark hair caught up inside a woollen cap. I was a dozen yards from her. I would have fallen for her hands alone, the way they were moving on the fretboard of the violin. These kids in front of me were blessed. They all belonged, there were no frauds or mistakes. I was the mistake, caught between two stools as the stools were pulled apart. How could I fit in? What could I do? I couldn't catch up to them. On current form, I probably wasn't going to even be in the department that long.

So I thought I would make the girl a tape. I thought I would make her the greatest compilation tape. I would make it from pop songs that all contained conspicuous parts for solo violin. It would be a challenge, but I felt I was equal to it.

I waited until the rehearsal had finished and then I got the bus home. I had some cereal. I prepared the living room for the ritual of taping. Richard was still at his parents', so I could spread the records all over the place and make myself a little island in the middle of the floor surrounded by vinyl. I thought I would start with songs that had a lead violin, or at least a violin solo in the intro or in the middle, or a theme carried on solo violin. So, I got "No Side to Fall In" by the Raincoats, because that starts with that crazy violin. Then I put on one of the best King of the Slums tracks—pretty much every one of their songs has violin all over it, she uses it like a weapon.

This is great. I got some indie momentum going.

> "Right Here"—The Go-Betweens
> "In the Rain"—The June Brides
> "It's My Turn"—The Servants
> "Take the Skinheads Bowling"—Camper Van Beethoven

But I only get so far with solo violin, so I start to stray towards Nico and Nick Drake and the Lovin' Spoonful. Jeez, I'm listening to this stuff in the living room and the purple starlight is pouring in over the blackened trees because I can't get up to put the light on, and everything sounds so great that I find myself with a slight dampening of the eye. Is this girl really worth all this magic? She deserves to hear it, and the grace and the magic of this little sequence of glory is all that I can offer as a match for her beauty and life. It's all I have, girl. And I don't even know your name.

I'm going to put a Thin Lizzy track on here. A vestige from my old rocker phase, but I love Thin Lizzy, I will always love Phil, he was my imaginary older brother; he died a few years back. He sings this one called "A Song for While I'm Away" and it has a genius string part. It's a pretty soppy song, but it's going on.

Now I'm into string sections big time, so "Cosmic Dancer" by T. Rex has to go on. If you listen to that song, you have to lose yourself in the section. The song is a dirge, it's a meditation, but the strings are the thing. It's the little story that goes along with the singing. The COUNTERPOINT. It's the motherfucking counterpoint. I should get up in that old bag Galbraith's class and give those posh schoolies a lesson on counterpoint. T. Rex and the Raincoats. Get it up you, you stuck-up classical arses!

Ha ha. Ok, not going to do that, but I feel a bit happier thinking that I have my own definition of counterpoint and what it can do to music. I put on "My Girl" by the Temptations. Don't want to get too popular, but the best bit of the tune is the string break and the "hey hey hey"s, so it goes on even though I like the Otis Redding version better. I know that Smokey Robinson wrote that one, so I stick "Tracks of My Tears" down. That is just a great song with a nice string and brass accompaniment, which is not really what I set out to do, but I've got the whole second side of a C90 to fill up. So I stick down that Beat track with the great strings on it, "Save It for Later," some Left Banke, some Commotions.

"Everyday Is Like Sunday"—I can't figure out whether they are real strings or fake. The pizzicato seems real, but the rest seems fake. Must be fake. But why would they get the guys in to just do the pizzicato? I'm going to keep it in. It's getting late, this room is getting cold, my knees are sore, and I haven't even eaten or peed. I can't not put the Three Degrees on there, it's majestic. Precious moments. And then the Simon Park Orchestra playing the theme to *Van der Valk*, the TV series about a Dutch detective. I know that if I put this on, there is no real chance that she's ever going to go out with me. I know that. This is the line, I can see the line, and I'm stepping over. I don't care. I love her and I love Simon Park equally and there it is. God, do the rest. Now that I'm safely over the line, I put on Dexys, and I know it's over. The tape is over, my life is over. My romantic life.

13

People Are Amazing

Bloody silly day. It was crisp of air and golden of leaf, I'll give it that, but it didn't really live up to its autumnal promise. I took the tape I made for the violin player down to the music department. I didn't know what I was going to do with it, I just went. I figured I could hang out there for a while, sit in the vestibule till something happened. Every music student had a dovecot into which went notes from the department. I thought she might come in to check hers, and then I might find out her name, and I could stick the tape in her box and be done with it. I hadn't even written a note with it. I had just stuck with my plan: that the initial letter of the name of the bands would spell out my address. So I started with 10,000 Maniacs and then the Four Tops—put those together, that makes fourteen. Then I went on to make my street with letters.

The music building was made up from a terrace of grandiose Victorian dwellings that had been converted when the university grew up around them. I went in and waited in the entrance hall. It wasn't a bad place to hang out. I took out the *Oxford Companion to Music* from a glass case and started flicking through it. (I didn't know that "a cappella" meant "in the church style.") I didn't mind this stuff. At least I had a bit of a purpose, and it seemed better than going to the library and learning about composition. I could just soak up more about music sitting here.

I'd hoped that by staking out the vestibule in the music department I would be able to observe some *Kids from "Fame"* type behavior. Maybe some kid in a top hat and tails would start to play mad ragtime piano on the upright I could see in the common room and that would set everyone off on a crazy jam, with even the staff letting loose with their oboes and tenor horns. Nothing much happened though. People came and went. The uni postman, the odd professor. The little glass window to the reception office would slide open now and again to accommodate some student's humdrum request. No top hats, no jam session. I just had to sit and wait for my own Irene Cara to show up.

I was there for two hours, almost about to quit, when she came in with a couple of friends. They were the loudest, most happening thing to come in all morning. Her and a girl and a guy. All business and bustle and self-absorption, and admirable because of it. I hid behind my hefty *Companion* and admired. She looked in her box for a second and grabbed a folded sheet of A4 out of there on the way past. It was like a blue tit grabbing a seed—you felt you might want to see it again in slow motion. But I kept my eye on her dovecot. Her little gang went up the stairs, and I went over to the box. It said: *Fara Joseph.* I went back to the seat and wrote on a scrap of paper: *Dear Fara, I thought you might like this tape, though I could be wrong. Have a great day. An admirer.*

I slipped my note into the cassette case, put it in the dovecot, reshelved my *Companion* and got the hell out of there. After I had taken care of that little bit of business, I went to the café. It was close by the university and seemed to provide a shelter in any storm. (It was called the George Café after the nearby Great George Street. Don't know who George was or if he was that great.)

It was a small place, often cramped. There were two lines of leatherette booths, divided by an aisle. From eight in the morning until ten at night the aisle was busy with uniformed staff taking orders and delivering food and drink. I used to come here at first with Vivian and her friends; it was a stalwart of West End living. Now I found that I came here all the time—not just for lunch or breakfast, and not necessarily to meet up with people. In fact, quite the opposite. I came here on my own, and I clung on to whatever hot drink I had ordered for the longest possible time so I could stay. It was warm, it was dry, there was free life here every time you stepped in. It was like a nice bus ride; you just sat there and the world moved around you.

I should have just told Fara that I'd be in the café, that would have been a better idea. She might come and find me, and we could talk. I was just thinking about going back and changing the note in her box when Carrie came in.

"Hi," she said.

"How did you know I'd be here?" I said.

"Who said I was looking for you?"

"You never come in here."

"Ok, I *thought* you might be in here, but I was close by, I had to see my doctor anyway." She took off her coat and slid into the booth.

"So what did she say?" I asked.

"Bloody nothing, as usual. Nothing useful anyway. Just some blabber. What does your GP say to you?"

"Not very much," I replied. "He called me 'dear' the other day as I was leaving, which made me think he was addressing someone else and hadn't been listening to me."

"Unless he really does think you're a dear!"

Gerry, the owner of the café, came over. He knew Carrie.

"Hi, wee bear! How are you keeping?"

"I'm ok, Gerry. I'm here!"

"I see that. That's great. I'm so glad you're feeling better."

She glanced at me. I knew that glance. As long as she was out of the psychiatric ward, she was "better."

"What can I get you?" he asked. Carrie ordered an Earl Grey tea and a scone.

"So, what's up with you? You look a bit nippy," she said, turning to notice me more.

"What do you mean, 'nippy'?"

"Not happy, out of sorts, of a constitution unbeguiling."

"I thought I was quite constant?"

"There's something up, I can feel it," she said.

I thought about telling her about Fara and the tape, but I went off on a different tangent. I didn't want to exploit her concern.

"Vivian's pal Samara said something once. She said that people can get used to anything."

"People can get used to anything?"

"Yes."

Pause.

"Well, what was the context?" Carrie asked.

"That's the thing. Now I can't remember if she was talking about me not being well or something else entirely."

"But you've chosen to remember it as the former."

"I *have* chosen to remember it as the former."

Carrie's years of studying psychology had evidently not gone to waste.

"And it's caused you no little pain over the years to think about it that way," she continued. She smiled over her Earl Grey.

"Why are you so funny today?" I asked.

"I'm not funny, I just feel ok. I'm here to work on your problems. You have a problem with what she said. It's been stuck in your head for ages. I get it. Of course I get it." She moved forward in her seat, onto her elbows, looking all the more like a psychologist might look. "I'm certain she didn't mean it to be bad. She probably said it real throwaway, and you took it too seriously."

"It definitely left an impression. I was annoyed. I thought, *That's easy for you to say. You're totally fine—dancing, drinking, rolling massive spliffs!*"

"People can get used to anything," Carrie repeated after a beat.

"That's what she said. I think I took it the wrong way. If there

81

was a wrong way to take something, I would take it, back then. I was bedraggled."

I took a sip from my coffee and settled back into the booth, slipping my shoes off, turning side on, leaning on the wall and lifting my feet up. There was a small window above us. A spider plant was there and had lowered a tendril with a spider plant baby on it. It was looking for the good earth. It found my forehead instead, but I found that restful.

"So, what about the question. Do you think she was right?" Carrie asked.

I pondered, then began. "I think people are amazing. They amaze me now, the things they can put up with. You hear about the lives some people lead and you think, *How the fuck are you doing that? How the hell are you dealing with that? You have children AND cancer, you're in a war zone AND starving, or even . . ."*

I looked around me, and my thoughts fell on one of the waiting staff.

". . . you're seventy and you're earning £3.50 an hour serving people in a busy café."

Carrie saw who I was talking about.

"That's Mary—she's not seventy. Sixty maybe. But look at her, she's bloody brilliant!"

"I know she's bloody brilliant, but how does she do it? She not only brings people what they want, need and desire, but she never gets flustered. She is always smiling. Therefore, the coffee and the scones that we are currently enjoying taste like her good mood."

"Your analysis is correct," said Carrie, polishing off the scone.

"So what about us? Can *we* get used to anything?" I asked. "Can we get used to this? *Should* we be getting used to it? Shouldn't we be more agitated, like Josie was talking about, or are we stuck here forever? Where do we fit in? What are we like—are we hopeless?" If Carrie was on a roll, maybe she had some answers.

"We're not hopeless. I don't think we're hopeless. There are many people a lot worse off than us." She sat back on the bench the same way I was sitting.

"People can get used to anything," she said.

"People are amazing," I said.

14

Frozen Fall

It is the autumn, there is no doubting it. I am no longer ambling; I'm having to pick up the pace to keep warm. The flood of new faces into the West End has faded somewhat. People are going indoors, and they are all getting down to business. I'm keeping my business light. I'm in the launderette at the "women's union"—the Queen Margaret building at Glasgow University (not that long ago, the "unions" were segregated between men and women).

This place feels different to me now. Back in my days of glory in the eighties, I was as much a part of this place as the regular drunks in the Steve Biko Bar, as Martin the doorman, and as the goths selling tie-dyed printed t-shirts and cheap jewelry in the foyer. Now I feel like a sneak. This was the building where I kept five hundred people dancing on my regular Thursday night slot. This was the building where I sat on the stage with so many bands, making sure they were safe from the overzealous attention of their fans.

That was then. Now I'm happy that I can still creep in with my laundry. Laundry is big for me. Richard goes to the one round the corner from our flat; I still drag mine on the bus down here. The laundry room is warm and zen—the buzzing and churning of the machines tends to mask outside interference and creates the feeling of a womb. In this womb I stay, occupying the corner plastic seat, always with an assiduously picked pocket novel to:

1. pass the time;
2. act as a conversation starter.

For example, with the arty girl in stripy tights on the next machine:

"*Lolita*—don't you think he's just a dirty old bastard?"

"Isn't that the point?"

"It's just art trying to legitimize child molesting."

"He's an awfully good writer."

"I wish you wouldn't read that in front of me."

That kind of thing. And here I sit. And I'm just happy to be here. I'm sticking around. I'm not moving. It pays dividends. A stressed sort of punky lassie with lavish brown curls, ripped tights, black velvet shorts and a frankly perfect brown suede jacket has dumped her load in the machine next to mine. She looks about the room for a bit, catches my eye, moves her eye away out the window for a second, then comes back to me.

"Are you going to be here for a bit?"

"I think so."

"Is there a chance you could watch my washing, make sure no one steals it?"

I wonder for a second how many people would make themselves a thief for a few wet t-shirts and pants.

"I can watch them. I will watch them." Luckily I wasn't reading *Lolita* or I might not have gotten the offer. I was reading *The Naked Civil Servant*. "You want me to switch them over to the dryer when they're done?" I ask.

She thinks for a second. I think I know what she's thinking: *Do I want this guy that I don't even know, this overly keen weirdo, to be handling my cold wet knickers and bras?*

"No, I'll be back in time." She smiles a weak smile, then pops off. It's a commission though. I feel useful. I will guard her machine against all comers.

I wish every day could be laundry day. This is my Saturday night. This is my peak socializing. I really appreciate the mornings now. I used to run from the clarity of the day, now I bask in it. It's kind of ironic that I fetishize busyness. I see people caught up in busy lives—involved, in love, in stress, achieving, aspiring. Just doing. It's great. If I could do it, I would. I'd dig the roads. I'd drive a bus (of course I would). I'd stamp library books. With glee.

What am I actually doing though? Do I have anything going for me? After the blush of September excitement, with the new academic year, everything slowed right down. I heard nothing from Fara, the girl with the tape. That doesn't surprise me. Maybe she hasn't had the time to appreciate the eloquence of the sequence I put together for her. Or maybe she just hasn't spotted my address in the code. I better leave that one to smolder. My bearded doctor in Fife? I went back to see him. I took his stuff. No difference so far. He did not provide me with any fresh revelation. He said six months. I'll give him six months. Then we'll see. I just wish I felt a bit happier. I have a bit of a dread feeling. I used to get it a lot, before I got sick.

What have I got on my side?

– I've got Carrie and Richard.
– I've got the music.

Occasionally I am reminded as I look at a leaf or sip my Earl Grey that creativity might be just around the corner. I haven't had any other songs come along like the first one. I sometimes wonder how close creativity and God are, whether they are close to being the same thing. They showed up at roughly the same time. They both give me a sense of: *This might be ok. This is bigger than you. You are part of something. Give in to it. This is the tip of the iceberg.*

I think I can now see that the merest hint of inspiration can lead to a song or a story or a picture. That's like a tiny mustard seed growing into a big plant, like the bit in the Bible said. I ponder these things as the dryer hums through its work. I feel suddenly a bit deflated—my laundry bubble has burst. I want to be in my room. I close my eyes and pray for a miracle before my laundry is finally done. I don't want the blues to fuck up my fluff and fold—it's the best part. I close my book and try to accept everything that is happening. I watch the gloom like you would watch a thunderstorm from an upstairs window. I wish it would go.

Suede Jacket comes back into the laundry room. She does not pick up where we left off, no more words are spoken. One day I am going to meet a person who has nothing better to do than talk about the laundry cycle and the book they're holding in their hand. They will have nothing to rush off to. Instead of a waiting room, we will both know that the laundry room is our destination. I don't want to be alone anymore. I was alone for years, and I liked it fine. Since I got ill, not so much. I love Carrie and Richard. Thank God for friends.

*****

Some days it feels like even God is not enough though. There's a Buddhist meditation center in the city, and I'm going to try it out. I figure I might get on a bit better if I'm meditating with other people. Richard is doing it, he's got it down. And he's happy doing it in the house. I, on the other hand, will take any opportunity to get out of the house and go looking for rest in another heated venue. So the next day I take the 44 bus to Sauchiehall Street, and I go straight up the stairs to the drop-in class. I'm a drop-in guy, no pressure, just slip in. Take your shoes off, grab a cup of something herbal, make your monetary contribution according to your means. It's peaceful. It's a respectful atmosphere, and it smells of incense. It's all the things you would imagine a Buddhist center to be. Student girls in baggy floral-print trousers. Older women in baggy floral-print trousers. The occasional man in a fleece and woolly socks.

They take us into the meditation room, and we grab cushions and the various paraphernalia that we will use to prop ourselves up while

87

we try to kneel or sit cross-legged. It takes us a while to get in position, and when I finally close my eyes I feel like I'm gently swaying. I'm trying to keep a straight spine and a tall neck. The teacher explains to us that they have two kinds of meditation here. One focuses on your breathing, the other encourages a feeling of loving kindness towards people. Today we're doing the breathing one. Now that I'm here, I feel a subtle slowing down, but I'm grateful for it.

Just by focusing on the breath I start to realize how much is going on in the mind at every second: it's a real party, with many guests all vying for my attention. The teacher, in essence, is inviting us to slip away from the party, to leave our guests, our multitude of badgering thoughts, and focus on ourselves. The teacher is inviting us to embrace the peace of a different room. It would be beautiful if I could just stay in that other peaceful room, the room that exists in the mind. I do believe there is a single window with ebullient light coming in. And I do believe the peace and that light are doing me a lot of good. I'd like to stay there, but I keep getting pulled back to the party.

In that short moment in the peaceful room, I got a taste for it. I saw the potential for how meditation could really work. That's the trick. If I can keep my mind on the breath, if I can just get my mind to shut up for a minute, if I can abide in that peaceful space without wavering, good things will happen. After the class I wandered out to a small park on Garnethill. I thought again about the meditation experience and I thought about a party game we used to play as kids. Let me explain.

It was called the Bournville Game. All the boys got in a circle, usually on the floor (at that age, and in that era of upbringing, birthday parties were usually single-sex affairs). A pair of dice were produced, a long scarf, ski gloves and a woollen beanie hat. Then a large bar of chocolate on a large white plate was put in the center of the circle, accompanied by a knife and fork.

88

When I say large, I can safely say that none of the boys in that room had ever seen a bar of chocolate so big. There was just no occasion that would call for such an excess of chocolate, not even Christmas. We assumed that these large bars were manufactured and sold only for use in this game. It was always Cadbury's chocolate and was usually the Bournville variety, which had the extra cachet of being dark and mysterious-tasting. Kind of grown-up.

The game was a simple one. Throw the dice and if you scored a double six you put on the scarf, the hat and the skiing gloves, you tried to pick up the knife and fork, and then you proceeded to tuck into the chocolate with as much speed and frenzy as the knife, fork and gloves would allow. The trouble was, you usually only got as far as one or two garments before the shout of "Twelve!" was heard, and then the scarf and hat were being ripped off you by the thrower of the twelve. On rare occasions, however, nobody could roll a twelve, and some lucky chap would have hit chocolate gold. Though it never happened to me, it happened to my friend Ian Prentice. He was a slightly portly boy and had acquired the nickname "Barrel."

Barrel had thrown a twelve, put on the scarf, the hat and the gloves, and though not in any particular rush had managed to get the knife and fork into his hands. He then proceeded, methodically and magnificently, to destroy the bar of chocolate. Nobody could throw a twelve. He looked as if he had been born for that moment and was grinning from ear to ear as he gleefully ingested the dark brown chunks of magic. Barrel was loving it. He kept looking straight at us as he shoved more chocolate in, his eyes shining. Long streams of chocolate juice flowed from each corner of his mouth, gathering at the chin, running down his neck. He showed no sign of slowing; the bar was disappearing.

Someone did eventually throw a twelve, but the spoils by that time were so depleted that it hardly seemed worth going on with the game. Barrel sat back and didn't take any further part in the afternoon's games. He made a little throne for himself and was happy to digest away. Even the adults realized his triumph and let him enjoy his role as King of the Party.

I thought about Barrel when I was meditating. I saw it all in a flash.

Barrel had that rare moment with the chocolate: when he was winning, he was flying, he was completely in the moment, he was harvesting the goodness. No one threw a twelve. I felt that if you could find that rare place while meditating, you could harvest peace of mind instead of chocolate. You could store up contentment, just like Barrel was storing up sweet goodness.

I was happy I had finally tried meditation. It could be another tool in my toolbox. It was a plausible practice, not just reserved for Richard the Meditator. For a brief, rarefied moment I felt the potential; my mind was balancing on a pin, and no one was calling twelve. It was altogether good, and I didn't doubt for a second that there was godliness involved somewhere. In *my* mind at least, God was sponsoring all serious attempts to find peace and happiness. God was quietly shoving me into all these new endeavors. He'd rewritten my curriculum entirely. He'd replaced the untenable with the possible, the irascible with the cordial. What did He want in return? Whatever He wanted, He could have it.

15

What Can I Give Him?

The year was tailing off, and I felt the life flowing out of the city with the Christmas conspiracy. I know that sounds like I'm being mean, but I just wanted things to stay normal.

Now that I'm a free-floating vagabond of the state, the fabric of my existence feels tissue-thin at times. When the 44 bus does something different, even on a Sunday, it's a wrench for me. Over Christmas the buses go haywire, and it gets me down. I know that maybe doesn't say that much about the health of my mind at the minute, but I don't want to think about it too much.

Richard had already disappeared back to his ancestral home. Even Carrie had given me the heave-ho, as she gave in to the rituals of her family Christmas. The flat was cold. I tried to warm up in the kitchen by draping myself over the one radiator there, but my core was chilled, so I just went to bed early, got under so many blankets. I was still cold, but I figured I would wake up warm. That sometimes happens. It was so quiet in that back bedroom with Richard away, nothing moving outside in the lane. I started listening to the sound of the feathers crackling slightly as I moved my head on the pillow. At least, I thought it was feathers. When I listened again, I thought maybe I had picked up head lice and that they were popping and crackling all over the place. Somehow, despite all the din, I fell asleep. I woke before the light. Christmas Eve. I hadn't gone in for gift-buying this year, but I knew that would be ok. My family would be happy enough if I turned up at all. I thought I'd at least make them a nice card and try and write them a poem each.

I made a silly Christmas scene on the kitchen table. Richard had a wooden Nativity scene that he'd inherited from his childhood. I added a few characters that were lying around. I had a Bart Simpson–shaped telephone that made it in there, a black mahogany elephant that used to be my gran's, some plastic figures from a Miss World game that used to belong to my sister (Miss Jamaica, Miss UK, Miss Italy). There was a wind-up frog and hedgehog, and a cute little angel and devil set where the angel was punching the devil out. It was quite a scene. I took a few pictures of it, the end of a roll of film. I shoved stuff into my shoulder bag. As I was leaving, I noticed Richard had left a little package for me. I put that in my bag and walked out.

I walked down to Byres Road, which wasn't far, and handed in my photo film to be done in an hour. I sat in the George while I waited, nursing my coffee, trying not to catch anybody's eye for too long. People were festive and I was not. There was such a gulf between their festiveness, chumminess, meeting-up-with-long-lost-pals-ness and my solo mission that I felt awkward. I looked around at the notices on the café wall, stuff that was happening. I saw that Fara's ensemble group was going to be part of a Christmas performance at the university chapel that afternoon. You would have thought that her stalker would have known this information far in advance, but it turns out I wasn't even that great a stalker.

An older couple sat down in the booth with me. It was the sort of café that if it was busy you had to share tables. I think because I was on my own they felt like they had to make conversation with me. They were nice, but I was not really in the mood. They were asking me questions about what I was doing for Christmas and so forth; the answers I gave them added up to a picture of me that I didn't really recognize at all. I had successfully negotiated the science degree I started six years previously, graduated, and was now working for a good company doing research. With a nice girlfriend.

Why did I make up stuff? Because I thought that was the kind of story they wanted to hear. Like I said, they were a nice old couple. The last thing they wanted to know was that the young person sitting with them had less energy, prospects and general stuff going on than they did. How was my generation meant to support their generation with stats like that? I said cheerio, paid my bill, picked up my photographs and went to the copy shop up the lane behind Byres Road. I made my cards, and I even got one printed on a mug for my mum.

I thought I would take a wander up to the Christmas concert, see if I could get in. I couldn't tell you if I was doing this for my soul or for Fara, whether I was attracted to the light of Christmas or the light of a girl. I got there pretty early. The zealous students in attendance told me that it was ticketed and that there were none left. I argued that I was in the music department, and after a while they told me I could go in and sit at the back somewhere.

I got myself situated in the top corner of the choir stalls, on an ornately carved chair that felt like a booth. It was above a heating pipe—bonus. I waited. My journey with God, welcome though it was, didn't up to that point necessarily involve Jesus and everything that went along with him. So now that I was in church at Christmas, drawn here to welcome his arrival, I was a little conflicted. I'd been given a gift, a hint, a glimpse, and I'd taken to it keenly, like a trusting kid. The gift of believing something. It was a rather nebulous belief so far, and maybe it didn't stand up to much scrutiny. My God could have been any flavor, any shape, any gender. But I did think God was good. I did think that much. I had no doubt he or she intended to be a guiding hand and a comfort.

There was a Labor politician called Tony Benn. I heard him in an interview on the radio talking about his faith or indeed his lack of it. He said that he'd never received the gift of faith. When I thought about that now, I got his meaning. It was a gift, no doubt. I waited up there in my corner and I was as passive as I could be. I just decided to give in to this moment. I didn't even know for sure if the trains were running late enough to get me back to my parents', but my steam had run out and I was heavy in the quilted pew with my carved chair and my willowing faith.

People came in—families and parents and students and staff. There were robes and rich red material and handbags and the aggregated perfume of older ladies. I realized that my class choir was going to be part of the concert, the choir that I simply hadn't gone back to. It made me shrink into my carved chair even more. Fara was there, part of the thirty-strong music ensemble that filled the space on the floor between the banked choir stalls of singers and watchers. I was lucky to be here, up high. Most of the audience had to sit further down the chapel on regular seats. I was close to the action.

It was more like a church service than a concert. Verses from the Bible were read, then they would sing something, then more from the Bible, all about Christmas. My favorite piece of music was perhaps the least "religious." It starts off just talking about the weather—"In the Bleak Midwinter." You know the one I mean. I always liked that one when I was young. The first verse was about cold and snow. It just made you think about the countryside and nature. I liked that. I think the next two verses were a bit more about Jesus; he started to come into it. It was when the last verse came in that I suddenly realized the strength of the whole.

> *What can I give him, poor as I am?*
> *If I were a shepherd, I would bring a lamb;*
> *If I were a wise man, I would do my part;*
> *But what can I give him: give my heart.*

Those were the words printed on the sheet. The "him" was Jesus. Considering that at that moment it must be noted that I didn't believe Jesus was everything the Church wanted you to believe, I found the whole thing pretty moving. I felt from somewhere a wave of emotion, and I didn't know where it was coming from. I didn't know if it was the music, the words, the occasion, me, Fara, Christmas, loneliness. Whatever. Something gave. Whoever had written that hymn or was responsible for that music was speaking to a part of my mind that wasn't my daily mind, it was a deeper mind, and I'd been found out. I was dizzy again, but this time my cheeks were wet with tears, not hot with blushing.

Did *my* heart know something that I didn't know? I looked at Fara, who hadn't been playing or singing but just listening. She was smiling, benign. She was light. As far as I could see, the music hadn't affected her the way it had affected me. Probably a good thing. I didn't want her to be sad.

After the show, I didn't hang about. I didn't hover around, trying to flash a significant glance in her direction. I didn't talk to her. I got back on the 44. I made it to the station and wrote my cards on the train. I opened my present from Richard. It was a framed picture of a young Rod Stewart looking wistful, dressed in leopard-skin, in a field with horses. He knew I liked Rod. I sat beholding the glory of the picture. It made me feel a bit better. It made me miss Richard.

When I got off an hour later in the coastal town my parents lived in, there were no more buses. I could have taken a taxi, but I decided to walk. It was ten o'clock. I suppose I was still running on adrenaline from being in the same room as Fara. The excitement seemed to justify a walk and a mulling over. I walked out from the center of town, and I immediately went down residential streets of large sandstone houses with big walls, big cars parked outside. Large trees loomed overhead. Lights twinkled inside as people settled down to enjoy Christmas.

My route took me past a hotel where certain groups of people from my old school used to meet over the festive period. When I looked down the drive, I could see the ground-floor windows were steamed up and there were the colored lights of the disco flashing within. I walked along the drive, careful to stay in the shadows, and I looked in a side window. I had a pretty good view of the lounge area, and I was surprised how many people I recognized on the inside.

There was a bunch of guys and girls from my year at school and the year below. I guess you could say they were all adults now and past the squabbles and pettiness of the decade before, but I wasn't taking any chances. I certainly didn't feel like going in and throwing myself into the crowd. I had left school a year before most of them and I honestly don't think anybody noticed I had gone. Our paths and thinking had probably done nothing but diverge from that point. Plus, if they knew anything about me at all now, they might have heard about my stay in Ashfield (the psychiatric hospital). It was a small town, after all. I didn't really fancy reminiscing about that.

There was an open log fire going. The way that people were stood around and draped over sofas, it looked a little like a picture in an American magazine, advertising knitwear. One thing that kept me at the window a bit longer was Alison Corbett. She was there, just to one side of the fireplace, sat in an armchair, talking to Peter Chadha, who was sitting cross-legged on the floor. I always liked Alison; she went all the way back to my class in primary school. She was a sweet person—I'm just kind of realizing that now, because who thinks that when you're ten years old? But she was that, and you could tell she had lost none of her sweetness as she sat and listened to Peter and laughed at his undoubted semi-crapness. I liked what she was wearing. She had on a cream-colored cotton dress, slightly ruffled, inch-wide straps over her shoulders, and a little paisley neckerchief. She still had the little gap-toothed overbite she'd had since primary school. And the long straight brown hair. She wore high-top black-and-white Converse trainers. She was quietly kicking everybody else's asses in the vibe department.

I turned away from the window. I didn't want to get caught

looking there, and I'd seen enough. One day I would like to be sat where Peter Chadha was, at the foot of Allie Corbett, listening to her chat, finding out what she was up to, cross-referencing old times and catching up on what people were doing now. I turned back into the dark, crossed the road and climbed over the stone wall that took me onto the golf course. Once there, away from the street lighting, it didn't seem dark or forbidding at all. It felt good to be on the springy turf, and there was enough light coming off the low cloud that I could see everything.

It was a mild night. A light breeze was coming from the sea, half a mile away. I knew the way so easily in the dark, I almost wanted to get lost but couldn't. This was the extended playground of my boyhood—the fields and the woods and the fairways. I got through the golf course, up to where my dad's allotment was. I knew by this time that my parents would be at the Watchnight service in the village, so I thought I'd go straight to the church, past more old houses with long driveways. Bare sycamores and beeches towered over the road. The streets were dead quiet and lights seemed far off. As I approached the church, it glowed like a Christmas card picture. I could hear the congregation singing.

I got right up to the building. There was no open doorway. They were singing "In the Bleak Midwinter." I could make out the words, and as I stood in the dark I was moved all over again. I felt sorry for myself, and I was crying again. I couldn't go in now, even if I found an open door. I thought about just heading back to the house, but I stayed around the graves and the old gray walls and waited for the last hymn to be sung: "O Come, All Ye Faithful." As people started emerging, I positioned myself in the shadows. I waited until I saw my mum and dad come out.

"Hello."

"Stephen. Did you just get here?" my mum exclaimed, a bit taken aback but happy to see me.

"Not too long."

"You should have come in."

She gave me a hug.

"I couldn't find the door," I half lied.

"Come on, you can drive, your father's had too much to drink already."

My dad looked at her with mock disgust. He did seem a little bleary though.

16

Winter Routine

January slid into April and I wondered what had happened to the momentum of last summer. I would go to the glasshouses in the Botanic Gardens to try and heat up. I found my bench and pretended I was invisible. It was hard not to ruminate. Carrie was always analyzing where she was at. She had a rather morbid graph in her room from the days when she never got out of bed. All there was to represent the day was a small block of color. It was the chronic illness version of scratch marks on a prison wall. Red for unspeakable, green for pretty awful, blue for ok.

Here on the bench, in an occasional moment of clarity, I realized that the trick is to get by without the analysis. If you can do that, you are much better off. It means that you are living and not just existing. For me, that would mean being defined not by illness but by other phenomena, even if those phenomena are deities, soft guitar music and undefined lust. This would be a start, to make a move away from the inert. I don't think anyone wants to be defined by what they can't do. What you can do? Lose yourself in *that*, no matter how tenuous.

Last summer was the chronic illness honeymoon period. The pit was behind me. Mentally, I got a boost from thinking, *I got through the worst.* It didn't last. Life makes deep psychological demands, and they are grinding and gurning away in the background. Carrie feels it, and it crushes her. Richard feels it, and it makes him fall silent and inward. I feel it clawing and coming after me, and I couldn't keep ahead, not through the dark and frigid winter we just had.

99

Overall, my tussle with the music department at the university had been anonymous. When I went to the sliding-glass window in the music building with another lateness excuse and a doctor's letter, the gray-haired woman at the window noticed me for once.

"Your health isn't great, is it?" she observed.

"Not really, no."

Her question qualified as a kindness, and it was also the seal on my university career. That's all it took. My emotional landscape was so arid, I was susceptible to any flicker of suggestion from another human. *Your health isn't great, is it?* You are correct. Thanks for noticing. I quit.

What was more worrying was the overall slowing down. I was quitting university again, but that was sort of ok. It was other things though. We never played tennis, the swimming faded out, and I had stopped giving Carrie pep talks about how we were all quite lucky, really. I used to tell her that we had been given a secret insight, that we could do anything with our lives. Other people were trapped in modes of thinking and acting; we had been freed from convention by dint of our condition.

I'm not sure she was really buying it, but I think she admired something about my speeches, the optimism, the bloody-mindedness. I told her that we were mad and that it was ok to be mad, in fact it was better. We had been in the madhouse, and the madhouse was where the truth would out. Nobody had anything left to hold on to or anything to hide behind. But now I was slowing down again, and Carrie was as powerless to help me as I was now powerless to help her.

At the ME meetings that we continued to hold every fortnight, I was the one who said "The body knows how to heal. If you give it the right conditions, it will heal." Again, another nice speech, but it wasn't happening for me. I was quieter at the last few meetings, and at the end of the meeting, when the girls hugged each other and some of them wept, I started to understand where the emotion was coming from.

I was really hoping that my Fife doctor would come through on his promise. The six months were nearly up, and he'd said I was going to feel much better. He must know something by this time. I wonder if there was any real wisdom in his tools, in his tidy beard and in his too little hands.

Someone at the last ME meeting mentioned a healer. It was put out there, a twig of conversation, but it never even budded. Except in me. I'd seen a healer before, but it was a circus, a visiting Irish chap in the town hall. A line-up, a quick hands-on, put your money in a bucket and good luck. I didn't like it, and it didn't work. But this mention of a lady that healed piqued something in me. I phoned Carrie, who phoned Nicola, who spoke to her mum, who said "Just be careful" but gave the number to Nicola, who told Carrie, who told me. Ok, I'll be careful. What's the worst thing that could happen while visiting a sixty-year-old lady in her house, and who, by some accounts, heals by the grace of Jesus Christ?

Judy Neal greeted me at the door. She didn't look old, didn't look young. She had short dark hair, slightly watery eyes and a smile that was fixed but not without meaning. We sat in her front room for a bit. I liked her house. It sat back from the road in a tree-lined inlet, so it was quiet and leafy green. You could have all the money in the world, but you still might not be able to buy the peace of a tree-lined inlet of Mosspark.

"How did you hear about me?" she asked.

"Through a friend of a friend's mum," I replied.

"I know about you ME people. I hear the cries and I feel the sadness," she said. "I'm glad you came. You don't have to give me any money, but you can make a contribution, just what you can afford."

"Ok."

"I practice Christian healing. That means I imagine Jesus working through me to help heal you. You don't have to be a Christian, you will still feel the benefit."

"Ok," I said.

"We'll go into the other room. It'll take around an hour."

We went into the room at the back, maybe a small dining room. It was her healing room. It was darker, a few chairs, a shelf with books, but most of the room was given over to the treatment table in the middle. I lay down on my back and immediately felt comfortable. The only sound was of a solitary bird outside chirping and whistling melodiously.

"I won't be laying hands on you, just over you," she said. "I will stay in one position for five or ten minutes, then I'll move round. You can just keep your eyes shut the whole time if you like. You might feel the area beneath my hands getting a little warmer—that's ok."

"Should I think of anything?"

"You should imagine the healing doing you good. That's probably the best thing."

I liked that since I got ill, funny things happened to me. I used to have the most energy in the world. I was the most energetic person I knew of. But I kept doing the same things over and over. I was moving around in the same circles. I went to the same shop for the same bread, lifted the same amps for the same bands. Unlocked the shop in the morning, locked it again. Read the same music papers, went to bed at ten. Now I was in the hands of a healer. Now I would ask questions in my head and get on a bus to find the answers. People liked being asked questions. I was going to keep asking them until I got the answers I wanted.

"How did you get started with this?" I asked her.

"I was a nurse," she replied. "When I retired, I went back to cut hair for people in hospital. When I cut people's hair, I imagined trying to heal them at the same time. I just got a feeling for it, like I might be able to help."

I thought I'd better offer something in return.

"I started going to church, but I'm not sure about everything I hear in there. I'm just going along," I said.

She thought for a second.

"That's ok. The main thing is that you're there. Did anyone take you along or did you just go one day?"

"I just went."

"You'll probably stay then. Sounds like there was something pretty strong pulling you in."

"Well, it was me that decided to go," I said.

"You wouldn't have gone unless someone really wanted you there."

I thought about this.

"Ok, here we go. I'll get started," she said.

And I shut my eyes.

She was up there somewhere. It was the most elastic hour of my life. I couldn't tell whether it was five minutes or five hours. I was floating. I was inside a Dalí painting, the one depicting Jesus that was in the Kelvingrove Museum. I came down from the sky and settled on the beach by the Sea of Galilee. Jesus was there. I wanted him to come over to me, but he wouldn't come any closer. There were splashes of sun through the evening clouds that felt warm, and those seemed to correlate with the warmth of her healing. I was on the beach. I *was* the beach. Jesus was there; he was looking at me from the corner of his eye. I somehow knew that all this was happening in my mind, but still I tried speaking. "I don't know what to say. It's not like I don't believe in you. I just want to be sure of the facts." He didn't reply. I felt like I was back in my own body again and that he was standing over me. I didn't want to miss this chance, so I repeated in my head, "I want to be better. I want to be well. I want to be better. I want to be well . . ."

She gently roused me by shaking me on the shoulder. I must have been asleep.

"How was that?"

"Good," I said, a bit bewildered.

"I could feel your spirit. It was knotted and boxed in. I tried to get it out, but it's stuck in there."

"Ah."

"You should come back and see me again if you can."

"Ok, I will."

I left her £5 as a contribution. I wish I'd left her £10, but all my extra money was going on the doctor in Fife. As I sat on the bus on the way home, I thought about how much better I liked her and the whole experience of going to see her than I did the Fife doctor. She didn't offer me a cure, she didn't promise anything very much, but I felt like she knew me better, and that counted for a lot.

17

Breaking It Down

I woke up thinking about Vivian. Maybe it's strange I don't think about her more. I mean, if you've only ever had sex with one person, what else is there to think about? If you've only touched one pair of breasts. If you've only touched one other person between the legs. If you've only ever reached over in the bed to see one neck, one shoulder, one mess of chopped blonde hair. Oh well.

This was the day I was due to visit my doctor in Fife. Tidy Beard. Even Carrie called him that now. It was a long trek up, all the way from Glasgow to the north Fife coast. Then up that bloody hill. Train, train, bus, walk.

"I can't do anything more to help you," he said.

This was a shock. I could hardly take in what he had said, it was so abrupt. We'd just had our "consultation," which was mostly me talking, telling him nothing had really changed. That's when he dropped this bomb.

"You said that you were going to make me better." I heard my own voice. It sounded weak.

"I had expected different results, that's for certain."

I sat there numb. "You were so positive about it, so sure about it, I just assumed that I would feel at least a *bit* better."

"I'm sorry. Nothing's guaranteed. Especially not with ME."

"You told me that you had a great track record with ME, that everyone improves."

"I'm sorry. I tried my best and nothing happened."

I felt like I had been punched or that someone was breaking up with me. It was like Vivian again. He had another patient coming

105

along. I paid him. In retrospect, I should have just walked out. I had rested so much hope on this doctor curing me. What did he do? Absolutely fuck all. In fact, I was now worse than I was a year ago.

I went back to Glasgow. I spent a few days at the flat with not much going on. I went to see Judy the healer again, and that was ok, but I think I was still in shock at the Fife doctor's verdict. What was I meant to do with that information? I was three years into this thing and I had firmly plateaued at a level that didn't allow me to work, love, study or do *anything* really useful.

Richard was away again, staying at his brother's. These days he often seemed to have more going on than me. He was pulling ahead. I didn't begrudge him it. I just felt a bit left behind. The place was deserted, and I was going really slowly. I didn't even make it down to see Carrie. I was in a kind of daze. A few days passed. My mum was joining my dad on the ship he worked on for their annual working holiday together, so the house was going to be free for more than a week. I said I would go down and look after the house and the dog.

It was a beautiful hot day in early June, Scotland was at its pinnacle of green loveliness, but the whole thing couldn't have been more of a contrast to what was going on with me. Sometimes it feels like the weather just comes along and *rubs it in*. Everyone is doing great, feeling great, making the most of these rare, halcyon days. What am I doing? Languishing. Bloody rubbish. I went down on the train. When the conductor asked me for my ticket, I fished it out, surprised that someone had spoken to me. He was a nice guy, and he tapped me on the shoulder as he went off. It made me well up. I didn't know why a friendly tap on the shoulder should make me cry. Maybe I did. I hadn't spoken to anyone for days. It was a shock that people could be nice. It was a shock that someone had spoken to me.

I got to my mum's, we had dinner, and I took the dog out for a short trundle to the grass at the bottom of the street. She was leaving the next day and in the morning was all ready to go.

"Will you be ok?" she asked.

"I'll be fine," I replied.

And off she went, driving north to Greenock to meet my dad. I was left alone with the dog. The house was monumentally quiet. I just moved from room to room, lying wherever the patches of sun hit the carpet. Occasionally a window frame would make a cracking sound, expanding in the sun. Occasionally a curtain would flap if the window was open. All the dog did was lie in his basket, licking his nose from time to time and moving his head from one side of his front legs to the other.

Suddenly I didn't feel so good. I thought about the next ten days of emptiness stretching ahead. I had looked forward to the prospect of peace, but now that I had it, I didn't want it. I started to panic. My heart was racing and I felt my blood turn icy. I had never had this feeling before and it was horrible. I didn't know what was happening and I certainly couldn't control it. I'd spent the last three years of my life keeping an eye on my pulse, doing pretty much everything I could to stay calm and relaxed, to never waste energy. Now here I was with an explosion of anxiety, heart thumping, almost passing out. This was irresponsible, this was not part of any plan. What was happening? How was I going to get through this? There was no one to call and I had to stay here.

The morning went on and it just got worse. I was shaking and sweating, I didn't know what the hell was happening. There was no one I could call, apart from maybe my mum, but I'd have to catch her somehow before she got on the ship. She had left early, but I didn't want to bother her. I knew she was really looking forward to the holiday on the boat with my dad. In the end I called the ship's office, which luckily happened to be in Greenock, where the boat was setting sail from. They managed to get hold of her.

"What's wrong?" she said.

"I'm not feeling well. You might have to come home."

"Really? Are you sure? What's happening?"

"I don't think I can be here on my own. I don't know why, but I feel horrible. It just started after you left."

I think she could hear the panic in my voice. I never panic. I have never panicked. Even when I was really sick before I had to go to hospital, when I was five-and-a-bit stone, I was always really rational—especially with my mum, because she knew me better than anyone, and she had always trusted me. But this time I think she could tell there was something bad happening. It was a rotten thing to ask her to do, give up her holiday.

"Ok, I'm coming home. I'll be an hour. I'll phone Doreen and ask her to look in," she said.

"No, it's ok. I'll see you."

I put the phone down. At least something was happening now. I sat beside the dog on the floor, not moving. The door went. It was Doreen, our neighbor.

"Your mum asked me to look in on you. Are you ok?"

"Oh yeah, thanks. Just not feeling too great. She's coming back now."

I don't know how convincing I sounded. I didn't want to freak Doreen out.

"Do you want me to come in for a bit?" She stood there with her arms crossed, half in, half out.

"No, thanks, Doreen. I'll be ok. I'm just sitting with the dog. She's coming back now."

She looked at me as if trying to assess a risk.

"Ok. I'm just across the road. If you feel any worse, just come over. I'll keep the door open, ok?"

"Ok, yes, thanks, Doreen. Yes, I'm ok."

She went away. I could feel my teeth sort of chatter, as if I was really cold, and my jaw felt like it was jammed shut. I stayed where I was. I don't know how long it was till I heard the car come up the drive. I got up to open the door. I didn't cry. I was too nervous and worked up.

"I'm sorry," I said to my mum.

"It's ok," she said.

I could see the concern on my mum's face. I have this thing, that I'm color-blind. So when people say to someone "Oh, you're turning red, you're getting a beamer," I can never see it. In a similar vein, if someone says a person "looks pale, has lost the color in their face," I don't see that either. I *felt* like my face was white, or the color of putty, but I didn't bother to look. I could tell from my mum's face that she could see it. My mum was a nurse, so not much freaked her out in the health department, and that was a good thing. She saw everything on a nightly basis down at Casualty. She'd kept me steady when I was at my worst before. I think I may have trusted her expertise a little *too* much before, when I got so thin and I kept assuring her I was ok. It took her a long time before she called the doctor on me.

This time she was her usual calm self, which was the best. I told her what I was feeling. She called the doctor's surgery straight away. It was getting late to go in, so they said the doctor would pop by as she was out already. It was 6 p.m. by the time the doctor came by. I hadn't eaten anything, maybe just a few mouthfuls of soup. I wasn't feeling any better. In fact, the approaching night was already making my nerves even worse, and I couldn't stop shaking. When the doctor sat with me, I think I'd got to the point of maximum distress without wailing and weeping. I was taut and wan, in a dark, walled place. She started off by asking me what I thought was wrong with me.

"I don't know. Never happened before," I managed to get out. I tried to talk more, but I was visibly shaking, and my teeth were still stuck together.

The doctor was less calm than my mum—she seemed pretty freaked, actually. She started by suggesting to my mum that I should be on anti-depressants. She wrote a prescription.

"Are you going to be ok?" she asked.

"I don't know. I don't think so," I chattered.

She fished a bottle of white pills out of her bag and gave them to my mum.

"He can take one up to three times a day. I'd take one now," she said, looking at me. "Do you have a history of mental illness?"

"No. I was in hospital, in a psychiatric ward for three months once, up at Ashfield. But I was never on any medication."

"What did they have you in for?"

"I've got ME. Chronic fatigue syndrome. But I lost a lot of weight and they kept me in while I put it back on."

"And have you been ok since then?"

"I've been living with the chronic fatigue and I've not got any better since then. But I know you guys can't help me with that."

She looked at me with a face that doubted me and was annoyed at me at the same time.

"Who was your doctor?" she asked.

"Simpson. I didn't like him. He never helped." The way I was feeling, I was just telling it straight. I didn't care.

"Ok, Stephen, we're going to try and help you. You should take the pills I'm giving your mum and try and get some rest. I've also written you a prescription for anti-depressants, and I'll arrange for you to see someone in a couple of days."

I was not reassured. She left. I took the pill, curled up on my side on the bed. My mum sat there with me for a while, and as the light started to fade, she asked me, "Do you want anything?"

"I'm ok."

She sighed. "I'm going to let the dog out."

"Ok."

She went out. Although I didn't want to be left alone, I used those few moments to think. There was something about the intensity of the experience that needed to be addressed alone and with concentration. It was all-consuming. I was beyond scared; I was petrified. I had never felt like this in my life. I couldn't even think of God. God was nowhere. There was darkness beneath the bed I was lying on. It was everywhere. A few hours went by. My mum said she was going to bed and was I ok? I tried to make out I was feeling a bit better, the pill had done something to me, made me shake less, talk with less teeth-chatter.

A while later, I thought I should go to the toilet. I got up, achy, groggy. When I got to the banister outside the bedroom a grim thought came to me. I saw suicide. I saw that it was an option. It wasn't scary in itself; it was a straightforward choice. All I had to do was proceed forward. How terrified I must have been at that point, that killing myself seemed like a simple, sane option. I'd never experienced anything like that feeling before, and I think I must have been quietly psychotic. I didn't actively fight the idea, but luckily that heaviest of black trains passed from me. Now I was just back to survival mode. I went into my mum's bedroom.

"Can I sleep here?"

"Of course," my mum said.

I hadn't been in my mum's bed since I was eight or something, and here I was, a twenty-three-year-old guy. But I didn't really stop to think about it, I just got in and tried to shut everything down.

It was a manic night, drifting between the worst kind of non-sleep and fully-awake panic. The anxiety and the doom were friends. They were a little tag team. When one was done, it would hand over to the other.

"You got him?"

"I got him, easy. He's all over the place, a real pussycat."

That's them talking—anxiety and doom. Big buddies, they had it worked out. Did I get a say in this? Did I just have to wait around and put up with this shit? Was I being changed? Was I being molded? Was this all for my own good?

*****

Day five after the breakdown. I'm on the anti-depressants. I'm still taking the Valium. I've seen the psychiatrist. I haven't had any more direct thoughts of killing myself. I stopped vibrating and I can talk without either my teeth chattering or my teeth sticking together. I called Carrie last night and told her what was going on.

"So what was your psychiatrist like?" she asked.

"He was the same one that I had in the hospital. Dr. Simpson. Complete ME denier. Was delighted to see me back, grinned like a cat when I went in. Talked to me like I was a naughty child who dared question his professional judgment. Basic cunt."

"Fuck sake. Usual pish. You need to get under the auspices of Doshi."

"Who is he?" I asked.

"She," Carrie corrected. "Dr. Doshi. It's my lady psych from hospital days, but I still see her."

"Do you need to see her? Is she good?"

"She's pretty sympathetic."

"That's the main thing, right? I mean, what else is there? You're not on anti-depressants, are you?"

"Yeah, I am."

"I didn't know."

"I didn't feel much like telling you before, but you're part of the club now."

"So how long have you been on them?"

"Two and a bit years."

"I didn't realize."

"Yeah. You always seem to breeze in here, so light and carefree. It's like the ME didn't seem to get you down at all. It was a bit intimidating. But I guess now you're feeling it."

"I'm feeling it."

The phone line was quiet for a second as we both felt it.

"Panic's the worst," I said, speaking quietly, like thinking.

"Yeah, there's nothing you can do with the panic. You can feel really shit, really down, really awful and still drag your ass through the day, and then you start feeling a little bit better and you have a cry and you can start the cycle over. But when the anxiety hits, it's shit in the moment and shit for ages afterwards, because it's so knackering."

"Will the pills help that? I feel like I've had full-on anxiety since this happened."

"Yeah, probably. They kill it a bit, they help you get it under control. Are you going to come back up?" I heard her voice get a bit pale, tail off.

"Soon, I hope. It will be good to see you," I said.

Then I could hear her choking a bit—a funny gurgle, a sob. She hadn't cried to me before. Even when the other ME people were crying, she was solid. Even when I didn't get it. I think I'd started to get it. I was trying not to join in. I don't know why—it would have been alright.

"Are you ok?" I asked.

"Yeah." *Snort. Gulp. Choke.* "Yeah, sorry."

"Don't be sorry. I'm sorry."

"What are you sorry for?"

"Dunno. Thought I was going to pull us through."

"Yeah, well, we're both fucked now."

*****

Day seven, I was in the park with my mum and the dog. Mum ran into a lady from church, who seemed to know a bit about my situation.

"How are you, Stephen?"

"I'm ok, Mrs. Kilgour, thanks."

"I'm sorry to hear you haven't been well. At least you're here to keep your mum company." She smiled at my mum. "Is it that ME that's still the problem?"

"Yes, that and other stuff."

Mrs. Kilgour was one of those perceptive older ladies. The kind you used to run from when you were wee, when you were up to no good—"I can *see* you, Stephen Rutherford! Your mother would *not* be impressed if she knew what you were up to." The thing about the perceptive ones is that they are often the kind ones too. She really could still *see* me like she did when I was wee.

"God must *really* love you," she said suddenly.

She said it in such a strong and certain way. She gave me a pat on the wrist, said bye to my mum and headed off.

We got back to the car, put the dog in. I told my mum that I wanted to walk home. I wanted to think about what Mrs. Kilgour said, and other things. Plus it was nice out, I wanted to linger in the green.

"Ok, see you back there. Are you ok?" my mum asked.

"Yeah, I'm fine. See you in a bit," I said.

I disappeared into the parkland of my youth and did the slow saunter I had got so accustomed to in the years that I had been back with my parents. I was the defiant oddball, the lanky streak of piss, the weirdo in the long coat. I stood out a mile in this low-walled suburbia. I didn't feel defiant now though. Even six months ago I'd felt sort of gallus, telling myself I was just biding my time on the way to being something good. Now I felt that the "me" had been completely stripped away. I didn't know who the hell I was or what I was meant to do. So, God must really love me? That was one way of looking at it. I assumed it was an ultra-positive way of looking at really bad times. But it did chime with what I had been thinking earlier. Maybe there was a point to all the pain and I'd find out one day.

I don't know what happened to those days. I had anxiety the whole time. One part of me wanted to get back to Glasgow, to some sort of living. The other part just wanted to stay there with my mum and the dog and the greenhouse. My anti-depressants kicked in. It felt like someone had double-glazed my nerve endings. I didn't mind. I just wanted to be less anxious and get as far away from the idea of killing myself as possible. I wasn't going to march out and kill myself. I wasn't going to walk into the water. I wasn't going to overdose. I wasn't going to jump off a building. No way. Didn't have the guts to do that one.

But that's ok, that's what you want with suicide. You want to not have the guts to do it. When you have the guts to do it, you're out of your fucking mind, and I wanted to stay in my mind. I thought that if I could keep putting layers between the thing that I had seen a few weeks back, layers between myself and that hideous void, that was all I could do. The layers were activity. The layers were human company. The layers were anything I could muster with my limited strength. The new reality was that I needed to forget about any sort of higher education. Get that out of your system. Also, I shouldn't put my trust in any sort of physician, madman or magician to make me right again. Forget that. There was God, but He seemed to have left me alone for now. I didn't know where He was. I was having difficulty getting through when I tried to engage in prayer.

I wanted to get back to the city. I knew it was going to be mentally tough, but I wanted to get away from this place. I couldn't stand the taste of my mum's Special K cereal anymore. My breakdown had been flavored with the "nothing going on" aura of my small growing-up town. At another time, the quiet wood walks and memories of bike gangs and heavy rock would be fodder enough to live off, but not now. My mind was hungry for the present to be enough.

*****

Richard was home when I got back to Glasgow, but Carrie was my go-to for confiding. When Vivian finished with me, over a year ago, she'd said something like "Carrie will just have to be your friend now." It had felt like she was dropping me off at the kids' table while she went out with the grown-ups. But here Carrie and I were—still together, still tight.

"Have you been to see your GP yet?" she asked me.

We were in a common position—her in bed, propped up; me on the floor, leaning against the bed; both nursing mugs of herbal tea.

"Going tomorrow," I said.

"Are you going to ask him about Doshi?"

"Yeah. I really don't want to see Simpson again."

At a tangent, Carrie said, "My mum and dad are going on holiday."

A jolt of fear went through me. The threat of Carrie going anywhere was enough to unsettle me.

"Where are they going?" I asked.

"To Majorca for ten days."

"Are you not going with them?"

"I was thinking they might want a break from me. Gillian is going, but Beth is staying here to help me. You can stay here if you like. There's a spare bed somewhere."

This canceled out my anxiety. I was happy enough with this result. It would be more fun if Gillian was around, but Beth and Carrie and the large sunlit rooms of summer were better than our moldering flat.

Carrie's folks went off the next day, and we easily occupied the extra space their absence afforded. Breakfast was taken lazily on the steps, looking out onto the street. We made a semi-permanent camp on the steps—it was a suntrap and an excellent place to watch what little action their side street afforded us. I happily browsed the family bookshelves, the largest of which lined both sides of the main hall on the ground floor of the house. Every afternoon, we ventured across the road to the pleasure gardens to set up camp there. It was all a bit *Brideshead Revisited*, without the drunken capers and boating blazers.

Their brother, Dan, showed up on the third day, back from college in Belfast.

"What's the place like that Mum and Dad have?" he asked Beth.

"It's a three-apartment or something. Three or four bedrooms."

"That's loads of room. We should go down there."

"All of us?" said Carrie, a little incredulously.

"Come on, Carrie, neck brace off—it's summer!"

Dan had a way of talking to Carrie that pushed her like no other. He could be a bit rough, but his heart was in the right place. Carrie had from time to time worn an invalid's neck brace when she had to sit up for long periods, to support the weight of her head. Now that she *seemed* to be doing a bit better, it quickly became a symbol, to Dan at least, of all the things she should and could leave in the past.

"I don't know . . ." she said. She looked at me.

"Would *you* come?"

"Would your mum and dad mind me coming? How much are the tickets?" I asked.

"The flights are about £120 return, and no, they wouldn't mind you coming," said Beth in her quiet, decisive way. Her deliberate tone surprised me and Carrie a bit. It seemed to suggest the scheme was really on. Dan and Beth left us to talk it over.

"I guess when you get there, you don't have to *do* anything. And it will be warm enough to just lounge about," I said.

"I suppose. It just seems a long way," Carrie mused.

"What can't you do there that you can do here?"

"Sleep. Eat. Watch TV."

I stayed quiet.

"Do you really want to go?" she asked.

"I'll go wherever you go."

"I thought you liked the quiet."

"I did. But it got too much and I went a bit mad."

She thought. "Ok, let's go. But we have to bring cornflakes. Will they have milk?"

"Jesus, Carrie, it's Spain. They'll have milk."

"I just thought . . . because it's an island."

"It's a big island. 'Majorca'—it means 'big.'"

A couple of days later, we were sitting in a package-holiday jet full of excited families and lots of kids. Dan was being goofy and keeping us all laughing. Beth was being steady. Carrie was chomping her figurative nails down to the nub. I—having accepted that the background hum of anxiety and depression would come with me—was quite satisfied to be there. I'd never been abroad. I'd never been in a plane. I'd never been somewhere hot. Here I was now, finally making my Spanish debut.

I know it's a cliché, but the blast of heat when I walked down the airplane steps threatened to overwhelm Carrie and me at first. How quickly, however, we were to get used to that spicy hot air and crave it forever after. We taxied to the resort, Carrie exhausted and fretting, but we knew we had made it. I could see there was enough calm in her that things were going to be ok once she had lain down for an hour and had her cornflakes. Her mum and dad were not quite ready for the whole invasion. Her dad quietly slipped off to the resort office and astutely paid for another apartment for the duration of the holiday. But the eaglets had landed.

The holiday proceeded thus—Carrie's folks did their thing, and all the kids did the other. But mostly the three fit kids plowed ahead, and Carrie and I followed at half speed. Carrie and I consulted with each other about the experience of taking pills and having anxiety in a hot climate. We were still waking up with a panicked start, when the first thought is *Oh fuck*, the heartbeat races and the engine sputters into life. Start of a new day. Did the panic give you more energy? Carrie thought it just exhausted you even more, drawing more from the bank of energy, which you struggled to pay back later.

I said to her, "But if you have this anxiety, and your pulse is racing, wouldn't it be best to try and put it to good use and do a bit more?"

"You could be right, Pant Man."

The family's name for me on this trip had already morphed from "Nature Boy" or "the World's Coldest Boy" to "Pant Man," because my swimming trunks were of the short, Speedo pant variety. I was behind in all sorts of fashion, especially to do with underwear, summer-wear and swimwear.

Can I just say that if my modus operandi since the breakdown was to be around people, then I got pretty lucky with this particular bunch of people. Carrie's siblings were a bit like intellectual super-heroes, at least compared to the groups of people I'd hung around with in the past. I guess with her dad being a filmmaker, it was all at a different level.

When the whole family were around, I felt they could be a little hard on Carrie; they could be impatient with her illness. Maybe I was too sensitive to her plight. I think I became her silent apologist, around the offspring at least. You could consider individual people, you could feel you were starting to know them, but groups have this thing; a family has an energy about it. They were clever guys, always bouncing topics around, drawing on their mutual history, jabbing and thrusting. They passed judgment on the world close to them or in the far-off news stories of the day. You didn't want to get in the way of that. It was something that I admired.

Carrie and I would wander down to the beach, catch the others up. I loved the walk, the baking stone, everything either terracotta or blue, the wee lizards running from us, the strange desert-like fauna. When we got to the beach, my eunuch status was confirmed—the girls all took their tops off to sunbathe without so much as a look at me. And that was it, their boobs were out for pretty much the whole holiday. It was never commented on, and I'm glad that I was not considered an obstacle to partial nudity. It was noble and beautiful of course—three Celtic sisters, the Paps of Antrim. I had only ever seen one other pair of boobs as an adult—they were Vivian's. Oh, and this one time I was at a golf tournament, when a woman streaked across the eighteenth green. The man in front of me turned to his friend and said "Dirty bitch" in a Geordie accent, but the incident passed quickly.

So here I was, in Spain, on an island, catching up on my boob time. The girls got kind of ripped off. All they got in return was me in my skimpy trunks. They got to see the outline of a modest, gerbil-sized package, if they cared to look over. I don't think my package was ever going to put arses on pews. But we holidayed, and the days were the best they had been. The beach was quiet and sort of lagoon-shaped. Carrie and I loved the water. It was magic to be able to luxuriate in seawater rather than simply plunge and cover, which was the Scottish experience.

The sun and warmth and sea and food and company were having an effect. If Carrie and I had been a couple of prize marrows, these would have been the ideal conditions to turn us into champions. With the swimming and the walking we were discovering some confidence in our bodies again. I had always been fit, and though my system was beleaguered, I had an idea that my body hadn't forgotten how to be athletic. We all got these plastic kayaks and it was just magic to row to the other side of the lagoon, to come up against the rocks, pull yourself out, panting and dripping, let the heat dry you, then paddle back again. We ate salad, chips and seafood twice a day, even chanced a little wine. We played Scrabble in the evenings, while the geckos climbed the walls around us. I loved watching them pouncing on the moths that were attracted to the lights. Carrie wouldn't play Scrabble as her head would hurt too much with the concentration, but that left the four other "kids."

I had a crush on Gillian and it was growing by the hour. She wasn't interested, she was never interested. I think the slightly queasy feeling that accompanied my crush arose from the fact she was the younger sister of my now confirmed best friend. Even if there had been something there, it still seemed like it would have been frowned upon somehow. But I was totally into her. Maybe the feeling it was never going to happen made it stronger. Sort of poetic, maybe? At least this was a living person that I could see and talk to, unlike Fara of the fiddle. Gillian couldn't run away; she was stuck with us. I got to look at the crunch of her forehead as she thought of her Scrabble word. I got to wonder at the shape of her nose, strong and sculpted, like a rookie boxer's, yet to be broken.

As I listened to her banter with Dan, I thought she was one of the funniest people I'd met. Funny ha ha. But dry. She could crack you up. I wonder if I thought I could never go with her because she was too smart for me. That might have been part of it. Best not to get too analytical, it just wasn't happening and that was that.

"Is 'bumhole' a word?" she said.

"Strictly speaking, probably not," said Beth.

"I'd give you 'bumhole.' It's a word—you use it," said Dan with a generous wave of the hand.

"But would it not have a hyphen?" said Beth.

"Only posh bumholes take the hyphen," said Carrie, without looking up from her supine position on the couch. We had the doors to the courtyard wide open so she could hear everything.

"My bumhole isn't posh," said Gillian.

"Truer words were never spoken," said Beth.

"Would anyone like any more red?" I offered, waving the bottle.

"I'll take a thimbleful, dear," said Gillian.

I wonder if she realized what calling me "dear" did? She was playing a character right at that moment. She was in a game of Cluedo or she was in a Brontë novel. But it still got me.

"'Archer' for thirty-six," said Beth, placing her letters on a double word.

"Remember Mr. Archer? What did they call him?" asked Gillian.

"Bullseye," said Dan, staring at his letters.

"Didn't he have a thing with Mrs. Cochrane, the biology teacher?" asked Beth.

"The Trembling Divorcée. She used to wobble when she got near you," said Gillian. "Shame," she added carelessly. Her forehead crunched furiously. "Someone play a 'J.' I've got 'blowjob.'"

I drank the red wine and it made me dizzy. Not in a great way. I wasn't meant to drink, on account of the pills and the ME. But the taste of the red was sort of heavenly. And my inner red wine copywriter was composing a letter to Gillian.

Dear Gillian,

This is a short note to say that I deeply fancy you. Please do not think that it's on account of the fact that I've seen you mostly naked for the past three days. I fancied you before. I fancied your brains and your furtiveness, and I fancy you as much in a polo neck as your topless swimsuit. Maybe even more.

I think, by dint of me having to write this note, my chances may be limited. I think what usually happens is that a boy and girl, or a boy and a boy, or a girl and girl, or a birl and a goy just end up kissing. I've heard about that, and I've seen it in some films. It always seems a little unreal to me that it just "happens," but I am inexperienced in these things. I've only had one girlfriend before, and she pretty much drove the bus in the romance department.

As I was saying, it's probably not going to happen between us. I know you have many suitors, and they are all able-bodied and splendid. Even if nothing happens between us, and that's looking more and more likely the longer this letter gets, can I just say that I am very happy to know you and that I think you are fantastic, and that's not just the red wine talking. That's me talking. Under the influence of the red wine.

I know that you know that I just had what they term in the business "a nervous breakdown." I hope that you feel I am not so much more unhinged than I was before. And that if I start lightly raising the topic of love around the place, it's not just because I feel desperate, or on the edge of some sort of emotional cliff or forced into it by the madness.

I think maybe the love was already there, but now I am a peeled switch, so you can see it. And you can have it. By the jarful. If you want it.

Wishing you bumholes and blowjobs aplenty.

Stephen

18

Summer Wanes

We got back to Glasgow. I was still spending quite a lot of time round at Carrie's place. I was sitting in the big-window room while she was off in the kitchen looking for biscuits. I thought about Carrie and her family, about their company, the things they think about and talk about. I've glimpsed the social and working life of the kids and the mum and dad and how people come and go in their house—there's an easy grace about how it all flows and happens. Still, I keep quiet. I'm still catching up to it. I sometimes wonder why they put up with having me around. Do they ever question why Carrie and I are not a couple? Maybe they think I'm gay, like Carrie did. Carrie says my trouble is I'm too "subtle." I'm ok with subtle though. No one ever died of subtlety.

Before sickness, I didn't have any friends like Carrie or Richard. I knew people, I saw them around, I talked to them, but I always retired to my little bedsit cave, on the run from responsibility and the threat of serious relationships. I knew roadies, because I was in a road crew. I knew little kids, because I was a youth leader. I knew great authors, but only because I read their books. I knew wonderful, poetic guitar bands, but only because I used to follow them and venerate them. I didn't know any normal people.

I had lost my friends as school went on, and I didn't make any real friends at university. I fell in with an odd bunch who seemed to like the same kind of music I did, but I think I was too intense for them. Maybe I had to go through illness, near death and a breakdown before I could relax in my skin. I'm only half joking. I mean, who's in charge here, who's driving the bus? I know there's God, or there *was* God—you've been awfully quiet lately. You seem to leave us for an awful long time without supervision. I mean, this was your idea, right? The illness, the shakedown, the breakdown—this was your plan? You revealed yourself to me on the piano stool. But where did you go?

The next day I drove Carrie to the country just outside of Glasgow. We were on a narrow road beside a field with horses. We could look back and in the distance see the city and the Clyde Valley sweeping from left to right. Further beyond this were lowland moors that stretched up to the horizon. It was a warm, quiet evening. We had the windows down and it felt good. I was breathing it all in.

Gillian had gone off to live in Edinburgh, to find a job and to prepare herself for life at the School of Art there. So that was that. Sightings of her were going to be even rarer now. Carrie had minimal sympathy for me at this moment, but that was understandable. She was thinking about the bigger picture, having her own little state-of-the-nation moment on the drive to get there. As we sat on the fence looking back towards the misty city, we carried on with the conversation.

"So you feel ripped off?" I asked.

"With what?" she said.

"With your life right now?"

"Of course."

"What did you expect?" I asked.

"A life, a man, a house, a few kids, a career. Not that much to ask. People have that, loads of people."

A sheep baaed. We took a second to let that sink into the senses. It was a balm.

"Don't you ever think you might be marked down for something special?" I pointed out.

"I don't feel special. Do you feel special?" she asked.

"I don't feel special. I still wouldn't want to be anyone else though."

"Really? Not for a while, if you could switch back when you wanted?"

"Well, yeah, maybe."

We both sat there thinking for a minute about who we would be if we could switch back. You know, people like Jesus, Buddha, Joan of Arc, Einstein—that type of extraordinary life. In truth, we both settled for the same person, the aforementioned Jennifer Beals's character in *Flashdance*.

"It would be good to dance like her," Carrie said.

"And have the welding thing on the side. Something to fall back on," I added.

"A life like that, a body like that, men are like flies round shite."

She seemed in a daze somewhat.

"Flies round shite," she repeated.

We looked out over the field again. I thought about something I had seen on a nature program.

"We need to be like the inland taipan," I said.

She snapped back in. "What's the inland taipan?"

"It's a poisonous snake that lives in the Australian outback."

"Why do we need to be like snakes?" she asked.

"Imagine you're living in Australia, under a rock. You're waiting for your dinner to walk past, but you've been waiting for quite some time. In fact, you haven't eaten for a couple of months. It's starting to get a little desperate. You hear something. Sounds like a rat. You're poised and ready to strike. You've only got one chance."

"Ok, I get it," she said. "We need to be poised and ready to strike. Because you don't get many chances in life. Especially us."

"Especially us. That's why we have to be ready, like the taipan."

"But why *especially* the taipan?"

"Drop for drop, it's the most venomous snake in the world. Plus they hold on to the prey and bite multiple times, like a mad stapler. The prey is completely immobilized within a second."

"So you're saying we need to attack multiple times?"

"I'm saying that we need to take our chance. And if it means sacrificing a little more venom than the next person, we have to do it."

Carrie stared at the nearby sheep. If this had been a movie and she was a smoker, she would certainly have taken a long draw on her Silk Cut at this point.

"Yeah, but wait a minute, Mr. Super Subtle," she protested, "how is it working out for you? Cos the episode with the cassette tape and the violin player was not the work of a deadly predator. You went after her with all the stealth of a koala bear."

"Yeah, I know. But all that is about to change."

Post-breakdown, post chasing the ghost of Fara and post being on my best behavior with Gillian Gallagher, I was ready to take a chance with the next vaguely suitable person that came along. The funny thing was, Carrie struck first. I'm not sure she was thinking about my advice, but she succeeded in hooking herself a man. And he was a real live tall, dark, Irish doctor.

She had managed to go to a ceilidh with an old school friend, and she was, in her own words, firing on all cylinders; she had really made an effort to look amazing. It turns out that this guy thought she looked amazing too, because he went straight up and told her. And from that point on it was easy.

"*Easy!*" she said. And even when she had to make her excuses and leave early, it only made him keener to see her again. Which he did. Day date. Coffee. Home-ground advantage. And that was it, she seemed to have got what she was after. I was really happy for her. I tried to give her a little more space, not be at her house *all* the time. I knew there was still going to be plenty of incoming information. The slide up from imagined relationships into a real one was going to be fun. Even for me, who wasn't strictly speaking involved.

His name was Quinn, by the way. Quinn Benjamin Eadie. He was training to be a doctor but wasn't quite there yet. Still, an Irish doctor he would be. With good health, good teeth, good hair, good upbringing and a poetic-sounding name. According to Carrie, he wore a watch really well. Good wrist action. The bastard had it all.

19

Fake Fur

Usually I tell Carrie stuff, especially about women, and she tells me everything about her men. But there was something that happened that I didn't mention; in fact, I'm not sure *what* it was. It started up at the Art School. I'd been with her and Quinn for a bit in the pub, and some of his friends. Carrie was toiling. I could tell she was out of her depth—she was struggling, energy-wise and other-wise, to keep up with the company of active medical men and women.

It was dazzling though, them all talking about cases and place-ments and where to stick a thermometer when you don't have any free hands. I was wearing silver trousers, a vintage yellow and blue cycling top, a wide-brimmed hat, black clogs, a little bit of eye make-up, and a long coat to cover it all up. I was trying to chip in to the conversation, but from my perspective it felt like I was a patient surrounded by junior doctors. Every time I opened my mouth, it was as if I was being examined. So I stayed quiet and felt out of it.

Quinn had met with Carrie a few times. He brought out his stethoscope the first time he was round her house. He talked about the Western plague of obesity and warned Carrie about cholesterol. He said she was "never too young to start." He told her during the ceilidh that her "lower back was pleasing," while they danced. But the way he said it made her feel like she was a test in anatomy.

So there I was in the pub with them, doing my sitting still thing, where I hardly move and don't contribute much. I found that if I could be unstimulated for the early segment of the evening, I had a much better chance of making it to the Art School to dance. At ten o'clock, I moved round towards Carrie and said, "I'm going."

This had been arranged, and she said in my ear, "I don't think I'm going to last long."

"You want me to stay?" I asked.

"No, I think Quinn will get me home."

"Ok."

I slipped out. I didn't really have to say bye to people. There were a few nods of acknowledgment, but I knew I hadn't made an impression. I felt a little bad leaving Carrie there, her eyes sunken and weary, but she had the Quimbo to support her lower back. So I left. When I got to the door of the pub, there was a gauntlet thrown down between lads on the way out. A big chunky blonde guy drinking from a pint glass announced "Must be a fucking poof!" to the rest of his pals. I just kept walking. I thought about all the smart things that I could have said as I walked up the steep hill to the Art School. I remembered Carrie's dad said there was a phrase for that in French—*l'esprit de l'escalier*, literally "the spirit of the stairs": what you thought of saying to a person after you left the house, when you were on the stairs.

I comforted myself thinking that "*L'Esprit de l'escalier*" might be the name of my band someday. (I love the French. Whatever I call my band eventually, it has to be French.) As I walked up to the Art School, I got lost in thoughts about having my own band and what the sleeve would be like for the first record. When I was at Yvonne's house last summer, I played the piano for them, and afterwards someone asked me if the piece had a name. I said "Belmondo," after Jean-Paul Belmondo, the French actor. And someone said, "That's so pretentious," and I kind of shrugged.

I continued my walk along Sauchiehall Street, dodging parties of drunk people. I remember in my first year of university I was caught up in a degree of pretension. I got stuck with a crowd of guys who were more political than me, more arty than me, more on the left than me. They seemed to care more, they were angrier, they despaired more about life, but ultimately they spent most of the time hating everyone. They had painted themselves into a corner of vitriol. I spent a whole year accommodating them and their ways, mostly because I liked the music that they purported to like. In the end, I just didn't have the stomach for all the nihilism. But the music had drawn me down a path. I started out with pretension—I wanted to like some of the music more than I really did—but in the dark of my room, my filter was on. I cleaved to all the new music that I was *really* in love with. The music, and therefore those guys, sent me down a path that ended with obsession, isolationism and an eating disorder.

These were not pretenses. These were me. Accidents can lead you to dark places. Pretensions can bring you to the truth. I thought all these things as I went up the hill to the Art School, and it started to cheer me. "L'Esprit de l'escalier" was the new single. "Belmondo" was the B-side. Picture sleeve, twelve-inch single with two extra tracks. I climbed the steep hill away from the crowds on Sauchiehall Street and got to the stairs of the Art School Union. It was just me there. I was first. Beautiful. Most folk sat in the pub till twelve, dead set on drinking till the pub chucked them out. By the time they got up the hill to the Art School, the queue was for miles. I didn't have those inclinations. I didn't want to drink. I wanted to dance.

I nodded to the two bouncers at the door and went in down the still, cool hallway. I walked into the bar, got a can of cold ginger beer and a glass full of ice and looked for my corner. I went through the archway to the dancefloor area and sat up on the covered pool table that had been shoved into the corner of the room. Soon enough, this table would be covered with piles of jackets and bags, but I didn't mind the heavy traffic. After being mostly in the house all week, I loved being surrounded by all humanity at close, intimate quarters. It served me for the rest of the week. I would soak it up. It made me feel calm.

Maybe I belonged here. I guess it was strange to not be the DJ anymore. It had been a couple of years now and I didn't care, I was over it. It's like I used to be in the team and now I was back on the terraces watching the game as a spectator. I knew the tricks for getting the night started. At this point, however, the guys who were playing the records were just warming up. There were hardly any punters in yet. They were doing what I would be doing—playing stuff you just bought, playing a favorite deep cut, trying out a new dance mix to see what it sounded like through the big speakers. No real pressure to get anyone up dancing yet.

I remember the glory of having the lights go down, pushing up the volume to club level for the first time, sticking on something that you truly loved, then walking out onto the floor, parading round the room as if you had a duty to test the speakers—but really you just wanted to revel in the sound of the record you'd picked.

I used to play new releases, album tracks early on. Sometimes you'd get the real indie scholars who could sniff out what you were playing and dance in a cool, knowing way, even though I didn't want anyone dancing yet. Marco and the Caveman, the Art School DJs, didn't have that problem. Most of the stuff they played was a throwback from way back—they were sculpting their own agendas from the archive of pop and soul history. When they played something "new," it was actually old, and it was unlikely that you'd ever heard it. It was good though. I liked it. Old soul, rare funk. Old garage, rare bubblegum. Old hits, rare misses.

It didn't take much to get me up dancing. I knew that there would be songs played now that would never be played later, and I was thankful for the space on the floor. For a weak person, I took up quite a lot of room when I danced. Marco put on one of my trigger songs, and I got up. "Let the Sunshine In" by Brian Auger, Julie Driscoll and the Trinity. I unconsciously slipped off a layer of clothing and stepped out onto the spotlit floor. Some people like getting into the swimming pool, or up on a horse maybe. Their moment of liberty and sensation. For me, it was dancing. Such a nice feeling, stepping out into the dappled light, into the sacred space. In the first week I came here, I waited till someone else went up before I stepped out. But from the second week on, I was usually first, and I didn't care. I liked it.

Frank of the whirling arms came to join me, Kim of the turtleneck got up, and the identical twin mod sisters. I never talked to them, just danced with them or near them. I used to run miles. This was my running now. Then, I ran for miles in exhausting isolation. Now I used as little energy as I could for maximum effect. I wanted anyone that was looking to see where every ounce of precious energy went. I twisted and floated. I used my arms to move my legs and my legs to move my arms. No energy was wasted. This was energy-giving, not energy-sapping. I rode along on the song, my body completely in tune with the track.

Kim joined me, and we moved around like snakes or shadows. They put on "I've Got Something on My Mind" by the Left Banke. There would be no room for such delicacies later on, but it was perfect for this moment. Frank joined us and crossed the floor on an invisible tightrope, wearing ballet pumps. He whirled his arms.

"A Lover's Concerto" by the Toys
"I'm Not Sayin'" by Nico
"Love (It's Getting Better)" by the Groove
"They Say I'm Different" by Betty Davis

And they even threw a couple of new ones in, which sounded great.

"Super-Electric" by Stereolab
"Sons of the Stage" by World of Twist

I felt as supple as I had done for quite some time. I was trying to turn my anxiety energy into something decent, and dancing seemed to be the best way to do it. And when I wasn't dancing, and when the wash of the lights came over me and the throbbing bass, the first clouds of dry ice mixed in, I felt the warm embrace of disco. Kids were trickling in all the time, the pile of coats and bags built up behind me on the pool table. Girls with too much make-up on looked good in the forgiving shadows.

Five years ago, my scene was still post-punk and shambling, embracing the humble efforts of disenfranchised guitar bands. Now the "thing" was the past. The whole scene was just loving the Small Faces. It was mod again, with a nineties twist. But not plastic seventies ska mod. It was mod of the sixties. Girls' hair, from short to longer, went from Twiggy to Mary Quant to Louise Brooks to a general Sandie Shaw vibe, all the way up to a few brave souls going for the whole Ronnie Spector. Dresses were short, checked, striped, floral. Nobody was trying *too* hard. And there was still a hangover from the baggy thing, so there were still lots of trainers and flares and sweat-inducing, boob-hugging polyester tops.

There was a smattering of rave kids too, but they mostly came down here by accident and soon found their way up the stairs to the big hall, to the coolness overflow, where you could dance more freely and be current. But here I was, sitting back against the wall on the pool table, resting, soaking it up. A couple came and leaned on the edge of the pool table, looking out to the floor. The Caveman put on Spencer Davis; the girl looked at the boy. She peeled off her fake fur coat, she turned to leave it on the pile. When she saw me sitting there, she gave me a look and shouted over the noise, "Can you watch my bag while we dance?"

"Of course," I said.

They went off and danced a few. The guy disappeared for a while, and she came back to lean on the pool table. She ushered me closer.

"Do you not have any friends?" She had to cup her hand over my ear.

"I have a friend," I said.

"Where are they?" she yelled.

"She's gone home."

"Your girlfriend left you?"

"Not my girlfriend!"

"Do you have a girlfriend?"

"No. Do you?" I don't know why I asked her that.

"I'm with my boyfriend, Simon."

"Does he have friends?"

"He's gone off to speak to them now. Boring friends. Would you dance with me?"

"Would he mind?"

"He wouldn't mind. He's always leaving me places."

I dunno—if someone asks me, I like to comply. She'd put herself out there. So I danced with her. I danced *near* her, at least. She wasn't *amazing*-looking, but she was nice. I watched a trickle of sweat go from behind her ear down her neck while we danced. She had brown hair in a general bob and dark eyes that sparkled. She looked a bit like Carrie Fisher on a night off from shooting *Star Wars*. We went back to lean on the pool table.

"I better go and look for him," she said. "Do you want to meet me sometime, for a coffee?"

"Erm, ok," I replied hesitantly. I didn't know what to say.

"Give me your number," she said.

She took out a pen. I complied. I wrote on the inside lid of her cigarette pack.

"What's your name?" I asked.

"Paula. What's yours?"

"Stephen."

"Ok, Stephen, see you."

And she went off looking for her man.

*****

Paula came round. It was raining, everything was lush and green. As she stood in the doorway with her colored umbrella and her long boots, her bobbed hair silhouetted somewhat against the backlight, I wanted to take her picture. I didn't have my camera at the front door, and the moment would never come again, but I can still see it.

My Olympus OM-10 camera had a look and a feel. It captured the depth, had a way of splitting the subject from the background. She would be framed in green light, the lens would ensconce her in the wetness at the front door, with the lime trees hanging behind.

"Hi," she said.

"Come in," I said.

We went up the stairs to the flat.

"Did you find it ok?"

"Yeah, I didn't come that far, just from Anniesland."

"Would you like a cup of tea?"

"That would be nice, yes."

I made tea and we went through to the lounge. I put on a Bobbie Gentry record. She tucked her knees up under her in the armchair and sipped her tea. I felt like she was waiting for something, but I didn't know what the hell it was.

After a while, she said, "This is a funny flat. What's through that door?"

"That's Richard's room."

"Is he in?" she half whispered.

"No."

She looked at the Scrabble board on the low table, half played.

"You guys like games? 'T-H-O-R-A-X.' Good word. What does it mean?"

"'Chest,' in a human or other mammal. Or the middle bit of an insect. You want to play?"

"No, thanks." She put down her tea and looked out the window.

"I like your dress. Is it vintage?" I asked.

"Yeah, second-hand. Got it at Starry Starry Night. You know that place?"

"Yeah, I've had a few things out of there. The woman's funny."

She chuckled.

"Yeah, the woman *is* funny! She always makes you feel like you shouldn't be in there."

"She's a snob."

"She's a total snob-a-job."

She looked at me steadily. I dropped my gaze. There were a few seconds' quiet and then she humphed a little. I heard her. A little *humph*.

I thought of something.

"I was going to have lunch, can I make you some pizza?"

"Uh, no, thanks."

She was still looking at me. I looked into my tea. Longer pause. Finally, she stood up.

"I'm just going to go, Stephen. Let you get your lunch."

"Erm. Ok." I got up and followed her to the door of the flat.

She grabbed her jacket.

"I'll see you at the Art School then," I said.

She turned and gave me a last smile.

"Yeah, I'll see you up there."

She turned and walked down the stairs. She anticipated my next thought.

"It's ok, I'll get the door at the bottom."

Ok. You do that, Paula. Bye, Paula. Bye.

Fuck.

What just happened?

I went back inside and sat at the kitchen table, playing out the little scenario that had just transpired. Was there something wrong with me, on top of all the things that were wrong with me? So much for a venomous snake—I had no fangs.

20

Be Like the Peacock

I went to bed early that night and had another crappy sleep. I woke up, felt the anxiety swell inside me and then run away with me. I took a Valium pill, and I tried to settle down again. When I woke up at nine, I put my trousers on over my pajamas, my long raincoat over my cardigan, and staggered down to catch the 44 into town. I figured I could just make the Buddhist class. I was conscious I was spending time with Christians and Buddhists. I would have them both. I didn't see any clash at all between the two practices.

I considered myself unreligious. I had God, and that was as far as I had got. I loved the Bible stories I was hearing and reading, especially the Gospels. They were speaking to me. But so was the stuff I was hearing at the Buddhist Center. Was there anything wrong with listening to both? I had no hesitation. I sensed they both had the potential to make me happier. I was glad to be in both places. These were my private passions. Some had lager, others had Celtic; these were mine.

This morning the teacher was Gen Pachen. She was a Buddhist nun, the real thing. I guessed she was Vietnamese or Filipino, but there was a hint of Australian in her accent. She smiled a lot and gave the impression from her stories that she had lived a life and hadn't just come out of a nun-shaped egg. We started with a breathing meditation. I was sitting upright on a small pile of cushions. I was imagining that my head was suspended by a thread from the ceiling and that my back was long and straight. This was quite an effort for me. It was a long fifteen minutes. My mind was still in spate, like a boiling river.

I viewed the room. Everyone looked so peaceful there, meditating. I was always going to be the rookie outsider, I thought. How come everyone always seemed so bedded in, so smug?

Gen Pachen brought us out of meditation.

"Ok, how was that?"

People nodded and smiled dutifully.

"Does anyone have any questions?"

Of course, a bunch of questions came to mind, but I knew I couldn't ask them. Stuff like *Why do I feel so crap? What's the point of it all?* And then I felt my lips move, and I did ask it.

"Why do I feel so crap? What's the point of it all?"

There was a mix of disquiet, people frowning through smiles but also some looking at Pachen to see what her answer would be.

"Plus I can't meditate. Not today anyway. My head is a mess," I added for good measure.

"What is your name?" she asked.

"Stephen," I said.

"It's not easy to meditate. It's easy to sit and close your eyes, but to quieten the mind, not easy. But to try is the thing. And in trying we get a little better each time. And even when we are having a bad day and meditation seems impossible, that is the time when it is most important—noble, even—to try." She paused, then continued. "You may think that I am sitting here with all the answers. I have some suggestions, but what use are they without experience? You must not accept what I am saying. You must always ask questions and test out everything in your own life and in your own mind. That way, you can build faith in the things we are teaching. Stephen, the reason you feel so crap is that you are human. We all feel like crap. Maybe not all the time, but a lot of the time. The important thing is to decide what to do about it."

She was looking at me and talking steadily, not unkindly.

"We must all try to renounce the crap." She looked around at the room and almost smiled. "I do not apologize for repeating the word that Stephen introduced, because really it will do. It is his truth, after all, and I am not in the business of denying truth. We must decide to leave the crap behind forever. Buddha realized that *every human suffers*. He saw it. It was the first thing that he saw when he left his royal palace. Our ambition is to leave the suffering behind through Buddhist practice and become enlightened. And when we are enlightened, we can help every living being become enlightened also. That is our ambition. That is the project of our existence."

There was a pause.

"How can we turn the suffering into good?" asked a girl.

"Be like a peacock," Gen Pachen said.

She smiled and then explained. "The peacock feeds on plants that are poisonous to most other birds. It finds the good in what is bad for others. We must try to be like the peacock. We must try to find a good outcome from the suffering we experience. We must try to face up to our negative moods. We must realize that bad thoughts or bad feel-ings in the mind don't last forever. Eventually they will fade, and we can learn from the experience. Thrive, even. Like the peacock."

Her steady enthusiasm might have been annoying to some. I could just imagine the average person out there in the world not thinking much of her talk. *If you feel bad, you feel bad*—that's what people would say. However, I was putting store in her pragmatism. I found the class to be helpful. I knew that you were meant to get attached to the teachings and not to the teacher, but I was absorbing the whole package. Her faith was giving me faith, and on a day like today I was going to take anything I could get.

21

Dr. Doshi

I finally got in to see Dr. Doshi. My "case" had been moved up to Glasgow and I had specifically requested Dr. Doshi, on the recommendation of Carrie. *Nihira Doshi*, I read off the card. She hung out on the campus of the big psychiatric hospital just a mile or so from my house. I was soon called in to see the doctor. She smiled kindly and offered me a seat. I took in the room. It didn't seem like "her" office as such; it was a typically generic-looking NHS office, but at least it had a window onto some grass and trees.

"So, how are you feeling today, Stephen?" she asked from behind her desk.

"Nervous," I said. "Actually, I feel ok right now, but on the whole I often feel nervous."

"What is making you nervous?"

"I would say nothing in particular. I'm just nervous. I'm nervous when I wake up and nervous when I go to bed."

She looked down at some papers.

"When did your ME start?" she asked.

Wow, she said "ME." She's actually asking me about it.

"Three years ago."

"And what sort of help have you had so far?"

"Income support and some housing benefit."

She looked up at me.

"I meant what sort of help with the ME itself. Treatment, support, that kind of thing?"

"Nothing."

"Nothing? What about your time in hospital?"

"Yeah, it helped me. I put weight back on and got out of bed. I sat in a chair instead," I replied, trying not to sound surly.

"Did they address the ME at all?"

"Whenever I mentioned it, which became never, they gave me a look as if I were talking about a magic land."

"A magic land?" she repeated, eyebrows raised.

"They just looked at me like I was talking about something that never existed. Some of the nurses—well, I would say one and a half of the nurses; student nurses, in fact—were sympathetic towards it and me, and seemed to accept that it was a thing for me. But no one else."

"What about Dr. Simpson?"

"I would say especially Dr. Simpson was skeptical. In fact, he was completely dismissive, and you could tell that was trickling down to everyone else."

"What do you mean, 'trickling down'?"

"I only saw him about twice the whole time I was there, because I was getting on ok with the regime that he set for me. But I was getting better despite him and his regime, not because of it. I'm pretty certain that during the little meetings they had, he passed me off as delusional to the staff and ward sisters. And that was that. I mean, that's what happens, isn't it? You set the tone for things—the psychiatrist is the boss, right?"

Dr. Doshi paused and seemed to withdraw a little bit. "I don't know the individual circumstance of every hospital, so I couldn't really comment on this instance," she said.

I then realized that I was doing the same thing to her that I had got used to doing to other people in her position, no matter how justified *my* position was. I was attacking her, and I was in danger of losing her interest.

"Dr. Doshi," I said.

"Yes?"

"I'm not mad, you know."

"I didn't say you were."

"I mean, I'm a bit affected by everything. And I went a little mental a few months back. But I'm not mad."

"I'm certain you are not mad, Stephen. I'm just trying to understand a little more about you so I can help," she said in a softer voice.

I thought about it, and I looked at her. I mean, she was cool and everything. I wanted to believe her, like I wanted to believe the rest of them. And I think most of them had wanted to help. But the *mind* was her business and I wanted someone to fix my body. Then *I* could fix my mind.

"My main problem is my ME," I said.

"Ok."

"If I wasn't so weak and sick all the time, I wouldn't be depressed."

"How does it affect you then?" she asked.

"It affects me every day. I feel ill every day. It's like having a cold or flu. But if you say that to someone, it's like 'Big deal. Everyone has a cold or flu.' But that's not the point. Imagine having the first day of a cold or the flu every day of your life. Feeling sick and weak and . . . poisoned every day. It's what *that* does to you. It's the days and the years. It fucks everything up. Sorry for saying 'fuck.'"

"No, don't worry, you're ok." She was jotting a few things down. "So what happened a few months back?" she asked. At least she seemed interested.

"I don't really know. I think my luck ran out or something. I've been ill a few years now. If you are restricted in what you can do, and you can't work, and you're always cold, and you can't have a girlfriend, it probably adds up."

"It probably does." Dr. Doshi looked at me, not unkindly.

"So, you really think you couldn't have a girlfriend?" she asked.

"Present circumstances, probably not."

"Why not?"

"They'd have to be too kind and too understanding. They'd have to accept the way I am and be cool with all the waiting and the inaction. It would be like having a third of a boyfriend."

"Do you ever meet other people with ME? What about them?"

"I do, that's the thing. We have a group, a support group. I started it, actually, with my friends Carrie and Richard—they have ME. We get on well and we understand each other, but everyone in the group is looking out for normal, healthy people—that's the goal. We couldn't go with another ME person. It would be too sad and claustrophobic. It would be like settling for sickness."

"Ok, I know what you're saying," she replied. "I don't necessarily agree with you about the relationship thing though. Also, it's good that you have a support group just now, but the goal of all support groups is that they should break up."

"Mm."

"You don't agree?"

"It's a fine idea. I just can't see it being as tidy as that, like we all graduate and go off and have families."

I didn't mean to come across annoyed or anything. She wasn't thrown though. She just asked, "And would you like to have a family?"

"What, like children?"

"Yes."

"I don't know." I felt like we were relaxing a bit. I smiled at a memory, then it came out. "I used to have gerbils. I used to breed them, in fact. I'm not sure I'd have the strength or focus to keep them alive right now. So I might have to wait on the kids. Do you have kids?"

"Yes. A boy and a girl."

"What age?"

"Four and six."

I looked at her and she didn't seem *that* much older than me. And she was pretty, and pretty together.

"I hope you don't mind me asking, but how do you do it?"

"What?"

I think perhaps she was a little taken aback by me asking questions. She looked at the desk, making a little circle with her pen. Then she looked at me.

"You have to decide what you want to do, and then do it."

"But with kids, you can't do anything. You're like a servant or something," I said.

"Stephen, it's not as bad as that. I like my kids, they're fun. And I'm here doing this job, which I like."

"Ok, sorry. It just seems so far off. It's amazing to me."

"So is there anything that you really want to do?" she asked. I could tell she was trying to get me talking about me again.

"That's the point. All the things I thought I really wanted to do are so far away now. They are impossible. They are so far away that I don't want to do them anymore."

"Like what?"

"I was a really good runner, and I thought for a while that I could do that."

"Ok, anything else?"

"When I first went to university, I wanted to be a nuclear physicist. I thought I would be driving a Porsche by now. I know it seems silly, but people do it. I mean, you did it."

"I drive a Toyota." She smiled, then continued. "Certainly a lot has changed for you. It's good to have goals that you feel may be attainable. Why don't you work on those and then come back and see me next month?"

I was getting the heave-ho.

"Ok. Do you want me to write them down or something?"

She laughed. "No, just tell me when you see me."

"Ok, thanks, Dr. Doshi."

I left her. I walked out through the grass and trees and thought about what my goals were.

22

The Weetabix Atlas

By the end of September it had started to cool significantly. Our flat got back into its non-summer ways. We started to huddle around the one heater in the kitchen again, and we were dressing like Sherpas on a Himalayan mission. Richard was an avid eater of Weetabix. Over the summer he had collected enough tokens to get sent the *Weetabix World Atlas*. It arrived mid-September and from that point we were improving our world geography on a daily basis. At the start of the atlas it showed the whole world multiple times, spread over two pages each time. The first spread was political, the second physical, the third showed population, the fourth climate. We liked to look at the climate page and dream about the sun warming our bones.

Light green was for Mediterranean. There were a few of these precious bands showing around the earth. The Mediterranean zone was the Goldilocks zone for me and Richard. Not too warm, not too cool. Just right. From the chart, it looked like the winters stayed mild. There were Mediterranean zones in Australia (along the south coast and in the west), in South America (Chile's mid-coast), a little bit in southern Africa, in California, and of course in the south of Europe.

"We should go live in a Mediterranean climate," said Richard.

"Aye, right," I said sardonically.

"No, really, we could go there and miss the whole winter."

Last winter, Richard's feet had never been warm. They were pretty much blue the whole time. He did have long legs and his extremities were quite extreme. Looking back at the map of South

America, his legs were like Chile, but his feet were right down at Cape Horn. A bit blowy and cold. So, in his rarely spoken way, I could tell he was being quite serious.

"Miss the winter, come back for spring," I said in a dreamy voice.

I saw that the possibility was good. I mean, what was holding us in Glasgow? Nothing. No partners, no jobs, no nothing. Could we do it though? Health-wise? And how could we pay for it?

"Where would we stay?" I asked.

"In hostels," he replied.

"A hostel?"

"Youth hostels."

I paused to think. "And you would really do that?"

"I dunno. I just thought about it."

"I'm going to think about it."

"Yeah, me too. I'm going to think about it."

We said goodnight.

I had a bath so I could think about it some more. I floated around in the suds and in the quiet night, and I tried to imagine what it would be like, traveling to a far-off land for the winter. One good thing about having ME is that you get good at contingencies. You get good at seeing three, four or five steps ahead. You have to. You ruthlessly and selfishly have to work out what you are capable of, but in the meantime sometimes you end up solving problems for others too, making it easier for everyone, finding the path of least resistance.

I could sell my records. I had a lot of records still—a lot of records that were rare and collectible. I could sell them all. Bloody hell, I spent the last eight years building up my collection, it would be a pleasure to break it down. It was like an albatross round my neck, a heavy weight, literally and spiritually. I thought about the Weetabix map, I thought about the green crescent shapes of Mediterranea!

- Australia: seemed too far away.
- Europe: Would anywhere *really* be warm enough? And wouldn't it be a bit sad and shut down in winter?
- Could go to Africa, but to be honest that might be a bit too much of an adventure for two guys who were practically on the disabled roster.
- South America. Chile—such mystery! When I was five, I had a poster for the 1974 World Cup, which took place in Germany. Chile was one of the teams representing South America. I don't know why I remember them so well, but on my world map it looked about as far away as you could get, and to my five-year-old mind it was "chilly" and remote there, just as Poland was full of Poles.
- Finally: America. I liked it when I was little. That's where the good films came from. And *The Rockford Files*. And *Cosmos*. And *Roots*.

As a teen and an adult, I dunno, Americans seemed a little crazy. I didn't like mainstream America; it was even further to the right than mainstream UK. We had a modern studies teacher who *loved* America. She was always pushing American values down our necks and justifying every move that the US made against Iran and Nicaragua, even Vietnam. I mean, I'm no history hotshot, but it made me feel a bit sick somehow, how American might always had to be right. If I met her now, I'd ask her how come "we" were all fighting Iraq now, when Iraq was our pal in the days of the Iran–Iraq War? There's a fuck-up in there somewhere.

I liked the Minutemen though, and I liked Hüsker Dü and the Meat Puppets and Sonic Youth. I liked the punky scratchy side of things. I loved the way America was portrayed in *Slacker* and *She's Gotta Have It*—I wondered if the real America wasn't more like that? And my obsession with the movies of Hal Hartley couldn't have happened at a more pertinent time.

"I want to go to California," I announced to Richard at breakfast.

He looked over his toast at me, took a bite. Chewed.

"I think I'd rather go to Europe," he replied.

"What's in Europe?" I asked.

"What do you mean, 'What's in Europe?' The whole world is in Europe, the whole of history, culture. We could learn a language."

"We've been trying to learn French for two years now. All I know is the little song that Jean-Paul Belmondo sings in *Breathless* about staying in bed on a Sunday."

"I'm getting pretty good," he pointed out.

He was getting pretty good, actually. He had this tutor at the Alliance Française called Yolande, and he was always meeting her for a cafetière full of something and a bit of je ne sais quoi.

"Well then, you'd have to be my interpreter. I'd be half a person the whole time, I wouldn't be able to talk."

"You just need to get a French girlfriend."

"How can I get a French girlfriend when I can't even get a Scottish girlfriend?" I said, a little exasperated.

"You just have to be charming."

"I don't have the energy to be charming. And neither do you."

He looked a little abashed at that. I didn't mean it that way, but it tired me out just thinking about having to show off to people or jump through hoops.

"If we went to California, I bet they would know much more about ME," I said craftily. "You know how they are always ahead with stuff, I bet they have a whole different way of looking at it. We could find a support group over there and soak it all up. The whole trip could be like an investigation."

This did pique his interest. We'd heard hints from somewhere that the Americans had different methods of treating ME. Over here, they had complete bed rest or graded exercise and nothing in between. Nothing. You were either Daley Thompson or a corpse.

"Plus I have a feeling that it would be warmer in the winter there than the south of France or Italy," I added.

"Where would we go?" he asked. "Not Los Angeles. I don't want to go there. I have no interest in going there. All those freeways and nowhere to walk."

"Ok, not LA."

He was thinking about it.

"We need to find out more about the exact climate of places. If we're going to go for a while, we need to know we're going to be warm enough."

"I couldn't agree more."

I was glad he had embraced the USA idea. We needed some sort of weather almanac though. We agreed to go to the library in the afternoon.

We got the bus down to the Mitchell Library, the big reference library near the city center. We were directed to the geography department. We found what we were looking for—mean temperatures for all the major cities around the world. What power we had! We looked at Marseille, Valencia, Rome, Athens, but all seemed too cool for the period we wanted to go, which was January till the start of May. Our plan was to go for as long as our money would last. The whole project would be based on getting by as cheaply as possible, because obviously we weren't going to be earning any money while we were there.

We looked at California. The cities of Sacramento, San Francisco and San Diego. Sacramento and San Francisco were still too cool in the winter, but San Diego was the baby bear—just right in every department, with daily maximums for the period ranging from 18 to 21°C. Pretty much the same as the Scottish summer. Richard was sold, and I was feeling it too. We would go to San Diego! We would go for three months. That was as long as you could go to the States on a tourist visa, and it was also the longest we could be away without our money giving out.

We couldn't just go and give up our sickness benefit though. We had to find a way to stay in the system in the UK while we were down and out in the USA. Because we were on long-term sick benefit, our respective doctors gave us a twelve-week sick line. That meant we didn't have to sign on every week, we could pick our money up from the post office every Monday with a voucher. I had sometimes missed a week and picked up two weeks' money the following Monday, which they didn't seem to mind. Carrie didn't get hers in person at all, her mum got it for her. Richard and I reckoned we could ask our mothers to pop in every few weeks while we were away and get it for us.

I had to go see my GP, Dr. Dean, to tell him what our overall plan was. He never showed much perturbation. I guess he saw a lot of funny stuff come through his door, and he just chose to stay unruffled. His demeanor was always like a cat who was considering their next siesta.

"I hope you know what you are doing," he purred.

"No, I don't. But like you always say, you don't die of this thing."

"Don't die of something else," he said as he looked over his glasses, signing the line at the same time.

I took that as a kindness. Of a kind. Funny he said that though. A few days before, Richard and I went round to see Richard's uncle Simon, who lived in Pollokshaws in the south of the city. Simon was elderly and was moving into a smaller house near Richard's mum and dad, and we were just helping him with some last-minute packing.

"SO *WHERE* ARE YOU GOING AGAIN?" he yelled.

He was a bit deaf.

"WE'RE GOING TO AMERICA, TO CALIFORNIA!" Richard shouted back.

"OCH, YE GET KILLED IN THAY PLACES!"

We both laughed at that. Either he had seen something on the news or he'd been watching too much *Miami Vice*.

Richard had got the line off his doctor too. He also had savings left from when he was working, before he got sick; he was ready, money-wise. I needed to supplement my America fund, however. This is where my records came in. I was going to sell them. I was feeling ruthless, this felt like the right thing to do. I wanted rid of them, I wanted to shed the weight.

First off, I took out the rare and collectible records that I thought I could sell in *Record Collector*. I'd got into the habit, while I was working as a roadie, of getting records autographed. I had a lot of autographed records, and even if I kept most of the records that felt precious to me, I'd have a lot left over.

I compiled my list. I had, autographed by the whole band in permanent black or blue markers, records by James, the Stone Roses, the Happy Mondays, the Pixies, Babes In Toyland, the Go-Betweens, Spacemen 3, Sonic Youth, Mudhoney, the House of Love, My Bloody Valentine, Galaxie 500, the Sundays, Dinosaur Jr., Nirvana, Hole, the Sugarcubes and the rest. I decided to keep the ones that they had written my name or drawn little pictures on. I kept at least one thing by all of them. The rest I would flog.

I got the ad together—the autographed records, along with another pile of indie and new wave rarities that I'd plundered from my time working in a shop. It came to about half a page of the magazine, in tiny writing. It would be in the November issue. Meanwhile, I borrowed my dad's car and with my brother Robbie's help we got the rest of the vinyl out of my parents' loft. (I don't think I ever saw my mum so happy with something that I was doing.) My brother and I drove up to Glasgow. He stayed over, and the next day we took all the records down to the student union, the one I used to work at. I'd put a few flyers around the place the previous week, stuck them on lampposts and in launderettes:

Record Sale: September 28th, 10 a.m.
Indie/Punk/New Wave/Dance/Classics/70s/80s
QM Union Foyer

It was good timing; the students were just pouring back into town, and the new ones were showing up too. The Queen Margaret Union foyer was a great place to hang out any day of the year, if you just wanted to see a nice mix of arty types and revolutionary communists. We had fifteen crates of records, some CDs, some singles. We sold A LOT. Frankly, I priced them generously. I wanted to give them bargains. I had been on the other side of the selling table for so long, I wanted to be one of the "good" guys for a day. Anyway, it was a nice sort of crazy day, and for my brother, who was an apprentice fitter at a shipyard, it was a day out with the "dafties," as he called them. Of course, I was one of the dafties, but I didn't care. At least he got to see me actually doing something instead of just sitting in our dad's greenhouse.

We cleaned up. I took in £750. We took the rest to a second-hand shop in the town. They gave us £250 for everything. I even left them the crates and all my plastic protective sleeves. Over the next three weeks, I got calls from all over the world "bidding" for the records in the magazine. It turned into a project, cos I had to keep calling people back until I had the highest bidder, then send everything out, but I made another £800 from the rare and collectibles.

We were going to America.

23

Vitamin Phillipa

We may have been going to America in January, but I was still facing my first October in Glasgow with no plan, no university. I started showing up at the George like I worked there. I'd just stake out the most coveted booth and see how long I could reasonably hold on to it for. I often had to share a table with other people as it got busy, but I didn't mind, I found I could tune in to or out of the conversations as I pleased. Plus it added to the dynamic of my day, as the people came and went, building up to the lunch rush, and out the other side into the afternoon lull.

I had all this time now, and I wanted to talk, but the crowd from a few years back had scattered like Larkin's golden arrows, shot into promising futures, just when I would have finally talked to them all. It was just me now, sitting. So I idolized the waiting staff, obviously — the waitresses of the George. I wanted to be one of them, ideally. I couldn't think of anything better than to have the energy to work in the café, do a shift, and retire to evening pastimes, shopping and reading, sleeping and dating, drinking and dancing. I wondered about their lives but was too cowardly ever to ask any of them. There was no time, they were always busy. A blur. I just sat and eeked, like a lowly mouse.

This particular Tuesday, Dominic from the group the Chairs came in. He worked in the record shop round on Byres Road, so I guess he had to eat somewhere. I just didn't expect him to come into the George. He sat in my booth; it was the only spare spot.

"Do you mind?" he said.

"Totally. Go ahead."

I had trouble saying those few words. It had been a while since I had spoken to anyone, and it always takes my tongue a few seconds to warm up. I guess I may have been slightly nervous on account of him being in a band. Cathy from the band came in a little time later and sat opposite him. I loved their group, had seen them a number of times. A few years ago, when I still lived in a bedsit on the other side of Hillhead, I used to hear them rehearsing. I threw open the window that looked onto the back court, and from one street down, the sound of the Chairs would float in on a summer evening. I thought it was the greatest thing ever. I used to close my eyes on the bed, and it was magical. I felt an intimate connection to the music and the city.

Now they were sitting in the same booth as me. I wasn't going to say anything, but Cathy turned to me after a while.

"What are you writing, if you don't mind me asking?"

I looked at my hands kind of dumbly and realized that they were still positioned over my jotter, left hand with pen, right hand in a claw shape, as if shielding my words.

"I was writing some thoughts."

"And what do you think?" she said with a wide grin, kind of cheeky.

"I don't think anything much. I was just wishing that I could work in here."

"I don't think Gerry employs guys," said Dominic, wiping his mouth with a napkin. "It's all women."

"You could be the first!" said Cathy keenly. "What's your name?"

"Stephen."

"I'm Cathy and this is Dominic."

"I know who you guys are."

"He comes into the shop," Dominic said to Cathy, still with his mouth full.

I nodded. I had been spotted.

"Are you making a record at the minute?" I asked.

"No, we're in between labels at the minute," he said.

That sounded serious. Imagine being in between labels—would that be treacherous or glamorous?

"What are you going to do with your 'thoughts'?" asked Cathy.

"I don't know. Maybe one day I can shape them into a song."

"Oh, do you write songs?" she asked.

"I try to."

"Do you have a band?"

"No. It's just me. I've never performed."

"Bands are overrated," said Dominic dryly.

"Don't listen to him," said Cathy, continuing to face me. "You should get a band together. I think that would be great."

I smiled at her. I didn't know what to say. She was so delightful and radiant.

"I will," I said. "One day."

*****

As the autumn moved on, I stayed camped out in the café. I moved on to writing letters. I had started writing to people I didn't know, but I wrote as if I did know them. I wrote to Quentin Crisp because his address was in a magazine article I read. I carried on writing to Harriet from the Sundays. I wrote to Hal Hartley a few times because I was into his films. And I wrote to Carla Camino.

She had a band called Smithfield. She was from Olympia, which is the capital city of Washington State, in the USA. There were only two people in the band, her and the drummer Bob Eisenberg. I'd been listening to their EPs incessantly. It's just her strumming away over his primitive beat, and her singing about unrequited love and circumstances. That's all there is to life, really—unrequited love and circumstances.

I wrote her a couple of times and I told her she was "A Siren for a Boy Beguiled." That was the title of a song I wrote, written in a Carla Camino style, partly about her. Anyway, I got a very nice letter back from her, first letter I ever got from a recording artist. She was planning a trip to the UK in spring, she knew Dominic and Cathy from the Chairs, maybe she would see me at the show? How did that happen? All I did was write a letter. I achieved more satisfaction from writing and receiving one letter than I did from taking three swings at a university education.

As well as the letters to strangers, I was still trying to write songs of course. It was slow going, every song seemed to take weeks, a month even. I'd chip away at the words until I was left with . . . just a pile of chips sometimes. Carla's songs seemed so easy; powerful, even. I thought that maybe I needed to get out and try and perform. So I persuaded Richard to come to a songwriters club in the city center. It was in the basement of a pub on a Wednesday night. People put their name down when they went in and then spent the whole night in a self-indulgent puddle of nerves waiting for their name to be called.

That was me, at least. Maybe others were calmer. I was just a wreck. I was trying to keep my pulse down with well-worn anti-anxiety techniques, but it wasn't working. What the hell was I doing? This couldn't be good for me at all. Richard seemed to be fine, but then he always looked calm. He said he would come with me, but he didn't want to accompany me, he just wanted to play a classical guitar piece. He got called up quite early on, and he played his piece, and people really liked it, they applauded, they listened. I had to endure at least another hour before I got my shot. The performers were mostly folkies, mostly older guys, some young women. Nothing too left-field. Acoustic and vocals, well played, nice voices, good techniques. I didn't like any of it.

When it was my turn, I said I was going to do mine on the piano. The guy was a bit surprised, but not unpleasantly so. He helped me get set up, pushed the piano out a bit. I sat as he positioned the microphone somewhere in front of my head. I was sort of hidden behind the piano, but I didn't mind that.

"Stephen Rutherford, everyone!" he said, and took his seat.

I looked at the sheet of paper with the words on it. The title was "Vitamin Phillipa." I had planned to explain a bit about the title and who she was, but then I balked. "Phillipa" was a girl I had seen hanging around outside the Queen Margaret Union. She seemed to be doing much the same thing I was doing, i.e. nothing, except she was much more out there. She wore a leopard-skin coat, ripped fishnet tights and creeper shoes with big platforms. She had a lot of bright red lipstick on. She was maybe twenty-five. She was pretty, but she looked ill. Too thin and too strung out, just a bit off. She hung out on the steps, smoking. She neither courted attention nor spurned it. A few people talked to her; most gave her a wide berth.

That was Vitamin Phillipa. That's who I opened my mouth to sing about. I started the song ok but got kind of lost as it went into the second section. I never really recovered, and the song just sort of petered out. No conclusions were reached about Phillipa. There was a smattering of confused applause as I reappeared from behind the piano and stole back to the place where Richard was. And there it was. I had done it. But it wasn't very good.

Back in my seat, I thought about Carla. I imagined seeing her in there and how she would light up the room and the true believer would see something special. How would she do it? Just by knowing she *had* to do it. When the special ones perform, they have no choice. They just have to do it, like breathing.

24

Chasing the Sun

A few days later, one aptly cold, gray December afternoon, Richard and I went into Sunset Travel on Byres Road to book our flights. The woman took us through our choices. She explained that we could stay in the States without a visa for three months. We knew that already. She also said that we would need to show up in America with enough cash so it looked like we were going to support ourselves and not work. And she said we should buy traveler's checks. Check. As the rain came down outside, and people cowered, and buses roared, and the light started to give up at four o'clock, we were snug in our little corner of the travel shop, smug in our plans.

This would only be my second plane trip, after the summer holiday with Carrie and her family. The notion that we were to be catapulted to the other side of the planet, that we would soon be looking out on the Pacific Ocean, that all the Scottish winter darkness could be so easily defeated was a lovely thought. We were shitting ourselves too though.

"What if you get sick and have to come home?" asked Carrie.

"Then we'll come home. Or I'll come home," I replied.

"Do they even have healthcare over there? You hear stories about them looking through your wallet for an insurance card before they sew your leg back on."

"We bought health insurance. We phoned up an advert in the *Guardian*."

"Did you mention ME?"

"No, of course not."

"Then you're living a lie."

"I'm living many lies." I smiled at her annoyingly.

She wasn't in the mood for games. "Seriously though, will you be covered if something goes wrong?"

"So far, ME has never been officially recognized by *anyone* in the 'health' industry." I did the "quotation marks" with my fingers. "Therefore, why would anyone pick the precise moment of something going wrong to suddenly recognize that it was there all the time?"

"Because they will. Because it's money," she replied emphatically.

I looked at her, then looked past her, thinking. I let go a breath.

"We'll be fine. There's risk in everything. This is just some risky business," I said.

"And you're Tom Cruise with his pants *way* over his head."

"I bet you loved that movie."

"I did love that movie."

We were in our usual positions, her on the bed, me on the floor next to the sofa, down in her basement room. She suddenly turned a bit sad.

"What am I going to do when you're away?" she said.

"You've got the mighty Quinn."

"He's not going to last. He's teetering."

"But he loves the small of your back. You said so."

"The small of a girl's back is not enough these days. The modern man wants more."

"What does he want?"

"Well, if I knew that, I would try to give it. But I don't think it's mine to give. He's running in fifth gear and I'm stuck in the garage."

She said it in such a matter-of-fact way that I felt sorry for her. Sorrier for her than I felt for me, which, honestly, was rare. We are, after all, just tourists in other people's lives, even our close friends'. And now it just so happened that while I was going to California to be a tourist, she would stay here.

"And now you're off with Richie Rich to San Fran Fucking Cisco," she said.

"San Diego."

"Whatever. Send me a postcard."

She turned to face the wall.

"Come on, it won't be for that long. It's not like I'm going to live there."

"I know," she said, her voice soft and muffled.

"I'll bring you back something good."

"A signed book of Armistead Maupin's," she muffled without hesitation. She turned around to me. "But you have to get it face to face."

"I'll try."

*****

January 28, 1993. A Thursday. Richard and I are at Glasgow Airport. We are scheduled to fly straight out over the North Atlantic, getting to Boston Logan in six hours. There, we change planes. We wait for three hours. We continue with Northwest Airlines to San Francisco International. Another five and a half hours. We are light, we are not fazed. We're just caught up in the moment. Excitement is the key emotion right now.

Richard's mum and my mum are here to see us off. We spent the last few days in Ayr at our respective parents' houses, gathering our strength, checking last-minute details. While there, we realized we'd better join the Youth Hostel Association. The plan was that we were going to spend the first week with Richard's cousin's friend Jackie. She lived with her boyfriend in the Outer Sunset area of San Francisco. Then we were going to buy an internal flight down to San Diego and find somewhere to stay there.

We thought there might be a few in-between days when we'd need to stay in hostels. So, on a chilly small-town Scottish evening, with not much moving around, we went down to the beach area. There were a number of huge old houses looking out onto the dark sand. At some point they'd perhaps been hotels or the Edwardian residences of rich merchant families. Either way, the biggest of them was now a youth hostel. We went into the reception, walking on a distinctive red-and-black tartan carpet. It was quiet, with an out-of-season feel. An elderly gent helped us to join, gave us a little "passport" in a plastic folder with our pictures attached. Hostelling International. We were good to go.

Richard had been to the States before. He'd worked in the kitchens on a Camp America program when he was a student. He was sent somewhere in New Hampshire. He saw the inside of a big kitchen, some woods, a cabin and some rich American kids that he was pretty certain had been told not to talk to anyone who worked in the kitchen. He told me it seemed like a long time ago. He was looking forward to going to the US on his own terms this time. Even though his energy was curtailed.

Now we were going to freewheel. I had missed out on Europe. When Vivian and the girls went cavorting in plimsolls round the Med, I stayed in Glasgow and tied myself in knots. Now, with everyone else getting on with careers and life, Richard and I were casting off into the pure unknown.

Richard's mum was bubbly and sweet, one of the nicest women you could ever meet. My mum was a little quiet. I hoped she was feeling ok about all this. All she would ever ask me was "Are you *sure* about this?"

She'd always trusted me. She'd trusted my decisions from the age of ten. There was one night that me and my brother were in the house alone with my gran. She had been living with us for a few years, but she hadn't been well recently. My dad was at sea, my mum was doing the night shift in Casualty. My gran was poorly that night, I could hear her coughing. I went and sat with her. I tried to persuade her that Mum should come home. She nodded eventually, and I called the hospital. I got my mum on the phone, and said she should come home. As I waited for my mum, I felt something had changed. It felt odd to suddenly be the one "looking after" my gran rather than the other way around.

Mum had always let me go about my business, was never nosy. When I went through my long "no friends" period, she didn't bug me. I just got lots of part-time jobs—delivery jobs and suchlike. From the age of thirteen I was always out the house early in the morning. Also quite a few evenings. And on Saturdays. When I think about it now, I was like a child from the deep past, studiously and seriously accruing wealth in case it might one day be needed to supplement the family income. Even when I went wrong, which was often (and sometimes spectacularly), she always accepted my explanations. Quite frankly though, some of those explanations were not very good.

I had increasingly not spoken to my mum during my bedsit years, aged eighteen to twenty-one. My explanations from this period weren't just "not very good," they weren't even explanations. They were circumnavigations. I was trying to tell her as little as possible about my real life so that she wouldn't badger me. Not that she "badgered" me as such. She was just insistent and worried. She had a right to be, but I preferred to be left alone. I wanted to make my mistakes and live my increasingly eccentric lifestyle.

My trajectory from twelve to twenty-one had read roughly:

> fun person,
> steady person,
> loner,
> craving change,
> craving excitement,
> dropout,

anti-normal,

anti-everything,

inappropriate,

unsustainable,

ill.

So now, at the airport, about to disappear to America for three months, off the back of three years of consistent illness, when my mum asked "Are you sure about this?" she was right to ask. What *was* the difference this time? What made me sure that we should do this, after all the missteps I'd taken before? In a sense, the stakes were higher than in the past. I was "healthy" then, and I got into trouble without even leaving Glasgow. Now Richard and I were crocked in the health department, and we were flying to the other side of the world.

But . . . it did feel different.

We took off in our Northwest Airlines Boeing 747. I had a window seat near the wing. You could have played football on that wing. It was a big wing. I looked at the Kilpatrick Hills close to the airport as we sat at the Renfrew end of the runway. I didn't feel much; I was in the moment. It was only my third flight, but after the hop down to Spain and back, this felt like serious business. Why were people on this flight? Not for a week's tanning and then home. There were people here who were leaving Scotland for good. There were oil workers and tech workers. There were people going to seek out distant relatives. There was a lot of luggage on this plane, not all of it in the hold.

The plane took ages to get in the air. It lumbered along, feeling more like a bus on a school trip. The lift was imperceptible at first. Then a few shudders. Water streamed across my window. Nobody talked anymore, people were quietly enthralled by the sound of the engines, the vibrations. My last glimpse of Scotland was of the River

Clyde heading down to the sea. I was hoping to see some of the islands to the west, but we were quickly in the cloud. It got bumpy in there, and it remained that way for the next ten minutes. Then a glorious moment. We got out of the cloud and into the gold and blue. We were above a thick layer of white cloud, the bumps disappeared, the plane leveled out, the buzz of conversation began again.

I looked at Richard. He was digging it too. There had been so many gray days this December and January, it was a shock to know all this was going on right above our heads. We knew the journey was going to be a bit of a marathon, but this bit seemed ok. Carrie would have struggled with the noises and not being able to lie down. I felt ok. I got settled with my book, *Dance of the Happy Shades* by Alice Munro. Eventually the cloud disappeared. I could see back behind the wing, enough to be able to check out the tiny whitecaps on the dark, indigo ocean.

I fell into just staring out, then I put my head back and shut my eyes. When something is finally happening, like a long-planned trip, there is a calm that descends. I felt a bit of that calm. I wanted to take stock. I felt nostalgic, so I thought about the people I went to school with. I used to think about them a lot when I was really ill in bed. I found it a comfort, then, to methodically recount everything I could about my earlier life. There were certain devices you could use as hooks when trying to recount your kid life. One of them, I found, was trying to remember the morning register of fellow pupils in my class. Working down the alphabet, hearing the distinct voices saying "Here!" seeing the hands being raised in your memory. The class I liked best was the one I was in aged nine to eleven. That seemed to coincide with maximum boyhood. I loved to close my eyes and picture the class, picture the groups of desks, try to name all the boys (easy) and then the girls (fuzzy round the edges). I felt like doing that now, miles up over the North Atlantic in a metal tube, leaving them all behind.

We landed at Boston's Logan Airport. We had to pick up our luggage and go through customs. We got pulled aside into a room. The guy wanted to know all about our plans. We'd heard that this could be a thing when you went to America. We had money—enough money, we thought—and we had a return ticket. But the officials were not satisfied. They kept asking us what we were going to do when we got to California. We answered that we were staying with a friend of Richard's cousin and that we were going to sightsee and travel around a bit. We didn't mention that we were ill. We both imagined that was the sort of thing that could get you quarantined and sent home.

I was wondering why everyone else had marched through so easily. It was a big plane, and we were the only ones pulled aside. I suppose that we did look a little raggedy, two guys coming off three years of chronic illness—young go-getters we were not. It never really occurred to me that we might get sent home. I felt like we had all this forward momentum. But still, if we were sent back, maybe it would be for the best. We might actually save ourselves a vast inconvenience. I was passive about the whole thing. I was so relaxed, even when they demanded to look through my diary, I didn't care. They took the diary that Carrie had given me (she'd got it free with the previous month's *Cosmopolitan*) and they flicked through it. There were addresses, emergency numbers, little doodles and notes. I had also written song ideas, in tiny writing, inside the day spaces.

Sometimes I would write backwards, like mirror-image writing. I did it:

1. because I was left-handed, and it was actually pretty natural for me to go in that direction; and
2. because from time to time I liked to write a thing that would remain private if someone I knew happened to pick it up and read it. Especially if it happened to be about

the person reading. I never intended nor anticipated this particular circumstance.

"What language is this? Is this writing backward?" the guard asked me.

"Yes."

And then I explained to him why it was backwards. He was not impressed. Richard had to explain to the other guy why so much of the writing in *his* notebook was in French.

"I'm studying French," he pointed out.

"But you're from Scotland, right?" his guy said.

"Yes."

"And you're not at college or university?"

"No."

"You just like France and the French?"

"Yes."

"But you're here in the US?"

"*Oui!*" he said, rather naively. It was a strange time for Richard to display his sense of humor. He wasn't usually a "funny" guy. Maybe he just got nervous.

The customs guy looked at him. He asked, "What's French for 'work'?"

"*Travail. Travailler,*" Richard answered.

He took Richard's notebook over to his desk and started flicking through it again, this time with even more zeal. I think he was looking for "*travail.*" That's what they were worried we would be doing, *travaill*-ing all over the place, taking jobs from Americans and then staying illegally. I wanted to tell them that I couldn't *travail* to save my life right at the moment, but it wouldn't have been helpful.

"Hey, Jimi Hendrix, how come you brought a guitar all the way over to America? What are you going to do with it?"

"I'm just going to practice," said Richard.

"What you practicing for? Carnegie Hall?"

They laughed. At least they were laughing.

"If I don't practice every day, my fingers forget."

Eventually they let us through. I wondered if Richard being black had any part in us being stopped. The irony was that from what I'd seen of America so far, there were more black people than in the UK, especially in the small Scottish town where we grew up. I looked at Richard and he was as neutral and nonplussed as he usually was.

Richard got called some things sometimes at school, but not the *worst* things. And the people doing the calling were idiots, like they had Tourette's and couldn't help it. We hadn't been best pals when we were at school, we only really became closer towards the end of school.

Nothing had ever seemed to bother him, and I shied away from asking him if he was ever affected by that stuff. I know that reflected badly on me. He also seemed so much more not-bothered about our situation than Carrie and me. I think I relied on his steadfastness more than I would ever admit to him. There was no way I would be in America without him.

We made it through. America smelled like cinnamon. We had a couple of hours to wait until the connection. We thought we would step outside, since we were only going to be in the East Coast winter for a moment. Richard wanted to see what the cold felt like. We left the terminal building and walked over to one of the car parks and went up to the roof. It was cold, but not scary cold. We looked across a bay to a neighborhood of big houses on a hill partly covered with pine trees. There was patchy snow on the ground. So far, so American. We went inside, back into the convected air and cinnamon. I felt good, I felt free. We were just here. Here to live and survive and find out about things.

The second flight felt different. There were no more Scottish accents on the plane, and that was good. We were really in America now. The atmosphere felt more relaxed. When we were young, we heard that Americans took a plane like Scottish people would take the bus. This seemed far-fetched to a young Scottish boy who had never been on a plane, but now that I was on one with real Americans, I could believe it. People were filling in crosswords, chatting to their neighbor. There was the hubbub of good-natured conversation and laughter. And every time one of the stewards spoke to us, or any time the captain came on the Tannoy, they looked and sounded like actors on TV. They were relaxed and assured. They knew what to say and how to say it.

"We're just approaching 24,000 feet, still ascending out of the Boston area. We'll soon be turning toward the west, flying over New York State and then over the Great Lakes. Then out toward the coast for a flight time of six hours and thirty-five minutes. We want you all to sit back and enjoy the flight. Mindy and the rest of the Northwest team will do their best to make you comfortable."

It stayed light all the way across the country, stretching out the January day like elastic. We were chasing the sun.

25

The Olympic Diner

We landed in San Francisco. It was the late afternoon. This time, we just walked off the plane, went to the luggage place, picked our bags up from the carousel and wandered out, dazed, through the Arrivals door. Jackie was there waiting for us. She gave us both a hug with the side of her that wasn't holding her coffee, and we stepped out into the curbside chaos that was San Francisco International. It wasn't cold, but it wasn't that warm either. I don't know what we were expecting.

We found her car, a messy little hatchback, and piled in and made for the freeway. Jackie drove one-handed, did everything one-handed. She never let go of her plastic beaker of coffee. I'd never seen that before. In the UK, we'd always been taught that driving was a serious business. She drove like we were on a fairground ride, like someone else was in control of the car.

"So there's been a slight change of plan," she said.

"Yeah?" said Richard.

"We can't put you guys up. We don't have the space just now. We just got a new dog and he's proving difficult to train."

Shocked silence from us, then Richard asked, "Where will we stay?"

"There's a hostel downtown. You guys got your hostel cards, right?"

"Yeah, we got them before we came."

"Ok, I'll drop you off there."

She said it all so easily, she didn't even apologize. My heart sank in the back seat. We'd had this plan for months—stay with her till we got acclimatized, rested, oriented, then hop down to San Diego. Did she not know we were ill? I couldn't say anything though. I didn't know her. She was Richard's cousin's friend. Why the hell should she care what I thought?

The freeway ducked and bobbed its way to downtown. There were bridges and buildings and hills, but I didn't take it in. I was worried. She dropped us outside of the Hostelling International on a busy street right in the downtown area. There were people screaming, cars careering into the multi-story car park opposite. She sped off without waiting to see the result of our inquiries at the front desk.

"Fuck," I said.

"Yeah, that's not so good," Richard said.

"I bet she doesn't have a dog. If she can have a dog, she could have a couple of people for a few days."

We went inside, and we joined a queue of younger, studenty, backpack types, which I considered we were not.

The next twelve hours were a bit of a blur, we were so exhausted. They managed to fit us into an eight-person dorm with bunk beds, one floor up, on the corner, over the street. It was the loudest room I'd ever been in. When you were in it, it just felt like you were in the street. It was one of my personal nightmares; I had a real thing about noise. We knew we had to try and get to sleep, but it seemed impossible.

Neither of us were hungry, our body clocks were in the middle of the night UK time. It was not good. I kept thinking about the vicious cycle of lack of rest, stress, illness. I knew that once you were on that downward cycle, it took a lot to reverse it. Later on, when the night had gone on for longer than any night I could imagine, I got up. I couldn't stand just lying staring anymore, listening to the mayhem outside—the screams of the quarreling homeless, the smashing bottles, the endless garbage lorries. I sat on the edge of the bed—and

I didn't offer up a prayer, and I didn't wish that the homeless were not homeless, and I didn't thank the Lord that we had a bed, and I didn't worry about my mum, and I didn't worry about Richard. I sat on the edge of the bed and despaired.

I would have wept if the anti-depressants had allowed me to, but they dried me up like a withered fig tree ready to be chopped and put on the fire. I despaired. I heard Richard say "You need to try and sleep," but I ignored him. There was a symphony of grunts and snores and wheezes from the other sleepers in the room, and I didn't care about them either. I was caught in a cycle of panic, and I wondered what the fuck we were doing here and why we had come.

I lay back down again, tried to sleep, but my dreams were like waking, and they were the worst sort—confusion, fighting cats, dreaming about not sleeping or trying to sleep in a cement mixer or in the gutter.

Morning came.

I like that sentence. It reminds me of the shortest verse in the Bible—*Jesus wept.* At Easter, Alec the minister based his sermon around the phrase "Morning came." He was talking about the hope engendered in any morning, but then he was talking about Easter morning too. After the darkness, the uncertainty and the anxiety, morning came.

Given we were up early, we decided we might as well get up and get out and try and find some breakfast. It was gray outside and in, and everyone in the dorm was still asleep. We stumbled out. The homeless circus from the nighttime was gone, the traffic was still flowing though, a steady stream of cars already going into the multistory, up its spiral ramp. There was a diner just across the street, the Pinecrest, but we walked past it. You never go in the first one. We turned the corner on Geary Street and walked along a few blocks. We spied the Olympic Diner with its flaming torch sign. We went in. A cheerful waitress immediately seated us in a booth and brought us water. The place was half-full. The TV was on, high up in the corner, and it was loud enough that you could tune in to what they were saying if you wanted or just let it be part of the background buzz.

The American day had begun, and we were part of it.

The menu was physically large, and large in choice too. You could have had steak, or pasta, or soup, or a salad, or a burger or half a grapefruit. There were things on there that we knew not of. Lox. Grits. Special scramble. Biscuits and gravy. Turkey melt. Gyros. Philly cheesesteak. Huevos rancheros. It was a whole new language.

"Would you like coffee?" the waitress asked. But she was already pouring. "Have you decided yet?"

"Not really. What's good?" asked Richard.

"It's all good, honey."

She went away.

"I think I'm going to have pancakes," said Richard. "A short stack."

"What's a short stack?"

"It's a pile of pancakes. A short pile. Look."

He showed me the picture. It seemed like plenty.

"Wonder what a long stack looks like?" I said.

She came back.

"Are you ready?"

"Yes," said Richard. "Could I have a short stack of buckwheat pancakes with bananas?"

"Perfect. And you?" She swiveled towards me, pencil poised.

"Could I have a short stack of the same, but with strawberries?"

"Of course. Is that all?"

"Is it possible I could have an egg as well?" I asked.

"This is America, honey. You can have whatever you want. Sunny side up or over easy?"

"What's 'over easy'?"

"We flip it. It's good."

"Ok. Over easy."

"Perfect." And she went off.

I think I was getting more rest from sitting in that booth than I did the whole night.

"What do you want to do?" I asked.

"Look around. Maybe we could go out to Golden Gate Park?"

"What's that?"

"It's a big park, massive. There's a poster in the downstairs of the hostel."

"We need a map."

"We definitely need a map."

The coffee sank in. The pancakes were vast. She refilled the coffee. It soaked up the pancakes. The TV played in the corner. People came and went, moving faster than us. People with work to go to, things to do, lives to live. We heard the rich American accents, the voices louder than the whispered Scottish café tones of old ladies back home. Here, people weren't afraid to let you know what they thought, or how they were feeling.

A man paused at the door on his way out to watch the American football highlights playing on the TV. Then he announced to the diner, "San Francisco would have been there if they let Montana play."

Straight away, the guy that looked like the cook or the proprietor said, "I'm not arguing with you. But we always got next year. We gotta look forward. Joe's got to move on."

The man at the door was still looking at the screen. Somewhat wistfully he said, "Yeah, next year." And he went out.

We walked out of the diner, and it hit me.

"I think I have to lie down," I said.

"They're throwing us out at ten," Richard said.

"I know."

The hostel closed its doors to its residents between ten and four. That was the hostel way. It was hostile. So we went back, cleaned our teeth, got what we needed for the day and went out. We were right round the corner from Union Square, so we walked round. There were benches there. We picked our bench. It was mild but certainly not hot. It was cloudy. From time to time the sun would break through and hint at what the Californian sun was capable of in January. Our bones soaked up everything we could get.

In Scotland, it was pretty much a done deal that the sun would not provide any warming of skin or bone from November through to the end of March. Maybe, just maybe, in the last week of March, if you stood in the apex of two brick walls directly facing the unclouded midday sun, you might feel a hint of convection. Here in San Francisco, for us, life had been reduced to very simple things. Heat, rest, food, shelter, peace. Back in Scotland, some of these things were vouchsafed us. We had chosen to come to a place where they were not. Why had we done that? Dunno. But we were here. It certainly gave us a purpose.

I lay down on the bench. I was wearing a long woollen winter coat, but I was glad I was. It was like a sleeping bag. I covered my face with my cap and tried to take a nap. Richard sat at the end of the bench. He tried to meditate. After a while, Richard rolled out the thin mattress thing that he had and lay on the ground next to me. Still the clouds flitted, and the ambience was dominated by the thrum of American traffic and the background humming of air-con units.

I was roused by a tapping.

"Are you ok? Do you want to come and have some soup?"

I sat up and it took a few seconds to realize what was going on.

"No, we're ok. Thank you though."

The well-meaning citizens of San Francisco had taken us for a couple of homeless guys and were checking in with us. I stretched and yawned.

"What do you wanna do?"

"We should look around," Richard suggested.

First, we dropped back into the hostel and asked if they could put us in the back, where it might be quieter. They couldn't. We said that we had health issues and they said "Sorry." But we found out there was another hostel down near the Marina called Fort Mason. They phoned over for us and booked us in there for a week. Then we headed back out. Richard had a guidebook. I didn't know anything about San Francisco apart from I vaguely remembered watching *The Streets of San Francisco* when I was little. With Karl Malden. Karlmalden—that's hard to say. Also, I had a View-Master when I was young that pictured the city. You looked through the View-Master and you were in a queer, super-real world of seventies San Francisco, in primitive 3D. I remembered the Golden Gate Bridge, Chinatown, Alcatraz, the cable cars and the funny snakey street with the traffic jam. That was it; the rest was new to me.

Richard said he wanted to go out to Golden Gate Park and check out an area called Haight-Ashbury. It was famous for hippie and flower-power culture in the sixties. We rode the 38 bus along Geary Street all the way out. We passed through many neighborhoods and it seemed strange to me that one street could have so many flavors. Downtown and busy, then a bit grubby, then it opened up, became tree-lined, passed through an Asian enclave ("Japantown," said Richard, reading his guidebook) and finally became residential.

We could see what we assumed to be the park, on our left a few blocks away, so we got off the bus and wandered over. The air smelled good out here. Richard said we weren't too far from the sea. He had a little map in the guidebook. We crossed a busy street and went into the park. It was different to UK parks—there was no fence around it, it just began where the road stopped. Plus it was wilder, and the trees were taller. We followed a path through the trees and eventually we came to a big field. There was no one in the field. We lay down in the grass, and the sun and clouds flirted with us again. There was a smell coming from the trees that was unfamiliar to me, but I was digging it. The peace was so welcome. The fact that we were lying under trees in January was already a quiet triumph for us.

"What was that? Did you see that?" I said, looking up as a large bee/hornet thing darted in and out of the branches.

We watched for a while and were delighted as it dawned on us that it was a hummingbird. A lady came by with a dog, a red setter. She didn't quite know what to make of us lying there.

"Hi," she said.

I was sitting up. "Hi. Could you tell us what type of tree that is?" I pointed up.

"That's a eucalyptus. They're all over the place."

The dog looked happy to see us and came over.

"They don't grow very well, some of them are in bad shape," the lady continued. "They planted them for timber a hundred years ago, then found that they grew too soft to work. So now we just have them. And the smell."

"Yeah, I like the smell. It's distinctive."

"It's the San Francisco smell," she said, smiling. And then she left.

We messed around in the park for a while, taking it real slow, trying to soak up the air and the soil and the goodness like the benighted eucalyptus. We came across a beautiful glasshouse that looked like the Kibble Palace in Glasgow except bigger and in a nicer setting.

"I've seen that, it's on a record cover by a band called the Rain Parade."

"Oh really?" said Richard, pressing on. He said it like he didn't believe me.

"Why would you not believe me?"

"I believe you."

We kept going, and finally the park gave way to streets once more. There was a record store there the size of an average Safeway store.

"If you go in, you'll be there all afternoon and we need to get back to check in to the hostel," Richard pointed out.

"Yeah, ok," I said with a backward glance. The store was called Amoeba, like the organism.

"This is Haight-Ashbury, where it all happened in the sixties," Richard added.

It was a colorful street, though its identity seemed to be a bit mixed up. There were bars, hippie clothing stores, "head shops," but then there were gift-card stores and Double Rainbow ice-cream stores too. There were a few characters who were carrying on the traditions of the sixties. Some seemed to have survived since then, others were kids younger than us. They were hanging out on the pavement, sitting on mandala tapestries, smoking grass, with their dogs, girlfriends and boyfriends.

Richard wondered whether perhaps they were paid to sit there to authenticate the reputation of the street, but I thought they seemed real enough. I mean, we were all capable of buying into scenes and dreams. I would have bought into worse if I thought it could make me feel healthy and normal again.

"I think weed may be the smell of San Francisco," suggested Richard.

"Certainly one of them," I agreed.

A guy came round the corner, just in front of us, who was universally the color of strong tea with no milk—his skin, hair, clothes, boots, and the sleeping bag on his shoulder. He was an angry man. He paused, looked around him, and said loudly to no one in particular, "I HAIGHT this street!" He was standing just under the sign that said *Haight and Ashbury*, so it felt like he was spelling it that way. We didn't stop to ask him.

We got back to the hostel in the late afternoon, picked up our bags and headed over to Fort Mason, the hostel near the Marina, which was an old army post. As we walked over the grass parkland towards the hostel, towards more eucalyptus trees, towards the Marina, the traffic died away. It got quieter with every step. It was already hostel luxury.

We checked in and got put in another eight-person dorm, but it just seemed warmer and more relaxed out here. The bed frames were wooden, and although my upper bunk was near the window, it was kinda cozy. I could hear birds. We passed a better night, and we chatted with fellow travelers at breakfast. I started getting a bit more of a feeling that things might be ok.

There was a large Safeway back towards the residential area near the Marina. We schlepped over there, we needed to get supplies. Even though I was an eating-out person, Richard was a whatever-option-is-cheaper person. I don't know if I was just lazier, or whether I just had different priorities, but it seemed to me that we could get by in America pretty cheap on food that was made for us and provided for us by other people. You could get a breakfast for $3.50 that would carry you for a long time, then get one of those massive Blondie's pizza slices for a dollar down on Market Street at lunchtime. After that, you were just looking for one more meal to get you through. We didn't need fancy. We didn't want fancy. It was all about the dollar rate.

When we went to the supermarket, the price of staples like cereal and bread seemed inordinately high compared to the price of pancakes in the diner. Cheese was expensive. Even raisins were expensive. I thought they'd be cheap because they grew them here. Still, the supermarket smelled good and gave us a little taste of real San Francisco as we eavesdropped on the residents in the checkout queue and got a feel for what people were doing. There was a high percentage of elderly people in the store, ladies with small dogs, gents who looked like they came here every day to stock up on alcohol. Wonder how they all got by? I felt like I had a lot of digging to do before I got down to the real America. And even so, was this the real America—the city by the bay?

Richard and I always needed a dedicated rest in the late afternoon. So by four we were waiting at the hostel door like stray kittens. We'd get into the bunk and the relief would be palpable. One of the guys that shared the dorm came and remarked "Resting again?" Funny thing is that he got into his bed and had a wee rest. Not such a bad idea, huh, dude?

The structure was important to us. It was important to me and it was important to Richard. Individually, we were two shaky structures. But two structures, when you prop them against each other, became stronger. We leaned on each other; we brought our coping mechanisms with us from Scotland.

Richard and I would make simple dinners in the refectory with our fellow travelers. Australians, South Africans, Germans, some Americans, some Canadians. A few families, mostly gaggles of youth. We weren't being *super*-friendly, just putting our little cat paws out so far. I must admit though that the lure of real people in the real city was stronger. In my heart I wanted to get out there. I was getting a taste for it. I had never been a tourist before and I don't think I wanted to be one. I had no desire to see Alcatraz or the Golden Gate Bridge. My business with San Francisco was elsewhere.

In the early evening I would play guitar, if I could get it off Richard. I had this need to play and create music. I hadn't left that behind in Scotland. If anything, it had grown keener. I felt the presence of music within me was a comfort on this trip, something I carried with me. My sudden wish to play guitar arose from the absence of any keyboard instruments. No piano on this trip.

"Aren't you going to teach me?" I asked Richard.

He looked up from his bunk.

"I don't need to teach you," he said.

"I can't play."

"But you know music. Make a chord."

"But what are the strings?"

He paused to think.

"Ok, I'll tell you the strings and then that's it, you're on your own."

He told me the strings.

"Try making a G chord and a C chord, that's all I'm saying."

And that's all he said. Tough love.

I went out and sat on a step round the corner of the hostel building. If I squinted down the hill through the evergreen foliage and red roofs of old army buildings, I could see the gray of the sea in the twilight. I sat there working out the notes. I don't know if the chords were right or if I was using the right fingers, but I made the guitar sound out a C chord. All the notes were either on the triad or were home. That means they were C, E, G or a higher C. I did the same for G. G, B, D, higher G.

It was awkward. My hand looked like a spider crab playing Twister. *This can't be right*, I thought. I considered going back to find Richard, but bugger it, he was making me feel like a child for asking. I plowed on with my C and my G. Over a couple of evenings, I started getting a little smoother. Practice and repetition, that was the thing. Landing your fingers on the strings was like a gymnast landing on the beam. My fingertips were ridged and raw. Richard said that after a while they would toughen up. So I stuck at it. The thing that kept me going was that I liked the sound. Those two chords, C and G, I liked them. That seems like an obvious thing to say, but it wasn't a given.

When I was eight, we had a chance to play violin at school. I was already playing piano, so I said no. My mum "advised" me otherwise, told me to get my name down straight away. It was free, after all. I was lined up with three girls in my tuition group, all of us scraping away. Linda, Linda and Shona. It was a bloody racket; I can still hear it now. The old teacher, Mr. Brown, would give us marks out of ten for everything.

"Play a D for me," he would say.

One after the other, we'd offer our measly Ds. He would "mark" our efforts.

"Seven out of ten, eight out of ten, seven out of ten, four out of ten."

I was the four. I was always the four. I gave it up. I think it was the first thing in my life I ever gave up. I don't think it was because damp-of-nostril Mr. Brown was biased towards girls. I just wasn't getting any satisfaction. It was a very negative feedback cycle.

Scrape.

"Four out of ten."

Scrape.

"Still four out of ten."

But the guitar was different. I pretty quickly found a sound. Two chords, that's all I needed. Maybe some would be inclined to try and play a beloved song of their youth or some heavy metal riff. I didn't want that. I wanted tools, I wanted bricks and mortar for songs. The sound of the guitar and the easy rhythm that those two chords made suggested a song to me. I started writing it. I started humming a mournful little tune over the top. It was a bit about me and a bit about an imaginary female. It was a song that felt sorry for itself and desired hope and happiness. It had a slight spiritual bent. I called it "Your Confirmation."

I felt I needed to shift to a different chord at some point, so I found that chord, putting my two raw fingers down. An E minor. That change from major to minor was surely going to come in useful. I played around for a while on the back step at Fort Mason, and no one bothered me. I liked the guitar—it was pleasing, it was personal. I hugged it into me. I could make it quiet; I could whisper over it. I could look out and sing, I could direct my gaze. I didn't have to look at my hands after a while. I'm not saying that it was wholly better than the piano, but it felt like it might be a *fast forward*. It just felt that this song was going to be ready quicker. I was actually molding the song as I went, as opposed to going away and writing words then coming back and trying it with a piano part. It was a one-stop shop—it accompanying me. I went round there the next few nights until I had a simple shape on the song and a few satisfying verses. By the third night I was getting better. I practiced until I was weary of my two, almost three chords. I could feel that the sunset and conversation were elsewhere, so I went back to look for them.

On the front stoop of the hostel a little group had gathered. Richard was there, slightly to one side with his book, but he was still listening. There were hostel folk seated all around the wooden steps. In the middle of them was a woman that looked distinctly non-hostel. She looked like she lived here. She was maybe thirty or thirty-five, and she was more smartly groomed than the rest. She wore a skirt and a blouse, a fine wool cardigan. She looked like she might work in an office. She just looked proper, like she had a proper plugged-in life. She held a glass of wine, the bottle beside her. Some others had beer.

I sat on the grass and tried to be included. (How long do you have to be there before you stop being the person who just showed up?) I sat still and was attentive.

The woman was asking people questions.

"Where are you from?"

"What brings you to California?"

"Do you like the city?"

"What's it like in Denmark?!"

When she got the answers she wanted, she took a swig of her golden wine.

"Where do you live?" someone asked.

"Over there," she said, pointing back towards the Safeway, to the Marina, to the lights of the houses beyond. As if answering the question that people were thinking, she continued, "I like coming down here. You guys are fun, you're young. You can do whatever the hell you want!"

"You're young," I said. "Quite young. Fairly young?"

I wasn't quite sure if what I said was too forward, so I was trying to reel it back. She snorted a laugh, more *at* me than *with* me.

"Are you going to play that?" she asked. The guitar was conspicuously still with me.

"I can hardly play."

"Come on, play something for us, it will be perfect."

"All I can play is a bit of a song I was trying."

"Play that then!"

I could see Richard out of the corner of my eye getting a little uneasy, ready to pounce and take the thing off me to save all our embarrassment. But she seemed genuine. She wanted me to play. So I started my strumming, and my hands remembered what to do. I sang a couple of verses of my song. The song was about a girl who came to our church for a couple of weeks. She was a student. Because the church was close to the university, we would get students coming through from time to time. Every year there would be a service where people would make an affirmation of faith. This was called a confirmation. I admired the people that could stride up there and say what they believed.

I think the girl was a little bit hip. She wore a floral dress that on some people would have felt like a mistake. But this person was wearing it deliberately, and it was a bold and enticing move. Swirls of orange and orangey-red with a bright white collar, the texture of crêpe paper. She had swollen red lips, lots of brown curls. I didn't know her name, but I had a good view of everything because the choir stalls were right up front. I imagined standing next to her. I imagined standing in solidarity with her. And I imagined that I would be in a bold dress too. And that's what the song was about really.

> *"I wore a dress to your confirmation*
> *Stood beside you and wished you heaven*
> *Are you ok?*
> *I lost my head in the ritual and wine*
> *You came around and we dressed together*
> *Matching styles for the balmy weather*
> *Will you wait?*
> *Life has stalled and my prospects are derelict of late."*

That's as far as I went. I had sung my verses and that seemed enough. You had to know when to stop, right? There was a polite ripple of applause from the steps, just to mark the effort.

The woman was looking at me, smiling. She drained her glass and said, "You're going to make it."

I looked back at her quizzically. The others went on with a different conversation, but then the woman came to speak to me.

"I liked your performance."

"I honestly have just started learning the guitar."

"So keep going. I'm telling you, you have something."

I mean, this was barmy talk, cloud talk. Nobody had said anything like this to me for so long that I had a problem believing her to be genuine. But I was in America, I was in California. Maybe the rules here were different?

I took what the lady said and I packed it up and put it in my pocket.

26

Getting the Hang of It

So we started to get the hang of it somewhat. If it wasn't so much about thriving but surviving, some golden moments were still scraped out in California. Every one day felt like a week. It felt like months since we left Scotland. I wore my long coat every day, it was the layers I needed. It mattered less what we looked like than at any time in our lives. We were unknown, anonymous. It was liberating. Ok, there might have been some tension ahead about what we were going to do with our lives, but we were pretty immune to that by now. I'm not saying we were burning super bright on the streets of San Francisco, but we were here. We were living and surviving. On pizza slices and burritos.

Our favorite place quickly became the Mission District. It was sunnier, and it was like no place I had ever been to. We got there by getting on a Mission Street trolley bus along Van Ness, from the Marina. It took a while to figure out the buses. Transit maps were hard to track down, but once I had one, I quickly realized this was a thing of beauty. There were so many lines and layers, beautiful names for routes, beautiful ways to crisscross the city. When you don't have anywhere to go and you have all day, transit becomes the end not the means. I fell in love with public transport in San Francisco.

You could sit on that number 49 bus and feel the transition as you moved across the city. On Van Ness it was a mix of people. As you crossed Market Street and on to Mission Street it became almost exclusively Latino people on the bus. It took a long time. Mission Street seemed to me to be in a constant state of carnival. The street was lined on both sides with bars, taquerias, cheap-price supermarkets, shops selling toys, fancy goods or religious knick-knacks, pawn shops, the occasional Mexican bank.

The pavements were rammed with people. Everything seemed bright, colorful, busy, vibey, different to anything I'd experienced. We made it along to an eating place called El Farolito, "The Little Lamp." We stuffed ourselves with burritos and sat back in the booths to digest.

"I want to go to a show," I said to Richard.

"Who's playing?" he asked.

"Ovarian Trolley."

"Ok, what have they done?"

"They formed a band."

"*Ha ha.* You know what I mean—what songs would I know?"

"None. None whatsoever."

Richard goes back to reading the paper.

"Henry's Dress are the support band."

"Oh, Henry's Dress—that's different, put me down for that."

"Really?"

"Not really."

"You know, sarcasm doesn't really suit you."

I went back to my paper. We were both reading the same paper, the *San Francisco Bay Guardian*, while sitting in the closed refectory of the youth hostel. We were mesmerized by the *Guardian*. How could this be free? How could it be so informative? How could it be so right on? How could the personal ads be so filthy? I loved it; it went with me everywhere. I felt like it was our hitchhiker's guide to San Francisco, helping us to get behind the tourist curtain and find out what the city was really about.

"The show is in the 'Best of the Bay,'" I said.

"Oh really?"

"Really."

"When is it?"

"Tomorrow night."

"How much?"

"$7."

Richard thinks. "That's, like, seven slices of Blondie's. A week of lunches."

"I'm still going to go."

"Ok."

"You mean, ok, you'll come?"

"I'll see."

The next night, Richard didn't end up coming. His relationship with *now* music was a bit flaky, so I got the bus over to the Mission on my own, to a place called the Chameleon. I paid my money and went in alone. I liked the bands, I just couldn't quite lose myself in it. I felt a little dislocated. I was used to going to things by myself, but in Glasgow I guess there would be a chance I knew someone, I could talk to someone at least, or wave hi or nod subtly. Here I was invisible.

The crowd was punky and cool. Cool as in the pages of the *Bay Guardian* cool. I don't know what I was expecting. The show finished, people were still congregating, the Saturday drink was talking loud, the vibe was funny and raucous. I had a feeling people were deciding what to do next, but I felt left out. So easy just to slip out into the night. Fuck it, I wanted to talk to *someone*. Surely I had a new city free pass for one night. Maybe I should have got drunk too. A group went out and I sort of followed them. They splintered to go to the bathroom. One girl was left standing at the bottom of the stairs. I went straight over to her.

"Do you guys have a car?"

"Yea-uh . . ." she said uncertainly. "Why do you ask?"

"I was just trying to get a lift home."

She nodded, looked at me a second as if trying to ascertain whether I was safe.

"Are you . . . ? Is that really your accent?"

"This is really my accent."

"What accent is it?"

"I'm from Scotland."

"What are you doing in San Francisco?"

She seemed like she was relaxed. Maybe I'd passed the non-crazy test. She had short bleach-blonde hair and was undoubtedly pretty.

"Just visiting," I said.

"Like Monopoly?" Half a grin from her.

"Like what?"

"You know Monopoly? The 'Just Visiting' square. Do you have Monopoly in Scotland?"

"We have Monopoly. I'm usually the dog. The Scottie dog."

"I always took the iron. I don't know why." She cracked a wider smile. This was immediately and easily the best thing that had happened since I got to America.

"Ok, you need a ride. Let me ask Eric. My boyfriend. He's got the truck."

Eric came back.

"This is Eric, and this is my brother Chris. This is . . ."

"Stephen. Hi," I said to them all.

"I said we'd drop him off. He's lost, he's from Belgium."

"Scotland."

"Yeah, Ireland, that's what I meant," she said, smiling the wide grin again.

Eric led the way to his truck. Chris and I jumped in the back of the pickup.

"Are you really from Scotland?" he asked.

"Yeah. From Glasgow."

"That's cool. You got the mountains and everything?"

"Everything. We got the whisky and the guys that wear the skirts."

"Woah. I have to see that one day. Isn't it cold there though?"

"Yeah, pretty drafty."

The truck took off suddenly with a few jerky movements, and we tumbled about the back.

"Where we going?" I heard Eric shout out the window.

"The Marina!" I shouted back.

"Ok," he shouted. Then I heard him exclaim "Jeez!" to the girl. I think I might have been taking them in the wrong direction.

"Are you from here?" I asked Chris.

"No. I live in Florida with my mom and dad. I'm just visiting Janey."

"She's your big sister?"

"By, like, four years."

"Is she a nice sister?"

"She's a pretty good big sister. My dad's a bit of an asshole, so we have to stick together."

"What does she do out here?"

"She does her thing. She's trying to do art, photography. And she's a drummer. There's more going on in San Francisco for her. You can make it out here as long as you set your sights."

I liked Chris, he seemed nice. It was just by talking that I realized how young he was. You could tell Janey and Eric were already street smart, while Chris, not so much.

"Did you like the bands tonight?" I asked.

"I did like them. It's not the usual stuff I would listen to, but I thought it was interesting."

"What do you listen to?"

"Hip-hop, Dr. Dre, Ice Cube, the Beastie Boys. Some metal too."

"Ok, here we are," said Eric.

We had made it down to the Marina. I jumped out onto the pavement side and said, "Thanks, guys. Thanks, Janey."

"Are you staying in San Francisco?" Janey asked.

"Just another few days. We're meant to be going to San Diego, that's the plan."

"Ha ha, *she's* going to San Diego. You guys should hook up!" Eric said from the other side of the truck.

I couldn't tell if he was being sarcastic. Janey shot Eric a look as if to say "Maybe shut the hell up."

"*Are* you going there?" I said to Janey.

"Um, yeah. Do you know anyone there?"

"No. We just thought we'd stay there awhile, me and my friend Richard. The weather's meant to be good," I offered a little feebly.

There was a bit of a pause. She reached forward in the truck and found a pen and scrap of paper.

"Ok. This is not my number, this is the people I'll be staying with. I won't be there for at least a week. But give me a call if you get *really* lost or something," she said.

I had no idea whether she really meant me to call, but she didn't say it unkindly.

Chris gave me a salute from the back as they went.

27

The Wise Men of Chronic Fatigue

That night, I didn't sleep so well. I felt sick. I felt panic.

I tried to pray; it wouldn't take. I wondered why I hadn't been praying so much since I got here. Too many distractions maybe? Distractions were meant to be good though—layers between me and the void. I gave myself a spiritual pass, for the moment.

"You were dreaming," Richard said at breakfast.

"How do you know?" I asked him.

"You were talking in your sleep."

"Really? What did I say?"

"You said, 'Why didn't I get any porridge?'" He started laughing. You didn't see Richard laughing too much, but he was chuckling away.

"I said that? No wonder I felt so bad last night."

Our big plan for the day involved the meeting for the ME Association of California in the afternoon. Richard wanted to spend the morning playing guitar, so I said I would meet him there, and I headed out. I took the 49 towards the Mission, just happy that an arm of the municipality of San Francisco was carrying me somewhere. How I wished it could provide complete mental comfort and solace also. I rode the bus right through the Mission till I got to the little hill at the end, and I started climbing up. The streets got suddenly twisty and steep, and then I reached an open grass area, turned around and sat down.

It seemed like I'd got up pretty high pretty fast. I was looking back towards the downtown area in the distance, but the Mission was spread out right before my feet. I could still feel the life of

Mission Street from up here; the main artery. I wasn't at the top of the hill; I didn't want to risk that it would be breezy. This was good for me. I burrowed my way into the hillside, into the wispy grass. There was enough intermittent sun to keep warming me up. I couldn't hear much of the city, but it was all there, laid out in front of me. I just wanted to sit there until I felt a bit better. I don't know if that was physically better or mentally better. I'd take both. I closed my eyes and pretended the sunlight was penetrating my whole being and flushing away the shit. Breathing in sunlight, breathing out the shit.

A lot of people would think this sort of "practice" was a load of bollocks. Hippie nonsense. But it was all about the mind, and we all have minds. You can change your mind. That's what Gen Pachen, the Buddhist nun, had said. Change your mind and you're changing everything. You are changing you. I was sitting on that hillside trying to change my mind, trying to show my depression the door marked exit. It was an exercise. It was like doing physio for a torn muscle. You weren't going to fix it in one session; it was a gradual thing. It wasn't voodoo. It didn't even require "faith," she said.

"Training your mind always works," she said. "It's scientific."

Underneath everything, the mind was as clear and calm as the blue Californian sky.

"Yeah, but that requires some faith to believe that," I said.

"Try it!" she said. "You come here in bits, in pieces. When you leave, I think you feel a bit better. Or else why would you come back?"

I wanted to change my mind. I wanted to do these things. I wanted the fear and the gloom to be lifted. But how did I do that when I was so physically beleaguered too? I wasn't going to be like this forever. I was going to get better and then I was going to be happy. That must surely be the hope and the plan. Physical health leading to mental health.

"Are you sure about that? Really, Stephen?" she had said when we were sipping tea after one of the sessions. "And you're going to wait till then, wait till everything is perfect until you start smiling again? That could be a long wait, maybe never. Best to accept what you have."

The ME meeting was back downtown, so I gave myself plenty of time to get there. I thought maybe it would be in a fancier place, but it was a room in an office building lent out by a conservation charity. It was packed. There were ME people and carers and wheelchairs and worried mums and healthcare types. It was like the meetings back home except busier, noisier, without the biscuits, but, crucially, *with* the healthcare types. Richard was already there. I went and sat next to him, the pair of us quiet, trying to blend in but probably sticking out. There weren't too many guys, certainly not guys our age. It wasn't like we were *too* scruffy, but we were the only ones that looked like we'd changed continents to get there.

To be honest, I don't remember much about the meeting. I was daydreaming. It was all well intentioned. I heard something about mitochondria, something to do with cells not working properly, but it was all very much at the speculation level. I looked round at the poor ME people in their various stages of distress, hope, calm acceptance, disbelief. I'd seen the same back in Scotland, but this was amped up somewhat. They don't have the NHS in America, and welfare here is not the welfare state. Getting ill in America has that extra layer of jeopardy: how do you survive if you don't have someone to take you in and care for you? I was guessing that at least the people *here* were ok. They were ill, but they hopefully weren't destitute. These were probably the lucky ones, informed and wealthy enough to be here. And we were also the lucky ones—the Scottish chronic fatigue poster boys.

The meeting moved from:

possible treatments—*none*;
to possible tests for ME—*erm, none*;
to coping strategies.

Everyone had one of those at least, and it got the crowd talking. From painkillers to Reiki, anti-depressants to saltwater baths, scary-sounding diets to therapeutic-pet visits.

A bright-eyed twenty-something woman came over and talked to us once the formal meeting broke up.

"So, where are you guys from?" she asked.

"Scotland. I'm Richard and this is Stephen," Richard replied.

"I'm Justine. I'm from here. Wow, I've never met anyone from Scotland before. Which one has ME?"

"We both do," I offered.

"And you came to California even though you're sick?"

"We came to California *because* we are sick," said Richard. "We came for the weather and to find out what Americans know about ME."

She stood there with her mouth semi-agape for a second.

"You are like the Wise Men of Chronic Fatigue. You came from AFAR! Wow. Except there's only two of you. I really hope you find what you're looking for." She smiled. "Are you guys staying in San Francisco long?"

"We're heading down to San Diego for a while," I said.

"But we'll end up back in San Francisco. We have to fly back to Scotland from here," said Richard. First time he'd mentioned coming back here. Good though.

"I live out in Sunset. You should come out and visit, we can all swap notes. I want to hear all about Scotland. And we have beautiful woods just across the bay. I go there when I need to recharge. I like to hang out with the redwoods. I can take you there."

"That sounds really nice, Justine. We could definitely do that," said Richard.

I wasn't dying to go to the woods, to be honest. There seemed to be plenty of trees in the city. But I was happy that Richard seemed to be enthusiastic about something; he was often impenetrable. We said goodbye to the friendly Justine and the other ME people and set our sights on San Diego.

28

Runway Lights of Point Loma

Sitting on the tarmac on a bright morning at San Francisco International. The Southwest stewards are doing their thing, and I sink deeper into my headphones. I brought a few tapes with me—a distillation of old favorites to get me through present worries. Starting with *that* Sundays song. Then the Cocteaus. Then some Erik Satie. Some John Coltrane. "Chill Out" by the KLF. It was a crutch, a comfort; it created a world of safety, of loveliness. Could you live in such a world? Not sure, but I was going to try. Music could be my home address. And in the meantime, I would take the feeling I got from the tape in my Walkman and I would try to replicate that feeling with strumming and singing. See if I can't keep the party going. The slow, sad party.

Around 1987 I got lost in pop music in a different way. It seemed to me that that was where the real party was happening. The music of the time was the blood that was pumping in my veins. Not only could you hear the music and play the music in clubs for people to dance to, you could go out and see the music in the flesh. Most of the music I loved was being played by current bands, and they all came through Glasgow. That was where the buzz was. The clubs and the venues, the music shops, even the record fairs. There was the artwork, there was the intrigue, there was the action, there were the performers. It was the whole package. I know some people managed to have jobs and still go to the club, or to go to university and still absorb the *Melody Maker* and go to the shows. I couldn't. For me it became a full-time job.

I can't believe they gave me a job on the crew, working with all the bands that came to the university. I kept bugging the guy for a job, and when he gave in and said he would give me a try, I thought, *Are you sure? I'm kinda nuts. Do you really think I can be trusted?* He took me aside for a chat. His name was Freddy and he really looked like a roadie. Denim and leather, high-top trainers, rock band t-shirt, silver chains, Dylan cap, home-rolled cigarette. Fingerless cycling gloves.

"Why do you want to do this?" he asked.

"I like music," I answered.

"Not good enough. Why do you think you can do this? It's hard graft."

"I'm strong. I may not look strong, but I'm quite strong, you know."

"See, that's what people think, you have to be strong. The most important thing about being on the crew is . . ."

He paused and let out a sigh.

"The most important thing about being on the crew is . . . ?"

"You want me to answer?"

"Yes."

I thought for a second.

"Make the show happen?"

"Well, yeah, obviously, make the show happen. But what else?"

"Help everyone have a good time."

"You don't have to worry about the punters, they're having a good time already. Everyone's drunk, everyone's dancing, everyone's *not* working, unlike us. Don't worry about them, they're having a good time."

Another pause.

"Ok, you're not going to get it. It would be better if you did, but I'll tell you, the most important thing about being on the crew is . . ."

"Teamwork!" I said.

"Swag," he said at the same moment. "But teamwork is good. That's a good answer actually."

"What's swag?"

"Swag is the stuff you get from the bands and record labels. Shirts, hoodies, jackets, records, shoes. I got a watch . . ." He showed me his watch. It was all black: black strap, black face, black hands. "You can't really see the time, but if you angle it a certain way . . ."

He leaned over to show me. I squinted.

"Oh yeah. *Gene Loves Jezebel*. Etched on the face. Very nice."

"Only two hundred made." He smiled, then put his serious face on again. "The pay is shit. £17 for a shift that starts at ten in the morning till three the next morning."

"Ok." I wasn't even counting on being paid. I was just going to show up.

"But you don't get paid for the first three times. I need to see if you have what it takes first."

"Ok."

"Report to me on Friday, ten a.m."

"Here?"

"Right here. Right on this spot," he said, pointing to the manky metal table and stools that we were sitting on. He gave me a piercing, serious kind of look.

Another guy came by.

"Who's that, Freddo?"

"New guy. Stephen."

"Good, good. Looks a bit fresh. Can he lift?"

"He says he's strong."

"I believe him. But we'll find out."

"We'll find out."

And that was it. I was in.

I daydreamed about the crew and some of the gigs I'd worked all the way to San Diego. We landed, then Richard and I stepped onto the tarmac. It was gray and overcast. We got a cab, and on the way out of the airport the digital sign said fifty-nine degrees.

"What is that in centigrade?"

"Fifteen? Fourteen?"

"That's nothing to write home about," I say. That reminds me, and I ask Richard, "*Have* you written home yet?"

We'd been in the States for ten days now, and neither of us had communicated with home. It was a little bit of a nagging thing, but then it seemed so difficult to do it. We couldn't find a post office in America. And to phone you had to buy an international phonecard or go to the phone box with a kilo of quarters. We could have done these things perhaps, but we hadn't. We had been wrapped up in survival. I think also the two of us had this innate sense that we needed to prove something to someone, and unfortunately for our mothers that someone was them. And perhaps Carrie.

"I'm going to write a postcard when I get to the hostel."

"Me too," said Richard.

The airport in San Diego seemed really close to downtown, we could see the tall buildings. But the cab turned away from there and took us to the hostel in a place called Point Loma. I was relieved when the neighborhood seemed quiet and the hostel seemed friendly. We checked in, got our beds in the dorm room. This time they weren't even bunk beds, there were four beds to the room. Virtually five-star for us. The place wasn't that busy. (Who comes to San Diego in February? In-between people like us. And Australians.) The plan was to stay here for a couple of days, then try and find a room for a month. Richard was determined that it be as near the ocean as possible. I was ok with that. If someone has strong feelings about something and you are ambivalent, then it's a no-brainer. You follow the enthusiast.

We went to the strip mall across the street and ate some good cheap Mexican food. Then we came back across and chatted to the folks in the hostel. I slipped off to one side and found a quiet patio to play the guitar. San Francisco had been something; it had been a lot. I was happy enough to be here though, to breathe out. Instead of rushing for the beds when the hostel had reopened for us, I was pushing myself, staying up to strum and watch the sun going down. I think my playing was getting a bit better. The hard skin was forming on my fingertips like Richard said it would.

I was learning to bar chord. Richard had at least told me that trick. He pointed me in the right direction. I assumed it was called a bar chord because your pointer finger made a bar across all the strings, shortening the length of the bit that vibrated, hence affecting the pitch. The good thing about the basic bar chord was that once you got the hang of the shape and built up the strength in your fingers, you could ping it around anywhere on the fretboard. Also, the bar had this extra quality—you could loosen or tighten your grip, and this affected if the chord would ring out or not. I found that if I wanted a standard "Sugar, Sugar" type strum (and I wanted that a lot), I could get what I was after by playing bar chords.

Ba da m-bum, Ba da m-bum, Ba da m-bum, Ba da m-bum

The little *m* before the *bum* represented a hit across the strings but with the bar "loosened" so that the chord wouldn't sound, so that it was just percussive. Rhythm—that's what I'm talking about. It would be easier to show you. It wasn't that complex, I'm no genius here. Furthermore, it was possible to play most of the chords as either a bar chord or not a bar chord, so that gave a range of sounds. There was also a device called a capo that acted as a permanent bar across the strings so that you could pick what key you were mostly playing in and play open chords instead of bars. But I was happy enough with my bars.

The next day was a slow day. We did laundry, and we wrote to our respective mothers. In the early evening I took a walk around the neighborhood. The day had been warmer, so it was pleasant to walk now. This was the most peaceful I had felt since we got to America. I was being careful with my energy of course—an evening walk was something of an extravagance—but I was just going with it. After walking for a while, it was getting dusky. The land dropped off, the houses ran out, I reached scrubby parkland. I ventured through it a little and I came out at the top of a hill with the San Diego airport below me and downtown directly beyond. The Marina was to the right. It was all a beautiful sight to me. I sat and let the dark come down. The runway lights were blinking, the jets took off flying directly towards me. They were silent as they came along the runway. They lifted almost imperceptibly, looked like they weren't going to make it. There was a rumble, and a roar as they went over my head, and I was on the business side of the thrust.

I sat there thinking about everyone, thinking about Carrie, thinking about Vivian, thinking about my parents. I thought about the people that were in my class in school again and what they might be doing now. This time I imagined my secondary school class. I imagined them grown up and doing adult things. I'm sitting there thinking I'm the messed-up exception, but I bet everyone feels that way. Everyone is exceptional. Every life is sacred and exceptional. Jeez, I'm not doing *that* bad. I made it to America. I've got a good view of the airport and the Marina. I have a traveling companion and a mum that gives a shit. I have a best friend and I have the round-about phone number of one of the coolest people I have ever seen or imagined.

I'm talking about Janey here. Even if her invite was only a semi-invite, I'm going to phone anyway. What else have I got? I have a blank page. San Diego is nothing to me but the ideal climate in a Weetabix atlas. I have nothing but her phone number. Of course I'm going to phone, and she probably knows it, though it might be slightly bothersome to her.

Remember Carrie and I talked about being sad snakes, starved of sustenance and company by our remote circumstance? We couldn't afford not to reach out with a sting to any person of interest that came by. In the Australian desert that person might be a rodent or lizard. In this case, the person was a high-smiling Floridian punk with Jean Seberg hair, a knee-length pleated skirt, battered leather Ramones jacket, Motel 6 t-shirt and stack-heeled loafers.

Of course I'm going to phone her.

29

Mission Beach

We saw the notice right on the board at the hostel. George and Poppy Geller had a room. Richard did the talking, he's politer than I am. We took it for a month. It was over on Mission Beach, even though Ocean Beach was closer. We didn't mind though, it seemed just right for us. *Room in quiet house beside ocean.* We gathered our stuff and we took the bus over. Richard explained we were spending too much money already to get a cab but there was a bus that would get us close.

George and Poppy were super-nice retired Americans. They greeted us like we were relatives and showed us into the ground-floor room that they had; they mostly lived upstairs. It was a plywood-paneled den, a living–kitchen vibe with a shower room attached. It didn't get much light, but it seemed like it would be comfortable. There were two cot beds that could be folded down, but to be honest the big sofa looked really comfortable to me.

They let us get settled in, and once we had dumped our bags and claimed our space, we took a look outside. We were just one street back from the ocean, on a narrow strip of land between the ocean and the inlet called Mission Bay. It felt good, like we inhabited our own spit of quiet land. Our "apartment" had a door that opened right onto the lane that ran down between the houses, but if you crossed the lane, took a shimmy between another two houses, you hit the sand. It was right there: Mission Beach. And if you went the other way two blocks and a half, crossing the main drag, you got to another beach on the inner side, Mariners Cove. Richard and I could go to separate beaches and never see each other, if we wanted lots of peace. It was ideal.

I really think Richard was happy now. He didn't show it much, he's not that demonstrative, but he was calmer than ever. He always did his thing, and his thing was to go to the beach, morning and night. That's where he did his reading, his meditation, his healing, his living. He really did seem like he was self-contained. Good for him. I wasn't so self-contained. I liked the beach enough, I liked watching the surfers. I particularly liked sitting out on the sand at night though, watching planes on their heavenly flight paths. They often just blended in with the stars if it was a clear night. I would sit wrapped in a blanket and observe them for a long time, like a person in medieval times lost in observing the moving flames of a fire.

We slept pretty good in the seventies den of the Gellers'. It was nice to carve our own space in the room, make our own den within the den. We ate Wheaties for breakfast, then mornings were for lazing. We did what we did back in Glasgow, except now that we were in San Diego we could be outside a lot. We were through the looking glass while winter was happening in Glasgow. This was a second-by-second harvest of advantage.

But that wasn't enough for me. My project was the songs. Every time I picked up the guitar and strummed a couple of chords, it suggested a new song to me. I was writing slow and steady. Every song was an effort, but at least I was still building something. Even though I had just picked up the guitar, I was writing simpler songs faster. Words were slow though, progressing the song beyond two simple chords was slow, looking for a chorus was slow, finishing was SLOW! But I had time, there on the beach. On the inlet, on the sunlit wooden steps of the Gellers'.

I would list the songs' titles on the inside cover of my notebook. I would list them before they were finished. I treasured the list. I liked titles. I figured if I listed the titles as finished songs then they would somehow become finished songs quicker. So I didn't wait, I just put them up there and I liked the way they looked.

"There's No Holding Her Back"
"Vitamin Phillipa"

were older ones I'd written back in Scotland.

"Your Confirmation"
"Soccer in the New World"

were the US guitar songs.

I didn't stop at actual songs though. I had titles, many titles, from things overheard, things read, new information coming in. I wondered when I would ever get the time to turn them into songs. I don't suppose it mattered, but in a sense a list of titles is a song nursery. Either a title reminds you of a feeling, or emotion or episode which you might later turn into a song. A handy reservoir of information. Or it was just a nice sequence of words that could come to represent anything.

So I wrote them all down. I thought that, at the very least, one day I, and the band that I might find myself in, could produce lots of great instrumental music—short, tuneful, self-contained pieces. My favorite group, Felt, had done similarly in their career. In fact, on one LP, called *Train Above the City*, the singer Lawrence had *only* contributed by adding titles to the pieces already composed and recorded by his bandmates. Looking at the inside front page of my notebook, I had such still-to-be-written classics as:

"Evolution of the Modern Horse"
"The Pacemaker Held On to Win"
"Hangover Hill"
"Romantic Saga Ahead"
"The Stars of Track and Field"
"Turkish Domes on the Isthmus"
"Puch Picnic"

"The Blue Ribbon of Celibacy"
"The Past Tense of Emotion"
"Heroin Skincare"

You see? That's an LP all ready to be made. It has structure, a backbone, some meaning. The notes are just waiting to be played by some future people in some future time.

*****

Richard saw a poster on a lamppost. It said that the Hare Krishna temple, in neighboring Pacific Beach, was giving out free food in the evening. He thought we should go along and get fed.

"Will it not be a bit awkward?" I asked.

"Why would it be awkward?" he replied.

"We're not Hare Krishna. I don't think I even know what Hare Krishna is."

"I don't think that it matters. They are feeding the needy."

"Are we needy?"

"We are *quite* needy."

So we went along. It was a bit of a walk. By the time we got to the temple, I was hungry. And if I was hungry, I knew Richard would be hungry too. I was hoping they would do the food first, but I suspected there was more to it than that and we'd have to wait.

We went in. It looked like a youth hostel from the outside, but it was very definitely a temple on the inside, with lots of Hindu imagery and decoration. They greeted us kindly, we sat on cushions on the floor, and we did a bit of chanting, which was cool. Then it was time to meditate, which of course was fine with us. The subject of the meditation was a little bit unclear to me, but I felt like I was in a pretty good place nonetheless, just letting the general sense of spirituality wash over me.

Then there was the chat. The monk was sitting up there in the chair, cross-legged, with the microphone. I was used to this scenario and I was ready for pretty much anything that he was going to come out with. He was dressed in pale yellow, with a shaved head, beads, and lines of painted decoration on his face. Other than that, he spoke in what I took to be a New York accent. (My reference for this was another TV show, this time *Cagney and Lacey*. I can't remember which one of Cagney or Lacey had the short brown hair, but his accent was like hers.)

He was referring to a particular passage that featured Krishna throughout. From what I gathered from the speech, Krishna was a Hindu deity, and they seemed to like him very much and revere his teachings. The monk addressed the room.

"We are pure spirit, we are not these bodies. The body is a covering of the soul. Very temporary, the gross body—the hands, the legs and the bones. Then the subtle body—mind, intelligence, ego. None of those are us. Without a source of higher knowledge, we inevitably fall into that identification. As spirit souls, we are eternal, we are pure particles of consciousness. We never were born, we never die. But we've been in this material world since time immemorial."

So here I was again, pecking around the edges of someone else's knowledge like a chicken scratching for a seed. I don't know if this was considered a good or bad thing. Were we interlopers or were we pilgrims on the road? I liked to think we were pilgrims. I looked across at Richard and he was calm and drinking it in. Look at him. Richard the pilgrim.

"We are not these bodies," the monk or the priest said.

I could have taken that one sentence and run with it. *We are not these bodies.* I believe that we are not these bodies. I firmly believe that. It was nice to hear that from another source, another culture, from this well-meaning and streetwise monk in this youth hostel temple.

One time, a year and a half ago, when Richard and I were still coming blinking into the light of our post-trauma ME world, we were lying on the grass near the beach back at our childhood homes. We were trying to stay outside as long as we could, with the open sky above. As I looked up to the sky and the gap in the clouds, with the blue beyond, and the subtly moving shapes, I was enamored once more with the mystery that had just begun with me. I had acknowledged God. I was just one small part of something vast. Once in a while I felt the vastness, I felt the otherness behind what constituted our normal lives, and I was comforted.

I was comforted by the contortions of the clouds and the shining sun. I allowed myself to be duped like a child, like these weren't just physical phenomena. I felt the essence behind the science and it left an imprint on me.

We are not these bodies.

This was worth the price of attendance alone.

Me and Richard were really hungry. We had enjoyed the chat, but I must admit that by the end I could smell the food coming and my stomach was going nuts. Also, with our ME bodies, we were used to making food a priority—regular meals at regular times. We definitely worked better when the fuel tanks were topped up. So we didn't stand on ceremony when they invited us to go through. We helped ourselves to the fabulous-looking veggie food on offer. In fact, we heaped our plates in case it ran out and there wasn't enough—not very charitable.

We sat in circles on cushions. It seemed like every circle had a junior-looking monk or nun attached to it. Ours started chatting to us.

"Are you interested in the Krishna movement?"

"Quite interested," said Richard.

"Really quite interested!" said I, with a face full of pakora.

"What interests you about it most?"

"Good question," I said. "What interests you about it most, Richard?"

He had just put a load of food in his mouth, so we had to wait for a bit.

"Well," he said finally, "the whole spiritual aspect of it."

"Me too. All that . . . spirituality."

"What do you believe in right now? Do you believe in the soul?" he asked with more directness.

"I suppose so." I remembered using that same phrase in answer to my music lecturer a while back and how I got laughed at for my inexactitude.

I was waiting for him to say "Ha!" and then whip my plate of food away from me. He did neither. He'd got me thinking though. *What was the soul?*

"I do believe in the soul. I believe there's a part of me that goes on forever. And I think we'll be going to a better place," I offered.

"So how are you going to get there?" asked the junior monk.

"Well, it depends. It depends on what system you believe in."

"We believe that we have to set aside certain earthly distractions, and then we can focus on Krishna, who will guide us."

"And you believe in God?" asked Richard.

"Krishna is the Supreme God."

"So only if you set aside the earthly distractions can you gain . . . heaven?" I asked.

"Precisely. To the highest of Krishna's spiritual realms. But there are lots of stages in between. Depending on how you live your life, you might take on many lower or higher rebirths before you get there."

I could never tell how interested Richard was in this stuff. He was taking it in, but he always seemed more passive than me. Yet he seemed to practice this stuff in daily life, he seemed more able to temper his emotions than me, and he dug his yoga and his meditation.

"To be honest, I struggle in life with what I have. I can't imagine cutting out more right at this minute. Partly the reason we are in California is because our health isn't good. We're just scraping by," I said.

"But you're looking for answers?"

"In a manner of speaking, I guess we are looking."

"Everyone is sick. Weakness in the body is a manifestation of negative karma."

The young monk was starting to bug me a little bit.

"Ok, then we will just wish ourselves better and everything will be ok."

"You could," he said with what I thought was a slightly smug smile. "Through prayer and meditation and going for refuge, you could get rid of your negative karma and hence your sickness."

"Go for refuge?"

"Pray to Krishna."

"I do pray already."

"Who to?"

"To God. You know, God."

"Are you a Christian?"

"I don't know," I said truthfully.

I wasn't sure I liked being backed up against a theosophical wall like this. Richard looked on, still quietly eating rice. Maybe this was his version of the Bournville Game from that kids' party I was at. As long as the monk was grilling me, Richard could continue to fill his face with free veggie food. I was not doing as much eating as I wanted to.

The monk continued. "So you pray to God, and you want to go to heaven, but still you are going round in circles, following your every desire and falling into every pit of fear that comes your way?"

I looked at the young monk. I think he was enjoying the spiritual upper hand that he clearly had, but I must admit he'd probably nailed the diagnosis.

"Yup, you're probably just about spot on there."

"And you're not going to do anything about it?" he said with somewhat exaggerated incredulity.

"I'm trying to figure it out. It's confusing. Pretty much yesterday I was in one of the holes that you're referring to. I know that I might be in one of them tomorrow. You seem like you are in a good place, I congratulate you for being so together. I'm just starting from a different place over here." I looked at Richard. "*You* know what I mean?"

He didn't leap to my defense like I hoped he would. Kept chewing, nodded a bit.

"I know what you mean," he said.

But it didn't really *sound* like he knew.

30

Janey's Coming Round

Janey's coming round. We're going to get tacos. I had called the
house she was staying in before she even got there. Lester, the
dad, was a bit surprised to hear from a "friend" of Janey's so soon.
Oops. But she's coming round. She's got her own car. She's staying
in a place called La Jolla, but she's driving over.

"Are you coming for tacos?" I asked Richard.

"Yeah, I'll come."

He said it without that much enthusiasm. Neutral. I'm doing him
a big favor though. I know I only met her briefly, but she is a cool
American girl, and who wouldn't want to have lunch with a cool
American girl? We walked up to the Mexican place beside the old
rollercoaster. It had become our default eating place now. It wasn't
classic like the ones in the Mission, but it was solid, cheap and did
fish tacos, which I loved.

We sat outside at the plastic tables with no menus and no service.
The streets and pavements were half-busy. Here comes Janey in
black dungarees, a stripy top underneath, blue Doc Martens, blue
sunglasses and a big smile. She looked pretty great. When you've
only met someone briefly, it's always a slight surprise when you
meet them the second time. Like, did I just make her up?

"Hi, you guys."

"Hi, Janey. This is Richard."

Richard stood up and shook hands. We sat down. Janey took off
her glasses and took in the scene.

"Wow, you guys are really close to the rollercoaster. Have you
been on it?"

"Not yet," I said.

"One day, one of those cars is going to fly off into the ocean. And that will be the end of that," she said cryptically, staring at the rollercoaster. Then she grinned. "You should definitely go on it before that happens."

I don't suppose it had occurred to either one of us to go on it. It had become part of our scenery almost immediately. Like if you lived next to Big Ben, it probably wouldn't occur to you to go up it.

"Did it take you long to get here?" I asked.

"About half an hour. It takes half an hour to get anywhere here," she said, smiling again. "So, you made it to San Diego. How do you like it?"

"It's good," said Richard.

"We like it," I said.

"Are you here to surf?" she asked, looking towards the ocean.

I kinda laughed. Right now, anything so complex and energetic as surfing felt like flying to the moon.

"No, not so much. I'd like to try it one day," Richard said.

"We see them pretty much every day though. They congregate at this one spot near the pier. It's fun to watch," I said.

I always feel a bit tense sitting at a café or somewhere when there's nothing happening on the service side. I always have to take charge and work out what's going on and get the ball rolling. Then I feel we can really start talking. To me, everything said before ordering the food feels like throwaway. Let's order, then we can talk.

"I think we have to go inside to order. Will we do that?" I suggested.

"Definitely," said Janey.

It felt like Janey was happy enough to be there, like she wasn't having her arm twisted. She was a little fascinated that we broke some traveler's checks to pay and were rewarded with dollars in change.

"I can't imagine the average American doing what you just did. It seems like financial sorcery," she said.

On our table was a jug of iced water and three plastic glasses. The sun was out and it was digging into our bones.

"So, San Diego. That's kinda random. Me and two Scotsmen. I feel like we should write an international declaration or something, you know?" she said out the blue.

"I'll sign it right now," I said. "Richard, you can write it. What should it say?"

"All good people of the earth shall have fish tacos."

"That's a great start. What about for the vegetarians?" Janey said.

"All people of the earth shall be given a veggie option?" he offered.

"That's good. That can be the first amendment," she said, laughing. "I would like the chance of a margarita on a Thursday and dancing on Friday," she added.

"We can definitely put that in. And something for dogs," I said.

"Dogs?"

"Yeah. General liberty from bad owners. Freedom to roam," I said.

"Dogs shall roam free on Wednesdays, Sundays and all public holidays," she replied.

"And food will be provided."

"For the dogs?"

"Yup. Little pavement troughs."

"Won't it just be chaos, with the big dogs eating everything?" asked Richard.

"You see, we never give them the chance. I think they would organize themselves," Janey postulated. "They would know to save food for the old, the weak and the chihuahuas."

"I'm not a hundred percent sure that's what would happen, but I admire your humanity," said Richard.

"My *dognity*," she said, and laughed.

When the tacos came, she asked, "So what *are* you guys doing here if you're not surfing?"

"We came for the weather, partly," said Richard.

"Yeah. We had to get away from Scotland, so we blew all our savings and came out. I've never been anywhere before, but Richard worked at a kids' camp in America."

"How was that? American kids can be a little . . ."

". . . bit too much? I thought the kids were fine, but I was in the kitchen all the time," Richard said.

"I heard from your brother you are from Florida. What brings you here?" I asked.

"I burnt my Florida bridges—I'm a West Coaster now. Then my friend Alicia sent me down *here*. She's super-sweet, she could tell I needed a rest from San Francisco, from certain things. She suggested I stay at her folks' place for a while. I'm tutoring her little brother and sister in art."

"Is art your main thing then?" asked Richard.

"Yeah. I was at art school in Tampa for a while. I'd like to go to one of the big art schools in San Fran, but they are *so* expensive to get into. So I'm just going to sell my wares around here for a while."

"But you play music too?" I asked.

"Sure. I was learning the drums, but I'm kinda removed from a drum kit down here."

"Were you in a group?" Richard asked.

"Not really. We just jammed, I guess. The kit was in this twenty-four-hour practice-room place in the Mission. When you got up from the stool, someone sat in your place and kept playing."

"We both play music. Well, he plays guitar, I just picked it up," I said, looking at Richard.

"You're actually playing more than me at the minute. You practice pretty hard," Richard said.

"What are you practicing for?" asked Janey.

"I just want to be good enough to play the songs I'm writing."

"So you sing too?"

"Ha, well, I sing *my* songs. I'm not a singer or anything. But if you ever want to play together, I'd be up for it."

"That could be fun." But I couldn't really gauge how much fun she thought it might be.

We ate our lunch.

When we were done, she asked, "You want to see my car? It's parked a block over."

We followed her over.

"Here he is—this is Casper!" She looked at us with a kid's smile, eyes shining.

The car looked to be from the 1970s, a Volkswagen estate, small and boxy, the babiest of blues.

"It's called a Squareback. Want to go for a ride?"

"Thanks, Janey, I'm going to go back and meditate for a while. It was really nice to meet you," Richard said.

"Great to meet you, Richard." She gave him a little hug and then turned to me and asked, "What about you? You coming?"

"Yeah, I'll come."

Richard left and we got in Casper.

"Was he ok? I didn't scare him or anything?" she said.

"No, not at all. He likes to meditate. We've been in each other's pocket for so long, he's probably loving the chance to have the room to himself for a while."

"You guys share a room?"

"It's nice, it's got everything in there, it feels like an American basement."

"What's an American basement?"

"You know, from *The Partridge Family* or something."

She snorted a laugh.

"Is your whole idea of America from seventies TV shows?"

"Pretty much. Yes. I feel like I'm in one right now."

"Yeah, this little guy is pretty *Partridge Family*," she said as she pulled out the choke. "Ok, here we go."

I was really happy to be in someone's car. I was really happy to be in Janey's car. The car had an old car smell, leather and fumes, but it also had her smell, which was kinda like musk. I mean, I think that must be her perfume. Kinda musky.

"Can you talk and drive? Want me to be quiet?"

"Stephen, I can talk and drive. That's what American roads were made for."

"Ok, just checking."

I didn't ask where she was going. Normally I would want to know because I didn't want to go too far. But . . . fuck it, I'm going with it.

"I'm still finding my way around here," she said as she looked at the street signs and negotiated traffic lights.

"Are you planning to stay awhile?"

"I don't really have a plan, Stephen. I'm just living in the present." Then she said, as if talking to herself, "Is it worth getting on the freeway? I'll get on here. I can always get off. I'm trying to find the park. Tell me if you see the park."

She got on the slip road and was soon driving at the 55-mph speed limit, though the engine complained a little bit.

"Double Nickels . . ." I said, gesturing towards the speed limit.

". . . on the Dime! You like the Minutemen?"

"I really like them. It's been a while though."

"I *love* the Minutemen! I love Hurley's drumming especially. That's so rad. I didn't think you'd be a Minutemen guy."

"I used to work in a record shop, they were my favorite of the American punk bands. Them and Hüsker Dü, obviously."

"Obviously. Ha ha. So you know how they came up with the sleeve and everything?"

"Yeah. I think because we're in an old VW it reminded me of the sleeve."

Ok, let me explain a bit about the Double Nickels. *Double Nickels on the Dime* was an album by American punk rock band the Minutemen. I liked the record a lot, and I liked the record sleeve just as much, even though at first it seems like a lazy sleeve with a bad picture taken from the back of someone's car of the back of the driver's head. But as I listened to the record and looked at the sleeve and asked around in the shop I worked in, I figured out the sleeve design wasn't lazy at all. It was a work of some sneaky genius.

There was a song by an old American rocker, Sammy Hagar, called "I Can't Drive 55." Fifty-five was the American speed limit. The song touched on the fact that Sammy felt restricted at that speed and felt like he wanted to go faster. The Minutemen thought about that and retorted, *Actually, we can drive 55. We can stick to the speed limit. You, Sammy, want to be a rebel. Our rebellion is going to be in the music we play. We're going to play free, we're going to play unfettered; we're going to break down the walls.* (In fact, *Double Nickels* is a free and unfettered record, which is why people loved it. A forty-three-song ramble through funk and philosophy.)

On the record sleeve they had the idea to show the car they were driving was going *exactly* at 55 mph. Mike Watt is driving the car; you can see over his shoulder, but you can see his eyes reflected in the mirror also. He looks pretty happy with himself. They also had to get the right spot on the freeway, underneath the sign for their hometown of San Pedro. It took them quite a few tries to get all the elements lined up—the speed, the spot on the freeway, Mike Watt's eyes in the mirror.

"Double nickels" is trucker-speak for "55." Two fives, two nickels, double nickels. "On the dime" means getting something exactly right, getting it on the money. They were driving at 55 mph, right on the money. *Double Nickels on the Dime.* Genius. His car was a VW Beetle. Janey's VW '72 Squareback had a very similar dashboard. Hence I was triggered.

We pulled off the freeway and started climbing. The houses fell away, and we pulled into a small road in scrubby parkland. The sign said: *Tecolote Canyon*. We got out and started walking up a trail. We didn't say anything for a while. I was just breathing in the spicy air. She was walking ahead, faster than me.

After a while, she turns and says, "I'm sorry, I must be a fast walker."

"I think I slowed down when I came here."

"California will do that to you."

She waited for me, and we continued up a shallow hill, on the sandy path. It leveled out, and we continued on a long straight path that was tree-lined and partly shady. It was good. I was enjoying being there. Then for a second I wondered what she was thinking, and that made me feel less at ease.

"Hummingbird," she said, pointing ahead. The little guy was darting in and around the branches.

"Oh yeah. We saw them in San Francisco too."

I looked over at her, from slightly behind. Her short hair at the back of her neck was tufty. I only looked for a second though. Like when looking at the sun, I didn't want to rest my gaze.

She turned to me as she walked.

"I don't have drums, you know. We'd just have to find things I can hit."

"We can find things. George has a garage."

"How old are you?" she asked me.

"Twenty-four."

"Ok." She let that sit for a second.

"Do I seem younger or older than that?" I asked.

"Both," she said.

"How old are you?" I asked.

"Guess."

"Mm . . . Twenty-waa . . . Twenty."

"Twenty-three."

"Ok. Twenty-three. Good for you. You look good."

She snorted a laugh.

"I look good? For twenty-three?"

"No! I didn't mean . . ."

"I'm just kidding you," she said. "You look good too."

"Thanks."

"I like that you're my age, almost."

"Why's that?"

"I think I meet too many teenagers, or too many older guys who act like teenagers."

The road turned a corner and dipped down.

"I think there's a creek down here. We should put our feet in, while there's water in there."

"Oh, ok."

We found a spot in the sun and picked a rock each to sit on. The stream was a little emaciated, but there was enough water to get the nature feel we were after. Janey's feet were outdoor feet, good feet. They were neat, tanned and sinewy. My feet were beat, white and pudgy.

"You know that guy Eric?" she asked.

"Yeah. Eric driving the truck."

"He's my boyfriend."

"He seems like a nice guy. That was a big truck."

"Yeah, he's proud of his truck. How old do you think *he* was?"

"Mm, twenty-three, twenty-four maybe?"

"He's thirty-four."

"Thirty-four? He's like a little pixie."

"I *know*. And *he* knows. He's like a little laughing pixie."

She was still light in the heart, but I wasn't sure where this going.

"He uses his pixieness though. He's no angel. He's a sprite, like Peter Pan, hopping from leaf to leaf."

"From flower to flower?"

"Not just the flowers, he liked the nuts too."

She laughed. I didn't really know what we were talking about.

"What are we talking about?"

"I dunno."

She looked at me over the rim of her sunglasses.

"Did you guys really come here to get warm?"

"We did."

"And are you?"

"Not entirely. I can't imagine a heat that will ever be enough."

"Florida in summer."

"I'll never go there."

"Why?"

"Cos it's Florida."

"Hey, that's my home state!"

"So go home."

"There's good things about it," she protested.

"Ok, I believe you. What about San Francisco? In the summer, does it get warm?"

"It can be warm, but it can be windy and cold. It's weird, there's a fog that comes in and then it's instant fall. But people like it. Some people."

"Foggy people."

"Yeah, people are drawn to that city. It cools things down, people go inside, people do art."

We looked at our feet. Mine pudgy and pale, hers brown and sleek.

"Would you go back to art school if you had the money?" I asked.

"Honestly, I would. I feel like I only just started learning, like my capacity to learn has opened up. I've been diddling around for a long time."

"I diddled."

"Yeah? What happened?"

"I wasn't satisfied. I felt guilty."

"Maybe you should go back to college."

"Nah, I've had my three strikes."

She put her arms over her knees, then rested her head on her knees. She looked at me and smiled a smile that wasn't punky or cool or wry. It was a straight smile.

"In Scotland college is free. My ex was at art school there," I said.

"They have a good one?"

"I think it's pretty good. She might actually be an artist when she grows up."

"Was she young?"

"She's twenty-one."

"So in Scotland everything is free? Like haircuts and dentistry?"

"The dentists are, not the haircuts."

Janey leaned back while the sun was out and closed her eyes.

"There was a girl used to sneak into the Art Institute," she said. "She was there a whole year before anyone realized she wasn't enrolled."

"Was she good?"

"I don't know. All I know is that after class she used to climb into one of the crawl spaces in the roof of the building. She had a mattress up there."

"And they didn't know?"

"She used to life-model too, so I guess they may have turned a blind eye."

"Are you sure about her? She sounds like a person from a super-hero story."

Janey stood up. "Are you doubting me, Stephen? Are you doubting the power and determination a woman can have?"

"What was her name?"

"Sabrina. Sophia. Sukie. Does it really matter?"

I didn't know if she was messing with me.

"It doesn't matter. It's a good story."

"She's real! She's still there. Up in that attic. Painting and mod-eling. Dancing and then . . . sleeping. Right there, in the building." She reached forward with her hand to pull me up. "C'mon, let's go."

We headed back. I didn't ask Janey any more about Sabrina/ Sophia/Sukie, the Spirit of the Art School, but I would be sure to look in on her when I got back to San Francisco.

31

Hillcrest

The next day I was back on the Mission Bay side, in a sunny spot, with a tape bought from the Krishnas, and my Walkman, listening over for any more wisdom. I noticed the monk said a trigger word for me: "sublimation." I listened back to the tape and what he said roughly was "The practice of devotional service sublimates our desire."

Sublimates our desire. That word again.

Back in the eighties, before I got sick, I was a confused person. All they did at school was scare the crap out of you for even thinking about sex. Sex leads to pregnancy, sex leads to misery, sex leads to AIDS, sex leads to death. Pretty much the line we got. It wasn't even so much the sex bit though. I didn't dream about it; I didn't particularly crave it. I just wanted to hold somebody's hand. My best thing when I was sixteen or seventeen was just wondering what it would be like to lie next to a girl in bed. Not do anything, just lie there. Consensually lie. Be accepted in a lying posture. With clothes on. That's all I really wanted to do. I never got the chance. I never lay beside anyone.

I fancied a barmaid at Butlin's. I worked at this huge holiday camp for three whole summer seasons. I had different crushes every time, but this one time I was working in the bars too, so I got to work beside this girl. I didn't want to snog her, or bed her, or grope her, or any of the other phrases that you might expect to come from the mouths of men of around that age. I just wanted to be her friend. I just wanted to hear her laughing, away from the heightened atmosphere of a teeming Scottish holiday-camp bar. But it never happened.

I suppose I could have asked her out on a date, but that was hideous, I'd tried that. This one time I made it on a "date," the girl sat back and expected me not only to have read the manual but to have work experience too. And I'm not just talking about kissing here. Or *making out*. I'm talking about just *being* with someone. I was too awkward. To be honest, I get why girls often drift towards older guys, because the older guys know what to do, they know how to drive, they know how to put a person at ease. Maybe? I don't know. The bottom line is that my early attempts at romance were rubbish, so I gave it up. I gave it up through sixteen, seventeen, eighteen, nineteen, twenty. In fact, up until Vivian, the last time I kissed someone I wasn't related to, I was thirteen.

Like I said, I had read in a book about sublimation. I can't remember the book. It might have been *Jane Eyre*; it might have been Proust; it might have been Nabokov. I can't remember the source. But it made an impression. I can remember looking up the meaning in my dictionary: *Divert or modify an impulse into a culturally higher or socially more acceptable activity.* So, this was a thing. I could divert. I could make my lack of success with women a "higher, more acceptable activity." Back in '88, I would take an idea and quickly run with it. In those days of bedsits and back-court windows, I was as impressionable as putty. Now I was sublimating. How long was I going to do it for? Didn't matter, let's just go along.

It made me feel slightly more involved and important now that there was a name for what I was already successfully doing—not having sex. Masturbation was another issue. But that felt so tawdry and lonely that I was already thinking that I should reduce the frequency. I worked on that. As well as stumbling on the idea of sublimation, I'd also heard about the straight edge scene from punk and hardcore groups in the States. I loved Fugazi, and I think it was the singer's previous band, Minor Threat, that spawned this "movement," seemingly accidentally, by writing the song "Straight Edge."

I can imagine why it turned into a movement. Young men like me didn't need much to get with a movement. If you are in the least bit leaning towards a habit or a way of thinking and there's a hint of a movement around, you will jump. I never called myself "straight edge," but sitting in my bedsit listening to American hardcore, never drinking, never smoking, no sex, no meat, never taking so much as a paracetamol . . . I mean, what was the difference? Sublimation, pleased to meet you.

Now I look back at the laugh-a-minute days of '88, I can see I was heading for trouble. Sublimate by all means, but you better really know yourself. You better know that your dogma will make you happy. I didn't really know what I was doing. I was trying to make my tenuous existence . . . plausible. Wouldn't it be great if someone came along, looked you in the eye and said:

"I know who you are;
I know what you're trying to do.
It's not all bad.
You're not a bad person.
But do 'these' things, and you will be . . . plausible."

And then they would proceed to give you some really good advice, every word of which you would store and use.

So I was up near the rollercoaster, heading back to our place, when a man approached me. He looked rough, like Charlie Manson. Rougher, in fact. Like Charlie Manson pulled through a hedge. The reason I made the Manson connection so clearly is that the man happened to be wearing a t-shirt with the aforementioned mass murderer pictured. So there were two Mansons coming towards me. Two Manson heads. One on the t-shirt, one on the person.

"Get back to Hillcrest, you faggot! Fuck off, get out of here, I don't want to see you on this street again. Go and suck someone's cock in Hillcrest, you fucking faggot!"

This was the first time in America someone had been out-and-out unpleasant. I'd had plenty of that back home, but it was informative to know where I stood Stateside. Not everyone was super-cool and groovy, even in California. My next thought was . . . Hillcrest. *Let's go check out this Hillcrest place.* It was a safe bet that wherever Hillcrest was, this guy, and maybe others like him, were not. I got the bus over there; it was away from the beaches, north of downtown. I settled into the bus groove, at the back, nose to the window.

I got off on the main drag. I didn't even have to ask where to get off; there was a nice, friendly *HILLCREST* sign traversing the main street. I got out and walked real slow up one side, crossed, and came down the other. Bookshops, a record shop, a cool little cinema and a couple of restaurants and cafés mixed with other busy storefronts of a more generic American "Main Street" vibe—a furniture store, a bank. I eventually settled on the coolest-looking café. This was way different to a standard American diner. I'd seen this kind of café, and it was definitely there for a different purpose. For a start, coffee seemed to be a BIG deal here. This was a "coffee shop," but coffee was the actual star. And people seemed to be treating it with a certain kind of reverence.

There was a queue at the counter, not for cakes, or beer, or pizza or rolls with egg. People were queuing for coffee. The people that were working there were doing weird things with the coffee. There were many choices as to what you could do with this steaming black liquid, and the people in the queue were making many of these choices. I heard the word "latte," I heard someone say "decaffeinated." I knew "cappuccino"—we had that back in Scotland, via the Italians. I saw things happening with steamed milk, I saw things happening with soy milk. There was also an enticing row of syrups. I saw vanilla, hazelnut, caramel, cinnamon.

"Hi, honey, what can I get you?"

"A black coffee, please."

"Espresso or drip?"

"What?"

"You want it from the espresso machine or just the house?"

"You choose, whatever's easiest."

"Ok, house it is. It is nice coffee though, we have the best beans."

She turned to get the coffee. The next song that came on in the café was a step up in volume. The server immediately turned to her female colleague with a dramatic face-to-the-ceiling childlike despairing gesture.

"I hate this song. How come Brad has this on the playlist? It's no good. Someone should tell him."

"I know, it's tragic. It reflects badly on *you*, it reflects badly on me," the other server agreed.

"I mean, do *you* like this music?"

She was coming back with the coffee, and she was asking *me*, which was surprising. It was modern American rock. The guy was singing "Two princes, princes who adore you, / Just go ahead now."

"Um . . . I can't say it's really my thing."

"You see," she said to her colleague. "*He* knows, and he's not even from here. Where you from?"

"Scotland."

"Ok, Scotland, this one's on the house." She handed me the coffee.

"That's very nice of you. I would like a muffin though."

"A muffin? We have muffins. What kind? I'd recommend the bran and raisin."

"Then that is what I will have."

She went and got it.

"I'll have to charge you for this though. We don't like you *that* much."

I laughed.

I sat down with my muffin, suddenly with a little sadness. Nothing dramatic, just some standard melancholy left over, still coming out in slow waves. Here I was, in a coffee shop far away from my point of origin. You would think the depression would have had the decorum to leave me alone on this miraculous, sunlit morning. Overall though, I was heartened, not frightened. There were too many good potentials happening. I liked Janey and wanted to see her again soon. I wanted to be beside her and chat to her and confide in her, and all at the fast-forward speed of an American, which also happened to be the speed that an enthusiast and a . . . I didn't know what to call the next thing. I'm not a disabled person, though some with ME are. Am I an infirm person? Probably, but that's still not a term you'd like to throw about.

Whatever I was, I was in a hurry mentally, even though my processes were slow. I didn't want the small talk; I wanted the big talk. I wanted to make up time emotionally, intellectually. Musically. Maybe I should do a concert? In a place like this? I looked around me. There were no booths, there was plenty of space here, it would take nothing to push aside a couple of low tables, make a semicircle with the mix of assorted armchairs and dining chairs and stools that people were perched on and draped over. I sat back in my plush red velvet chair and pondered.

"He didn't even pay for utilities. He never paid for *anything!*"

Two men behind me were having a conversation, and, this being America, you could hear every word. Here, it seemed like people didn't mind personal stuff leaking out into the café-sphere.

"I was in thrall to his penis," the first man said in conclusion. "He met someone else on the golf course, can you believe that? You know he caddies up at Riverwalk."

The second man replied, "It's a target-rich environment, that's the trouble, being with buff golfers all day."

"What am I, Leonid Brezhnev? Just because I'm not swinging my balls all over San Diego."

"You know what, you are right," the second man said. "Fuck golf and fuck Garth."

I could hear the smile kindling in the first man's voice, though I wasn't looking at him.

"Let's go get drunk."

Man number one started getting up. Number two followed him, and they brushed past me. They were both mid-twenties, I'd say; jeans and t-shirt. I would have said they were both pretty "buff," if that meant fit-looking. They were ok, they were going to get drunk, they were seizing the moment. Fuck golf and fuck Garth. I tended to agree with them. My dad had been a golf fanatic and that had pretty much put me off that whole scene for life.

Back to my thoughts. What would I need to do a gig? It could be just me and Richard. It would be more fun if Janey played drums though. If she was going to play drums, I'd need someone on bass guitar or else there would be a big hole in the sound. I thought for a second and looked around the place. There was a noticeboard, a community thing with local ads. I could put up a notice there for a bass player. A bit of a shot in the dark, but you never know.

I went over and took a flyer for a local theater group and wrote on the back:

BASS PLAYER WANTED FOR POP GROUP.
PHONE STEPHEN

And I left them the George/Poppy number. I asked the server behind the counter if I could pin my notice.

"Sure thing, just don't cover anyone else's. And stick a date on it."

"Do you ever have shows in here? You know, gigs?"

"We don't. Not really. It's more of a poetry circle vibe in here.

Sometimes someone will play an acoustic guitar, but we don't have any speakers."

She looked at me with an apologetic scrunch of her face. I posted my note on the board, right on the edge, hanging off. That looked about right; that's about how much I belonged to this community.

*****

"Are you Stephen?"

Here was a young guy, slim and wide-eyed.

"Hi, I just saw you put your note on the board there."

He sat on the chair next to mine, perched at the end.

"Are you a musician?" he asked.

"No, not really. I'm just starting out."

"And you want to form a . . ." He looked over his shoulder as if he needed to reference the notice. " . . . Pop band?"

"Um, yeah. I just thought of it since I came in here. I have a few songs. I thought I could get up in a place like this and sing them."

"Wow, you would just do that?"

"I don't know, I'm just thinking about it. Are *you* a musician?"

"I like music. I'm studying it at the moment."

"At college?"

"I'm still in high school. I finish this year."

"Is this not a school day? I mean, I don't know how it works here."

"I have an 'art in the community' module, so I usually just come in here."

"Wish they'd had something like that when I was at school," I said.

"Where did you go to school?" he asked, relaxing back in his chair somewhat.

"It was in Scotland, where I'm from. I'm just visiting here."

"Oh, that's *awesome*! I've never met anyone from Scotland before. It's next to Ireland, right?"

"Pretty close."

"And you came here to escape . . . the bombing?"

"Ha! No, I came to escape the cold, amongst other things."

"You know, I could play bass guitar for you. I'm learning guitar as part of the module. There's a bass in the store, I could probably pick it up fast."

"You could play bass? You just saw my notice right now and you think you could play bass? I'm not going to refuse that offer. That would be a dangerous offer to refuse."

"Alright then," he said, and leaned over to shake. "I'm Samir. Sami."

"Ok. I'm Stephen—as you know. This playing thing, it probably won't last too long as I'm not going to be here for long, just a month. Hope that's ok?"

"That's ok. It'll be a good experience for me. Art in the community." He looked off to the middle distance and said reflectively, "I'm finally doing something. This is great."

32

Riding on the Equator

I'm on the mattress next to the sofa. I just woke up. I can't see Richard, he's over there somewhere. We have the sofa between us, so we each have a "land." At least he is a quiet sleeper, that's crucial. I hope I am a quiet sleeper; I think I am. I always wake up in the position I fall asleep in, even though I wake up quite often. I reach over and put on my headphones. Hopefully quiet enough that he can't hear it. I put on Felt; I put on a track called "Riding on the Equator." I want to set a groove in my mind for the new morning, and this is a great track for that.

Felt, for me, was one of those groups that I stumbled across in the eighties but stuck with me. They came in like so many other guitar groups at the time, the jangly ones, the ones that had guitar sounds the color of copper and amber and refracted gold on a late September morning. You know those bands? You know those guitars?

Well, it turns out I thought you knew, but maybe you didn't. Falling for Felt was like a paperchase in which I was giddy, breathless, caught up in the thrill of the music and the running. Everyone liked music, everyone liked guitar music, everyone liked soft, poetic guitar music, everyone liked vocals spoken not sung, everyone liked a guitar melody that went on forever, without resolution or explanation, played over three chords, positions 1-4-5. Everyone liked record sleeves with no band name on, often just soft, unfocused patterns.

But the thing is, you didn't. Every time I made a statement in the last paragraph I lost half of the people, or three-quarters of the people or nine-tenths of the people. They all went the other way. Not everyone likes music, not everyone likes guitar music, not everyone likes soft poetic guitar music. In my enchantment there was an assumption that everyone was with me, but they were not. At every narrowing of my category of likes, I lost most of you, until on my musical paperchase I turned and looked back. It was a copper and amber morning in late September, and I was standing alone in a silent wood. My hair was wet with the chase and my breath smoking just a little, but I was completely alone. And that is how I stayed.

But it didn't matter to me. My relationship with the music became more fierce and desperate. I needed those three chords to keep tumbling over each other time and again. I needed to hear about the waiter and the caravan and Panama City and "the best woman you ever had." I didn't know what you were thinking when you wrote that, Lawrence, but I didn't have to know. I didn't want to know. It was *my* dream now, it was my journey. *I* was riding on the equator, I went there and back again. I was wearing Panama hats and I was your foreign correspondent. And I didn't even have to take my headphones off.

Every time the song finished, I died a death. Every time the song finished, I woke up a different person. I looked around the woods and no one was there; there was never anyone there. But that's ok. I knew back then that if I wanted to, with a bit of effort, a bit of resolve, I could find the paperchase again. I could listen and listen and follow the long tendrils of sound back to the last place I saw a person, back in sunlit July, in a gap in the trees, and from there they could show me back towards life and the mainstream. But I was happy in my solitary place for now. I let the song finish and I didn't even dare to think I could make music like that. I let the song finish, and thinking on my own plan for music was like looking at an emaciated acorn compared to the forest Felt had created.

What did I have? A few scratchy songs, uneven, unsure, a bit cringy. A gut-string guitar between two people. One could play well, one could hardly play. A promise from a schoolkid in a café, and a tenuous nod from the punk Jean Seberg. Maybe it was something. As I thought about it, I liked the uncertainty of it, I liked the possibility, and I liked the unlikeliness of it. Unlikely groups, unlikely meetings, unlikely sounds. What about the Pixies? How did those guys ever get together? In '89 I loved that band like no other, and they actually played at the place I worked in. It was the most exciting day of my life. It wasn't just about Black Francis, it wasn't just about Kim Deal, Lovering or Santiago. It was all of them, and it wasn't *just* about the sound. They didn't look particularly "cool," and that's what made them cool.

I don't know who answered whose advert, but I bet that's the way it happened. They didn't look like they went to college together, they didn't look like lovers. They looked and felt like four average citizens, four newspaper readers who got lucky in each other's presence. But that's what made it magic. Ordinary people touched by magic. I could be wrong about this but hey, this is my music. Give me the story, not the facts.

The waitress in the café had recommended another place where I could do a little show. It was called Café Chabalaba. I went round there and spoke to them, and they said we could play on a Friday afternoon in a couple of weeks' time. They wouldn't pay me anything, we just had to advertise it, but they would have a small PA set up in the café area.

I was having all these thoughts, then I heard Richard get up. A little later, we were both sitting at the table eating our Wheaties. Not saying much, just munching and reading about this guy Ken Griffey Jr., who was a baseball player for the Seattle Mariners. The information was all on the back of the cereal box.

"Can we practice today?" I asked.

"I'd rather not today," said Richard.

"Ok. Maybe tomorrow then. I was going to see if Samir could come around and bring his bass."

"How about the weekend?"

"That only leaves a week before the show."

"Oh yeah. Listen, I might go down to Tijuana for a few weeks."

"But not until after the gig?"

"I don't know, I'm not sure. I might just go."

"I booked the café for the Friday!"

"Yeah, I know. I didn't ask you to though."

"I thought it was a good idea."

"It's quite a good idea, I suppose. For you. I'm not so sure I want to play though."

"Why not?"

"It's not really my thing. Not like it is for you."

We went back to our Wheaties. It's funny that I felt at that moment a little like I felt when Vivian had finished with me. Depleted and helpless. I hadn't seen this coming at all. I just assumed he wanted to play; I really liked his guitar playing. With his classical picking it was a bit like the way the sound was colored in for Felt. I was back alone in the silent wood. I had lost the rest of the paperchase.

33

Practice in the New World

When I go to sleep at night and when I wake up, I get these funny moments when my mind gets loose and starts racing. Not in a worried way; it doesn't go over and over the events of the day. It just feels like, if it was a dog, I had let it off the chain and it was gone. It does its own thing for a few moments. But in those few moments it shows me images and people and feelings and art and music. It races by like someone flicking the pages of a color shopping catalog, but a color shopping catalog from Venus.

I accept these moments, but I thought I'd take a second to note it down. It's almost two years ago that God crept into my mind, ushering in a firm notion of eternity and a hint of what I should be doing about it. It's almost two years ago that I found I could formulate music, and the experience of music coming from "nothing" was quite similar to how God crept in. Now, I'm observing that there is a chasm in the mind that appears at bedtime and in the morning that appears to show different worlds and memories that I never lived. What is that?

Maybe for just those few seconds a day, when the mind is loosed and limber, it takes you and shows you a pool of collective memory. Maybe you get to see other people's thoughts and experiences? Like when you used to tune a radio at night and you slipped in between a myriad of European voices. If the mind is meant to go on forever, like the Buddhists suggest, then maybe we get a hint of that forever-ness in those nebulous seconds. For certain, there's more going on at this present moment than just your conscious thoughts — your tea, your heartache, your sofa, the view from your window.

The mind is an uncommon thing.

Janey and Samir came round yesterday. It was fine and it was fun, but the effort of actually having people come over and making them tea and trying to keep up with them and being social to a limit expected by normal human standards is still so hard. I think about them now and they are so appealing. It is so nice to have bright and active people in your life. The talk is rare and funny, Janey so positive about everything, Samir so delighted to be doing something that actually constitutes "art in the community."

He followed me slowly on the bass guitar he brought round. I was actually still working on a song called "Soccer in the New World," and when I played a bit for them, I had an idea for a new place it should go. This involved playing a chord I had never played before. Samir was particularly interested in this process.

"So you don't know what the chord is?"

"I can hear it in my head."

"And it's not one you know already?"

"I don't think so. I thought I had tried them all."

I tried a few more shapes. Richard was watching on, and he maybe could have helped me, but he was sticking to his "you can play the piano, it's the same thing" rules. I eventually found the chord; it was an A-flat with a sixth in it, leading to an E-flat with a seventh in it. Samir was impressed.

"This is great. You're making it up as you go. That's an impressive way to learn an instrument."

"It's a *slow* way to learn an instrument," I said.

"He's not really *learning* it," Richard pointed out. "He's just using it."

"Yup, I predict I will never really learn the guitar."

From that point on, I gave the guitar back to Richard. Samir said he would liberate a six-string electric from his school cupboard for the next time. I went back to singing and playing this little fan-blown battery keyboard I got from Toys"R"Us. It sounded a bit like a harmonium, one that you would blow. We got through "Your Confirmation" and "Soccer in the New World," we played a bit of a traditional Scots song called "Green Grow the Rashes" (in the style of a version by Scottish group the BMX Bandits), and we tried to remember as much of the Kim Wilde song "Kids in America" as we could.

Samir was fine on the bass. He was sticking rigidly to the tonic note of the chord that either Richard or I played, not trying anything fancy, but that was working. (Aside: the tonic note, or the "home" note, is the signature note of a chord. If you heard a chord and were asked to sing a note along with the chord, this would be the note you would be inclined to sing. So what Samir was doing was underpinning the chord I was playing, giving it depth and fullness. If you want an example to check out, listen to any AC/DC song. Cliff Williams is mostly playing the tonic, but everyone is glad he is. Check out "Riff Raff," for instance. He takes a while to come in, but when he does, he comes in on the tonic, and sticks to it, with a few jiggy bits. I picked that song at random, but it's a good one. Enjoy yourself.)

I liked Janey's drumming. She was just hitting a few upturned basins and buckets from George and Poppy's garage, but she was hitting them right, heavy and steady. She had a sleeveless shirt on and was just beaming and having a good time. The racket we made reminded me in small instances of a group called Dolly Mixture from the early eighties. They were an all-girl trio I had on a tape someone made me. After we were done, we stood outside the G&P house, in the little in-between street that we lived on. We chatted for a bit, then Janey said she had to go. She came up and gave me a kiss on the cheek. I must have looked at her a little bemused; startled, even. I'm immediately thinking, *What does* that *mean?* But she looked back steadily at me, then gave Richard a farewell kiss on the cheek. I'm sure she would have kissed Samir too, if she hadn't been driving him home. I would be analyzing that kiss later on, when the world was quiet, when outside stimulus had been subdued.

The next day finds Richard doing his yoga, and me on a bus. I'm looking for a record store. This is a typical morning for me. I'm like one of those old folks in beige you see riding tourist coaches. I'm well aware that I've become old before my time. I've given in to it, lowered my expectations. I'm stuck marveling at the moving world from my seat at the eternal plate-glass window of life. The record shop I was planning on visiting was way out in La Mesa. According to the ad in the free paper, it specialized in rock and pop memorabilia, t-shirts and posters. As the bus got going, I could tell from our progress on the map that it was going to take a while. I settled into my journey.

I had mail from home. I had a letter from Mum and a letter from Carrie. I had saved them up for the bus to give me something to read and absorb. The sentiment from my mum's letter was mostly relief. She was so glad to hear that we were doing ok, that we were settled in San Diego. Nothing much seemed to be happening at home. My dad had read the lesson in church, and that had gone ok. My mum had moved back to day shifts at the hospital, which was a relief. The dog had kennel cough.

Carrie wrote a bit more. She was amazed and glad at our progress and was keeping her toes and fingers crossed for us. She admitted that she missed us, that life was even slower than usual. She had been fighting with her mum, nothing more than minor irritations, but in the events-starved world of ME, the tiffs had left her wounded. I felt sorry for her because I knew that if I was there, we'd be able to laugh that stuff off together. I missed her for those moments on the bus. I allowed myself to miss the slate gray of Glasgow for a brief reverie. I imagined the cozy dusk and spotting rain-kissed marginals at the checkout queue of the Byres Road Safeway.

Carrie had reported that the Artful Dodger, a brief addition to the Byres Road café scene, had closed its doors. We had only gone there so that we could hipster watch. It had the best window in Glasgow for that, but the man who ran the place didn't know what he was dealing with and didn't know how to exploit it. He was a ferrety little man, unctuous towards his few customers, desperate that they stay and validate his business and his life. He poured the tea himself, each table being served with a different kitschy teapot, some in the shape of cottages, some of fruit. Our favorite was a teapot shaped as the head of a cartoon lamb, wearing a hat and a bow tie. We secretly, quietly rooted for the lamb. We didn't indicate our preference, but we knew if we got the lamb, good things would happen.

Anyway, the Artful Dodger had closed. It seemed that, without me, Carrie hadn't gone in so much, and without Carrie, the whole operation had folded. Carrie had taken the mighty Quinn there, the big Irish doctor. But mostly he just wanted to tell Carrie that he was going to stop seeing her, at least in a romantic sense. What other sense was there? It's not as if she was going to bump into him around the wards of his hospital. I felt doubly sorry for her. I felt sorry for the thing with her mum, the thing with her man, the thing with the café. That's trebly. We could have laughed off the café, laughed off the argument with her mum, but the Quinn was a tricky one. I just hoped her sisters were rallying round.

The bus rolled on. The buildings got lower. The space between buildings got wider. The occasional empty lot started showing—basically, wee bits of desert that San Diego hadn't spread to. We went under freeways and over freeways, through residential bits, past a few schools. We even passed the rarest of American institutions, a post office. But I let it slip by. I am in transit torpor. I just have to sit here. But it's ok. I got the sun through the window. I got my legs. Got my arms, got my fingers, like the song says. I got life.

I read a story somewhere about an athlete. She trained so hard, running was everything to her. There was a huge race in a stadium, one that she'd been building towards for years. She felt good, she felt like she would win. The race was harder than she thought, she was bogged down in the pack. When they broke for the last lap, she went with the leaders, but as they approached the last bend, she felt them stretching away. She had nothing left; she faded. She ran from the stadium after the race, lost and inconsolable. She ran, and her body and mind were separated in madness. She ran, she jumped over a barrier in a car park and fell three floors onto concrete. She was crippled, her beautiful legs smashed to pieces.

That was the end of the news story. I don't know what happened next. But I think about that girl, that athlete, that woman. I had it all a few years ago. I had health, energy, opportunities, freedom, friends, family. I was driven, but I didn't know where I was driving. I was pulled apart by forces. If I couldn't be the best, if things didn't go my way, I got angry, I got frustrated. Maybe I had to be laid so low to start seeing the beauty again. My fall lasted a year and a half rather than the two seconds it took her to fall three floors. In my unconscious crumpling, in my protracted collapse, I was protesting against life.

Life had pulled me back, it had tried to show me the error of my ways. Now I see the good stuff, now I see the possibilities from a different place. I feel so fortunate that I didn't die three years ago. I've got the rest of my life to make up for my mistakes. I was saved for something. I hope to God that the athlete eventually realized that she was saved for something too.

After an hour on my sleepy, empty bus, I got to the place where the record shop was meant to be, but it had shut down. I waited in the sun and the dust for a bus back.

34

The Nabisco Cats

The Nabisco Cats?" said Janey.

"Yeah, why not?" I answered.

"Why Nabisco? Why cats? How about . . . Quaker Dogs?"

"It has a significance."

"Tell."

Janey wasn't exactly digging the proposed band name, but she was mostly just feigning indignation, I think. I tried to tell her the reason for the name. Carrie and me had a joke that her younger sister was cooler than her—her sister always knew the right things to say, knew the right people, she was number one. She was the Kellogg to Carrie's Nabisco. Janey cracked up laughing.

"You know, like 'Original and Best' on the side of every Kellogg's box," I said.

"Yeah, I get it. It's funny you guys sit around aligning yourselves with crappy cereal companies." She reflected. "So we're the Nabisco Cats. We're the losers, we're second best."

"We're plasticky and make-do. We're the cats you call when you can't get the other cats."

"What's going on the flyer?"

I took a little sketch out of my pocket. It was a picture of a cat with a man's head. The cat/man was playing guitar.

"No cereal?" asked Janey.

"No, just this guy. With the guitar," I responded.

"He kind of looks like Oscar Wilde."

I looked at the cat man.

"It's not intentional."

"Must be subliminal."

"Oscar Wildcat, I'll call him."

"Good one."

We went into the printer's and created our little flyers right there on the counter. The guy working there was young and hip. You could tell he fancied Janey, and she did her thing. Suddenly our flyers went to the top of the pile, he would go to work on them right away, he could fit us in, and we could wait there in the office. Once we had our flyers—printed A6 size, black ink on light green paper— we took them into Café Chabalaba and laid them proudly on the counter. The person who I was dealing with before was almost a little surprised that I had followed up on my request for a spot in his café, but, again, the Janey magic seemed to be working. Everyone wanted to believe anything the girl said. Her believability rubbed off on me, and suddenly I was plausible.

Now we had the fun task of putting out the rest of the flyers, of knocking around downtown San Diego together, deciding which coffee shops, record stores, dry cleaners were worthy of our flyers. We became king and queen of the disco for the day. With our scruffy piece of A6 paper, we deign to bequeath coolness upon you. *Come to our fiesta and escape!* After we had hit a few spots, it was clear Janey was just getting going, just warming up. I was already lagging. I needed to sit down for a while.

"Can we take a break?" I asked.

We were in a falafel place. I wasn't sure if we were going to garner much support for the gig from there, but I liked the way our flyers looked beside the pictures of Lebanon and the Levant.

"You hungry?" she asked.

"Not yet. Just want to sit for a bit."

I got into a booth and leaned up against the wall, trying to morph into recovery mode. I'm not sure she was fooled. She went up to the counter and got some water.

"Are you *ok*?" she asked sincerely.

"Yeah, I'm good."

I have noticed that a sudden lack of dynamism in me can freak people out. She didn't seem freaked though. That was good. She sat with the free paper for a while. Then she looked at the menu. Then she looked at me. Then she looked back at the menu.

"I'm getting something—this looks good. Want me to order something for you?"

"Sure, I'll have what you're having."

Janey was up at the counter for a while. I appreciated being in this place. Maybe I would feel better after food. Trouble was, I didn't feel hungry, I just wanted to lie down. But if I could trick my body into taking on fuel, ingesting sustenance, then maybe I could spark a revival. Also, I felt "better" around Janey. I felt like her spirit was helping to carry me. I could have loved her for that alone. I looked around. It was half past three, a classic in-between time. America doesn't care though, it's usually ready to serve you whatever time of the day or night it is.

Suddenly, this booth, and the café beyond, was an officially recognized ME/CFS sanctuary. And as I sat there, I actually thought about designing a shield with those words on it and sticking it up on the doors of places I sanctioned. I thought about the lettering, I thought about the color, the motif. Janey came back and got me out of my design daydream. She produced two falafel plates, with hummus and salad and pita and other good stuff.

"Maybe I should paint you?" she wondered.

I wasn't sure whether she meant painting me a specific color, to blend in with the surroundings, or painting me on a canvas.

"You can paint me anytime. That's one job that I think I'd be quite good at."

"How so?"

"I'm good at sitting still and doing nothing. Plus I can project a feeling, and keep doing it." I made a sort of pitiful face.

"It's ok, I'll take the neutral face, thank you."

"Seriously though, I'm your man."

"Ok."

She smiled, and I wondered whether my response was a bit too keen. But then she was helping me with my music. Surely it was ok for keenness to be reciprocated. We ate our falafels.

"What other jobs do you think you could be good at? If the musician thing doesn't work out?" she asked.

"I think I would do anything," I replied.

"Like, become a soldier?"

"Maybe not that, though there was a time I did think I could be one."

"Really? Who did you want to kill?" she asked.

"I didn't want to kill anyone. I just wanted to get away."

"Why didn't you go?"

"Too young, too clueless."

"So what did you do?"

"I hid in my bedroom."

"And how did that work out?"

I thought about it. I held up my hand and counted out each word with my fingers.

"Bad, middling, good, bad, really bad, terrible, ok, bad again, then . . . now."

"Oh wow, that's an album right there, dude. I take it that all took a while to happen?"

"Yeah, a number of years."

"And now?"

"Now, I'm not sure. Some good days, some not so good. More good days. Today is good."

"I'm glad to hear it, Stephen."

I took a sip of my water, then asked her, "What about you? Ever hide in your bedroom?"

"Like, for a few hours at a time. When I was fourteen or so. Just trying to get away from my parents, my brother. Then I went outside, and I never really came back."

"Where outside?"

"In Florida, you could do everything outside if you wanted. My friends and I were pretty bratty. My friend Michael had a car, even though he didn't have a license, and we just went around in that. Swam, smoked weed, skated, played saxophone."

"Saxophone?"

"Yeah, really. I was Lisa Simpson before Lisa Simpson."

"Where did you play?"

"I didn't play in a band, I was mostly just messing with it. They gave me a few lessons at school to get me going, but it's pretty straightforward to play. I used to take it to the park nearby, and when I was confident enough I would play it when my friends were there."

"Do you still play?"

"I brought it out here from Florida, but I don't get it out so much. I think it suited me playing it there—no one was listening, or if they were, it was like 'Wow, is that a saxophone?' I feel like if you start playing in San Francisco, you better be good. People are more discerning."

"That's a pity."

"It was my Florida thing. I was Saxophone Girl."

"I have such a narrow view of Florida. Somewhere between Disney and *Miami Vice*."

"There's actually much more to Florida, I like my home state. But yes, beaches and theme parks and drugs and murder, that's the headline. We used to drive to Miami and hang around the beaches. One time, a group of us were out late. We spotted these guys at the shoreline and thought we could go down and give them shit." She laughed. "Like, 'Hey, mister, you know it's not the best idea for you to be out here at this time. There's a lot of bad people around.' That kind of thing. They looked kinda surprised to see us, and then I sort of recognized them. It was Duran Duran!"

"Ha ha, really? What were they doing there?"

"I don't know, but it was the eighties . . ."

"They didn't want to party with you?"

"No way, we definitely came across as brats. They didn't hang around for long."

We finished our falafels.

"Ok, what you wanna do?" she asked.

"What do I wanna do?" I replied.

"Yeah, you're the boss."

"I know a spot that's pretty good. Can I take you somewhere?"

We circled back to get Casper from the parking lot, and I tried to remember the way back towards the youth hostel in Point Loma. Between us we worked out how to get pretty close, and we turned into the neighborhood I remembered walking in when we first came to San Diego.

"Here—you can pull over here," I said.

We got out the car. It was quiet enough, the streets still smelled their perfumey and flowery best.

I led the way towards the dark end of the street. The street ran out, but there was a trailhead into the scrubby trees, which we followed. It was getting dusky again, but I found that particularly relaxing. I love being out in the dusk. I think it has a similar effect on me as it does when you put a blanket over a parrot's cage—it just relaxes me, an inbuilt reaction. Instead of flicking off a light in your room, it's like the day is tugging at you, flirting with your body clock, saying "It's ok, this is how you are meant to feel. You are built into this day, you are meant to be here."

"What are you thinking?" she said.

"I'm just thinking about the light. I like it."

"Me too."

"I always like dawn and dusk. They're much more interesting than the rest of the day."

"Yup, they should put in something for around noon, to look at. Like a solar eclipse," she suggested.

"Every day?"

"Once a week. On a Friday."

"Nice. Who wouldn't like that?"

We came out of the trees, and we were at my spot, where the land fell away and the lights of the airport were right there. I put my coat down, and we sat on the grass.

"I'm surprised no one else is here," I said.

"Everyone's down at the beach applauding the sunset," she said. "This is better."

The first jet moved quietly towards us out of downtown. Then it whined and blasted past us, tucking its landing gear away.

And there we sat. I hope you realize how gallant I was being by letting us sit on my coat. It was a bit cool up there by this time, and usually I'd be clinging on to my layers. But it was worth it. We had to sit close, after all. I could feel her warmth, I could smell her smell. She was letting me sit that close; there was no awkwardness, she accepted my proximity. There's a bit in the film *The Breakfast Club*, near the end, the makeover scene, where the goth girl asks the prom queen, "Why are you doing this?" And the prom queen answers, "Because you're letting me."

I thought about that moment. *Why are we doing this?*

She was letting me, that's why. I was scared to move in case she shifted or got up. I soaked up that modicum of heat from the boys' Lyle and Scott jumper she wore and the scruffy canvas khaki of her thighs. I looked at her feet, and that's where her movement went; it was the only bit of her still moving. But her feet were moving in slow, concentric circles, and you could guess the shape of her feet inside her flimsy Converse. It felt like a cat twisting its tail slowly in satisfaction and comfort. We sat there and let the day disappear completely. The park vanished around us, and the lights of the city took over.

Two fleeting souls sitting on a coat, looking at the airport and the dusk.

35

Question Answer

So here's what is happening with the gig.

Richard is staying to play; he isn't going to Mexico until next week. Phew.

Samir is meeting us there and bringing the other guitar.

Janey is also meeting us there, and she's actually on the trail of a basic second-hand drum set. Bonus.

Me and Richard are going to get the bus into town.

I'm feeling pretty wiped out, but we're not turning back now. Richard is very relaxed, but then he's not as invested in this. These are my songs, and I'm singing them. We ride the bus and get into the café in plenty of time. It's quiet, just a few people having drinks, coffee. Samir shows up, but he is a little crestfallen.

"I couldn't get the guitar, just the bass. Someone else has taken it for the weekend. No one ever takes that guitar, but just this morning it disappeared."

"It's ok, we'll manage," I say, but I'm already getting a bit of a bad feeling about the day.

The guy that was supposed to help us set up is not exactly helpful. It's like he is totally uncommitted to his duties. I don't think they often put on shows this early.

"Are you sure people know about this?" he asks me.

"We advertised it, we made flyers."

"Yeah, but do you have friends coming? Does anyone know you?"

"Not really."

"I wish I could have brought the class down, but it's still a school day," Samir chips in. "I would have had to get permission."

"O . . . k . . ." the guy says in an ominous way.

He goes back to reading his magazine at the bar. Richard sits and plays classical guitar on a stool. Samir looks for somewhere to plug his bass in; the guy says he will plug him "straight into the desk," but he's going to wait for the drums first.

"I'm not sure the drums will really need amplification," I offer.

"They'll sound pretty lame. But whatever you want."

He goes back to his place at the bar. There's no sign of Janey. There's no sign of anyone. We're meant to be on in half an hour. I want to disappear. I want not to be here. It occurs to me that this is the first thing I have organized since I got ill. I mean, I guess I helped organize the ME group. And I did organize selling all my records. That worked out ok, but this is the first time in years I've done anything musical. Maybe my organizational powers have gone the same way as . . . my power. Maybe I was *never* any good at organizing things? Whenever I arranged my own nights with bands that I loved, I always lost money. I just picked the band I loved, picked a place I loved and gave them the soundtrack I thought they would love by playing records. I dunno, maybe I'm just too niche.

I sat fidgeting with the jotter with my lyrics in. Samir smiled. Richard kept playing his pretty arpeggios, completely unruffled. Maybe he knew what the deal would be all along. Or maybe he was ready for any eventuality. He did seem to float through most things. He's probably going to float right through ME.

While I was thinking this stuff, showtime arrived. I hadn't rushed the guy to get the rest of the gear set up. I hadn't rushed to do a sound check with the limited line-up we had. I could have done, but I didn't. There was no one there and I just wanted to go back to the beach house. I didn't want to sing. I didn't want to raise my voice in song. Who was I kidding?

"Hey, I'm sorry this isn't working out," Samir said. "I was really looking forward to playing the tunes."

"Yeah, I'm sorry too, Samir. I think I overestimated something."

Even though I was harassed, tired and in a bad mood, I think it would have been better if "something" had happened and we got to at least play the songs. If there had been one person to listen. But it was just the sound guy, sitting at the bar. There weren't even any other customers; they had moved off when they saw us setting up. We packed up to go, and we were just considering sharing a cab when Janey came rushing in. She was properly vexed.

"Did I miss it?" she asked.

"No, you didn't exactly miss it," I said.

"Have you played?"

She was gulping down air, with a bag on each shoulder.

"No, it wasn't happening, no one came."

"Oh my God!" she said, almost in a half whisper. Some of her panic deflated and turned into indignation.

"Are you ok?" I asked.

"I'm ok. The car broke down—Casper broke. I was halfway here, I had to find a garage and find a cab. My stuff is out on the curb there." She gesticulated.

I almost thought she was going to cry. I thought, *If she's going to cry, I'm going to cry. I'm due a cry, we can just cry together. We can find a corner away from the non-cryers.* We didn't cry though. Samir called his dad. He came and scooped everyone up. He was nice. I sat in the back with Richard and Janey. She was in the middle, and I held her hand where we were squashed together. It was meaningful handholding. I felt like I was getting a lot of new information about her through the hand; it was as if we were exporting information and feelings to each other. Solidarity? Companionship? Relief? Loneliness? Comfort?

Definitely comfort. Offered and received.

"Samir, why don't you ask the guys to come by the school? You can play a little concert for your classmates in the music department," Samir's dad said. It was nice of him to think of that.

"May-be . . . ?" Samir answered. "I mean, *I* would like it. I'd have to ask Thornton and Baggley, get them both onside," he continued.

"You've been talking about music in the community and found art for a while," said Samir's dad. "Well, you found these guys. In the community. What could be better?"

"Ha ha. Yeah, maybe they would let this count for some of the exam . . . I'll ask them. If it's ok with you guys?"

I looked around, and the car seemed to be in general agreement.

"Yeah, fine. Thanks," I said.

I took my thumb and was rubbing it into Janey's hand. I pretty much did it all the way back to the beach. Wonder if that was too weird? I held Vivian's hand, though I'm not sure I held it like that. But I don't think it was to do with her. I think my handholding capacity had increased in the time since. My handholding game had come on in leaps and bounds.

Samir came through. He asked his teachers if he could present us as part of his ongoing assessment for environmental art or music or something. He said that they were happy to have us if we didn't mind answering some questions about where we were from and how we got together. I said that sounded fine, and Richard was going to hold off going to Mexico until the next day. This time we planned to get there extra early.

We got there at twelve and set up in the performance space they had. Brad the tech guy was there to help us, and I got to play the electric guitar that had been promised before. After playing the gut-string acoustic exclusively for the past month, the electric felt smaller and therefore easier. I tested the microphone, checked that it didn't feel weird. I could hear myself ok, there was no need to play loud or anything. We jammed along together for a bit, and it did feel a little ramshackle, but not too bad, I thought, considering.

The students came in and sat on the bank of benches. Some of them looked keen, some of them were just there because they were there. That was ok. I didn't find it weird at all. I relished the forensic nature of this gig—it was more like a show and tell. We said hi to the teachers, Miss Thornton and Mr. Baggley. We used the titles "Miss" and "Mr.," but they honestly didn't seem that much older than Richard and me.

We started with "Your Confirmation." I came in with a lightly chugging guitar. It was so nice to play. The amplification and the effect on the guitar made it so you didn't have to do much at all, it made you sound alright. Janey was tapping around her drum kit, just following, not really hitting a beat. She was using her cymbals for atmospherics. Samir was sticking to those home notes, with a little syncopation. Richard was playing very little, just waiting for his moment. It was cool, they made a space for me, for my voice to step easily in.

> *"I wore a dress to your confirmation*
> *Stood beside you and wished you heaven*
> *Are you ok?*
> *I lost my head in the ritual and wine"*

Janey sang in answer to some of my lines:

> *"Oh, and I should have known!"*

I don't know what she should have known, but I liked that she was singing. Brad had given her a vocal mic. Richard eventually came in, filling out some of the sound, picking out a few sinuous parts. We built the sound up together and we finished all at the same time. That was kind of lucky; I wasn't sure what was going to happen at the end of the song.

"This next song is by a poet from Scotland called Rabbie Burns. He died about two hundred years ago. He wrote very keenly on the subject of women. This is his song to them. He calls them 'lassies' in the poem. It's called 'Green Grow the Rashes.'"

Richard harmonized with me on this one, which was much more upbeat than the first one, and seemed to go ok. I could tell that our performance so far was dividing the audience somewhat. There were a few people who were engaged in the music, a couple even that were quite taken by it. The rest seemed a bit bemused. I was just happy this was actually happening and that we were playing. Even Richard seemed to be enjoying it. The next piece was him playing solo. He played a thing called "Mood for a Day" by a guy called Steve Howe in a band called Yes that we had both loved back in school. It was his party piece. There were a couple of trickier sections that he simplified, I think, but it sounded really good. He could really play that guitar. He got the biggest applause. I looked at Samir and Janey, and they had their mouths open.

Next we played "Soccer in the New World," and we tried to find that space that we found in the first number, and it was ok. I tried not to be *too* earnest, but I think I probably came across as pretty earnest. Finally, I handed Richard the electric, I used my little battery keyboard, and we played a very shambolic version of "Kids in America." I'm not sure if those guys had really heard the tune before, and if they had, they weren't sure if they could get behind it.

And that was it. Our funny little show had happened. Five tunes—hopefully we hadn't outstayed our welcome. We came and sat in chairs closer to where the audience were. Miss Thornton stepped in.

"Thank you so much to the Nabisco Cats, featuring our very own Samir Kassis. I thought that was wonderful. Now, do we have any questions?"

"How did you guys get together?" a girl in the audience asked.

She was one of the people who had been really engaged in the performance. I spotted her straight away. Her diligence had made the performance worthwhile. Samir told her the story of me and him in the coffee shop, and Janey told her how we had met in San Francisco. She made it sound like I was a bit of a weirdo, but not in a bad way. I suppose in a sense I was. But the stories seemed to amuse the people. I'd be willing say they were better received across the board than the music.

"I loved your drumming. You don't see many girl drummers, have you played for long?" another girl asked.

"Mm, not too long. I did play at school, then I didn't have access to a kit for ages. This is the debut of my new kit—it's nice to be playing again, thank you for having us."

"You're so rad!" said the first girl.

"Thanks," said Janey, her eyes smiling.

"So, Stephen, the songs you wrote, what were they about?" Mr. Baggley chipped in.

"Erm, I'm not sure. Disappointment? Dreams? Desire? I think when I write the words, it's what I would say to an invisible friend and to no one else."

People chuckled at that.

"I suppose if you can't be honest in a song or a poem, or even when you are painting a picture, then what is the point?" Mr. Baggley added hopefully. Think he got it about right there.

That afternoon, as I said goodbye to Samir, he pointed to Janey and said, "You should really be a couple. I mean, even I can see that."

36

Oh, the Places You'll Go!

I'm trying to come off my anti-depressants. I just came down to a half dose, which means I take a tablet every second day. I started this a week ago, but already I'm getting these little jitters, short flashes like electric shocks in my brain. I think that means they're loosening their grip. I don't feel like marching up a hill and shouting "I'm cured!" of either the depression or the ME, of course, but something is happening. I did still wonder, when we were singing our songs yesterday, if it is possible that I can entertain these people—or any people? Can a sick person really entertain? Surely they will feel my impermanence? Surely they would prefer to be in the hands of a non-invalid?

I still felt like a bit of a charlatan when I was performing, like I was going to get found out. I'm always on the lookout for creative people who were sick. Apparently, Robert Louis Stevenson was fragile his whole life. Sylvia Plath was depressed, of course. So was Dostoevsky. Proust had something, didn't he? The Brontës were plagued by failing health . . .

I woke up feeling bad and a bit panicky. Richard left for Tijuana yesterday, so it's just me. My arms felt numb, I felt dizzy, I felt weak, I had to lie down again. Isn't that a thing, when your arms are numb? Dizzy, fainting, that's no good.

I called Janey. "Can you come? Erm, I need to see you, can you come over?"

She was a little mystified, took a little persuading, will have to change plans with her "family," but . . . she's going to come. I start to relax a bit now that I know she's coming. I sink back into my bed sofa and listen to *Victorialand* by the Cocteau Twins. I think I listened to the whole album, but then I must have dozed off. I heard faint knocking, then I noticed that my tape was jammed at the end of the side and I clicked it off, got up and went to the door.

"Hi. You look sleepy!"

I must have looked pretty bedraggled. She came in. She gave me a little kiss on the cheek on the way past. This was the first time she had been in our dumpy little space, but it felt ok, I didn't feel like I had to make it look presentable or fuss around.

"You want some tea?"

"I would have some tea," she replied.

She sat at the kitchen table and watched me. I was moving slow, taking my time. Eventually I sat down.

"Are you ok? You seem a little fragile this morning," she said.

"I *was* feeling queer this morning, that's why I called. Thanks for coming over."

"That's ok. What's up?" she asked.

"I was feeling pretty weak and dizzy, like I was going to faint, so I thought it was best if I called someone."

"Aw, I was your someone."

"You were my someone."

"And how you feeling now? Better?"

"Well, I feel better now you're here."

"But you're still feeling dizzy and weak."

"Yup."

"You want me to take you to the hospital?"

I thought about it for a sec.

"Don't you have to have a leg hanging off to go to the hospital?"

"I don't think so. You don't have a cold or flu?"

"No."

"And you didn't eat anything suspect?"

"No, it's not that."

"Well, if you feel bad and you don't know what it is, then you're probably safer getting it checked out."

I took a drink of my slightly bitter rosehip tea.

"I do know what it is."

And I proceeded to tell her about ME, and Richard and Carrie, and the reason for the trip and everything, bar the breakdown stuff. She sat listening patiently, asking a few kind questions along the way.

"I mean, if you don't mind me saying so, you don't *look* so bad. And I never really suspected you of being sick."

"Yeah, I guess it doesn't really show on the surface. If you spent a lot of time with us, you'd see how our day was. We creep away to rest a lot. If I was meeting you, I'd save my energy up."

"Thanks."

"You're welcome," I said.

She got up to put more hot water in her tea.

"So you and Richard are on a mission?"

"We're on a mission. Partly we came to California because we thought they might have a cure, or at least better treatment."

"They have ME in California?"

"Oh yeah. There's a lot of it, you just don't hear about it. It's not a very dramatic condition, it doesn't get in the news."

She paused for a second like she was considering.

"Ok," she said, jumping up. "Let's do something healthy." Then she froze. "I mean, if you're ok with it?"

She looked at me slightly anxiously, as if I might just crumble like a sand statue.

"I am in your hands."

I really meant it as well. I wanted to be in her hands. She came over and rested her hand carelessly on my shoulder as she thought. It's funny, here was this slight, punky girl from Florida, we hardly knew each other, but I was in her pocket, if she wanted me.

"We can go slow. You can tell me more about ME or whatever you want to talk about. You want to go for tacos?"

We drove the few blocks to the fish taco place. It was breakfast for me, but I figured the protein would do me good.

"So how did you pull this thing off? How did you pay for the trip?"

I told her about the fact that we were still under the doctor's supervision, that the state paid us a weekly stipend and that we managed to receive it while we were in America.

"Wow, that's amazing the UK is unknowingly sponsoring your trip. It's a liberal dream."

"I did sell my records to get here too. So it was partly a liberal, partly a capitalist venture."

"I congratulate you for embracing both ideologies for the common good."

"It was for my own good."

"But I'm glad you made it. Samir was too."

The sun came out and warmed our skin and bones.

"So how was your love life back in Scotland? Good? Are you popular? People love that stray puppy thing." She had that mischievous glint in her eye.

"I'm not a stray puppy," I said with genuine surprise. "I don't have that thing. At least, I don't mean to."

"Trust me, Stephen, you got the puppy thing. It's like your paw is in a sling."

"I didn't mean it. I wasn't aware I was giving that vibe. And if I was, it hasn't been doing me any good, at least not in Glasgow."

It crossed my mind, a thing Frankie from the crew said to me once—"Whatever it is you've got, use it!" I didn't know that the puppy thing was a thing or else I'd be using it.

"Ok, sorry. Does the ME make a difference with relationships?"

"It makes all the difference. I dunno, it's not like I had that much luck before, but I've been out of that particular game for ages now."

She looked like she wanted to say something. "Does it affect your . . . your ability to . . . ?"

"No, not really, nothing so dramatic as that. More just a long slow abstinence brought about by not being at the party."

"Stephen, you have that British way of talking. I'm not sure what you mean."

"Ah. I'm sorry. It's just that things seem so different at home. If you were there and I was there, you wouldn't be talking to me."

"I'd be talking to you!"

"Maybe, but you'd be doing a million different things."

"I'd still be talking to you."

I paused to think how daft this conversation was. I decided to drop my proposition.

"Janey, I accept that you would, and I'd be glad of the company. I'd be really chuffed if you talked to me."

She laughed her laugh—a snort, then a chuckle.

"Ok, I know, I'll take you to La Jolla. It's peaceful, there's a beautiful park."

"I could go to a park."

So we drove off. On the way she was talking about how she was getting on with her friend's family—how Alicia's family were more well off than any family she'd ever known. How she kept saying the wrong things at the wrong time, but she thought it was ok. The kids seemed to like her, and as long as the kids liked her, she was in. We pulled into the car park. It was quiet, no other cars around. It was a weekday, in the afternoon. Just as we pulled in, it started raining big heavy drops on Casper's windscreen.

"How long does rain usually last here?" I asked.

"Could be a few minutes, could be an hour. Could be three days."

"We're stranded."

"Looks that way."

It did occur to me that this might be a good time to try and kiss her. She was just sitting there like a pudding. How do you do this again? I was all belted in. If I took my belt off, would that be a tell? I can't stand the tell, can't stand the telegraph. How is this meant to go? I took my seat belt off. I looked at her neck. I thought, maybe I could just put my head on her neck. So I did that. I leaned over and headed for her neck. I nuzzled in. I went for the nuzzle. She put her hand on my head or my neck, somewhere. I nuzzled a bit more, then the next thing I'm brushing my lips on her neck. I did it lightly. I liked doing it. I did it for a bit. She still had hold of my head. I brushed her neck, her cheek, her ears, even, with my lips. She started doing something similar. She was taking her chance, dragging me with her lips, brushing lightly over skin. I could feel it. We were both at it.

The rain tapped on the windscreen. It covered us over like a blanket. It encased us in her funny old car. I didn't really know where to go next. I'd only kissed Vivian, and a couple of girls at school a long time ago. I sometimes think sex is like a fight in the playground. Where does it stop? How much are you meant to hurt the other person? It escalates. Like kissing and making out. *It* can escalate. Where's the limit? Does it always have to end in sex?

She paused and looked at me. Then we touched lips. I wasn't expecting it, so my mouth was still closed and kinda dry. But we got the little shock you get from touching lips. At least *I* did. I was getting big breaths of her smell. I think I could smell her more because she was warmer. That would make sense in a scientific way, convection and all that; the inverse square law. We kissed more on the lips, this time our mouths opening, blood flowing more, more heat, more moisture.

And then we stopped.

We looked at each other. She smiled.

"Hey, the rain's stopped. Shall we go?"

"Ok."

"We don't have to if you're tired."

"No, I want to."

We got out and began slowly walking up a wide trail that was really a road, but there was no traffic. The sun came out strong, and soon the road was dry. Everything smelled really good. I was taking in big wafts of spring flowers and eucalyptus.

"Dr. Seuss lived here."

"Really?"

"Yeah, look at the funny palm trees, don't they look like Dr. Seuss trees?"

"Yeah."

"He lived here. He drew them. This place definitely affected his drawings."

"Is he still alive?"

"I think he just died. Last year. Or the year before. He lived at the top of one of the hills here." She pointed vaguely in the direction away from the ocean. "Alicia's little brother Josh has one of the last books he wrote. It's called *Oh, the Places You'll Go!* We love to read it together. It's like a manual for life, his last will and testament."

I sat down on the curb.

"I just need to sit for a bit."

"Sure thing. Can I see your camera?"

I took my old Olympus out of my bag.

"No wonder you're tired, this thing is solid."

"It's a well-made piece of machinery. I call it 'Old Faithful.'"

"Can I take a few shots?"

I lay on my front. The grass was still a bit damp, but I didn't care, I was glad to be on the ground. It was only then I appreciated how peaceful this place was. When you get away from cars in America, it makes a big difference. I opened my eyes and noticed she had the camera trained on me.

"*Oh no.*" I lifted myself onto my elbows and screwed up my face at the prospect of being snapped.

"The pickings are rich around here," she said as she took a few more.

"I don't want pictures of me," I said.

"You'll thank me in a few years. You look good."

I got up and we walked on again.

"So, your ME, do you think it defines you?"

"What do you mean?"

"If you had a label round your neck, would the ME be up top, in big letters?"

"I don't want it to be. Probably more on the inside. It still gets to me."

"I didn't know you were ill before you told me. You could get away with it if you wanted."

"That's what we do, we sneak by. It's a game of how much can you do with the least energy. We arrive last, leave first, take breaks, go off alone, sit down first, disappear without warning. It's basically a disease of no manners."

"Hey, if you ever tell me you need to go off, I'd get it."

"Thanks for that. But you're the exception. You can stay."

We took a smaller path. It was bushy on one side but on the other we could still look down over La Jolla to the sea about a mile away.

"What about you, what's on your label?" I asked her.

"Ha ha, mm. Artistic, opportunistic, high functioning, comes with drum set. A free girl in San Diego."

"Free?" I asked.

"I travel pretty light. I'm not tied down."

"What about your family?"

"Yeah, I feel sorry for my brother. He's stuck with those guys for now. My mom and dad are going through a divorce. I think they waited until I was gone and my brother was almost gone to have the divorce. Then our house burnt down last year. That was the last straw. It was almost poetic, the timing and everything. It was like, there goes the house, there goes the marriage."

"Do they know what happened?"

"No, they couldn't work it out, but to be honest I wouldn't be surprised if someone set the fire deliberately. My dad had some pretty shady connections, real assholes."

"Did your brother want to come stay with you?"

"He hinted at it, but he's still got his Florida thing going on, he's got some good friends. And he always got on better with my mom than I did, so he's doing a good job staying with her. Hey, look at this . . ."

We had come to the edge of a little pond. There was a small wooden pontoon there. It was still dead quiet, no one around.

"I would go for a swim."

"You'd swim in there? It's probably pretty cold." I looked closer. "I can't see through the water, could anything be in there?"

She laughed. "In Florida we swam with snakes and alligators. There's nothing in there."

She sat on the deck, I sat down with her. She started taking her shoes off.

"Really? You going in?"

"Let me just dip my feet in." I took my shoes off too, rolled up my trousers, and we sat side by side with our feet in.

"What do you miss most?" she asked.

"About home?"

"No, about not being sick."

"I don't know. There's a part of me thinks this was meant to happen, like it was a big wake-up call or something. I really want to get better, but I don't want to go back."

"That's good. You shouldn't want to go back. You need to keep looking around the next corner."

"Around the next corner . . ." I repeated lazily. "I miss not being able to live carelessly. I know that's when interesting things happen. Just not thinking about things too much. You don't want to have to think about every moment like you're wrapped in cotton wool. You just want to be in it."

"Are you in it now?"

"Yeah, pretty much."

"Ok, I'm going in."

"Really?"

She stood up. She took her jeans off. She took her cardigan off, her shirt. She started taking her bra off. She was fast. I didn't know whether I was ok to look, so I just checked it all out in my peripheral vision. Pants off, and there she was, naked, lowering her tanned, slim, boyish body to the edge of the dock, two legs over, elbows bent, down and then gone.

"Ooh, wow, yeah, it is cold!" She panted a little as she trod water. "But it's good."

She started effortlessly swimming round. The water wasn't clear, so I only got glimpses of body when it came near or broke the surface. She just took her clothes off in front of me. Either she just does that, or she feels pretty comfortable around me. I hope it's the latter. I could sense that she might be generous with her nudity around other people, but I wanted to think it was just for me.

"Are you coming in? I'll keep you safe."

"I may be safe, but I'm ok here."

I didn't know what the protocol was. I could go in, but I'd keep my pants on. Was that unfair? Think I'll just stay here. Oh bugger it. I stripped off down to my underwear and lowered myself in. It was cold, a little shocking. What was I doing? Showing off.

When I surfaced, she said, "Maybe this will help you!"

"Help me how?"

"Get the blood flowing, kick-start something."

I knew that wasn't how it would play out, but I didn't hold it against her for saying that. I swam up close to her, and she was beaming in her usual ebullient way. She certainly looked like she was in her element. I trod water close to her, wondered for a second if we should or could try to pull off a midwater kiss, but then I suddenly felt queer. My arms weren't doing what I wanted them to, I couldn't feel them so good. My legs felt draggy. I didn't feel good at all. She got it straight away.

"Are you ok? Maybe we should get out. Come on, I got you."

We made our way back to the bank; she helped me to clamber out on the side. It was muddy, a bit slidey till we got to the gravel. We went back to the dock and I kinda collapsed there. I probably looked like a frog, one you find squashed on a path. She grabbed my clothes, wrapped my hoody around me from the back, then fairly wrapped herself around me also, like the blanket they give people when they're in shock.

"I'm sorry, Stephen! Oh my God, are you ok?"

"I'm ok, I'll be ok."

I could feel my heart beating hard. Way harder, I thought, than this enfeebled body needed. I thought at that moment, where was all that energy going? *If my heart is beating like a racehorse, how come the rest of me feels like a landed jellyfish?*

"Argh, I'm so dumb, putting you up to that after everything we talked about."

"No, really, it was my own choice," I responded in a small voice. "I just wanted to try and keep up with you."

She kept the holding position, and she bowed her head into the back of my neck.

"Ok, you're good, you're safe, your body's recovering. It had a bit of a shock, but now it's fine. It's safe, you're safe, everything is good. This is part of the healing. I'm healing you."

She gave a hard squeeze. We stayed like that for a minute or so.

"You should do this for a living," I said, only half joking. "People would pay for this, really."

She laughed into my back.

"This is a service only available to certain people," she said, somewhat muffled. "Let's go to my place, it's close by. I think the guys will be out. We can sneak round the back and get dried up and warm."

We pulled our clothes on over our wet bodies and got back to the car fast. I was still shivering.

She didn't have to drive far before we were in streets of quiet housing, more of the big spread-out bungalows that I'd seen before. She turned in at a gate and it started to open magically in front of us. We drove up a curvy front drive to a pretty house in pretty grounds. I could've said garden, but it was way bigger than the standard garden we're used to in Scotland.

"That's good, nobody's home, no cars. I'm at the back."

We walked round the garage, walked through the back garden and came to a little outhouse, like a cottage. Inside there was a lounge/kitchen/porch area that she was using for painting in. There was painting stuff all over the place.

"I'm just getting started," she said.

As she headed into the back somewhere, I looked at the sketches. It was everyday stuff—palm trees and road signs and buildings and kids running around, all very southern California. I liked the feeling of it all. She was back quick; she had a towel wrapped around her.

"You wanna get dry?" She held up a towel for me.

I nodded. I did want to get dry, but I wanted to stay and look at her in the towel. It was a pretty scene. She threw the towel. I went into the bathroom. I started stripping off. I started rubbing hard with the towel, trying to get the blood going again.

I looked in the mirror. I had the towel around me, I was still pale and disheveled. Would she want to see me like this? Is something going to happen here? I put my hand down on the towel at my waist and felt around down there. There was nothing much to speak of, no life, no action. I think it was still in shock from the plunge in the water. I gave myself an extra hard rub with the towel. She came to the door.

"I got a few things," she said.

I opened the door. She looked in the crack and smiled.

"Everything ok?"

"Everything is fine, thanks."

"You still look a bit blue."

She came in the bathroom, got another towel and started rubbing my chest. She stopped to give me a little kiss under the shoulder. Then she rubbed some more, got a little closer. She put the towel on the rack, put her hand around my neck, and we kissed.

I stopped. "Are we ok here?"

"I think so. They don't usually bother me out here. I think they will be out for a while longer anyway."

We started kissing again. I was stalling. I wasn't sure I could really remember what to do next. I hugged her closer and put my hands on her backside, still covered with the towel. In a microsecond, she unhitched the towel at her chest, and it fell away. There she was, naked, cuddling into me. She looked up at me.

"You wanna go on the bed?"

She grabbed me and we went to the bedroom. She quickly dragged the curtains closed over the floor-to-ceiling windows. The curtains still seemed pretty see-through, but I guess it was going to be harder seeing in. And there were trees and bushes close enough that we were protected from all but the most prying of eyes.

I was surprised it had come to this. Sure, she had been flirty in a warm and hip way, but I didn't know the American rules. As much as I knew of America, the way she acted could have led to us being good friends, pen pals, bandmates, or she might just have been leading up to selling me her car. Who the hell knew? Sex was never a given. Not until she dropped that towel did I think, there's going to be sex at the end of this.

I really liked her. She was beautiful and kind and smart. We had talked and talked and now we were in a secluded pool house at one of the ends of the world. She lay on her front but then turned towards me and propped herself up on one elbow.

"Is this wise?" she asked.

"I don't know. It feels ok," I said.

"You're going to go away soon, is it really a good idea?"

I thought it was a good idea at that moment. I wanted to live day to day. I thought that if we were going to be separated for a while, we should have this thing in common. I didn't think beyond that.

37

Janey and the Kids

So we did it, and we came at the same time. I'm not giving myself any credit here, I'm sure that was down to Janey knowing her own body and everything, but it was nice to cross the line together. We lay for a while, pleased with ourselves for pulling off this international tryst. We jubilated quietly about the closeness of bodies, about the finality of skin meeting skin. This made everything alright for the moment. I wasn't thinking about leaving—this was only the beginning, life was just getting going, someone somewhere had fired a celestial starting pistol.

I think we would have stayed there a long time, and let the dusk fold in on us, and we may have done it again, and taken our time, and then talked and talked, and had showers and drinks, and listened to music, and dressed up and danced, and done the things that people do when they are alone and happy for the evening.

But then the family came home.

"Shit!" Janey said, jumping up.

She ran into the bathroom. I heard the tap running, the toilet flushing. She came back out.

"Sorry, Stephen, you need to get up. I've got to go to the main house to take care of the kids; it's better that you come with me and say hello."

I was wondering why all the rush, but then I guess she didn't want them to think she was hiding someone in the pool house.

"I'll come back for you in a minute."

She went off. I got up and got cleaned up and dressed.

When she came back, she said, "Ok, the kids are named Josh and

Naomi, they're nine and eleven. Their mom has gone back out, but you're ok to stay and entertain them for a bit while I make their dinner."

"I can do that."

We went over. The advertised youth were there, they existed. They were in the large open-kitchen/family area. The girl was already hard at some drawing at the counter, while the boy was flipping channels on the massive TV in the lounge area.

"Hey, guys, this is my friend Stephen."

The kids said hi. Naomi looked up and smiled at me. Josh kept watching TV.

"Ok, I'm going to make you . . . raw poodles and cabbage for dinner, is that ok?"

"Noooo!" they both cried.

"Ok, thanks, it'll have to be baked bicycle tires again with chocolate sauce."

"Nooooooo!" This sounded like a ritual.

"Mac and cheese, with sausages and . . . salad?"

"Yeeaa . . . ?" They sounded unsure as to whether this was a serious offer or another dud.

I thought Janey was serious this time. "That sounds delicious!" I said, to add some enthusiasm for the cause of dinner.

"Josh, maybe you could leave the TV a second and talk to Stephen. He's from Scotland. Do you know where that is?"

Josh looked at me properly for the first time. "Is it near . . . France?" he guessed.

"Not bad. Really not that far away. Have you ever been to France?"

"No, but we're learning about it. In geography."

"Have you ever been to another country?" I asked.

Josh thought about it for a second. "Texas!"

"That's still part of America. But it's pretty far away. What did you do in Texas?"

"We went to Aunt Mimi and Uncle Brett's."

"I bet that was fun."

"They had puppies, and mine was called James."

"Your puppy was called James?"

Naomi commented from the kitchen without looking up from her drawing. "I told you it was a silly name. That's not a name you give a puppy."

"Did you have a puppy too?" I asked her.

"Yeah, mine was called Priscilla."

"Priscilla the puppy."

"Yeah, but we had to leave them in Texas."

"Do they still live with your aunt and uncle?"

"I'm not sure," said Naomi. "They said they might have to go live in another house with another family."

"But they said they were going to still be James and Priscilla," said Josh. "When they went to the other house. There's a picture of them on the fridge."

I went over to the fridge, and there was a picture of the two kids with about five fairly big-looking puppies of a hound variety.

"There's five puppies here."

"Bruno, Pooch . . ." said Naomi.

"And Chrysler!" said Josh, laughing.

I watched Janey in the kitchen, preparing food, moving around purposefully. I wanted to go rest my head on her neck, but that would not have been wise. But I went over to her and said to her quietly, "What if you're pregnant?"

"Then I'm having your child," she said without pausing what she was doing.

"What will we call it?"

"Well, Pooch and Chrysler are already taken. Any ideas?"

"What about Hurley?"

"Hurley's good. Like George Hurley, the Minutemen drummer."

"Exactly."

But then I really thought, *What if she is pregnant? What are we going to do? Where will we live? How will I work?* I think she could sense my rising panic. She brought a plate of food to Naomi, then to Josh.

"I'm not pregnant. You're fine," she said to me in passing. She came back and gave me something, a little gold biscuit-bar thing. It said *Tiger's Milk* on the wrapper, with a picture of a tiger. "Eat that," she said. "It's a protein bar, full of good stuff. I don't want you to feel . . . depleted." She smiled.

38

Luna at the Casbah

L una's playing at the Casbah," Janey said.
    "I know," I said.
"It's sold out."
"I know."

Luna had formed from the ashes of a group called Galaxie 500. I loved Galaxie 500. I had seen them first onstage supporting the Sundays at the Queen Margaret Union. I didn't know who I loved more that night, the already beloved Sundays or this hardly known American trio of soft surfers who blew us all away. I democratically put it down to one of the best nights of my roadie life and loved them both the same. Luna had released their first LP, *Lunapark*, late last year, and it was one of the few tapes I had with me; it had sort of become the soundtrack to the trip so far.

"We have to get in," she said.

"Can you get us in?"

Janey only knew of the drummer from Luna, who was called Stanley Bukowski or Beroski or something . . . Demeski? That was it. He used to drum with the Feelies, and she loved the Feelies, especially the drummer of the Feelies, her being a drummer, and so she loved this Stanley guy. So we really had to get in. (Her favorite drummer was Georgia Hubley from a group called Yo La Tengo, by the way.)

We showed up at the heaving Casbah on Saturday night. I had a plan. The music paper the *NME* had given out a collectible set of playing cards free with four consecutive editions. One week you got the hearts, the next spades, and so on. The cards pictured what the

NME conceived to be the fifty-four most important musical pop artists historically and contemporarily. They put a different picture on each card.

I really liked Rod Stewart—you know, Rod the mod, Rod from the Faces. He was the jack of spades; there was a picture of him looking his seventies best, wearing silk, shades and a silly grin. For some reason I put that card in my wallet and carried it with me for good luck. When we got to the Casbah, we went right to the front of the queue and asked for the guest list. I figured I would turn the card around in my wallet—the reverse side of the playing card had the *NME* logo printed white on black.

"I'm here with the *NME* to cover the Luna show," I said in the broadest Scottish accent I could muster.

The doorman looked at me, looked at Janey. She was just smiling away, and she looked amazing.

"That's the UK music press," I added.

"Are you on the Luna guest list?" he asked.

"I just got in from London, I don't think we had time to arrange that."

"Well, do you have some sort of ID?"

I fished out my wallet and showed him the card. He took it out of the wallet and turned it over. I thought the game was up. But he looked at the picture, he looked at me. I guess I might have been grinning inanely, a little like Rod in the picture.

"Ok, Mr. Stewart, you can go in."

We didn't hang around. We ran into the venue, and when we got far enough in, Janey let out this whoop of glee and laughter. I guess Rod wasn't as well known in San Diego as he was in most other places. The support band were on, they were called Trumans Water and they were angular and obtuse in just the right sort of way. We liked them. We got a seat at the back of the club when they were done, but really we were just sort of perched because it was so packed. Right in front of us a little scene played out. There was a young wild-haired kinda feisty girl who seemed like she was a little wired. She bumped into a guy, then turned on him.

"Watch what the fuck you are doing! Are you stupid? Didn't you see me?"

It was a bit ridiculous and unprovoked. She was prodding this guy, shoving him, and he was rightfully annoyed and bewildered because he had just been standing there with his friend.

"Don't fucking touch me," she said as she got in the guy's face and was pushing *him* back.

He put his hands up, one of them holding a beer bottle. "Can you *please* just back off?" he said in an exasperated voice.

Right then, out of nowhere, a guy flashed into the scene, followed by another guy. The first guy knocked the bottle out of the bewildered guy's hand, then punched him pretty hard on the head. The bewildered guy went down. The second guy started pushing the bewildered guy's friend around, while the girl stood over the bewildered guy, still yelling at him, calling him "bitch" and "pussy." The three "attackers" moved on pretty quickly to another part of the crowd. We waited for a moment for them to clear away and then we helped the beaten guy. He just sat there on the floor for a minute.

"Fucking assholes," he said as he rubbed his head. We got him on his feet. Someone gave him a beer. "Fucking assholes," he repeated to his friend.

The whole episode was over fast though. It was like the scene when Alec Guinness cuts off the man's arm in the bar in *Star Wars*. There was a ruckus, everyone looked, but then they returned to their own business quickly afterwards and the band immediately started playing again.

Luna came onstage. They said hi and went into the first number, which was called "Anesthesia," my favorite from the LP. We got to the front of the crowd so we could see everything; in fact I sat on a part of the low stage, and no one came to yell at me. The band played pretty much all of the debut LP. I guess if that's what you have, that's what you play. I really liked the whole record, so it was fun for me to hear it. It occurred to me that they would make more records and that they might only ever keep a couple of these songs in the set and that they might never play most of these again, so we were lucky.

At one point, the singer, Dean Wareham, looked out over the crowd. "There's a mirror on the back wall here, and I can't help looking. I can see the band playing, and I was watching me play during the last song. Now I'm in the middle of an existential crisis. Maybe this isn't what I'm meant to do with my life?"

The crowd shouted "No!" and "Boo!" to confirm that they approved of what the band were doing and that they should keep doing it.

"Ok. Well let's do a cover of someone else's song, maybe I'll feel like less of an imposter. This is one by a singer called Evie Sands. It's called 'Take Me for a Little While.'"

They played this song, so sweet and simple and soulful. Dean had a natural falsetto that he flirted with, but he used it to good effect on this song, which I loved. They played a bunch of covers throughout the set, but it never felt like padding. I remember his previous band Galaxie 500 played some covers, and they had people scrambling through their collections to see if they had the originals, so great were the band's interpretations of the songs. This time they played "Indian Summer" by Beat Happening. I knew this one really well, released a few years back on the K label.

The last cover they played really surprised me. It seemed so familiar when they started it, but I could hardly believe it. It was a song I hadn't listened to since my "prog rock" phase, when I was around fifteen years old. My favorite band then were Yes. This song was early Yes, before they got prog. It was called "Sweetness." Luna played it straight, it sounded very cool. I had been so fast to drop Yes when I moved up to Glasgow. I needed to reconsider their early stuff.

Janey had her hand on my shoulder, and occasionally she would rub the back of my neck and my hair at the back. She was having a good time, she was kinda jigging along with everything, but she never really took her eyes off the drummer. It was like she was feeling every hit he made, that was how she felt the gig.

It was a great show, we loved it. We got back into Casper and drove to George and Poppy's place. We walked down to the beach, down to the surf. This was my last night in San Diego, so it was good to go down there, take a last look at the stars from the beach and the arc of jet-plane lights on the flight path.

"Are you going to write to me?"

"Constantly," I said.

"I'm going to miss you, Stephen."

I think she almost had a tear, but she turned it around real quick, it was fleeting. I kissed her just in case, and I did taste salt, though it could have been from the ocean. We were pretty close to the beautiful crash and drag of the waves. Shit, I'm going to miss her. I don't want to think about it right now, but it's going to hurt. I am the one who's leaving, I am the lucky one, I'm the one who's going to San Francisco, otherwise I might feel sicker right now.

We snuck into George and Poppy's. There was an understanding that there wouldn't be sex on the premises, I knew that. We came from the youth hostel, we had been a couple of sick boys from Scotland on a recovery retreat, there was going to be no issue. But I snuck Janey in there, and we got cozy on the sofa, and we tried to stay quiet. She found *Jonathan Livingston Seagull* on a shelf of books Poppy had left for guests, and she read a big chunk of it to me as I lay there perfectly comfortable in her presence.

She was sitting up beside me, and I took the chance to kiss her belly now and again under her t-shirt, and she would rub my head and keep reading. And eventually we got rolled together onto the little cot bed I had been sleeping on for weeks. We pushed it up against the sofa so we could sleep side by side. She fell asleep with her head on my chest, with a leg over my legs, and I lay awake for a long time, enjoying the feeling of being so close to someone and soaking up her weight and her presence and her smell and her heartbeat.

39

The Spring Earthquake

Janey ran me to the airport. I was meeting Richard inside, then he and I were getting the same plane back to San Francisco. Janey was all smiles at the airport. I was being a bit of a wimp.

"San Francisco is going to be great to you," she said. "Go to the Greenpeace office, like I said. They'll find somewhere to put you up."

"I wish you were going to be there."

"I know. I've got to deal down here for a while, and you have to deal up there. That's the deal."

She smiled the trademark smile. I knew what she meant, but then I also didn't know. I checked my bag in. She hugged me. We kissed.

"You have my address, I have yours. Now go and write lots of songs, Stephen. Beautiful songs."

"Paint me a picture. A self-portrait. Send me your picture of you."

"Ok, it's a deal."

She hugged me and left. I watched her walk out of the building. She turned at the door, waved and smiled. If, in the recent past, a person like that had waved at me and smiled at me in that way, I would have leapt towards them. I would have snaked my viperish way towards them. Instead, I was going the other way, purposely leaving this person. But I had to deal. With it. And I had a deal with San Francisco. And once you decide to go, you have to go. With both Doc Martens facing in the same direction.

It felt like ages since I'd seen Richard, but it was just a week. He had gone to Mexico and had fallen in with two girls from Tijuana, and they drove him out to the desert and they had cooked together and played music. He seemed like he was in great shape, and he was looking forward to San Francisco.

On the plane, I put my headphones on and listened to the Luna LP as we left the ground for the short flight. At some point I looked in my bag and there was a little bundle of Tiger's Milk bars wrapped in a note fastened with an elastic band. On the note there was a sketch with a sunrise and a beach and a graphic that said: *YES, YOU CAN DEAL!* There was also the address of the Greenpeace office, with the line: *Try these guys, they're sure to put up any stray puppy that comes their way! XXX*

*****

We phoned the Greenpeace office from the airport; no answer. Then we phoned the hostel at Fort Mason, and they were full. They put us through to the hostel at Union Square, and we got lucky. They had a "family" room that we could have. It cost a little more, and they would need it back in a week, but we could take it and share that. A family room was their name for a non-dormitory room. Compared to staying in the dorm again, it felt like a good option, so we told them to hold it for us.

When we got to Union Square, I think we were both relieved. The room was high up and at the back of the building and, crucially, was "ours." It was almost twice as much a night for each of us, but I didn't care. I was tired. I threw myself down thankfully on the little bed, while Richard dragged his bed over to the further side of the room. Even if they would let us, we couldn't afford to stay in the hostel for longer. They charged on a nightly basis; it added up fast. We needed to get a room somewhere in the city for the month and a bit that was left of the trip. We asked downstairs, and they said we should check the classifieds in the *SF Guardian* and go to neighborhood stores and check the noticeboards. That became the project for the next week. And in between times we would rest. The weather duly complied with our plan as it rained for three straight days. It was kinda comforting in a way, it gave us no choice. Just stay in and hibernate.

I had two books. Both of them were cool American second-hand paperback editions that I had bought back in a store in Hillcrest:

Zen and the Art of Motorcycle Maintenance—Robert Pirsig;
The Hotel New Hampshire—John Irving.

I had read the *Zen* book before, in my crazy book-reading days of the late 1980s. These were book-reading nights more like. I used to stay up all night, glued to my book, moving under the covers without taking my eye off the page, not even going to the toilet. I don't know how my elbows ever stood it. The edition of *Zen* I had this time was from 1976, with the Monty Pythonesque illustration of the flower turning into the wrench. Such a classic cover and layout, I liked having it around with me. It was more than a vessel of words, it was furniture for me. It was like a mini coffee table; wherever I put it down, it made that space look better, and when you are traveling, that can suddenly mean a lot. You cleave to small possessions when you are all at sea.

The other one, the John Irving, looked almost as good. A 1982 edition, covered in repeated lines of text, title and author in a very 1982 font. There was a small picture of an American football player superimposed on the design, seemingly at random. I mean, who gets to design this stuff? What a great job. Imagine getting paid for that. I would do it for nothing. To have these little slabs of design joy sitting around windowsills and coffee shops, draped from fingers on subways and buses, the greatest accoutrements of intellect and escape. I chose the John Irving first because I hadn't read it, and I allowed myself to be lost in this very American novel. It was a sweet antidote to missing Janey; my mind was quickly subsumed by the life of the book. As the rain came down and the radiator hissed into life, we took shelter in the hostel blankets and politely asked the cleaner if they wouldn't mind leaving us alone to our squalor.

Jewish prayers flowed up into our room via the air vent three times a day; there was someone reading out loud. Whoever this guy's rabbi was, he would have been pleased to know that his pupil was not stinting on his practice. Even though he was in a hostel in San Francisco for God knows what reason, God certainly knew he was there. He literally prayed morning, noon and night. It was making my feeble attempts to connect with the Almighty seem like such an afterthought. It made me realize I had neglected the Lord since I came to America. I hadn't been to church, and any pattern that I'd had in my praying had gone out the window. There had been distractions of course, but the chap at the other end of the vent was managing to attend to his devotions.

"I wish that guy would shut up sometimes," I said one evening.

"It's comforting. I like it," said Richard.

He *would* like it. Richard had a trick of turning irritations into causes for jubilation. A handy trick to have, especially while traveling. By day three, we thought we really better get out. By day three, I thought I really *was* living in the Hotel New Hampshire; my mind was melding with the pages. On opening the *Guardian* classifieds, we spotted a few things. We reckoned the Mission was the best place to stay for vibe and heat and neighborhood-ness. My eye strayed to the personals. America was so funny, right there on the page. People were propositioning the whole Bay Area. They put their wants and needs, often sexual, right there in the newspaper:

Play guy needs play girl . . . with prominent ideals and a prominent derriere!

My name is Sasha and I'm looking for fun. I'm 120 lbs and stand at 5'2"

... must be good, giving and game

God-fearing—Be my everything! Listener, friend, soulmate ...

And from a guy, who put his picture in too:

Family oriented—I want to start my own family one day with an amazing guy beside me

I couldn't imagine all this going down in Glasgow. San Francisco was way ahead. But then that's what we always suspected about California. Or maybe it wasn't a case of being ahead, maybe they were just further out there. People here were straight up about what they wanted and how they were feeling about things. In Scotland, it just wasn't done. At least not out in the open. At least not with anyone I knew.

But back to our mission—we had a couple of leads from the paper, but we also had Justine, who we'd met at the ME meeting, and we had Greenpeace. I took Greenpeace, Richard took Justine. He went all the way out to Outer Sunset to see her; I went to South of Market. I didn't get anywhere. A woman took my name and the number of the hostel, but I don't know if she really had any idea what I was talking about. I tried giving her the puppy eyes, but it didn't work. I think she thought I was either demented or I had facial palsy.

Richard was away at Justine's for ages. I didn't mind because I got plenty of cozy book time in the room. He finally got back at eight at night. I thought that had to mean good news, but she couldn't do it. Her apartment was really small, one bedroom, and she didn't want to give up her living room/kitchen for a month. Plus she wasn't allowed to sublet anyway. Fair enough.

In the morning we got up and went to see a room down in the Cow Hollow near the Marina. A woman came to show us the room, which was in her apartment. She wasn't much older than us, and she wore seventies-style clothing with long brown hair like Karen Carpenter. It was a nice room, but it was really small and there was only one bed, albeit a double.

"Yeah, we'd probably need more space than that. Where would we sleep?"

"Surely you guys wouldn't mind sharing a bed?" she said with a sweet smile.

I looked at Richard and he at me. I wasn't feeling it.

"I really don't think we'd get a good night's sleep," he said to her.

She smiled again at us and said, "You guys are cute."

We left her and schlepped all the way over to the Mission. We took the 22 Fillmore most of the way, and then we transferred to the 49 along Mission Street to Army and Mission. It was a sweet transfer. When we came back to San Francisco, I made a big decision. I was going all in with a monthly pass for the Muni (Municipal Transportation). This cost $60, which was a chunk out of my traveler's checks, but it was an investment I wanted to make. I wanted to travel the hell out of this city and see every corner. The beauty of it was that while I was sitting on all those buses and trolleys, I was getting some rest. I really managed to find a place of zen on some of the routes; it could be my recovery place. Richard didn't go for it. He was never a follower; he didn't want to splash out on the pass. It's not like we were doing everything together anyway. I didn't mind because I felt free when I was on the Muni. I liked to drift. Having someone else along on your particular ride wasn't fair on anyone.

The place we'd come to see was near the corner of Army and Guerrero. It was a regular San Francisco–looking house. Anne met us there. She was a schoolteacher, a single mum with two teenage sons. She seemed nice, if a little tense. She showed us the room, which was big and bright, with a bay window looking out on the street. There were two single beds. It was good, if a bit noisy from the traffic. We were stuck looking for a place though, so Richard and I quickly agreed we should stay here. Anne seemed happy enough with that, and she gave us one key for the house and asked that we go get another one cut. We caught a glimpse of her sons, who were almost as big as we were, maybe thirteen and fifteen years old? They didn't seem to want to say hi. We gave Anne $400 for the month, and we said we would be back on Saturday, two days from now. Sold.

Finally, there was a whole city out there, and we were right in the action, not tucked away at the beach, not a bus ride away from the salient parades, we were here in our own corner of the Mission. All we had to do was walk a couple of blocks over and we were on Valencia, where the sulky, hip coffee shops are, decked out with thrift-store standard lamps and house-clearance sofas. Walk a little more, and Mission Street has everything you want—the best Catholic souvenirs and the best cheap Mexican food.

*****

Anne goes out to work; the boys leave with her. We go down and get our cereal and our tea and then head straight up to the roof. There's a little stepped wooden ladder thing that takes you up to a hatch door then out onto the silver roof. It's great up there. The sun in March is getting stronger, and there's a brick structure on the roof that gives shelter from the breeze so that effective sunbathing can be enjoyed. And that's what we do. Richard is a keener sunbather than me. When he gets on the towel, that's it, he doesn't want to move. I get bored after half an hour.

"You wanna do something?"

"In a bit."

I always sound like a kid when I ask him that. Like a kid pestering his dad. But I don't want to bug him. If conditions are right, he'll stay there most of the day. He doesn't need me around to enjoy himself.

So I went along the street to the big Salvation Army place to have a rummage round. I hadn't bought anything since I got to America. I picked out a nice blue-and-yellow checked shirt for a dollar, choosing from about two hundred checked shirts. On the way to the checkout, I looked over at a big table piled with shoes. I wasn't tempted, I was doing ok with my boots, but I noticed a pair of Adidas Rom sticking out of the middle. I had always been an Adidas Bamba kid. The black trainer with the white stripe and natural-colored midsole seemed to go perfectly with everything else I wore from ages eight to eighteen. The Adidas Rom, however, was a state-ment trainer. Bright blue stripes and trim on brilliant white, it took a certain kind of person to really pull off the Rom look.

Graham Percy was that kind of person. At eleven years of age, he was the tallest, the fastest runner, the best footballer and the best kisser in the whole of P7. This was understood and certified in all categories. He wore Rom, and even I had to admit that the way the bottom of his Levi's fell over the shoe to give only tantalizing glimpses of the famed blue and white . . . well, I joined the gaggle of girls in crushing on that. Dunno what Graham was doing now. That's a lot of expectation to live up to. Maybe it was easier to be a late developer. Us mutts just cruised along in the slipstream, trying to stay away from major beatings, until it was time to leave school.

Still, we got there. I got there. I was in San Francisco fishing fourteen-year-old Adidas Roms out of the Salvation Army, ready to party like it was 1979. This was the glass slipper of my generation — perhaps I was to be a crowned prince after all. I pulled at the shoes, but they wouldn't come. They must have been stuck to the other shoes. Gave them another tug. Nope. Got hold of them both properly, and they started to come. Felt like I was pulling at a large potato plant, feeling something heavy underneath the ground coming up . . . They were indeed attached to something heavy. Big metal joints and big chunky wheels. They were roller skates.

The trainers had been attached to heavy "four on the floor" style skates. I'd never seen such a setup. The skates I had seen as a boy were basically a metal plate on plastic wheels with a strap. I didn't care though. I looked at them with wonder. They seemed like they would fit me. I tried them on; they were snug. Oh my God, Cinderella, we are going to the ball.

They were quite expensive, $20, but when I thought about getting some perfectly flared Levi's to drape over them, I was in no doubt. I was finally going to be Graham Percy, even though everyone else in that story had grown up and was having kids, cars and careers. I didn't care, I had my beautiful Roller Roms.

I got back to the house around three. Richard was hanging out in the room, reading.

"Justine invited us to her house tonight for dinner, is that ok?"

"Yeah. I'll maybe have a quick rest. When do you want to go?"

"In about an hour?"

"Ok. Did she call here?"

"Yeah, I gave her the number, but I told her to let it ring twice and then hang up so I knew it was her, then I called her back."

Anne had made it clear she didn't want people calling us up on the phone and blocking the line. She seemed a little nervous, her list of house rules kept growing. It's like she wanted the rent but didn't really want to know we were around. That was ok though, we were pretty good at making ourselves scarce. So we headed back out, and I was quite glad that I had been swotting up on my SF transit, because without hesitation I led Richard to the J Church trolley stop.

The J Church was a tram, at least that's what we would call it in the UK. It was an attractive, boxy-looking mini train, with two carriages. It was white with a yellow band, and *Muni* written on the front in very particular seventies writing that reminded me of the pattern of Swedish butter biscuits that we used to get when we were young.

There was lots of glass, big windows to look in and out of. The whole thing looked very friendly, like a Lego design come to life. It felt like we were meant for each other, us and the J Church. I flashed my pass at the driver and he waved us both on like we were San Franciscan, Richard scoring a freebie. That's it, we *were* San Franciscan now. You are what you imagine yourself to be.

Here in California I had started to flow. Richard had started to flow. Something was moving, I had to admit to myself—quietly, on deep background, but it was moving. Something was lifting; maybe it was mood, maybe it was attitude, maybe it was musical, maybe it was spiritual. Didn't want to think about it too much. Best just to move forward. Like Willy Wonka said, "You can't go backwards. Got to go forwards to go back. Better press on."

Better press on. The J Church was singing along Church Street, stopping to let the occasional person on. The road started going steeply up, but something was happening. The tram swung off the main road and seemed to be going through people's back gardens. I swear we were passing through trees, passing through white, snapping bedsheets hung out on lines to dry. We could see into people's houses. The tram slowed right down to negotiate the gradient and the tight turns. It moved like a ghost train. I looked in the house windows, I saw crockery, I saw knickknacks, I saw a piano in someone's house. I saw a man doing woodwork at an outside bench. He didn't even look up when we passed.

No one in the tram seemed much bothered by what was happening. Some looked steadily out, some seemed caught up in their own thoughts. I rattled from one side of the tram to the other, trying to take in all the wonderful detail of this unique excursion. We were high up on a hillside. We caught tantalizing glimpses of the city beyond the houses on the right-hand side. As I looked forward, I saw we were on a discrete path that the cars couldn't get to. We went into a gulley, and it got deeper. It had a bare wall on the left that went up a long way, with houses way up on top.

We weren't in the gulley for long. Quite suddenly the tram straightened out, and on the right-hand side the view opened out as the houses fell away. We were looking at a crazy vista of downtown San Francisco, with the Mission in the middle ground and the palm trees and green of a sloping park right outside the window. I looked at Richard, and he was smiling away in appreciation too.

"It's a great town, isn't it?" he said.

"Not too shabby," I agreed.

We got off at Market Street and switched to another tram called the N Judah. That one took us through a tunnel and out to the western side of the San Francisco peninsula. We got to Justine's house around five. She was welcoming and friendly, and it was nice to feel the warmth of her hospitality. We went in, and we sipped on Spanish vermouth, which was new to me but delicious. And we chatted of course about ME and how we were all doing. We touched base about any progress we had made and any new therapies we were thinking of trying.

My only therapy at that point was the therapy of living, and I was getting happier with how things were going. I almost didn't want to talk about it, because I feared that in the observation of a positive phenomenon, the phenomenon might decide to disappear in a puff of ephemeral smoke. Justine had a *lot* of ideas about therapies and supplements, medicines and protocols. It was a lot to take in, but Richard was definitely taking it in. He was engaged in what she was saying in a way I don't remember him being with *anyone* else before.

We had dinner, which was of the stuffed peppers and couscous variety. It was getting pretty late. Justine had an acoustic guitar there, and she asked Richard if he could play something. He played "Cavatina," the theme from *The Deer Hunter*. Even though this was probably recognized as the Spanish guitar tune best known to man or woman, it was still a very nice piece of music, especially if played well. Richard played it really well. He was pretty flawless. I admired his determination to quietly succeed in what he chose to do. Justine was enthralled with his playing and seemed delighted with our visit, with Richard in particular. She looked at the clock.

"It's pretty late, guys, you can stay here if you like. I have an air mattress."

I half expected Richard to say that we needed to get back, but he just smiled and said "Great!" Then Justine brought out the single mattress and some blankets and I started to blow it up with the foot pump.

"Ok, good night, Stephen. Just help yourself to anything that you need," she said, waving carelessly in the direction of the kitchen. She said this as she left the room to go into the bedroom.

It was then that I noticed that Richard had already gone in there too. Maybe there was an extra bed in there I didn't know about. I didn't think about it too much. I set to making my bed on the floor as comfortable as possible. I was sleepy, happy to get comfortable fast. Luckily, I had my headphones and Walkman with me. I put on a tape I had of all the Felt instrumentals on one side, and I got all wrapped in the blankets like a sausage roll.

It was good to be in a house that was away from a busy street. I was getting used to the traffic on Guerrero in the Mission, but this felt especially soothing. I was drifting off, listening to the music, my eyes still opening now and then, just checking the room out and the shadows on the ceiling. The light hanging from the middle of the room was slowly swaying. I froze and watched it to check it was actually moving.

Even before we came to San Francisco, we were aware that it was in an earthquake zone, especially after the big one in 1989. People had been talking about another one happening soon, saying that we were due one. Richard and I had joked about it, calling it "the Spring Earthquake," almost daring it to happen. But it wasn't really something to joke about. For Bay residents, it was serious. There were "Duck and Cover Tips" posted on the walls in every room you went into. The serious side of it struck me again as I watched the light fitting sway. There was no doubting it. I couldn't hear anything, didn't experience any real shake, but the shock of seeing the light moving on its own was enough to have me roll across the floor.

I rolled in my blankets and made for the wall. There was an old-fashioned sideboard there, with shelving on top. If that lot had fallen on me, it would have been bad. Getting underneath it was the best thing to do. I would be protected from any falling shelves and from everything else as well. I fitted beneath the sideboard pretty snugly and I had my back to the wall, looking out. The light was still swaying. I wasn't sure how long these things went on for, but I wasn't taking any chances. I think between the fright and my already tired state, I passed out quickly.

I woke. It must have been seven or something, but it was already getting light. I was still under the bookshelf. The house was still here. San Francisco was still here. The light had stopped swaying. I drifted back to sleep for a bit. Justine came into the room around eight. She tried not to disturb me, moved quietly into the kitchen. I could hear morning kitchen sounds, and then the smell of coffee and something baking. Justine's ME must have been on a different level to ours, as she was still holding down a part-time job at the university. She set us up with breakfast and pretty much had to split. The speed at which working people get up and out in the morning never ceases to surprise me.

As Richard and I sat at the table eating the fresh-baked rolls with jam, I remembered about the earthquake the night before. I was just about to tell him and then I stopped. I was like the only person in the room who didn't get the joke suddenly getting the joke. I stopped myself just in time. Maybe it wasn't an earthquake. Maybe it was something else. There was a shift in the Richard/ Stephen dynamic after that night. Not a *seismic* shift, if you get my meaning, but a shift nonetheless. Those guys had found something in each other, and they weren't waiting on me or anyone else to cement their relationship.

From that point on, Richard got steadily more taken up with Justine. Sometimes he would be at our place in the Mission, mostly he would be at Justine's. It was cool though; I was happy for them. They would invite me along to things they were doing, outings and so forth, and that was cool, especially when we escaped the confines of the city and would head over the Golden Gate Bridge to the woods north of the bay. But if it did leave me with a lot of alone time, at least he left his guitar at the apartment in the Mission.

40

Gold from the Mold

The first night I was on my own in the Mission, I hit a bump in the road. Not an actual bump, a metaphysical bump. I got a wave of weird panic, an echo of the feeling I had last summer, an unwelcome reminder that the mood stuff hadn't gone away. Of course, when you feel that way, you start questioning. Like, *Where the hell did that come from, why did it spring up, what did I do to bring that on?* I was thinking, *If I can understand where this came from, I can simply avoid the steps leading up to this feeling and it will never happen again.* But it doesn't work like that.

As I sat wrapped in my blankets on the small single bed, with the occasional car still passing on Guerrero, I felt bewildered. I guess Anne and her boys were about somewhere in the house, but it was midnight and I sure as hell didn't want to go wake anybody up. And even if Anne was up, I had the feeling I really didn't want to get into it with her. I think she had problems of her own, but it struck me, and I don't mean to be unkind, it struck me that sharing a problem with her wouldn't be a problem halved. I think the deal with us staying there was that we were very much meant to be problem-free.

I sat up in bed, and I thought about praying. God was tugging at me again. I felt a bit like Solomon in the temple when he got the call. Very quietly, I took my blanket and a cushion to the little wooden steps that led to the roof. I climbed up there, pushed out the oddly shaped door with the corner cut off, and there I was, in the Mission night. It wasn't too cold, there was no wind, there were a few clouds, but there were enough gaps between the clouds to pick out some stars. I placed my cushion in the spot against the wall, wrapped my blanket around and started to pray. It had been a while since I had done this, and I was ragged, apologetic, a little bit desperate.

After a while I opened my eyes and looked at the subtle change in the clouds. I could see more stars, different constellations. I thought, *Maybe I should get dressed, go down to Valencia and find one of those bars that's bound to be open. Maybe I'll find a soulmate there, someone to talk to.* I thought about that for about ten seconds and realized this was probably pretty high up on the list of things not to do at that moment. I was ok here. I felt a little better after my prayer.

Was I really the cause of my own sadness? Probably. Was I going to do better in future? Hopefully. Wasn't the answer to depression to simply do more things that made you happy? Maybe. I was limited in what I could do, so did that mean my happiness was limited? I had a feeling that there were plenty of fit and able people, some of them accomplished and high-flying, who had problems with their mental health too. And that suggested that man, or woman, could not live by bread, or even a full diary of happening events, alone.

I had been pretty quick to drop my prayers when things were going well. Now that I was uncertain again, here I was, under the stars, looking up, with my head and heart wide open for any spiritual help I could get. I wrapped the blankets tighter and prayed again until I was numb and swaying from cold and tiredness. Eventually, I staggered back to the room, put my earplugs in and got to sleep.

The next day, I took my sneaker skates to North Beach. I thought I'd practice along the esplanade. This was a nice area of San Francisco, full of bookshops and lovely-looking old Italian restaurants, plus standard San Francisco architecture on standard crazy San Francisco slopey streets. I couldn't get enough of that. How many cities in the world feel like a treat walking up just about any street for the timber and the vistas, for the angles and the crazy cats that tumble out of the doorways? That's the way I saw it, and it made me wonder and it made me want to *be* San Francisco.

I passed the Art Institute, where Janey's legendary friend allegedly spent a rent-free year by hoisting herself into the loft space at the end of the working day and made money on the side by posing nude for the life classes. It made me wonder if I could pose nude for the sake of art. I don't think I'd have the balls for it, literally or metaphorically. Maybe one day I will find my thing to be the king of. Did I tell you I wanted to dance? Like be a modern dancer. For a couple of years. But I never did anything about it. What a stupid waste. I put all my energy into God knows what when I might have been training as a dancer. I admired the modern dance troupes so much. I used to go see dance like I would a gig. The music would be just as loud and the performances even more raucous than a band, people throwing themselves and other people all over the place. Why didn't I put myself forward? I could have found a class or a group. I was young, lithe, strong. I could have done it but didn't. I was lazy. Spiritually lazy. I just wanted to stick to things that were safe and familiar.

I came along Columbus Avenue, the main drag through the neighborhood. There was a nice big grassy square there with a beautiful cathedrally-looking church on one side. That's a nice way to show off a religious edifice—build it beside a park and then stand back. I passed further down Columbus and came to a large recreation ground. There were many tennis courts and a couple of basketball courts, but there was absolutely nobody around. I wondered if they belonged to the school or to the city. I didn't care; I was here, they weren't. It was a perfect space to practice my skating.

I got on my skates. I looked down with some satisfaction to see that my brown semi-flared pencil cords were resting over the shoe in a relaxed fashion. I was wearing a cream-colored bomber jacket over my t-shirt, and I felt right about what I was doing. I set off around the recreation ground. All I wanted to do was the simple stuff, without falling on my arse.

I'm skating, and the world is quiet and warm. And the quiet and warmth and the movement are getting to work on the angst, and the angst is lifting like North Beach fog when the sun burns through. I'm getting the hang of it. I think the trick is not to look down. I skate around in slow circles. The trucks feel smooth, the ground is forgiving, and the air is still, just full enough of ambient neighborhood sounds, reminders of the city beyond.

I had been skating for quite a while, and I slipped into a sort of reverie. At one point I did notice someone watching me, but I managed to airbrush them out of my perfect revolving picture. Eventually I started to slow down and I went back to my bench. The person that had been there before was still there and was close to the bench, hanging over the railing, smoking a cigarette. I looked over and smiled an acknowledgment of his presence.

"I like your skates," he said.

"Thanks," I said.

"Are you training for something?"

"No, I'm just taking them out for a run."

"Nice, I like them. They suit you."

"Thanks."

I went back to changing.

"Are you Irish?"

"No, I'm from Scotland."

"Oh really? I'm part Scottish, I think. Well, they gave me a Scottish name. I'm Alex. Alexander." He said the last bit in what he thought was a Scottish accent.

"Stephen."

"Do you live in San Francisco?"

"No, I'm just visiting." I turned to face him; he was still leaning over the railing, but close enough to carry on a conversation.

"You don't look like you're visiting, if I may say so. You look like you belong here."

"Ha ha. Thanks."

"Are you staying in North Beach?"

"No, the Mission."

"Oh, that's cool, that's cooler. So expensive here."

"Do you live here?"

"No, Lower Haight. Duboce Triangle."

"Near the J Church."

"Jeez, you *do* know the city. It took me a year to find that line. I work over there," he said, pointing over his shoulder. "I'm on a break. I need to get back actually. I work in a garlic restaurant called the Stinking Rose. It's on Columbus."

"A garlic restaurant?"

"Yeah, I know, right? Only in San Francisco."

"Does everything have garlic in?"

"Even the ice cream."

"Whoa! I'm not sure I could go there."

"It's not for everyone." He checked himself. "Ok, I got to go, this is too much fun. I enjoyed talking to you, and I hope you don't mind I watched you skating."

"Not at all."

"Hey," he said, "do you like football?"

"American football?"

"No, your kind. Soccer."

"Sure."

"Me and some Italian friends are watching Milan play tomorrow at midday. There's a bar called Enzo's on Haight Street. Come by if you have nothing to do."

The next day I went off to Enzo's Bar on the Lower Haight. I met Alex and his flatmate Erica. She was the center of a lot of attention. She was surrounded by men—by the looks and sounds of it, Italian men. She was young, dark-haired and pretty, and the men were young, dark-haired and vivacious. The pre-match excitement was in full swing. Me and Alex positioned ourselves to one side of the main group, and we had a good view of the large television set. The game was the Milan derby, AC Milan vs. Inter Milan.

Erica waved over to us and shouted, "Who are you for, Inter or Milan?"

"I'm more of a Roma guy, but . . ."

"Did you say Roma?" said one of the Italian boys.

"This guy's a Roma fan," said a second.

"Is he going to bring us bad luck?" said the first.

Erica looked a little unsettled. "Yeah, but you're shouting for Milan today, right, Stephen? Right, Alex?"

"Definitely. *Forza* Milan!" said Alex.

"Yeah, what he said," I said, agreeing.

She seemed happy with that and went back to the center of the gaggle at the bar. I was liking this; this was a lot of Italian. Alex was liking it too. Maybe not so much the football.

"I mostly come here for all the cute Italian men. I mean, they are all hetero and all over Erica, but I figure that one day I might get some Erica runoff."

Erica was doing a great job keeping everyone happy, yelling at the screen, berating the referee. She certainly knew the game and the teams. She didn't seem to have a boyfriend among the boys. The bar got busier as the game progressed. It was Saturday, but neither Alex nor I were having a drink. We sat with our coffee, and in between the roars and gesticulating ragazzi, he told me something about himself.

He had been in San Francisco for a couple of years but was originally from Washington State, from the town of Olympia. He knew he was gay early on, and though he liked his hometown, he was happy to get away from family life. His mum and dad had divorced, and he didn't really get on with his big brothers. So he moved south, lived in a bunch of places and had a bunch of different jobs, but people kept letting him down.

"It's tough. This city is tough on people. Everybody's crazy. Nobody can pay rent on time, nobody cleans properly, everybody is trying to sleep with everybody, people are still taking risks. There's a lot of drugs. I don't know if I'm going to be able to stick it out. If you have a lot of money, you can get a nice place, you can get further away from this crazy street." He gestured at Haight Street. "I mean, it's a nice street to visit, but our apartment backs onto it. Too much street life for me. But anyway, I don't want to sound like a moaning Minnie, I can always leave, right?" He made a face where he puckered his lips and stared at me before breaking into a wheezy cackle. "What about you? What are you doing here?"

"I'm here sort of by mistake. My friend Richard and I traveled over to San Diego to escape the Scottish winter and to look around, but we've ended up back here."

"Yeah, I guess there's not *too* much to do in San Diego."

"Unless you're a surfer. We liked it, but I wanted to come back here."

"Where's Richard?"

"He's with Justine. He just met her, but they seem to have made quite an intense connection."

"So you've been jilted for a woman."

"That's the rule, isn't it?" I said.

"What do you mean?"

"If a friend gets with someone, the other friend has to step aside."

"Huh? Maybe. I'm not sure it has to be so definitive as that."

"I'm not complaining. I think it's healthy that we're spreading our wings."

At that moment, Milan scored and the place went berserk for a few minutes. I liked watching football, I really liked the Italian games, but it was nice to talk to Alex too.

When things settled down, he asked me, "What's your plan for the rest of the trip?"

"I just like walking around the city, on and off the Muni. I have some songs I want to finish that I'm working on."

"What kind of songs?"

"Just me and the guitar. I'm still learning. Richard is a really good guitarist, and we were playing together, but I'm pretty certain he doesn't want to do it anymore."

"Yeah, you can't force anyone. They gotta want to do it. So you're on a solo mission?"

"Looks like it. I just started writing though, so it's a work in progress."

"You can sing to me. Once you think you have something ready. I'm a good listener. And I have great taste." Alex said that last bit with a wide grin.

The game ended. We decided to get some fresh air. Alex waved at Erica, and she smiled and waved back. She was in her element. We walked on down Lower Haight Street and came to a record store. I stopped to look.

"You wanna go in? It's a good one," Alex said.

I was already transfixed by the vibe in the place. It was called Gold from the Mold, and it seemed from first glance to deal only in seven-inch vinyl. You would think that someone who had just sold hundreds of kilograms' worth of vinyl records would not be interested in stocking up on more. But this was a new, different me. In the past I bought a lot of records speculatively and in the service of others. Some of them I never listened to, or maybe just once. It took a while for me to work out which records I truly loved, which tracks I couldn't live without.

I was working on a new set of music, much smaller, much more selective; music for me. This record store seemed to cater exactly for the place I was at with my listening. I just wanted that one piece of Gold to stick out from the Mold. And I wanted to treasure it and play it like I did when I was ten and had only a handful of singles.

Alex and I delved into the racks. It seemed to be mostly soul, and some funk, some pop, from the sixties and seventies. This was pretty much precisely what I liked most at this moment.

After about ten minutes of looking, I pulled out "You Turned My Bitter Into Sweet" by Mary Love. I'd heard this song at a soul night in Glasgow. I think I remember there was something great about it. I asked the proprietor behind the counter if I could play it.

"Sure. Knock yourself out. I'll put it on the speakers, it's a great one!"

I didn't expect him to be so friendly; record shop people can sometimes be a little cold, especially in such a precious emporium like the one we were in. I went and put it on the turntable myself, it was right there in the public domain. I heard the rumble, and then the soft coo of Mary Love came in, accompanied by this perfect velvet groove, great backing vocals, easy horns filling in behind. "Sensational, unexplainable / Every time that you are near . . ." she sang. On the whole, I had heard a lot less music in the last two months than I normally would, so this was so rich and welcome.

"What you gonna play next? You got everyone going with that one, you better follow it up." The store guy was this funny, camp, avuncular fellow, beaming from behind the desk.

"Here." Alex handed me a disc. "Play the A-side. 'California Soul.'"

The track was by Nick Ashford. As soon as it came on, the proprietor shouted, "You guys are good. I like this version, sung by the guy who wrote it with his wife."

It became a bit of a game. Keep the kettle boiling, taking a chance with something that you thought you knew, or a killer title, or stumbling on one that you knew was classic. I put on the Velvelettes' "He Was Really Sayin' Something," Alex put on Betty Davis's "Anti Love Song," I put on "Do You Know the Way to San Jose?" and Alex put on "Downtown."

"That's my favorite song in the whole world," he said to me.

"'Downtown'?"

"Yeah. Doesn't it just make you feel great?"

"I've always liked it too."

"Of course you have," said Alex.

As Saturday afternoon became Saturday evening, we gave over DJing to other people, but it was a nice scene, the music and folk spilling out onto the street. Alex and I sat down on one of the benches outside. We were only there a few minutes when Erica came along. She was pleased to run into us again; she gave us both a hug, then she heard the music.

"I love this song!"

"What song?" said Alex.

"*This* song!"

And she started doing a little dance on the pavement outside the open front of Gold from the Mold. Alex gave me a look that was like a shrug, and he got up and joined her. I watched them for a bit, then someone put on the Miracles with Smokey Robinson singing. I didn't know the track, but it was a "dancer" and enough to get me on my feet. Erica tuned in to the music and was really moving well. Alex was cute; he had on heavy boots and was dancing like he was at an eighties disco playing Depeche Mode, but it worked. We danced like that for a while, out on the pavement, until the music got a bit slower, and I had to sit down. I told them I was going to catch the J along to the Mission. They both gave me a hug and a kiss. Alex's kiss on the cheek was scratchy with his beard, but I didn't mind it. Erica's was about as sensual a kiss as you could ever expect to get on the cheek. The memory of her lips on my face is still there.

41

Quiet Riot Girl

Monday morning. I woke up in an empty house. Richard still at Justine's. Anna and her sons had left for their school day/ work day. I got my cereal and took the guitar up onto the silver roof. I made a little den up there in the angle formed by the wall of the next house and ours. The sun is on me and will be until one, when I will slip into shadow. I wrote a letter to Carrie, giving her the barest details of what's been happening. I don't even mention Janey. I'll tell her when I get home. I wrote to my mum. To my dad too, but mostly my mum. She's the one that's worried about me, after all.

Actually, that's a little unfair to my dad. He was good through my illness; he had to adjust a lot. Before that, we just used to fight about what I was doing with my life. When I got so sick that he had to carry me into the ambulance, it neutralized everything. Survival trumped ambition; even he felt that.

I could imagine him looking over my mum's shoulder in the kitchen, and when he couldn't read what the letter said, he would demand to know "Where is he now? What's he doing?"

And my mum would say, "Let me read it first and I'll tell you. He's fine. He's still in San Francisco."

"San Francisco? Sailed in there many a time."

And he had. He was a sailor in the merchant navy, and he'd sailed into most of the great ports of the world at some point. Perhaps there was something in this trip I was on that was oddly analogous to my dad's experiences. In a way I was following in his footsteps, even though you couldn't have picked a different sense of purpose. Him serving the empire, me serving nobody. Except myself. I'd like to think that I could serve Carrie and Janey and Richard. And I do aspire to serve God, I think. But mostly I'm probably serving me.

I wrote my letters, and I lay out on a blanket, and I let the guitar go out of tune in the sun (which Richard told me never to do). I stripped down to my underwear, and I thought about taking my underwear off and standing like the statue of David and seeing how long it would take the traffic on Army and Guerrero to spot me. Would someone call the cops? I decided not to.

I have written a song called "Hurley's Having Dreams." It's a song about the kid Janey and me could have had if our union had been "blessed" and we had followed a completely different path in life. It's about her and it's about an imaginary kid called Hurley. I'm putting the love into a song. I mean, I'm glad she isn't having a baby, cos that would be a situation. But I'm writing a song baby instead.

So I was flitting between that song and another one. The other one just has a couple of chords so far, but I really like playing those chords on this lazy silver-roof-and-blanket Monday. I don't know what the chords are called, they seem like some sort of sixth or seventh, maybe major sevenths? They just have that wistful sound that could go on forever and cast a spell. I keep playing the two chords and I start writing words about me and a girl and some political grievances.

I was in one of the Valencia coffee shops the other day, and I got talking to a woman. She was from Seattle and she seemed a little spiky. She was bothered about a few things, and she was telling me about men and where it all went wrong, and I wasn't disagreeing with her. I was just listening; I didn't want to say something to piss her off and show my ignorance.

Then she started talking about music and how much she loved Huggy Bear and the Spinanes and the Pastels and Heavenly and Bikini Kill and the whole Olympia thing. She was great. She had on really shiny, really tough strappy shoes, like the kind you might expect a poison spike to appear from at the toe. And pink tights and an old pink dress and a hat. She looked like Miss Marple, to be honest, or at least someone just out of school who was dressing up as Miss Marple. I gave her my phone number, or at least I gave her Anne's house number, and I told her she had to ring twice then hang up and I would call her back. And she sort of nodded like she'd taken the information in. But she didn't call me, and I don't have her number to call back. It was a pity because I think she would have been a nice person to hang out with in San Francisco, someone with a really different perspective.

So that was my other song. I thought I would call it "Quiet Riot Girl," even though that phrase doesn't appear in the lyrics. "Quiet Riot Girl." I get the feeling that if you ever write a song about a person, you should never tell them. They're probably not going to like it, like it sells them short or sells them wrong. But then it wasn't *really* about her, because I didn't know her. It was about me and the two chords I'm playing, and the San Francisco morning, and the way that I can see partway across the Mission, and I'm flying and falling into all the backyards, and thinking about back home and how there's always a fucking Tory government, and trying to convey to Valencia Miss Marple that I hate what she hates and love what she loves, and that I just want to drink sherry in her kitchen, nothing else. Sherry, books and a hard-tiled fucking San Franciscan kitchen floor.

And after a while of just playing the two chords, I realize that I need to get out of here. I'm in this city and I have a travel pass; I need to get out. I was drawn down to the waterfront, listening to the *Kind of Blue* LP by Miles Davis. I went right out along the curved pier, out into the bay. I met a man at the end who tried to sell me drugs. I told him I didn't want any and he called me square. I walked back along the pier and along a length of shore. Such a nice little beach. I don't know why it surprised me that there should be a pretty cove here, but I dug it. I dug that when I took my headphones off the tiny sound of the rippling waves at my feet were equal in volume to the ambient sound coming from the city behind. The mighty and the minuscule balanced in sound perfection.

I shifted to my beloved Cocteau Twins, the *Blue Bell Knoll* LP, and kept walking round the cove and back towards people. I walked through the Fisherman's Wharf area and bought a crab sandwich. It was about the best thing I'd ever tasted in my life. I think it helped that I was walking and eating and free and happy. That'll make most things taste good. A crowd of people were gathered around a man who was standing on a box with a microphone. He looked towards me and seemed to say something, and I could see the crowd laughing in response. I took my headphones off, and I heard him say something like "Look at this guy! Have you never heard of Supercuts?"

The people laughed again, some looking over towards me. I didn't have the energy or the wherewithal to come back with anything snappy, so I just let it go. I liked my hair just now. It *had* grown out a bit shaggy and raggedy, right enough, but I didn't care. It was still a pretty rich auburn from the henna I put in before I came to the USA. The red color seemed to be growing back towards the roots, though realistically I knew that couldn't be so. Fuck it, I liked my hair. If they had a problem, then that was their problem. I walked all the way along the Embarcadero, back towards the tall buildings of downtown. What a word that is, "Embarcadero": "leaving," with a flourish.

As I got to downtown near the Ferry Building, I heard music — rock music, outside music. Of course I followed it, and I tumbled into a plaza between buildings that was pretty busy with people watching a group. I would say about three thousand people on their lunch hour, enjoying some free music. The female voice was familiar to me, though I couldn't pin it straight away. As I worked my way through the crowd to get closer, I recognized the singer as Tanya Donelly. She had been in a group called the Throwing Muses. I had a vague idea she was trying her own thing, but I had no clue she was suddenly so popular. People seemed to be into it.

I got a seat somewhere along the side, in the sun, on some big concrete steps. I had a complete view of everything. I took in the music, it was nice. It didn't mean anything like as much as the music of her previous group to me though, but I guess that was about me changing more than her changing? Maybe sixty–forty. The Throwing Muses had been one of my crucial late eighties bands. I was in love with them. They came to play the venue I worked in, so I got to hang out with them, and I followed them around Scotland. The Sundays were supporting them, so really I didn't know which way to turn. I was mute with admiration.

I was glad that I was past that stage, being in crippling thrall to folks in bands. It meant so much to me at the time, meant everything. It was cool people, interesting people, people I wanted to be with, people I wanted to be. Plus it involved this magical activity called music. Still, there had been a way that I was taking things to extremes that obviously wasn't very healthy. I used to think that if I loved the books and the music, that was enough, that would be my complete focus, there would be no room for relationships. That model fell apart with Vivian, as reported elsewhere.

A girl sat next to me. She had a whole stack of vinyl in a couple of cloth bags. She was on her own, drinking out of a purple Slurpee cup. She had black hair in bunches, a bit like Lucy from *Peanuts*. But she also had thick, black-framed glasses. I don't think Lucy from *Peanuts* wore glasses. Maybe when she was being a psychiatrist? I can't remember. Either way, the girl here had the heavy-framed glasses.

I took a peek at her records, tried to guess as many as I could from the top edges of the covers. She had a Gil Scott-Heron record on top, and I think on the top of the second bag was *Ege Bamyasi* by Can. I was fantasizing that the white, blue and red edge of a record somewhere in the middle was the "Safety Net" twelve-inch by the Shop Assistants. She caught me looking though.

"I thought I saw a Shop Assistants record in the middle there. I got nosy."

Without saying anything, she looked at her pile and flicked through. It was the Shop Assistants.

"Jeez, you're good. You could tell that from the top?"

"I used to DJ, so I was always looking at the top edge of records. I used to carry that single everywhere."

"It's my boyfriend's. In fact, most of these are his. I'm borrowing them for my radio show."

Tanya's band, who were called Belly, finished their set, conveniently for conversation.

"So were you a DJ?"

"Yes, in Scotland, in Glasgow. Not on the radio though. That must be a nice job?"

"Well, it's fun, but it's not really a job. It's the college station down in Stanford."

"The college has a radio station?"

"Yeah, that's a thing over here. It's not just the campus, we broadcast to Palo Alto and the university, as far as the airport and San Jose."

"And you play whatever you want?"

"Pretty much. Every show has a vibe—as long as your vibe is good and fits with the overall plan for the station."

"What's the overall plan for the station?"

"Do you know what, I sit in the meetings and I try to work it out, but it keeps changing. Things get hazy. I just try to keep my nose clean. My name's Shirin, by the way."

"Stephen."

"Hi, Stephen. And you're here in San Francisco?"

"Yeah, just looking around, playing a bit of music, getting away from Scotland."

"Playing, as in . . . ?" She motioned as if to play a guitar.

"Exactly. My friend Richard and I have been performing under the name the Nabisco Cats."

"Ha, that sounds nice. Do you have a tape?"

"Nothing on me."

"Ah, pity. I could have played it on my show. If it was any good," she said. "Do you guys sound like the Shop Assistants? Or the Pastels? Or are you more like Orange Juice, or the Blue Nile?"

"You know a lot about Scottish music."

"I do seem to love a lot of Scottish bands."

"I like all the things you mentioned, but there's only two of us just now, so maybe imagine something between Love and Beat Happening. At least, that's where I'd like to aim it."

"The Arthur Lee Love?"

"Yeah, the Arthur Lee Love."

She turned to me. "Ok, Stephen, I have an idea. What if you just come on the show? You can play your songs, you can play some records, we can talk about Scotland . . ."

"Really? That sounds great!"

"Are you here awhile?"

"We go back home in a couple of weeks."

"So you could do it next week maybe?"

"Sure, I think so."

"And you'd be able to get down to Stanford?"

"Where is Stanford?"

"Well, do you know the way to San Jose?" She chuckled.

"That's funny," I said. I said it in the cool way Americans say "That's funny," without necessarily laughing. But it *was* funny. She got away with it.

"It's about a half hour south of San Francisco, on the way to San Jose."

We chatted a bit longer, swapped details, made sure I knew where and when I was going, and parted company. We were going to be on the radio.

42

Berkeley

Alex and I went to Berkeley on his day off from the restaurant. I got on the BART at 24th Street and Mission, then stepped off at Civic Center. Alex was already there, so we waited for the next Berkeley train and traveled over to the east of San Francisco Bay for my first time. "BART" stood for "Bay Area Rapid Transit." It worked on a whole different level of speed and sleekness to the rest of the Muni and extended one's horizon beyond the seven square miles of SF. *And* it looked like something from *Blade Runner*. It had a seventies-vision-of-the-future vibe that was starting to look a little tatty, like a Hewlett Packard mainframe computer, soon to be obsolete.

We settled into the brown cloth seats in the wide, low cabin and felt the velocity. After a couple of stops we had the long stretch under the bay, which seemed to last a long time, even though we were going at considerable speed. I wasn't sure if this was a journey that Alex took often, but he looked suitably nonplussed while he waited for the train to emerge.

"You like the train, huh."

"Can you tell?"

"Yeah, you're like an excited dog. If the window was open, you'd stick your head out."

"Oh, wait, here it comes—Oakland! Don't you think that Oakland is cool? I've always liked the Oakland Bay Bridge, it's the working man's bridge, as opposed to the Golden Gate, which is more for the tourists."

"What in God's name are you talking about?"

"Oakland! Original home of the Raiders."

"You actually like football?"

"They started showing it on British TV when I was a kid, and I got into it. The Raiders were my team. I even had the uniform."

"Jeez, poor thing, you got duped. They sold you the American Dream all the way over in Scotland."

"We were always force-fed America, but we liked it."

"And we were over here dreaming about your castles and your queens and princesses."

"You can have them."

We looked out the windows as the train slowed and seemed to weave and bob between freeways and other rail lines, elevated above the streets of West Oakland. We stayed on until Berkeley. I couldn't go to Berkeley without the music of Simon and Garfunkel ringing in my ears. All I really knew about Berkeley was that it was where Elaine Robinson went to college to get away from Ben and her folks in *The Graduate*. I mentioned it to Alex.

"Oh yeah, I know that movie. We can go there—you better go get it out of your system."

We walked up through the campus and it looked just how you would imagine an American campus to look, carefully laid out, lots of paths and grass and big, big trees, and on each side, in the distance, palaces of learning. We walk up to the bit with the plaza and the tower, where Ben stalks Elaine in the movie. It was nice, but they must have been in class, cos nobody's around. We sit for a while.

"You hungry?" asks Alex.

"I suppose. Are you?"

"I'm *always* hungry. Especially on my day off."

"Ok, where do we go?"

"The main drag is over here."

We go over to a street called Telegraph. And we have to cross a street called Bancroft to get there.

"Do you think they called it after Anne Bancroft from *The Graduate*?"

"Maybe," Alex says offhandedly.

We pass a store called Buffalo Exchange. I'd been in one in San Francisco, it was great for second-hand clothes and wasn't too expensive, so I asked Alex, and he said he didn't mind going inside. We drifted around the racks. Alex was less interested than I was. I suppose he'd been here for a couple of years; he wouldn't get the same thrill I was getting, seeing all this great stuff.

I pulled out a leather jacket. It was so heavy, I nearly dropped it. It was a brown leather flying jacket, with a fur collar and thick lining. It was in great condition. I didn't look at the price immediately. I went to try it on. It was big, but that was ok, it would do good for a Scottish winter, but I could still wear it on a chilly SF evening and not look like I was on an Arctic mission. I headed for the changing room. I put it on and immediately I wanted it. I came back out wearing it and looked for Alex.

"What do you think?"

He had a good look, then said, "I'd fuck you in it."

I'd never heard such sexual frankness come straight in my direction before.

"Ok. But the jacket?"

"It's really nice," he said in a sweet voice, getting on board with my enthusiasm.

"All right, here goes."

I lift up the paper tag on the string. $45. Yeah, that's not a gift, that's a lot. Screw it, I sold a lot of records to get here. This is a Spaceman 3, plus a My Bloody Valentine rarity. I can go for that. I pay, we leave. We go get something to eat, we get a window seat on Telegraph.

"Get the catfish."

"Really? Catfish?"

"Catfish and greens, it's classic. I guarantee you will like it."

"Are *you* getting it?"

"No, I've had it. This is for you though. I'm getting a club sandwich with a side of sweet potato fries. You can have some."

"*Sweet* potato fries. With sugar on?"

"No. Fries made from sweet potatoes. Also very good."

We ordered. The food came. The sun was out. The waitress was nice. The people walked about. It wasn't *too* unlike *The Graduate*. But it didn't need to be. It was a perfect lunch hour.

"Food's good, isn't it?"

"Everything is good."

I was watching two girls get out of a car, really stylish. I was just soaking up their look, their sass. I leaned over the table a little so I could watch them cross the street. Alex was watching me, apparently. He was looking at me intently but also with a sort of bored look.

"You're HH, aren't you?"

"What do you mean?"

"Hopelessly heterosexual."

I didn't know what to say to that.

"Do you ever go back to Olympia? I want to go there one day."

"Yeah, I go there to see my mom sometimes. I just take a bus."

"You take a bus?"

"Yeah, it takes a *long* time. I take this one called the Green Tortoise. It goes in the evening, and then they turn all the seats flat so everyone gets to lie down and get some sleep. It's pretty good. And they stop in the forest and make pancakes."

"You made that bit up."

"Seriously, they stop in the woods somewhere in Oregon in the morning, and they make a fire. And you think they're going to kill someone and it's probably you. But then they just make pancakes, and some people go for a swim if it's summer."

"When do you get to Olympia?"

"Maybe about four hours later. Then the bus keeps going to Seattle and Vancouver."

"What do you do when you get there?"

"I mostly just stay with my mom, fix things that need fixing, get the groceries. My dad isn't around. He's a bit of an alcoholic, so I don't see so much of him, though he's in Olympia too."

"Do you see friends?"

"Yeah, I see some. I'll always go to the Smithfield Café and see what's going on."

"Oh." I felt a penny drop. "Do you know Carla?"

"Carla Camino?"

"Yeah."

"I know her, she's cool. She's got the band with Bob. He's a good drummer. She was at my school—she was a couple of years above me, I think. She was friendly."

"Her band is called Smithfield."

"That's right. Olympia was called Smithfield for about five minutes. It's funny how that stuff sticks."

We wandered around Berkeley a bit more, then got back on the BART to San Francisco. We got off at Civic Center and wandered slowly back towards Alex's house. Alex asked me if I wanted to see his place. I didn't really feel like being on my own just yet, so I said yes. We walked up Lower Haight to Haight Street "proper." The entrance to the flat was on Masonic. We walked up two flights of stairs. The flat was nice and bright, a bit noisy in the living room, as it faced Haight Street and the window was open. We went into the kitchen. Two guys were there. It looked as if one was talking the other through some difficult times. They acknowledged us, but it was clear they wanted to be left alone, so we left them.

"Let's go to my room," Alex said.

His room was at the back, so it was quiet but still bright. His bed was pushed up against the window. We both sat on it.

"That was Zack and Lucien. Lucien is my other roommate. He was the sad one, the good-looking one. He's got a drug problem; he needs to get off them, it's not doing anyone any good."

Alex got up and put a CD in the machine. It was sort of music hall music, or maybe songs from films from the thirties and forties. It sounded a bit scratchy, but the playing was amazing.

"I like this stuff," he said. "It relaxes me."

I was tired. Now that I'd sat down on the bed, I felt my energy draining further away. Alex seemed to register this.

"You can just kick your shoes off and lie down, honestly. I don't have any plans—take a nap."

I was too shattered to argue. I put my head back on the pillow and got close against the wall, but I was still looking out the back windows at the sky, which was less bright than it had been. Alex pottered around in the background for a while, putting clothes away, tidying up. Then he got on the bed beside me. I didn't mind, it was his bed, and I was getting sleepy. After another bit he started rubbing his hands softly through my hair. I wasn't sure I liked that so much, but again I was just so tired. And I did appreciate his company. I appreciated that he was being nice. I think I made a trade-off in my mind: ok to stroke the hair as long as I can just lie here and maybe go to sleep. I did fall asleep, and he did too.

When I woke, the sky was purple outside, and I could feel the warmth of Alex's body next to mine. Was I bad? Was I being a tease? Just cos I didn't want to go back to an empty room just yet?

"Hey, Alex?"

"Yeah."

"I need to get going."

"Ok, buddy, will you be ok?"

"Yeah, I'll just get the bus along, I'll be fine. Thanks for the day out."

"It was fun. Let's do it again."

43

On the Radio

We're going home soon. Just over a week. I've been soaking up San Francisco. I've been doing all my favorite things one more time—riding my favorite bus routes, walking my favorite walks, standing in my favorite places, eating my favorite things. When am I ever going to be back here? How much have I changed? What am I going to do next? What about Richard? I think he's seriously conflicted about going home at all. He's so close with Justine, it's now difficult to imagine Richard without Justine. What about Janey? She said that she's going to move back up sometime; not too long, she said. I could wait for her. Maybe if I told her I was staying, she would come sooner, we could get a place?

But I'd be illegal. And Richard would be illegal. And we'd soon be broke. And I'm a long way away from having enough energy to hold down a regular job. And I'd have to take whatever illegal work I could get. Richard too. And we'd get caught and sent home. And we'd never get to come back to the States.

When I was a kid in the seventies, America was a dream. It was *Starsky and Hutch* and Blondie, it was fast food and Disneyland. Nobody went there, we just got it poured down our necks through TV, films and music. And news. One of my earliest memories as a kid was night after night of color footage of people bombing the hell out of Vietnam, and those people were Americans. Still, the overall impression was alluring. It seemed to be the place where life happened, and we were getting the sloppy seconds.

In the high Scottish summer, when school was off and we were ragged and free, I used to watch jet planes going over, really high and small. You could hardly see those silver darts, but you saw the vapor trail. It started out true and straight, and then expanded, puffed out, drifting. You could watch those trails for hours, lying on your back in some deserted park. Those planes were going to America. I knew enough geography to know that America was to the west, over the sea we lived beside. They were all heading there. From where, I didn't really know or care. I just liked thinking about the jets heading to New York or Chicago, some such place. I felt connected. The people in the planes were like gods, but it felt good enough to watch them fly over. Then go home and watch *M*A*S*H*.

The Bay Area really did carry the essence of what I had imagined. The sparkle in the air, towering buildings, boats like Quincy had, evergreen trees like in Hanna-Barbera cartoons. The feeling was satisfied, the far-off dream was recognizable.

A couple of days later, Justine took Richard and me over the Golden Gate Bridge to Muir Woods to look at the massive coastal redwoods. They had already been there, and they told me about John Muir. Apparently he was Scottish, and he was a great naturalist and was called the father of the national parks. It was lovely to be out there surrounded by nature, to be away from cars and buildings. Justine and Richard looked and felt completely at home here, and with each other. On the way out I broached the subject of the radio program down at Stanford. I could feel Richard pondering, but I could also feel Justine's enthusiasm.

"That would be fun! I could drive you guys down."

I think her keenness maybe worked on Richard. When we got to the woods, he said he would do it, but I also had a distinct feeling that this would be his musical swan song as far as "we" were concerned. It was never really his thing. For someone who liked classical guitar *and* Deep Purple so much, he really was an ace accompanist. I never had to tell him anything, he always made my tunes much better when he was playing, but he never went too far either, never encroached.

"You need to keep the music going, Stephen."

We were sitting in a sunny patch at the foot of one of the massive trees, all of us leaning against it, getting as close to the living thing as we could.

"Yeah, I'm going to. I can't really think of anything else to do."

She was grinning in a way that seemed like she had more to say. "Richard and I went to see my clairvoyant, did we tell you?"

"No, I didn't know that. Did you learn anything useful?"

"She told us a lot of stuff about our lives—you know, the usual clairvoyant stuff."

"I've never been to one. I think I'd be a bit worried to find out about tough times ahead."

"Yeah, well, there is that, but I felt like it was the right time to consult with her. I always get a feeling when it's going to be most useful."

Richard wasn't saying much; in fact he wasn't saying anything. He seemed happy to let her talk for him, like he was saving energy for the things he liked to do, rather than waste it on communicating. It occurred to me that he might have preferred to talk a lot less over the last few years, but I kept starting conversations. Maybe he was relieved that he could finally sit there and say less.

Justine continued. "So, do you want to know what she said?"

"About you?"

"No, it's best to keep that to ourselves. I mean about you?"

"About me?"

"Yeah, she specifically mentioned you. She asked if Richard was traveling with anyone. When Richard said your name, it prompted her to say a few things."

I *was* a little hesitant about this kind of stuff. Weren't you meant to take the adventure that was coming to you, accept it, not look ahead and dodge around it? At least, that's the sort of thing I always read in the kind of books I loved when I was young. Take the adventure that comes to you. Maybe though, this was part of the adventure? I hadn't asked Justine to go to the clairvoyant, and the lady wasn't asked about me; she offered.

"What did she say?" I asked.

"She said that you should certainly carry on any artistic, musical, creative passions that you have. That was the main thing that she said. It's going to be a big thing for you."

I looked at Richard and he kind of smiled and shrugged, his way of corroborating what Justine was saying.

"O-k," I said. "No problem there. I'll try my best."

Justine continued. "She mentioned gold discs. She saw you with gold discs on the wall."

"No way! You're kidding? That's so funny. She sounds a bit whacky."

We all laughed, but I could tell that Justine was sincere about all this. She was enjoying the dispensing of the prophecies.

"One last thing. She said that you will meet a childlike person and that they will have a big part to play in your life."

This threw me. I didn't know what to say. I thought about it, then said out loud, "I really don't think I should be having babies. I mean, that doesn't seem right."

"She never said 'your child.' She said 'a childlike person.'"

"Ok. I'll watch out for that."

I should be able to watch out for a significant childlike person sneaking up on me. I'd nip that in the bud. I didn't need any more distractions at the minute.

*****

Alex couldn't come with us to the radio station, he was working. He was worried he wouldn't be able to tune in to the session as he was in San Francisco, so he asked me to get a tape of the show. He had become my musical adviser. He had listened to me sing and had given me some useful pointers, or at least told me what he liked and didn't like.

Richard and I had worked up a few things to play. I had the little battery keyboard from Toys"R"Us. It produced the noise by means of a blower, and the blower sound was almost as loud as the music sound, but it had a certain charm.

When we got out of the car in Stanford, we immediately noticed how balmy it felt. It seemed much warmer than San Francisco.

"We should have come and stayed here," I said.

"That's what I was thinking," Richard agreed.

"Yeah, the city seems colder because of the proximity to the water. Welcome to Silicon Valley," said Justine.

Shirin met us at the radio station, which was called KZSU Stanford. It was a low brick building with a simple entrance, a few stairs down to a wooden door, but once you were in, it was cozy. There were a few people moving around. Everyone was friendly, but everyone was purposeful. Even though they were all students, it seemed like the place was run professionally. I wasn't often in a place where people had purpose and the alluring air of busyness. I liked it. We set up in the booth where Shirin did her show. We had a mic each, Richard had borrowed another acoustic guitar from a friend of Justine's, I had the acoustic and my funny keyboard, and that was it.

"Come with me," Shirin said.

We followed her through to a room that was floor-to-ceiling vinyl, shelf upon shelf.

"We have more recent stuff on CD here too. Why don't you pick some stuff you want to play, then come back through."

I picked Orange Juice, De La Soul, Josef K, the Go-Betweens, Stereolab, Funkadelic. Richard picked Bert Jansch, Hendrix,

Fairport Convention, Billie Holiday and the soundtrack to *Jesus Christ Superstar* (Original Cast). It was lovely to play and hear the music, just for us, never mind the other people listening. Shirin was a good presenter; she seemed genuinely curious about Glasgow and about Scotland in general. She had never been there, but like she said, she loved a lot of the bands, so we did our best to paint a picture for her and for the people listening.

It was funny to reverse the roles for a second, to be not the enchanted but the enchanters. Our description of Glasgow was of this lush green place with live music pouring out of every tenement window, enlightened, lazy students picnicking in every municipal pleasure garden, and the pubs oozing with Fender-Jaguar-wielding protagonists of ace guitar music; political yet beautiful, spiteful yet forgivable. If only that Glasgow existed. The way that San Francisco existed.

But then San Francisco was soon to be gone. I suppose from the point we leave this city, it will exist for all time as a painted memory. And Glasgow will hover back into view. There, the cynics would be out to greet us on our return, the haters of weakness and strangeness. We could turn our collars up to the cold and damp, but it would find us out eventually and keep us stunted and low of libido. Glasgow, of the swift shoe in the nuts.

We sang our songs—a little wobbly, I guess, but spirited. We did two of mine:

"Your Confirmation"
"Hurley's Having Dreams"

And two by others:

"Kids in America"
"Downtown"

327

After we were done, Shirin thanked us, and we said it was fun and that she should come visit with us in Scotland one day. We went outside, into the late-afternoon sun. When we got up the stairs and into the warm Stanford air, there were two people there. It was a girl and a girl-maybe-boy, I couldn't tell which. They were sitting on the curb, but they stood up when we came out.

"Hi," said the girl-maybe-boy. "We were listening to the show, and we liked your songs."

"Wow, so you came to say hello?"

"Yeah, we're close to the campus, so it didn't take us long. I'm Sandy, and this is Myra."

Sandy had on a white shirt and gray trousers, like they had just finished work at a stationer's. They had blue hair, but apart from that reminded me a bit of Billy in the *One Flew Over the Cuckoo's Nest* movie, except not as nervous. Myra was cool in jeans and boots and a powder-blue velvet jacket. She looked like she had Indian heritage and was beautiful. I know I say lots of people are beautiful, but I guess I think lots of people just are.

"We play music too," Sandy continued. "We live close by, if you guys want to come over for coffee?"

We followed their ramshackle little car for about ten minutes and came to a quiet residential street and an older-style apartment building. We went up the stairs into a nice room that felt comfortable and boho and still had that San Francisco apartment smell, which may have been damp, or eucalyptus or incense. Whatever it was, I liked it by this time. The coffee was served, we established a few things. Myra was studying statistics; Sandy was floating free at the minute. They had been together a year, but I didn't know whether that meant musically, apartmentally or as a couple. Pretty soon, Sandy got their guitar out, and Myra produced a portable keyboard, kneeling at the coffee table. I was in the mood to hear what they would do.

"This first one is called 'Why I Had to Split Up with You.'"

Sandy and Myra looked at each other as if they were about to share a secret, and then Sandy began playing, and the keyboard came in barely perceptibly underneath. The first thing I noticed was that Sandy's playing was metronomic. They picked with their fingers surely and steadily, and the noise was very good. Because it was something I couldn't do, it came across to me as a little miraculous. Their voice was a little deeper than I expected when they came in, but it was immediately engaging and didn't shy away from the message.

The song moved to strange places, chord changes I wouldn't have predicted or expected. Myra would sing with Sandy in some places; not obvious chorus marks, but when she came in, they were like two kites sticking close to each other in the air, moving in perfect synchronization, a couple of notes apart. It was at points exhilarating; it reminded me a little of the way that Kristin and Tanya from the Throwing Muses moved. The song ended. It was *much* better than any of my songs. So accomplished. They played another. This time, Myra started with a theme played with a piano sound; she took more of the lead instrumentally, but Sandy still sang the lead part. The song was called "Chapman's Homer"; the subject was a little dense with imagery, but it was still completely engaging and interesting. I could tell Richard was really impressed.

I didn't feel dispirited; their music was just different, it was all there. I just had to keep working. There is room in the world for endless song. I had to try and play my part as well as Sandy and Myra.

"Do you guys play concerts?"

They laughed.

"We don't really have enough songs together yet, we're just starting to play at parties."

"We left a tape at KZSU, but they haven't played it yet," Myra added.

"Really? That's crazy. I guess we got lucky. Maybe the Scottish thing helped."

We got their details in case they made it to Scotland one day. It was a nice way to end our trip.

44

Back Through the Wardrobe Door

Got to go home, got to get on a plane, got to come back from
Wonderland, got to come back through the wardrobe door
into the dusty upstairs room and be a Scottish person again. It was
the last night in San Francisco. Richard was over at Justine's, and
they would pick me up in the morning. I took a walk down Mission
Street and went into El Farolito for the last time, our favorite burrito
place. It was a good place to go to on your own; I was into cantina
dining, when you could go in a crowd or on your own. Nobody
cared, it didn't need to be a big event, you were just in there to get
fed, get your foil-wrapped little donkey full of goodness, served in a
modest plastic basket. If you were really good to yourself, you'd
have a Negra Modelo on the side to wash it all down.

Tonight, I was on the agua fresca. I didn't feel like beer. I was in
a sober, reflective mood. We were going home. I was ok with that.
We had done it; we had made it. And we were not in too bad shape.
Richard especially seemed to have had a transformative experience.
I didn't know what I was going to do when I got home. It felt like
we had been away for years. I guessed that it didn't feel like that
for my parents and for Carrie. Time was stretchy, it was all about
experience—our experience had been rich, whereas all the people
we knew had just passed a regular Scots winter.

When I got back to the house, I went up on the roof to think, to
say goodbye, to pray a bit. I thought about all that had happened,
going right back to the start of the illness. I'm pretty certain I was
being guided, or maybe I was being shaped, molded somehow. It
should have been some consolation to think that there was a reason

for everything, that someone was watching over us. It was still painful though. In reality, every time I had taken a wrong turn—and there had been many—it had ended in a painful correctional move.

Maybe I should have stood up to my parents, to my peers, to the people who said they had my best interests at heart, and told them "No, I'm going the other way. I'm going to follow a different career path, or in fact no career path. I'm going to follow the path of non-profitability. I'm going to follow a path ridiculous to an almost-middle-class, don't-get-ideas-above-your-station, don't-stand-out, serve-the-country, serve-the-machine, serve-the-system upbringing."

But I couldn't do it. I tried to do it. I ran from both sides. God eventually came looking for me, and He got my cookies out of the fire. But it was a painful deal. He put me in the hospital, He put me with Richard and Carrie, He sent us into the wilderness, He set us on a journey of exploration.

I love C. S. Lewis. I love his grown-up books, his biographies. I even like his science fiction. When I was a kid, I read the Narnia books and they were my special ones, and I went back to them when I was in my late teens for comfort. In one story there is a boy called Eustace, and he's a rotter, a bad 'un, a wind-up merchant, a dick. An interesting thing happens to Eustace, of course it does. He sneaks off from the others while they are all stranded on an island. He finds a dead dragon lying beside a treasure hoard in a lonely valley. He fantasizes about all he will do with his new riches and the revenge he will have on the others, who he perceives as being enemies. Eustace falls asleep on the treasure. When he awakes, he is terrified to discover that with his dragon's hoard and his dragon-ish thoughts, he has turned into a dragon.

Poor old Eustace. I never related to him when I was younger, but now I feel like him. I've been him; I am him. An exceptionalist, looking out for myself—snobbish, scared. One night, Aslan comes to Eustace. Aslan is the magical, powerful lion, the spiritual heart of the story. Aslan suggests to Eustace that he needs to undress. If he wants to be a boy again, he needs to scratch off his dragon scales. Eustace succeeds in taking off a layer of skin, even though it hurts. But he's still a dragon. He tries again, goes deeper, but he can't do it. The lion has to do it for him. The lion digs its claws in deep and pulls the dragon's skin off. It hurts Eustace more than anything he had ever felt or imagined. The lion throws him in a pool of water. He is a boy again.

I feel that with each misstep I make, God is around to take a layer of skin from me. He removed the skin I could never remove. He goes in deeper than I ever would. His commitment to change me goes beyond anything that I would remotely contemplate. I think about the things that have happened, and the way that the bad times have molded me. I didn't like them happening to me at all, but still, maybe it was for the best.

Alex showed up at ten. He was coming out to the airport with us.

"I never go anywhere. It's fun to come to the airport," he said. "I'll stick around and get the train back. I like to watch everyone, look up at the board and imagine what flight I would take."

"Why *don't* you take a flight somewhere?"

"I will, one day. Maybe I'll come to Scotland."

"You definitely should. You should come stay with us."

Justine and Richard arrived, and we packed into her Volkswagen Rabbit. It was a tight squeeze. I posted my keys through the door of the house. My goodbye to the landlady had been most unsentimental, just a note on the kitchen table saying *Bye*. I'm not sure Anne realized that we were disappearing today, but we were up to date with the rent. When we got to the airport, we left Justine and Richard to say goodbye to each other. That took a while but was not unjustifiable of course. Those guys were a proper couple. I didn't know what was going to happen, if they had made a plan. I felt certain their story was not at an end.

I said bye to Alex, and he went off to drink coffee and hang out at the airport. I was pretty certain I would see him again at some other time, in some other place. And then we went through, and then we got on the plane, and then we were quiet and reflective all the way to Boston. We changed planes for the nighttime trip back to Glasgow. When we got on the plane, we started to hear the Scottish voices, and it was a bit of a shock. The layers were peeling back.

We flew through the night. I couldn't sleep much sitting up. Richard had moved to another row, an empty one, so he could lie down. I watched the black turn to twilight, looked down over the dark gray-blue of the sea, then saw the land come in—some green outcrop, some crag of a Scottish island. I watched the inlets turn into sea lochs, turn into glens. I saw the first wee cottages and roads, and they turned into bigger roads. It was mesmerizing to me. Scotland—there it was; it existed. Scotland in May. I could see that the woods had greened and I could see specks of yellow gorse.

It was good to get a clear morning. I saw it all, tried to guess where we were, composing a map in my head with what I saw, but it was confusing. We were coming in from the northwest, so the map was upside down. I saw what I thought were the islands of Loch Lomond. Soon after that we came in low over some hills, and I could see the city spread before us, stretching out to the left and right along the Clyde Valley, glimmering and glinting in the fine, clear morning.

We got off the plane, and customs was a formality. No one asked us any questions, nothing like the grilling we got on entry to the US. The UK gave a shrug as if to say "You're back. Big deal. Walk faster." Our respective mothers were there at the airport. They were respectfully tearful, though we were not. We were glad to see them of course; I was just a little numb from all the travel, and I think Richard was too. We were huckled off to separate cars even though we were both heading back to Ayr, the small seaside town where our families lived.

It was May 3, and on the drive home I was dazzled by sunshine and green. It was surprising but very welcome. The trip over the Fenwick Moor towards home gave me time to get used to the Scottish terrain again. Then I got the first glimpse of the sea sparkling and saw the far-off hump of Ailsa Craig island as we raced down the hill of the A77 towards the coast.

Richard and I stayed for a couple of days in Ayr, lazing, reflecting, eating. We were keen to get back to Glasgow though. We needed to get new sick lines from the doc so there wouldn't be a disturbance in our benefits. Our mothers had managed to pick up our money from the post office while we were away, but the three-month lines were about to run out, just as our tourist visas had. All very neat, but it did make us feel a little like Phileas Fogg and Passepartout, rushing to get home before the clock ran out.

Richard's brother Jason had been living in our flat while we'd been away. He was in between jobs, or courses or something, back from living in London. It was a little funny coming back to the flat with him there. He was a nice guy, but it didn't quite feel like our flat straight away. He had changed things round, and cleaning didn't seem to have been big on the agenda. We had a couple of days settling back in, hanging with Jason, eating the curries he made. I was happy to be with my books and music again. Even my plants had survived.

45

Ever Had a Little Faith?

The West End felt fresh and green. Pretty much as soon as my rucksack had been dumped in my room, I took the fox's path to Carrie's house. I luxuriated in the journey. I went round the back of our house, I went under the arch at the end of the terrace, took a detour through our pleasure gardens, through the gaps in the fence. I lay down for a few minutes on the still-damp grass just to prove I could. I took another lane behind the primary school and followed it through to another set of streets, surrounding another set of pleasure gardens, this one being the king of all gated sanctuaries, Campsie Gardens—luckily, the one Carrie had a key to. I wasn't sure if she knew I was back. I tried the door, her mum answered. She was pleased to see me. She asked me if I had managed ok, health-wise.

"Yeah, we did ok, we got the hang of it. It helped that the weather was good."

I think there was a little regret in her eyes, as if wondering why her daughter wasn't making similar progress. She showed me downstairs. Carrie was in bed. It was ten thirty in the morning.

"I've got to pee so bad."

She got up, her eye mask still on her head. She gave me a brief hug, a funny pat on the back, and said, "Welcome home, I missed you." And then went off to pee.

I made her tea, and she had some toast. I didn't manage to get her Armistead Maupin's autograph, but I did get her a nice second-hand hardback edition of *More Tales of the City*. The American artwork was chunky and beautiful. I also gave her a picture of me in a little frame. Richard had taken it in our first few days in San Francisco. You could tell because my face was so pasty, and my hair was a bright copper red from my recently applied henna. I was pictured next to a plaque that said that Robert Louis Stevenson had lodged at this address and had written essays and prose there. I was in my winter coat, and I was pretending to also write something in my notebook. The picture was a little corny.

"I thought it was warm in San Francisco?"

"It took a while to warm up. But you know me . . ."

"The World's Coldest Boy?"

"Yup. The good thing is, it's almost as warm outside as it was in San Francisco. Let's go sit on the blanket."

She pondered. "Front step or gardens?"

"Let's do Campsie."

"Ok, go and build a camp in Campsie Gardens. I'll be over soon."

I took the world-famous Gallagher plastic-backed tartan rug over, with a few cushions. She came over soon enough, still a little shaky from the sleep, but I was so pleased to see her. I suddenly wondered how I had made it without her the whole time, so easily did we settle into each other's company again. And how the fuck did she make it without me? Ha ha.

"So where's Quincy?"

"Gone. Graduated. Off to the fresh-flowing pastures where junior doctors drink and fondle each other's fibulas."

"Has he got someone else? Fucker."

"I dunno. He doesn't have me though," she said. "I'm over it. I'm relieved."

"Glad to hear it."

"What about you?"

"What about me?"

"America! Everything!"

"Yeah, it was nice."

For about fourteen different reasons, I didn't feel like telling her the story of America. I felt like leaving it behind for a while, to be honest, or at least I felt like letting the present in.

"I guess you'll tell me when you feel like it."

"I'll do it in installments, like Armistead would."

"How is your mum?"

"She's fine. I think my dad is driving her up the wall more than usual, now that he is at home more, but she is good. Still working, still loving the day shift at the hospital rather than the night."

"And Richard?"

"He's good too. Very good, but he's a little melancholy of late."

"Why is that?"

"Because he left what I suspect to be the love of his life back in San Francisco."

Carrie propped herself up on her elbows for this.

"Really? What's he going to do?"

"I think something is going to happen. Either he is going back there or else she's coming here."

"What's her name?"

I suddenly felt happy to tell her the first installment of the story, the ballad of Richard and Justine, including the spring earthquake, which made her laugh her arse off.

After a while, I left Carrie to do Carrie things, and I took a walk along Byres Road. I felt a little like Moses coming down from Mount Sinai. I thought people would see my face shining with a Californian glow, but nobody gave me any notice. I was hoping to bump into someone, but I didn't spy anyone. I made it to the Botanic Gardens, and I lay on the grass for a while, pondering my next move. There were quite a few people lying out, as the sun in Scotland doesn't come out much, and when it does, people lie down like haddocks trying to turn into smokies. I was quite near the path. An elderly lady wearing a long, pragmatic raincoat came over to me.

"Is that you relaxing?" she says to me.

I was a little surprised by this intervention, but at least I had someone to talk to.

"I'm just having a think," I said to her. It was the first thing out my head, but it was honest.

"And that's work, is it?" And she took off immediately.

I was a little bit sleepy, right enough, but I was trying to work out, did she just shit on me and my morning? Welcome back to Scotland!

I decided to go back down Byres Road and go to the café, surely a haven for those either unable or unwilling to do a shift in the name of country and empire. I got in there, got the little sliver of a booth that was only good for two small people. It was like riding at the back of the bus; it faced one way, towards the rest of the tables, but that was ok.

I got my coffee and pondered anew. I wondered how long my glow would last. I know that we hadn't climbed Everest, but in a way I was altered. I didn't want to be unaltered. I was scared to go back. I wanted to keep the momentum going that I'd had in California. I wanted to live a Californian life, in Glasgow. The waitress came over; she was new to me.

"What would you like?"

"Can I get a tuna salad croissant and a small black coffee? And an idea. What should I do next?"

She stopped writing on her pad. "What?"

"I was just wondering what I should do next. With my life. I'm at a crossroads."

The waitress looked at me, nonplussed.

"We have yum yums. You want one of those?"

My momentum was waning.

"Yeah, I'll have a yum yum," I said resignedly. "Not heated."

"Ok," she said, her pen still attached to her pad, as she backed away from me.

She looked like an extra from *Gregory's Girl*, and she acted that way too. I guess I had stepped out of a different movie—*Diner*; *Working Girls*; *Fast Times at Ridgemont High*—where everyone gives you sass back, with interest. *Gregory's Girl* is fine though. I love that film. I needed to chill out and get back into my Scottish groove. My tan was not going to last anyway.

We settled back in. I got back into most of my routines. I went back to the after-school club with the kids. I went back to dancing at the Art School on a Saturday night if I felt able, and I went back to singing in the church choir on a Sunday morning. And I went back to hanging out with Carrie.

Richard lent me his second-best guitar, which was the first guitar he owned. It was a steel-string acoustic, as opposed to the gut-string Spanish-style one that I had been used to up to this point. It was a "Martin copy," which was fine by me. I didn't know Martin or why anyone should copy him. I carried on with my tunes, and I reflected on my time away. The ideas slowed a little; it seemed harder work than it had been over there.

I did go to see Dr. Doshi again, and she was really impressed with our trip to America. Obviously it gave the outward impression that I had taken a real step forward, mood-wise, and that I had the wind in my sails. I was happy enough to go with this optimistic narrative while I was with her. You want to believe it, you want to walk away unscathed into a bright new future. Who wouldn't? No one wants to be stuck, everyone wants to be happy. People can be coy about it, cool about it, abstruse about it. They still want to be happy. I wanted someone to tell me that I seemed well and that it was all going to be ok, that I was on the right path, that the prognosis for life was positive. I wanted to jump on my own positivity bandwagon. I had no wiggle room for "cool."

I tried to get a job as an usher at the Glasgow Film Theatre, the arty cinema that we loved. I reckoned I could do that job. They only seemed to work for about fifteen minutes, ripping tickets and waving people towards the seats. Then they got to sit through the movie. And the people that ripped the tickets always seemed so louche and attractive. Maybe I could be one of those? Trouble was, everyone wanted that job. The reason that louche and attractive people had the job is that hundreds went for it, and the only way they could discriminate between all the hopefuls was to give it to the most louche and attractive. I never got it.

I did get a job at a popular theater nearby. Same drill, just without the coolness. I only lasted two shifts. The supervisor insisted that I had to stand at the back during the performances, not sit. A lack of slovenliness was what they were aiming for. I couldn't hack standing for two hours. I quit.

A week later, at my appointment, my GP slipped into the conversation that he'd seen me cycling down Great Western Road and that I'd looked like I was brimming with health. I tried to insist that the bike was carrying me and that I only ever cycled downhill with a breeze behind, but he was not convinced. I wasn't trying to fool him. It's obvious that at any given moment you might look normal, you might look like anyone else doing normal stuff. He had been generally supportive of me since I'd moved back to Glasgow, but he perhaps thought I could do with a shove in some direction.

Apparently there was a government-sponsored course for would-be musicians in Glasgow. "I think you should give it a go," said my GP. I really had had enough of courses. And the government-sponsored thing made it sound even grimmer. The implication was that he wanted to sign me off the sick or at least make a change in my status. I had a sinking feeling, and my emotions gave way. I started crying right in his office. Man, I really didn't want to do that, but there it is. You know when you feel things are just starting to move in the right direction, you earn yourself a little breathing space, there's some blue sky ahead, and someone or something always comes along to blot out the sun. It was apparent that my dance with the benefits system wasn't going to be the waltz it had been. I told him about my recent dalliances with employment.

"I'll still sign you off as unsuitable for work," he said. "Just go in and give it a go. That's all I'm asking. I'll give you till the end of the summer to build up to it."

At least I had the summer. The season of green. The season made lovely by the quietness of the streets, by the warmth of the breeze, by the midnight congregations of mooch foxes in the hinterland of humans. Summer was approaching. Summer in Scotland can be a fleeting, ephemeral thing. I can write a better summer than the one I can see. So before the humdrum comes in, let me imagine a Scottish summer. Before I sign up for a course designed to get the unemployment figures down, designed to make the government seem like they are on top of a problem. A problem like me.

*****

I went back to church. People were glad to see me, though they were a bit confused as to where I had been and how long I had been away. They thought I was still a student, they didn't know about ME, but that's all ok. I can get by for an hour on a Sunday morning with a minor misunderstanding.

Alec was still talking about Easter; we were in the season of Easter. He was talking about his personal experiences. He was talking about his wife dying of cancer, only two years ago. He compared the way he felt to the way the apostles felt about the death of Jesus. All hope lost. A darkness that came and overtook everything. Then one day a morning came. In the Bible it was the third day, when Jesus rose from the dead, when the stone was rolled away, when the tomb was found to be empty. The followers of Jesus were told by angels that their Lord had risen. Hope rose in their hearts.

A morning came for Alec, when he felt the sun rise in his heart once again, when he knew life had to go on, when he acknowledged that God meant him to make the best of his life, when he acknowledged that his wife's death, and the horrible time he had been through, had to be put in the perspective of earth and heaven. Morning came, and hope rose in Alec's heart. I couldn't imagine. I couldn't imagine the darkness that Alec had had to go through, and I couldn't imagine being a follower of Jesus. I couldn't imagine resting all my hope on one person, leaving everything to go with him, then for it all to disappear when Jesus was branded a criminal and killed. All was lost. But then it wasn't.

I like Jesus. I like him more the more I read about him, the more I hear about him. When I got my faith, I wasn't given Jesus. I was gifted a fleeting vision of God and heaven, but that was enough to set me on a path of sorts. It was enough to keep me praying, keep me in church, keep me believing. I wasn't given Jesus. He was just there, always the starring role, always the brightest son, putting up with humans, apologizing to God for our behavior. Even when they nailed him to a piece of wood and hanged him, he would say "Dad, they don't know what they are doing. Can you let this one go?"

I have two friends in Glasgow—Carrie and Richard. Before I got sick, I saw a lot more people, but I'm starting to see more people these days on the "scene"—the Art School scene, the coffee scene. It's mostly casual nods and inconsequential chat. My point is, I don't think any one of them would want to talk about God or Jesus. I think if I managed to get Jesus into a conversation with any one of them, it would quickly turn awkward. That includes the era of Vivian and her friends. Maybe I'm not giving some folk enough credit: it was Richard that suggested I should go to church, after all.

When church was over, I didn't go home, I just felt like walking. I came right through Dowanhill and carried on along the Great

Western Road, in the general direction of the city. I was walking slow, helped by the fact it was another warm day with little breeze. I nearly walked with one foot in the gutter and one foot on the pavement like I was eight again, but I caught myself. I thought about Alec's sermon. I gave the whole concept of Easter a good mental workout as I walked. I went over the Biblical events in my mind. It did make me feel hopeful, but maybe I was just feeling hopeful anyway.

I wished I had someone to talk to about this stuff. Sundays, I pretty much had to walk past Carrie's house. I felt estranged from her at the weekend, I knew she was deep in family stuff on Sundays. And Richard is completely taken up with Justine. Did I tell you she's coming to Scotland? She's coming to stay with us for a while. The me and Richard days are coming to an end. But I'm happy for those guys.

I walked along the Sunday strip between Oakfield Avenue and the Philadelphia Chippy. The sun was good, the people were out. For some reason this area is magical for me. I remember stumbling out at this junction back in '85, perceiving the Great Western Road flowing like a great river towards the city center. I felt like Lewis and Clark stumbling on the Mississippi for the first time. It was the start of a long love affair with a thoroughfare.

I was stood at this happening junction, luxuriating in a patch of sun. There was usually an interesting mix of people waiting at the lights to cross. I kept imagining I was going to walk into someone like me, someone as loose and malleable as me, except they would be female. Where are all the female loose-end wanderers? Girls always look like they have somewhere to go and are going there in a hurry.

I imagined a person, so I started singing to her, and I started to write a song to her, but just a conversation, like we had both walked out of the church together and the sermon had thrown up questions in her head.

With your headphones on
Through the drizzled pane
Of a wet slate roof
Sun will turn to rain
Why are you the one?
Couldn't take the pain
Something good will happen, wait and see
Something good will happen, wait and see

Do you spend your day
Second-guessing fate?
Looking for a way
To live so divine
Drop your sad pretense
You'll be doing fine
You will flourish like a rose in June
Ever had a little faith?

Morning came
Hope rose up in your heart
You felt ashamed
When morning came
Roll away the stone of doubt, girl.

So she went from street to street
Looked up and down
She must have missed him
If she could only find him
She would throw her arms around and kiss him tenderly
She would give herself on bended knee
Never thinking if it's wrong or right
Hurry sister, there's a little light
Ever had a little faith?

Maybe the "she" was Mary Magdalene. I think she became her by the end of the song. Mary Magdalene hiding in the shadow of some Renaissance masterpiece. Come out into the light, Mary. Throw your arms around the one you love. You won't have him for long. Do what no one else dares to. Everyone else is standing back and doubting, criticizing. Show the love that no one else will.

I took my song back to the flat and tried to work it out on the guitar. It took a long time with a bit of resting in between, but I got it going pretty good, got it down on tape.

46

A Night with the Stars

I don't know what I'm meant to do. Do you put up with what you've got or get out there and hustle? My hustle has lost its . . . whatever. Sometimes Carrie and I are just sitting on her front steps with a few cushions. It's early June, and if this were P. G. Wodehouse, he would say that it was the sort of morning you could hear a snail clear its throat a mile away.

I love Wodehouse. You see, as long as there's things to love we'll be ok. As long as this blanket remains here, as long as there's a few cushions and a patch of sun. And as long as Carrie's dad pops out to make a wry comment on the hour every hour, as he is wont to do. He just came out holding a tiny jar of honey, one of those individual portions. Carrie must have brought it home, she's a collector of table detritus. Her dad held out the tiny jar.

"I see that you keep a bee," he said in a theatrical tone.

He waited for a reaction. And when he got little from Carrie, and just a smile from me, he chuckled anyway at his own humor.

Delight in the small things, they say. I don't know that it will be enough though. If this were one of those big Victorian novels, I wonder what sort of character I would be. The one without the prospects, the idiot son. The drinker of teas who barely gets a mention. I have no plotline.

"The trouble is that if this were a Victorian novel, we would have no plot," I said.

"Half of those books have no plot," Carrie said, rising immediately to the subject. "They come in, they have tea, they talk about their prospects and the plight of the poor, then someone gets consumption."

I pondered this.

"Now that you say it, it doesn't feel too far removed from us," I say.

"Exactly."

"But surely you have to have more of a stake in your life than this?" I said, a bit exasperated.

"Stephen, if you are going to be restless, I might have to ask you to leave. I feel oddly calm today; you're ruffling the ambience."

"Sorry."

"It's ok."

I listened out for Wodehouse's snail. I was rewarded by hearing a man fart in an adjacent house. I knew it was a man because you could see his substantial outline through the crinkly glass of an upstairs bathroom window.

"Did you hear that?"

"I did." Carrie put down her book, looked up at the window, looked at me and asked, "Did you fart in front of Vivian?"

"No chance. Did you fart with Marcus or the farmer?"

"Nope. Held it in. I'm not very farty though."

"What about if you get married?" I asked.

"What about it?"

"You'll have to fart sometime."

"I'll fart, but with discretion."

We listened again to the warm peace of the morning.

"Do you think you will get married?" I asked.

"I don't know. I used to always want it. Now I'm wondering who would have me."

"Because you're ill."

"Obviously. What about you?"

"I don't know about marriage. It's never been a big topic for me. I think having a girlfriend would be something to aim for," I said brightly.

"Are you ready for it?"

"I don't know. Maybe it's like America, you just have to throw yourself in."

Carrie looked at me, then looked past me, thinking.

"You could be right," she said.

I think I'd hit a nerve though. I don't think she believed it for herself. I think she felt a regular relationship was the moon to her still.

"When does Justine get here?" Carrie said, changing the subject.

"Two weeks."

Justine was coming, but before that something else was happening. Remember the singer that I used to write to, Carla Camino? Well, she is definitely coming to Glasgow, all the way from Olympia, Washington. Like I said, she is friends with that group the Chairs, she's staying with them while she's here to do a show. She is going to be here for a couple of days, and she mentioned there was a guy who was writing to her, i.e. me. The Chairs must have been like, "Oh yeah, we know that guy." When I ran into Cathy I suggested that people might want to come to our flat to play some songs, and Cathy thought that was a great idea, so it's going to happen. Thankfully Richard agreed that it was a good thing too. He said that he'd help me out this one more time. I told Carrie about it.

"God, that's quite glamorous."

"Can you come? I know music gives you a headache after a while, but it will be fun."

"I'll try. I would like to."

The day got closer. I got some snacks and drinks in. Cathy was in touch and said a few more people might come along. The thing was growing more legs apparently. On the Thursday night, people started to arrive. Not just people though, people *in bands*. The Chairs came with Carla, and she was lovely and hugged everyone straight away. Duglas and Francis from the BMX Bandits turned up at the door. And then the Pastels came. The Pastels! Jeez. And they brought . . . *gulp* . . . Norman from Teenage Fanclub. I didn't really know what was going on, it was exciting. I just hoped I wasn't going to make a fool of myself. Carrie came. I went down to get her, told her who was here.

"Bloody hell! Are you ok? Can you handle this?"

"Well, it's happening, so we might as well enjoy it!"

Of course, she knew about my veneration of these titans of the Glasgow jangle scene, even if she didn't share in it. I got her a comfy seat in the corner. I liked that she was there, she made me feel calmer, almost like I wanted the vibe to be chiller so that she would be ok for longer. We made a sort of performance space in front of the fake fireplace, and everyone formed a natural curve around it. People had brought drink and stuff, so we didn't have to do too much in terms of hosting. Carrie was the only one drinking tea.

The last person to arrive was Eugene from Captain America, previously from the Vaselines. He seemed like he'd already had a couple of drinks and claimed to have got lost in the back streets. Dominic suggested they thought he'd been taken up into the bowels of an alien spacecraft, to which Eugene replied, "No, but I may have been taken *in* the bowels by an alien spacecraft."

Everyone seemed to be in a band except me, Richard and Carrie. I wanted to say that we were the Nabisco Cats, but Richard was like, "Let's just be Stephen and Richard tonight." There was one other person who came with Duglas and Francis. A girl was there. She stayed very quiet, just smiled. She gave the impression that she could have been a ballerina from inside a music box. Or someone who had just narrowly failed the audition to be in a Spangles advert in the seventies. Or somewhere in between. She sat and listened. Mystery girl.

It was a bit awkward at first, but thankfully Duglas was a good party icebreaker. He and Francis got up first. I'd seen the BMX Bandits on numerous occasions, but in this stripped-down way the song they played seemed more sober and thoughtful. I think Francis had written it; it was good. Carla was up next, and she ripped right into my favorite song of hers, and I was in heaven. I couldn't believe the evening was happening.

The Pastels did a beautiful version of the Everly Brothers' "All I Have to Do Is Dream." When it was our turn, we played an older one called "Vitamin Phillipa," the one I had tried to sing at the open mic last year. With Richard strumming through it, it gave it a bit more backbone, so at least it didn't fall apart completely this time.

Norman came next, just him on a guitar. "This is a new one, doesn't really have a name yet. Let's see how it goes."

He launched into a tune that was both moving and accomplished. It wasn't a folk tune, you could tell it was meant to be a pop tune with his band, but he put it across so well. The way that the chords moved around under the elegant vocal was so clever. It just sounded as good as one of those tunes by Todd Rundgren or some other hero of the seventies, like it would sit on the radio for a hundred years. People applauded, as they did for everyone, and we went round a couple more times, everyone taking a turn except Eugene, who was happy to have a night off and be the main contributor of humor.

Finally, Norman said, "If I play 'September Gurls' by Big Star, would people join in?"

People said they would. He played and sang it, and we joined in like we were scouts round a campfire. All coolness evaporated, we were united in our appreciation for classic pop. The rest of the evening, folk were chatting and drinking. Carrie lasted well. Though this might not have been her usual crowd, she was of course glad to be around people, making the most of it while her energy stayed intact.

I cleaved to Carla, gleaning information about her, her songwriting, her upbringing in Olympia. She seemed to remember Alex, which was brilliant. A small world we lived in, littered with cafés, second-hand record stores, people looking for and finding the same inspirations, the same loves, just oceans and time zones apart.

Carrie had to get going. Francis had a car and said he would drop her home. Everyone else took this as a cue, and they all got up to go in a oner. And that was our night with the stars.

47

The Wedding

This is not one of those stories where everyone gets what they want, or even remotely what they want, and goes happily into the sunset, and every day is better than the one before. Does anyone even write those kinds of stories anymore? This is not a heavenly story, this is a slow human story, where people keep trundling along, jostled and occasionally pricked by circumstances and tripped up by their feelings. Maybe I'm being too cynical.

Today, however, on this summer morning, I feel ok. Richard is getting married. I'm the best man. I have to make a speech. I'm worried about that, but that's nothing, he's got his whole life mapped out for him now; he's taking on a mighty promise. I mean, I really hope those guys get what they want and live happily ever after, that would be a result—what was I talking about before? I wish them heaven.

The wedding is of a humanist nature though, in a hotel in Ayr, and the reception is at the same place. Handy. Me and Carrie are there. Richard's brother and sister too, but aside from that the gathering is vastly weighted in favor of his mum and dad's circle, fifty-year-olds and upwards. Richard and Justine didn't even want a reception, but they did it for his mum and dad. Her family are absent, but she's cool with that. One sister made it across, but Richard and Justine are going to live in California after this, so she's going to be around her family more.

I get up for my speech. I've never done this kind of thing before. I tried to make it light, funny, a bit spicy, get a few digs in at Richard, but the staid and elderly audience aren't really having it. I tell the story about the spring earthquake in San Fran, and how it was really them shagging, but it goes down like a lead balloon. Only Richard's sister squeaks in laughter, but I think maybe she's laughing at me trying to sell the story to a whole room of legendary non-laughers. The reception was slightly better when Richard and I got up to sing "Green Grow the Rashes." A bit of Burns in Burns country will always do well, even though the arrangement was probably a bit too folk/rock for them. Carrie told us afterwards that the song had moved her, that she wasn't usually into Burns and all that but that the words in this case, and the performance by the groom, were highly appropriate.

There was a meal, but no one was really drinking. I looked around and I thought, *You go, Richard and Justine. Get to California and do your thing, carry on in the vein of the trip we had, and don't look back. Live well and live free, and together maybe you can put the curse of ME behind you. You're giving yourself the best chance, supporting and understanding each other.* Me and Carrie thought they were so brave, especially Richard, heading off to a new life where they would have to support themselves financially and otherwise. It still seemed a long way off for us, but Richard and Justine had a plan. They had each other. And that was a lot.

Carrie and I drove back to Glasgow. Carrie had had a lie-down after the meal, so she was doing ok. I was driving the Bop.

"So what now?" I ask.

"I'm going back to university, that's what." She had her head back on the rest and her eye mask on, even though it was getting dusky outside.

"You're going back to uni? Since when?"

"Since you and Rico went to America, that's when. I needed something."

"What are you going to study?"

"English lit. Bit of psychology too."

"Part-time?"

"Yeah, part-time, but it still counts towards my original degree."

"Wow. You kept that quiet. Do you have a reading list yet?"

"No, not yet."

"Will you be a fresher again?"

"No, I think that ship sailed a long time ago. I will be a ripe old lady of letters. What we used to call a 'mature student.'"

"They'll love you. I used to like a mature student back in the day. All that life experience—you'll be sought after."

"I'll be shunned."

"It could go either way," I admitted.

We came in over the moor and started seeing Glasgow appearing ahead. We could see right over the Clyde Valley to the hills at the far side. Hills and moors, and a bit of city in between. I think that's part of the reason Glasgow is so dreamy. You can get out fast and be by the sea, in a forest, by a loch, up a hill within an hour, even if you do it on a bicycle. We hadn't been in the country lately, but it was nice to be reminded that it was all still there, waiting for us. There and back, country and home, nature and tenement, yang and then yin. And then maybe someone to cook you a nice veggie dinner at the end of it. That's the dream.

"What about me then?" I asked.

"What about you?"

"What will I do?"

"You've got your music course."

"You do realize it's a retraining thing for people they don't know what to do with? It's not university."

"What did university ever do for you, Stephen? Maybe you're just past it."

"Oh great, thanks."

"I mean that in a good way. I'm just going there to have something in my life. I don't really know what I'm doing. You *have* something going on. You have your songs."

"I suppose."

"Just do *them*. Do whatever it takes. When you do other people's stuff, you get ill, have you noticed?" she asked.

"Is that bad?"

"It hasn't been great. Ditch the idea that you have to do anything normal. We're abnormal. It's good."

I continued the drive. Yeah, I was probably done with proper jobs and education. I'll show up to the "course" in September. I don't have a choice anyway—they'll cut my money off. I'm trying to think of a new philosophy, a new superpower. Back in the green mornings of 1991, before breakdowns and America, we sometimes thought we could do anything. Or at least I did. Back then I was enjoying the emotional freedom of not going out with Vivian, even though I moaned about it. I had come through hospital, I had bypassed an early death. I thought we could do anything. I suppose I still think we could do anything. But the *anything* has to turn into *something*. Working out what the something is, that's the tricky part. It takes work, perseverance. It takes a long list of words that you would find in motivational speeches. This is not a motivational speech.

But . . . we *could* do anything. Normal rules did not apply. Carrie could lie down in supermarkets, Richard could marry a woman who listened to fortune tellers, and I could keep strumming the same chord over and over until a melody and a philosophy were evoked.

*****

I woke up feeling quite shady. I called Carrie and she was feeling pretty bad too, but I still said I would come down to see her.

"Let's do some healing," I said when I got there.

"What?"

"You know, I could do healing on you, like the lady did on me."

Carrie was always tolerant of me going to church and everything, but I could tell she wasn't really feeling the spiritual stuff on a personal level.

"It couldn't do any harm," I said. "You just have to lie there."

She thought about it for a second. "Do you put hands on me or something?"

"No, they just float over. That's what Judy Neal did anyway. She left her hands in the air, then went round the whole body, holding for a few minutes each time."

"Ok, I'll try it. Just don't give me a worse headache than I already have."

So we tried it. Her on the nearside of her bed, me kneeling on the floor with my hands hovering over her. I started at the head. I honestly didn't know what I was doing. I was trying to channel healing vibes from God through me into her. I floated over her face, her throat, her shoulders, her arms, her chest, her legs, her feet. I didn't say anything at all, just tried to focus and pray. From time to time, Carrie would have a spasm. Her whole body would judder, like the shock response a tiny baby has when you pick it up. We were used to the spasms; we both got them, her more than me though. They happened when we were becoming relaxed—instead of just becoming still like other folk, it seems like we had to fall down a series of physiological jumps rather than a steady descent to sleep.

I got to what I thought was the end, and she was limp, asleep. I pulled the duvet over her; she didn't move. You could hardly make out her form with the blanket over her, she seemed to shrink in sleep, becoming part of the bed that was so used to embracing her. I went back to my prayers, sometimes reaching for unimagined futures, mostly just asking for guidance in getting us through the day. I hoped that she would recover, I hoped that university would be good for her. Mostly I hoped that she would find a key, something that would unlock the thing in her that had helped cause her to get so sick.

48

We Could Do Anything

The summer came and began to go. The tartan rug had plenty of use. We drifted, we had adventures close to home. I leaned on the café, on music, on God, on Carrie, on Carrie's family to help me through. Richard and Justine lived in the flat with me and it was nice, but the three of us knew it wasn't going to go on forever. They quietly planned, their eyes became set on California, and this time it would be for good.

Carrie was getting ready for university. She *actually* bought new pens and pencils, and a pencil case. I picked it up to smell inside, see if it would give me a "back to school" feeling. It did, but it cast me right back to 1980, the last time that I had anticipated school with a semblance of enthusiasm. Who would truly be a kid again?

"They are having a cheese and wine," Carrie announced.

"Who's having it?"

"The English lit class. They're having a get-to-know-you thing."

"That's nice."

"It's on Thursday. Do you want to go?"

"Why would I go? Is it not just for people in the class?"

"I thought you might want to get me along?"

I was trying to work out whether Carrie was feeling sorry for me. If she was, I didn't really want to go with her. If she wanted a pal, I supposed I could go.

"I don't want to get in the way of your new classmates."

"You won't. I'm sure there will be plenty of room there to meet them."

"I will be an interloper."

"No you won't, don't be daft. If you like, I can tell people you are my assistant."

"How do I assist you?"

"You can get my cheese and wine."

I mean, I could go, I didn't have anything else on.

"You don't have anything else on, just come with me," she said. There was something funny about her insistence, she wouldn't usually be so emphatic.

"Why can't it be fish and chips?"

"What?"

"Instead of cheese and wine. Cheese and wine is such a moldy combination."

"Oh shut up. Are you coming?"

"Yeah. Ok."

"You can dress funny, I won't mind."

"What do you mean 'funny'?"

"You know, you can go full Stephen, be untethered."

"I never think about it, I just leave the house in what I'm wearing."

"You think about it."

"I don't."

"Well, maybe you should start thinking about it." She was trying to get a reaction, but she was too kind to really want to wind me up. She held her breath while I looked up to see what expression she had, then she burst into a snorty giggle.

"I like my clothes," I said.

"I know. I like your clothes too. Especially that Raleigh top."

She said that kind of ironically, because it was hers. It was a tight black knitted bicycle jumper that you zipped up so that it hugged into you. It was from the seventies. It had a band of rainbow stripes across the chest, and the team's name, *Raleigh Campagnolo*. It was the most perfect garment. A friend of her dad's had given it to her, and it was just lying around, so I started wearing it, and then I started wearing it home, and then I just started wearing it every-where.

"It's ok, you can have it. It smells of you now, I don't want it back," she said.

"Do I smell?"

"Everybody smells."

Come the English lit cheese and wine, it was a warm, still, early-September afternoon. I did feel a bit of a spare part as we walked slowly up to the nearby campus of Glasgow University. The gather-ing was in one of the old terraced Victorian townhouses that had become university property. English literature was just a couple of doors up from my old music department. My memories of that place weren't fond, and I was glad to be a hanger-on-er rather than a candidate for learning.

We followed the printed A4 signs to the second-floor annex, to a wide and bright room with a school classroom vibe. There were long tables along one side, adorned with the promised wine and nibbles. It was busy, there was a hubbub—people chatting noisily, all excitement and new starts.

"Will I leave you here?"

"*No,*" I said indignantly.

"I'm kidding, but I do want to mill around."

"Mill. I'll tag along at a safe distance. No cramping, I promise."

Carrie went off and mingled. I'd not often seen her in this situ-ation, looking normal, being equal to people around her. I know she was working hard to keep it there, but she looked good, she didn't seem nervous; in fact I could see her putting people at ease. She had a way of finding the people who had good chat, she gravitated towards the interesting—maybe this was another labor-saving device she picked up in ME world, zooming in on crucial people while her window remained open.

I stood there for a bit. I didn't really want to talk to anyone, I didn't want to open up false avenues of chat. I leaned on the cheese table. I caught a glimpse of someone. Just a flash of an eye, then they were hidden in the crowd. Then once more there was a burst of contrast, someone both darker and brighter than the rest. But they got submerged again, they must have been small. Carrie was over there somewhere. She was in a group, talking. The people seemed to thin out in front of me and I could see that Carrie was talking to a group that included the contrasty person. They were indeed smaller than most of the people in the room, but my attention was immediately drawn to her. I couldn't stop looking towards her. I tried not to be rude, but I wanted to look at her.

Carrie gestured to me, and the girl looked over. They talked for a few seconds more, then broke off from the group and came towards me. The girl was smaller than Carrie. She had long dark hair in bunches, she wore a navy two-piece dress outfit with orange piping and pockets, very sixties, very stylish. She wore boots with a big stack heel and silver tights. Her make-up was pronounced but expertly applied. She was very pretty, unique-looking. She was the girl from the music night, the one that never spoke. The mystery girl. The music-box dancer.

This afternoon at the gathering, her air was changed, she seemed relaxed and open. Carrie turned to speak to someone else, and the girl stood in front of me.

"Hello," she said.

She smiled, and her face dimpled around the smile. She put her hand up to her mouth to try and get a bit of control back over the smile, but it wasn't happening. Then the smile really burst out, teeth and lips and dimples. It was quite a performance.

"I went to your music night thingy. It was nice."

"I saw you there. You're Rebecca?"

"Yeah, just Becky. And you're Stephen. So you're not in the class?"

"No, just came with my friend Carrie."

"I spoke to her, she said I should come talk to you."

"She said that?"

"She did."

I was already getting a funny feeling about this. She was still there, the girl. She didn't run away. I didn't have to try and think of anything smart to say to her to stop her moving on. She was just there, waiting.

"Do you like cheese and wine?" I asked.

"I like wine fine, and cheese is good, but I wouldn't put them together."

"What would you do?"

"Drink the wine and save the cheese for a toastie."

"Ah."

"Have you ever met someone so small?" she said suddenly, smiling.

"You're not that small. How old are you?"

"Nineteen. I know, I look younger."

"Not that young," I offered.

"You're quite tall. What are you?"

"Five foot ten, I think."

"Are you wearing clogs? They make you taller."

"Are you from Newcastle?"

"Nearer Durham. That's hard to say. Nearer Durham . . ."

There was a pause.

"Look!" she said. She lifted a flap on her dress at the waist and showed me a bit of her belly. "What are you meant to do with that?"

"With the dress?"

"No, with my tummy. It's puffy. Sorry, it's the wine. Should have had some cheese first. You want to sit down?"

We went over to the other side of the room, where there was a stack of benches, and we perched there with a view of the room.

"Did you not want to meet your class?" I said, regretting I had as soon as I said it.

She took a second. "Nah, I'll see them all this year. I met some already."

And we sat up on the benches, and we just talked, easily, comfortably. We talked for a while, without giving ourselves completely away. And when things seemed to be drawing to a close with the event, I said, "I better go get Carrie. It was really nice talking to you, Becky."

"Likewise, Stephen."

I turned to go, awkwardly, in slow motion.

"Ahem," she said.

"Yes?"

"Would you like my number?"

"Yes, of course. Definitely."

I held out my wrist for her, but she took a piece of paper out of her bag and wrote on that and gave it to me. I waved her goodbye, and with a final look I went to get Carrie.

As I walked back from Carrie's, walking slowly to savor every crunch of gravel, I thought about Becky. This was a rare thing, I thought. Seeing her there today felt . . . consequential. When I got to the house, I didn't go in. I found the hole in the fence where Richard and I had broken into the gardens. I went in, and I sat down in the middle of the lawn. There was a large moon, so I was illuminated. There was a real brightness. I kept thinking about Becky, playing over the conversation we'd had. She gave me her number. I would definitely call her. I felt like phoning her now. Would that be silly? I'd only just met her, and it was late.

I lay looking up at the gap between the clouds for a bit more. I couldn't think of anything else. I *could* phone her. It wasn't *that* late. I got up, left the gardens, walked to the flat, went up the stairs and called her. It rang four times, five, six . . .

"Hello?"

"Hi. Becky?"

"Oh, hi, Stephen."

"I'm not calling too late, am I?"

"No, you just made it. Nobody's in bed yet."

"I wanted to say that it was nice to meet you today."

"It was nice to meet you too, though I had already met you, remember?"

"Oh yeah, of course." There was a pause. "I could come round and say hi if you like?"

"No, don't come round just now," she said. "It's a bit late. Come tomorrow."

"Come tomorrow?"

"Yeah, come and get me in the morning."

"Ok. What will we do?"

"I don't know, we could do . . . anything."

"Anything?"

"Just hang out, spend the day."

"Ok, I'll come round in the morning."

"Not crazy early."

"Not too early." A thought occurred to me. "Becky, I might have to rest at some point during the day if we're hanging out."

"That's alright, Carrie already told me."

"That's ok then," I said.

Another little pause. I could hear her breathing.

"It was *really* nice to see you today," I said.

"It was really nice to see you too," she said brightly.

"See you tomorrow."

"See you tomorrow, Stephen, love."

She put the phone down.

I had a date for the morning.

We could do . . . *anything*.

Acknowledgments

The author would like to thank, along with sporadic thoughts of loving kindness for all the everlasting support and inspiration:

Marisa Privitera Murdoch, Denny and Nico Murdoch, Ciara MacLaverty, Michael and Valentina Mair, Heather Snider, Steve Dunn, Victoria Morton, Audrey and George Doherty, Fraser Murdoch, Fiona Morrison, Stevie Jackson, Sarah Martin, Chris Geddes, Bob Kildea, Richard Colburn, Dave McGowan, James Sandom, Sarah Willson, Fraser Tannock, Stephen MacDougall and the fabulous Belle's crew, Jud Laghi, Angus Cargill, Dan Papps, Pete Adlington, Catherine Daly, Lucy Ridout and all at Faber, Alexa Frank, Tara Parsons and all at HarperVia, Matt Stevens, Sean Daily, Laura Taylor, Al Mills, Chris Lombardi, Patrick Amory, Gerard Cosloy, Miwa Okumura, Sam Carlin, Iain Thomson, Sarah Holmes, Prof. W. Wang, Andrew Irons, NHS staff everywhere, Amanda and Gary Heather, the Rev. George Mackay, Carole MacGregor, Ann Henderson and all at Broomhill Hyndland Parish Church, the Very Rev. John Christie, Arthur Calnan, Gen Kelsang Machig, Gen Kelsang Zamling, Gen-la Kelsang Kunsang, Gen Kelsang Tubchen, Ven. Geshe Kelsang Gyatso Rinpoche and all at Kadampa Meditation Center Glasgow, Jennifer Brea, Linda Tannenbaum, Sonya Chowdury, Claire Sehinson, Amanda Waring, Paul McGuigan, Natasha Noramly, Hannah McGill, Barry Mendel, Linton, Matt Brennan, Anna Miles, Michael John McCarthy, Pete Ferguson, Rachel Mooney, Andrew Symington, Sean Hamilton, Peter Miller, Kyle Lonsdale Jackson, Yvonne Kincaid, Brian McNeill, Shirley Scott, Jean Stewart and the class of P7S at Alloway

Primary School (1979/80), Robert Funai and the class of 1 Kintyre A at Belmont Academy (1980/81), A. M. Stefani, Cressida McDermott, the MacLaverty family, David Brand, Robert White, Stephen McRobbie, Katrina Mitchell, the staff at the Grosvenor Café (1988 to 2001).

Here ends Stuart Murdoch's
Nobody's Empire.

The first edition of this book was printed
and bound at Lakeside Book Company
in Harrisonburg, Virginia, December 2024.

A NOTE ON THE TYPE

The text of this novel was set in Stempel Garamond, a typeface originally published by the foundry Stempel in 1925. It is considered to be a more faithful reinterpretation of Claude Garamond's iconic sixteenth-century design, eschewing the larger x-heights and soft shapes of Garamond's American spin-offs. Angular in detail with a bold contrast in stroke thickness, Stempel Garamond cuts a lively figure across the page. However, it maintains the same charms of the Garamond family at large. Elegant, warm, and incredibly readable, Stempel Garamond is a natural choice for all forms of continuous text.

HARPERVIA

An imprint dedicated to publishing international voices,
offering readers a chance to encounter other lives and other
points of view via the language of the imagination.